P9-DXT-701
3 9311 00259 0913

Advance Praise for *Of Another Time and Place*

"Schaeffer's *Of Another Time and Place* brilliantly weaves a modern-day mystery with stirring depictions of aerial combat in World War II, while deftly addressing the moral issues raised by that war. This first novel clearly vaults Schaeffer into the ranks of accomplished storytellers whose next novels are anxiously awaited by his legion of fans, of which I am now one."

—ERIC L. HARRY, author of the series *Pandora: Outbreak*

"I love Brad Schaeffer's writing, and *Of Another Time and Place* is no exception. Buy it and read it. You won't be disappointed."

—BEN SHAPIRO, bestselling author, editor-in-chief of *The Daily Wire* and host of "The Ben Shapiro Show"

Fic
SCHAEFFER
12/18
Cochise County Library District
CONFIDENTIAL

A POST HILL PRESS BOOK

Of Another Time and Place
© 2018 by Brad Schaeffer
All Rights Reserved

ISBN: 978-1-68261-663-5
ISBN (eBook): 978-1-68261-664-2

Cover art by Christian Bentulan and Cody Corcoran
Interior design and composition by Greg Johnson, Textbook Perfect

This book is a work of fiction. People, places, events, and situations are the product of the author's imagination. Any resemblance to actual persons, living or dead, or historical events, is purely coincidental.

No part of this book may be reproduced, stored in a retrieval system, or transmitted by any means without the written permission of the author and publisher.

Post Hill Press
New York • Nashville
posthillpress.com

Published in the United States of America

This book is dedicated to my wife, children,
and the scattered-but-still-close Schaeffer clan
whose unbending encouragement and faith in my writing
gave me enough fuel to see the mission through.

ACKNOWLEDGMENTS

A work of historical fiction requires the writer to immerse himself or herself in an ocean of archives, books, articles, films, and technical data. I am no exception. But without a literary agent who believes in you, and a publishing house willing to take your story beyond a stack of papers on a desk and bring it to the public, not much can come from writing a book beyond personal satisfaction.

As such, I would especially like to thank my tireless agent Bob Thixton at Pinder Lane & Garon-Brooke for taking a chance on an unknown, and Anthony Ziccardi and all the staff at Post Hill, especially Billie Brownell and Madeline Sturgeon and their diligent editing, for making this book a reality. I would also like to thank those who encouraged my writing along the way. They include: Rich Hull, David Frum, Dominic Magnabosco, Jason Hanna, J.D. Griffin, Linda Habgood, Jason Wolfe (now climbing with angels), Ben Shapiro, Hank Berrien, Mark Lasswell, formerly at *The Wall Street Journal*, and Josh Greenman at *The New York Daily News*.

AUTHOR'S NOTE

Many years ago I discovered that my next-door-neighbor served in World War II with the USAAF 8th Air Force as a navigator on a B-17 Flying Fortress; he was shot down over Bremen and spent a year as a POW in *Stalag Luft 1.* I had the honor of helping him craft his memoirs. A veteran of several missions, his tales of brutal combat in the skies over Germany prompted me to wonder in particular, who were those men flying the Luftwaffe fighter planes, about whom he spoke with grudging respect? How did these young pilots muster the intestinal fortitude to climb into their cramped cockpits and rise up and meet the ever more powerful Allied bomber armadas and their accompanying buzz saw of fighter escorts day after day until the very end? What was their story?

And so I began researching Luftwaffe archives, letters, testimonials, and even gun camera footage. What I discovered was that perhaps the most dangerous place to fight in Western Europe in the last two years of World War II was in the cockpit of a Luftwaffe fighter during "Defense of the Reich" missions.

Oddly, the German fighter pilots' story of waging a defensive war against hopeless odds—with some squadrons facing no less hazardous conditions than those of their oft-celebrated U-boat compatriots—has largely been ignored. Sources vary, but according to the *Gemeinschaft der Jagdflieger*, from 1939 to 1945, out of 28,000 day fighter pilots, a total of 8,500 were killed in action, 2,700 went missing or were POWs, and 9,100 were wounded or injured. This is a stunning casualty rate of 72 percent. And the vast accumulation of these losses occurred in 1943–1945. Such a story demanded a voice as a subject among the pantheon of war novels. I hope I have in my small way brought their tragic tale to life…even as they died fighting for a wretched cause that had to be obliterated. Still, their suffering was real, and they paid a severe price to be the spear point of a nation led astray by a madman who was, in the end, a dark mirror held up to us all.

"I would say that if we were not all guilty of crimes, then we were at least accomplices."

—Roland Kiemig, Ostheer soldier, 1991

"We cannot and should not be allowed to win this war."

—Lieutenant Colonel Helmuth Groscurth,
in a letter to his wife after the execution
of ninety orphaned Jewish children, 1941

"How much longer can it continue? Every day seems an eternity. There is nothing for us now. Only our operations, which are hell. And then more waiting for the blow which inevitably must fall, sooner or later. Every time I close the canopy before taking off, I feel that I am closing the lid to my coffin."

—Luftwaffe Captain Heinz Knoke,
from his diary, August 1944

PART 1

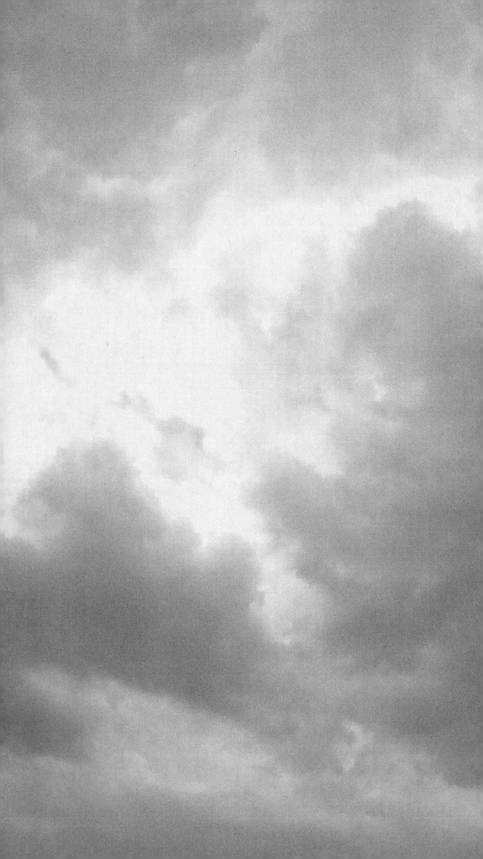

1

Whenever I find it difficult to sleep, I try to count the number of men I have killed. By the time I approach one hundred, I have usually slipped off to a netherworld of agitated dreams of fire and swirling ash, mixed with the cries of children in the dust. But for my last victim, they were souls I never knew. I see their machines breaking apart into shards of flaming metal, tumbling end over end and disappearing through the clouds below me. Sometimes I follow their death spiral all the way down until they slam into the earth, atomized in churning fireballs. Like me, I must believe they were young and full of hope and promise. Unlike me, they are bright-eyed ghosts now. Rumors. So many years later they still fill my windscreen during the interminable nights. Memories follow a man like a vapor.

The mornings are especially difficult. That's when I'm alone with thoughts so clear, staring wide-eyed yet unseeing into the deep blue shades of the pre-dawn darkness. In the past, whenever the images would take hold and torment me until I jackknifed upright in bed, a sheen of sweat gluing my nightshirt to my pasty skin, a gentle hand would touch my shoulder and bring me back home. A soothing voice assuring me that all is okay. That she is here. But she is no longer with me. And once my eyes open, I find retreating back into sleep impossible.

Today's date is circled on my calendar, reminding me that I'm to receive a curious visitor. I have no idea what a journalist from the States wants with me, other than to pick at the scabs of my old wounds. Americans are a forceful lot. The mystery of her insistent calling intrigues me. Yet, I'm uneasy all the same. My roiling stomach warns me this could be a painful encounter.

So, with my nerves now charged, I struggle out of bed with a groan. When you've lived eighty-two years, as I have, you learn not to get up too swiftly; one misplaced step could mean a shattered hip…a death sentence at my age. Would that be so terrible? I shoo the thought away like a pesky fly.

Once steady on my feet, however, I move with the purpose of a man who's held command in the past. Shuffling to the hall, I pause at the bedroom doorway and glance back through shadows at the sheets that lie in a tussled, frustrated bundle. My bed is empty. Amelia has been gone for one month, yet I still expect to see her. She should be lying on her side, the mound of her hips gently rising and falling with her breathing as if bobbing in a current. A phantom visage.

In my robe and slippers, I feel my way through the narrow corridor and down the stairway to the second floor. As delicate as I try to be, one of the steps creaks under me. I pause and grit my teeth as if a grimace will muffle the sound. Dora, my fifty-year-old daughter and only child, stirs in the guest bedroom. She's temporarily abandoned her family in Dover to stay with me since her mother was buried. She knows I'm lonely.

She calls to me: "Papa? Are you okay?"

"Fine, Daughter," I assure her from the bottom of the stairwell. "Go back to sleep."

"I'm already up. If you wait a moment I'll come down and brew you some tea." Dora's mother and I grew up in Stauffenberg, Germany, a village tucked away among the rolling hills of the Oberfranken on the Main River. Thus we never lost the telltale "zis" and "zat" that afforded us so many looks of suspicion immediately after the war. But Dora's a product of London and, as such, developed a curious continental brogue.

"That would be kind," I say. "If it's no bother."

"Of course it's no bother," she calls from her closet. I hear her fumbling through a rack of clothes, searching the armoire for her robe.

In the dimness I creep away from the banister to a pair of French doors. A surly November wind howls through the streets of Westminster. This place leaks like an old vessel, and drafts push through the hall.

I nudge open the doors and lazily move into the conservatory, gently closing them behind me. Two leather couches sandwich a mahogany table, which in turn pins a Persian rug to weathered oak floorboards. Bookshelves line the far wall. On the other wall hang photographs from my life. Frozen snippets of my past. I have to turn away from them before the memories build…and I come to face a richly stained grand piano that waits for me in the recess of my bay window. The Steinway's been my constant companion this past month.

I see from my window that it promises to be a crisp, clear autumn day. And as I take in the first hint of pink ribbon peeking over the eastern London sky, I sit down to play. Closing my eyes, I strain to hear in my mind the sonata before my fingertips touch the ivory. Then I lay them gently on the keys and step into the musical world that has sustained me throughout my life. And I whisper to myself a question implanted in my bleeding head by a French priest who was witness to my complicity in the slaughter of innocents. One I have repeated every morning for the past sixty years: "Will God forgive me for what I have done?"

2

Rachael Azerad sits quietly in the back seat of the taxi and views the whitewashed stone and auburn brick facades as they whiz past her window. A *New York Times* reporter, she instinctively caresses the portable tape recorder, no bigger than a cigarette box, in the pocket of her raincoat. She leans her forehead against the car window and, catching her reflection, she studies herself as if viewing a painting.

At thirty-five, the shapely brunette Queens native with her full lips and athletic build can pass for ten years younger. This despite the rugged nature of her demanding career, which often exposes her to harsh conditions. She attributes her youthful appearance to her olive skin, a gift from her Sephardic father. In an alluring contrast, her eyes are light blue, almost gray—a contribution from her German mother. Rachael turns heads wherever she goes, and deflects heated advances from men and women at press club dinners. But her foreign-correspondent life is a lonely one that allows for only the rare, torrid affair. More often it's a life of holidays spent isolated in strange, sometimes hostile, places few have heard of and fewer would care to ever see. But this is her choice. It's a course that suits her. The pay is good, and her learning about the world never ceases. And sometimes it even offers her that rare glimpse into the nobility of the human heart. Today, she hopes, will be one such occasion.

And yet, she finds her mission distasteful. If he is not the man, then she's flown three thousand miles to sit down with a war criminal. A brute who marched with the barbarian horde that almost drove her people to extinction. She finds her stomach churning in aggrieved protest, but knows it's not car sickness despite the cab driver's treating the London streets like his own personal Le Mans course.

"A bit fatigued are you, madam?" inquires the cheerful taxi driver from the front seat. Glancing up, Rachael reminds herself to shift her gaze to the right, as she's now in a country where they drive on the left side of the road through these ancient and impossibly narrow streets.

She forces a smile at the jolly fellow, whose bushy orange mustache completes the image that could have been ripped right out of a tourism brochure. "A little jet-lagged, yeah," she manages in reply. "Just touched down from the States about two hours ago."

"I see. Well, it *is* early to you, no matter where you are then." The car executes a series of screeching twists and turns through roadways that in Manhattan would have passed for alleys. "Business or pleasure?" The driver's benign eyes, studying her in the mirror, are framed by cherry-red puffs of thick brows.

She shrugs. "I'm not sure."

Rachael glances up at the ornately crafted buildings jutting up from the sidewalks. Each is remarkably elaborate, yet one follows the other so that their exquisite architecture becomes commonplace. Offices and apartments, occasionally adorned with "To Let" signs, with their heavy stone construction and chunky wooden frames surrounding thick panes of narrow glass. She muses to herself how much older is London than even the most historic colonial sections of lower Manhattan. The taxi follows the bumpy curves of Lancaster Terrace and whips around Westbourne Street, where it pours onto one of the tributary roadways emptying into the greenery of Hyde Park.

"That's the Lido on your right across the water," says her driver, who doesn't quite understand how New Yorkers value silence because they get so little of it. "The Diana memorial walk over there. Holocaust memorial to your right." At that, Rachael takes notice. It's a reminder of why she's made this journey across "the pond" in the first place. It took her a week just to convince her editor it was a potential story. A month more to convince her family that it was worth the investment of time and money.

A silent prayer passes over her lips as they bank around the obelisk of the equestrian Wellington monument and eventually join the noisy bustle of jammed cars, black taxicabs, and iconic red double-decker buses that flow along the Piccadilly. *Please let me be right about this man.* Otherwise, she knows, her trip to see me this bright morning will have served no purpose but forcing her to spend time with a man who, in another time and place, she might have wanted to kill.

3

"Come in." My daughter ushers Rachael into the first-floor parlor. Rachael's surprised at the relative quiet of this tiny back street lined by ancient brick pubs and booksellers just two blocks off the hectic Strand. The journalist pauses at the threshold. The music hits her like a blast of air. Dora perceives the appreciation on her guest's face and smiles. "Papa plays more than usual these days."

"It's beautiful. Is it Mendelssohn?"

Dora nods. "From *Songs Without Words*. Come and meet him."

Rachael follows Dora from the entranceway up the stairs to the main flat. She studies her hostess. My daughter wears her graying hair in a tight bun. Streaks of her original sandy blonde reveal themselves in the light.

The reporter poses a hypothetical question in her mind to the broad-backed woman who smiles over her shoulder as they climb the stairs. *What would you have done? Sixty years ago? Would you, Dora, have helped me?*

At the head of the steps are the French doors. Dora halts there. Rachael peers around her and catches the shadows of the piano and the music maker weaving back and forth like a human metronome.

The doors gently swing open, and Rachel follows Dora into the conservatory. Her hostess offers a comforting remark: "Don't be intimidated by Papa. He's more songbird than raptor now."

Rachael nods and clenches the strap of her shoulder bag. She moves past her guide and steps into the salon where I, the decorated Luftwaffe flier, now fill my remaining days with serenades to a world that has passed away.

At the end of the grand piano the two women stand before me as if I'm a display. But I ignore both my daughter and her attractive guest. I'm wholly absorbed in the music.

"Can I get you some tea?" Dora whispers to the fidgety reporter.

"I'm good, thanks."

My daughter nods. "I'll leave you two alone then. You have much to talk about I gather, considering the distance you've traveled." She retreats through the double doors and closes them gently behind her.

Now it's just the two of us. I play on, giving Rachael a chance to study me with a professional acuity, like a grid overlaid. A silver mane caps my pale face, gouged like a dry riverbed. A heavy gray cardigan and white oxford shirt shroud a rapidly withering physique. Hints of a robust youth. Heavy, powerful hands, broad shoulders. A firm chin. My eyebrows are white as flour. But beneath them it's my eyes that grab Rachael and hold her fast. The green is a shade of serenity. She searches them for the heart. And I in turn decipher her thoughts. Am I the man she seeks?

Rachael retreats to the far wall, splashed with photographs. The pictures are a mixed bag of the old and new, black-and-white and color prints. Various sizes. Some are moments captured from decades ago, others just this past summer.

She focuses her attention on a fresh image of me as an old man cradling a woman, frail and ashen, in my arms. Sporting colorful nautical jackets, we lean against the rail of a boat off the Channel Isles, the slate-gray waters behind us. A cold spray whips through our white hair as we smile spryly for the camera. We are two old salts in the twilight of our lives and still very much in love. Rachael feels a twinge of compassion for me now.

But then her eyes fall upon more sinister images. Their bleak, faded sepia a stark contrast to the sublime color of my later years. A portrait of a young Luftwaffe officer. Supremely confident as I leer back at her from under the brim of my visor cap, tilted at a rakish angle that was the style of the *Jagdflieger*, a fighter pilot. I wear the old uniform of a Germany that I find hard to imagine ever existed. The dark blue flannel frock lined with brass buttons, the choker collar, the stiff medallion of the black eagle over my heart, its wings spread in flight, clutching the swastika in its talons. Another tattered photo. An action shot of that same young man in a baggy flight suit, hoisting myself out of the cockpit of a fighter plane. Again, the confident, swaggering grin. My leather flying cap has been removed to reveal a tuft of disheveled honey-colored hair.

Another framed portrait, this one of a family, dated August 1940. A freshly commissioned Lieutenant Harmon Becker, in full dress uniform, cap in hand this time, stands next to my teenaged brother. Paul, a darker version of his blond knight sibling, is dressed in his Sunday best—a Nazi emblem pinned to his lapel. The boys' taciturn father, Karl, sits in a chair sporting the less bellicose attire of a local constable. Our round-faced mother, Greta, sits beside her husband, her hand in his, wearing the traditional frilled blouse, heavy dress, and apron dirndl of the Bavarian country Frau.

Rachael is set to turn back towards the piano when her eyes lock on one last photo from my war years. She stiffens. The shot is of a line of German soldiers in crisp dress uniform standing at attention like statues. I am leaning forward to receive a medal while I shake the presenter's hand. Rachael, of course, recognizes the master of the cold ceremony in the picture. The very lines of his face, his every nuance and contour, from the dark square mustache to the searing crystalline eyes, have been seared into her consciousness as sure as the numbers burned into the forearms of his countless victims. This young version of me formally shakes hands with Adolf Hitler. My guest boils inside. How could I display such a vile photograph on the same wall as one of my wife? Now she feels deceived by the old man behind her. To her I'm nothing more than a tired, broken-down old Nazi. A war criminal.

Rachael turns away from the wall as she would from a foul odor and comes face-to-face with me as I stand right behind her now. She hasn't noticed that the song ended minutes earlier and silence but for the comforting tick-tock of a grandfather clock saturates the room.

I point to the picture. "Yes, that's me," I admit with a scratchy voice. "I was awarded the Knight's Cross by the Führer himself."

My thick German accent visibly repels her.

"It's nice to see you no longer wear it," she offers acerbically.

I'm unfazed by her tone. "I no longer have it. I keep that photograph not as a treasure, Miss Azerad, but as a reminder."

"Of the good old days?" Her sarcasm is a razor.

I shake my head. "Of how foolish I was." I extend a veiny hand to her. She glances down, her combative nature disarmed by the tone of my contrition. She takes it. "I'm pleased to meet you, Miss Azerad." I lead her to the couches and motion to one as I ease into the other with a sigh. "Sit. And then you can tell me."

"Tell you what?" she asks, lowering herself to the cushions.

"Tell me why you are here."

4

Sitting across the table from me, she clears her throat. I can tell she's never met a German veteran of the big war before. I wonder what she's feeling inside. What images of my youth are parading through her mind? After some hesitation she says: "Well…you're one of the last of the great World War Two flying aces. Your book's earned some acclaim."

I guffaw heartily. Even she smiles at her transparency. "From whom? *Aviation Week*?" I laugh again, then cough violently, cursing the dampness of the English autumn as I hack a wet marble of phlegm into a handkerchief I whip out from my back pocket.

The book she refers to sits on my coffee table. It's an insignificant, and rather dry, memoir of just one more soldier's experience during the war. Very few have read my book, as the publisher reminds me every so often. History, it is said, is written by the victors. I glance down at its jacket. Is that young pilot really me? *Bitter Skies!* the title shouts. *Memoirs of a Luftwaffe Fighter Pilot.* I sometimes forget my days in the Wehrmacht. But never completely. That's my burden, I suppose.

I tap the cover with my finger. "Everything you need to know about my war years is in this book. The interesting part anyway. Tell me, Miss Azerad. Why have you come so far to talk to a retired concert pianist who a lifetime ago flew fighter planes in a lost war?"

She remains silent, so I press the issue. "You're a foreign correspondent."

She nods.

I lean into her now: "So why am I not talking to *The New York Times* literary critic as opposed to one who writes about Fallujah and the Golan Heights? What about me is so important to you?"

She lays her little tape recorder on the table and fishes through her leather bag for a notebook and pen. She presses the record button. "Do you mind?" she asks.

I shrug. "What's the harm?"

She touches the pen to her lips. This woman is a true beauty. A real spitfire—if a German flier dare use that term! Even in my advancing years I can appreciate the fairer sex. Her sultry features are so much the opposite of my porcelain Amelia's.

She says nothing more, until the silence makes me uncomfortable. "Well?" I say, growing slightly irritated.

"I'm sorry," she responds defensively. "I've never met a German war veteran before." As I'd figured. Then she adds: "A Nazi." And the way she says that makes me suddenly look down and fiddle with the crease of my trousers.

"Is that who you think I am?" I say in a near whisper.

She looks up at me. "You wore the uniform."

I meet her gaze and rub a contemplative hand through my fine hair. "How can I put this? Good men sometimes fight for bad things, Miss Azerad. The question is, can they redeem themselves?"

"A good question," she agrees. "One I intend to answer. We can get to that in time. But first some background. You say in your book you were shot down over the English Channel in June 1944?"

"Ah, so it begins," I say. "Very well. Yes, that's correct. I became a prisoner of war after that."

She stares at her notes as if taking insurance information at the doctor's office. "It must've been frightening."

I shift in my seat. "I'd been brought down once before."

She pauses, draws in a breath, and looks up from her pad. "But this time was different. Your book doesn't tell everything. Does it?"

The grandfather clock chimes. I hear Dora rummaging about in the kitchen. And I sit motionless.

"Please, Mr. Becker, tell me. Tell me the whole story."

At my age I'm always cold. Yet now a heat wave ripples through me. "You're a good reporter. But why should I confide in you?"

She answers sternly: "Because then, and only then, will I tell you why I care."

5

I slide open the coffee table drawer and produce a tattered envelope with a yellowing piece of paper folded and stuffed inside. I carefully slide out the paper. The note is creased and has grown soft as tissue over the years. I discovered this letter when, at Dora's gentle prodding, I finally forced myself to start clearing out Amelia's personal effects from our house. Her death, though not entirely unexpected—a cancer had been robbing her of her life for over a year—came far earlier than the doctors predicted. I've just begun the unbearable task of packing away her life. This fragile epistle, which I've read every day since I found it, is one last link to the beginning of our long life together.

Rachael observes me as if I'm about to perform a card trick. "My wife, Amelia. She died recently."

She nods. "I'm sorry."

"Of course the reporter knows," I say. "I wrote this letter to her during the war. When she and I were sweethearts. Naturally it's in German. But I'll translate it for you."

Rachael begins to scribble something but then catches herself and pauses. She glances at me with sympathy. "I don't want to pry. That's a personal cor—"

"No," I cut her off. "If you wish to understand what happened, then I should start here."

"Alright, Mr. Becker," she says. "I'm listening."

I unfold the delicate letter and smile up at my guest, whose professional curiosity is piqued. She looks at it as if trying to discern the lettering through the light.

"You see? No need for glasses," I say with mock pride. "My eyes are still sharp after so many years." I reflect on that a moment. "I can see it all so clearly now." Then I begin to read.

6

December 14, 1943

My Dearest Amelia,

The war goes on. The killing. Still the Americans come. Things seemed so simple not so long ago. I miss the old life. My home, my music. Most of all you, my love. But I suppose it is unhealthy to dwell on such memories here. I must stay focused on the ugly business at hand. We fly every day now. And, in a sense, it suits me. I know that sounds odd but it is an odd life we live. We bear the mark of death, yet because we fly we are more alive than most. I cannot adequately express how it feels to be so high. The sky a deep blue…the color of your eyes. Silence but for the hum of the engine and the occasional voice on the radio. The earth below seems so peaceful. Yet I do not have long to contemplate my false reality, as the skies will soon be filled with death that I have come to know like an old friend.

I pray the winter finds you well. When this trouble subsides, we will be together again. But for now my duty pulls me aloft and into harm's way, for this is a different war. It is not like the heady days in the beginning. We are on the defensive now. And as I curve into formations of Boeings so thick they block out the sun, my past sins flash before me.

But do not worry, my love. I believe I will survive this test. And then, my dearest Amelia, a clear horizon beckons us to a better day.

With all my love,

Harmon

Bundled up in my flight suit, I penned those words sitting at my desk in my cozy hut on base while a gentle snowfall added a thin layer of fresh powder to the Belgian countryside. No sooner had I finished the last sentence and sealed the envelope than the alarm sounded. I jumped up and scrambled out into the cold, racing to my fueled and armed fighter, which sat at the ready on the tarmac just outside the snow-covered hangar.

As I hurried across the wet ground to my waiting aircraft, I handed the letter to my ground-crew chief, Sergeant Ohler, with orders to mail it whether or not I returned.

Before climbing into the cockpit of my Focke-Wulf fighter plane, one of many lined up along the field with propellers whirring, I paused and gazed up into the steely overcast of clouds frowning down upon us. After so many years of going to war in the sky, I came to dread the ferocity of air combat and to embrace the words of Shakespeare: "*...this brave o'erhanging firmament, this majestical roof fretted with golden fire, why, it appears no other thing to me than a foul and pestilent congregation of vapours.*" This could have been the soliloquy of every German flier in Western Europe by this time.

Then it was off to the war once again. My moment of quiet reflection obliterated by the roar of engines and their promise of battle...up there somewhere, beyond the blanket of gray, waiting for me.

7

At fifteen thousand feet the sky was a rich blue, like a Caribbean lagoon. Outside my canopy, the thin air was minus thirty degrees Fahrenheit and so clear it seemed like I was flying through a vacuum. As we cruised along, heading for the intercept waypoint, for a brief period between takeoff and combat I could forget the war. A plush carpet of thick gray clouds beneath me made the ground and its troubles seem to be part of a separate universe.

There were sixteen aircraft in my squadron. I was flying the lead fighter in the lead arrow, each consisting of a four-plane "swarm" element in "finger-four" formation. Each swarm consisted of a loose two-plane "pack" with leader and trailing wingman. I'd logged five hundred-plus combat sorties by now and so wasn't preoccupied with the minutia of keeping formation or maintaining altitude and airspeed. Instead, lulled to passivity by the humming of the bulky radial engine in front of me, my eyes drifted to the tattered, wallet-sized photograph taped up against the console. Amelia's smiling face gazed longingly up at me. Although the image was black and white, the color of her eyes was a match. An image so feminine and fair and enchanting, it seemed obscenely misplaced among the coldly sinister dials of this war machine. My thoughts traveled to the letter I'd just penned. I yearned for several winters ago. The looming war had been still a thing of abstractness then and I just a happy boy, so very satisfied that the girl of so many dreams had taken me as her own. All had been right with the world then. I longed to see her in—

"Attention, Nebel-One."

The crackling of the intercom in my ears abruptly snapped me out of my daydreaming. Ground-control wanted a fix on my position. As acting group commander of the entire Three Group made up of aircraft from several bases as well as my own sixteen-man squadron, I was in charge. Suddenly I was Captain Harmon Becker, the warrior again.

"Nebel-One calling Bodo," I replied, speaking into the radio molded into the oxygen mask that covered my face and prevented me from passing out at this altitude. "Three Group on course two-zero to waypoint Berta."

"Victor, Victor Nebel-One."

I then spoke to my squadron. "Can anyone see them?" I was referring to a convoy of American bombers over the North Sea and headed this way.

"Nothing yet, Herr Captain," responded Lieutenant Josef Mueller, my jovial wingman. "And our petrol's running low," he added.

"JG 32 Three Group," the ground controller chimed in again. "Heavy babies now in sector Gustav-Paula. Go to Hanni eight zero. Vectoring Two Group to support you."

"Victor, Victor," I replied. " Message understood."

My gloved hand brought the control stick of my aircraft closer in to my groin. The other members of the squadron followed suit as we executed a gentle climb to twenty-five thousand feet and turned towards the new heading to intercept the targets. After five minutes we leveled off in position to meet the caravan of American B-17 Fortress bombers chugging towards us and Germany beyond.

I admit I disdained the bomber crews for wreaking destruction upon our cities. But unlike many of my comrades whose hatred bordered on bloodlust, my animosity was tempered with a desire to understand why they were here. I would in time question the war in my own way. But not today.

For now my duty pulled me north by northwest to stop the Americans. I honestly thought they were mad to even try to break through us. We had known well in advance they were coming, the thick clouds would make accurate bombing impossible, and the Luftwaffe had every available fighter in the air, just waiting to meet them. I scanned left then right to see my pilots' aircraft buffeting up and down on gentle cushions of frigid air, so close to each other that you could have jumped from wingtip to wingtip. A formidable flock of determined young men in their fighter planes.

My FW-190A fighter was a fearsome aircraft. Its sobriquet, "Butcher Bird," was well-deserved. Its sleek cylindrical lines came to an abrupt nose at a flat cowling that housed a robust fourteen-cylinder BMW radial engine. With seventeen hundred horsepower at my fingertips I could throttle the little plane to over three hundred seventy miles per hour and still turn inside any fighter the Allies had at the time except the British Spitfire. Although its performance fell off at these high altitudes, its deadly array of four twenty-millimeter wing cannons and two synchronized 7.62-millimeter machine guns made it the ideal weapons platform for taking on the four-engine "heavy babies," as we called the American bombers.

What we did not yet have to deal with in any great number was enemy fighters accompanying the bomber streams. I'd tussled with them over Russia, and in areas nearer the English Channel, but never over Germany as we were flying now. Our air marshal and Luftwaffe commander-in-chief, *Reichsmarschall* Hermann Göring, insisted that the Allies would never have a single-engine fighter plane with the range to accompany the bombers from their bases in England all the way to Germany and back again. So we thought we'd always have an unimpeded crack at the heavies that were so brazen as to raid the Fatherland in broad daylight.

But I've always had a cautious nature, and so I called out to my wingman over the radio waves. "Mueller, can you see any fighters?"

"No, Herr Captain," came his reply.

"Keep a sharp eye."

I glanced over to see Mueller in his cockpit swiveling his head, scanning for any sign of the enemy. Josef Mueller was the man with whom I'd been flying longer than any other. For over two years he and I had kept each other from dying young in the violent skies like mutual guardian angels. We'd come to depend on each other in the air. Once again we were headed side by side into combat against a determined and ever-more-formidable foe.

At that moment an ominous dark blotch appeared in the sky above Dortmund, which lay somewhere underneath the colorless tarpaulin of thickening clouds below us. At first indistinguishable, then the individual forms of warplanes began to take shape out of the amorphous glob.

"Boeings at twelve o'clock below," Mueller reported in the clear with his usual excitement.

At closure of over five hundred miles per hour, it didn't take long for me to make out the stacked formations of what looked like three hundred B-17 Flying Fortress bombers. At this altitude their engine exhaust formed long contrails in the sky, white ribbons that led us right to them.

The ships were a menacing sight. Powerful four-engine leviathans coated in olive drab. The white stars on blue circles painted boldly across their wings and fuselages were instantly recognizable as American markings. As we formed up for the attack like lions preparing to pounce on a herd of wildebeests, I heard young Sergeant Heinz Kluge in my headset.

"I don't like those guns up front," he observed with agitation in his nineteen-year-old voice. Kluge had just joined us from flight school and this was his first mission.

"Don't worry, boy," said Mueller, laughing. "They're saying the same about you right now."

"Alright," I interrupted. "We'll attack in echelon, head-on, into their high squadron. Fan out and claim a target. Two and Three Squadrons, follow in order. There's plenty to go around. New fliers, remember, you're never as close as you think. Use your guns to sight and then count to five before switching to cannon. And aim for the cockpit."

"*Jawohl*!" I heard several voices click in unison.

I flipped the safety lid on the control column that covered the gun buttons. Then I switched on the Revi gunsight, and a yellow circle and bars appeared in the sighting glass. I sucked in a deep oxygenated breath and tried to relax.

"Ready, Mueller?" I said to my wingman.

"I'm right behind you," he replied.

"Good hunting, lads," I said in a sporty tone that seemed ill-suited considering our prey were aircraft crammed with crews of ten men inside. I put that grisly notion out of my mind as I throttled up and bore in for the kill. We had a job to do. And that was that.

8

Texas Totty, the lead bomber of the high squadron, loomed large in my windscreen. Once in position, I went to full throttle, the G-forces pressing me back into my seat like an invisible hand. My breathing grew rapid and heavy. Beads of sweat popped on my brow as I steadied my gunsight to rest over the cockpit of the green monster.

"It's yours, Captain," said Mueller. "Take the shot!" I could see white muzzle flashes, like blinking lights, as both the nose and top turret gunners tried desperately to dispatch me before I opened up on them. The glowing tracer rounds zipped past me, but I was too elusive a target. I rested my index finger over the gun trigger on my control stick. "Hold steady, Ami," I breathed. *Closer…closer…*

Mueller's fighter dropped slightly behind me. *Steady…steady…FIRE*!

I squeezed the trigger and felt my little craft shudder as the four wing cannons thumped away, hurling explosive rounds into the stunned fortress bomber. I watched with fascination as flashes of my shells hitting their mark methodically traced a path from the Plexiglas nose cone up to the cockpit and then top turret. It was at most a three-second burst, but it was on the mark.

In an instant I sped past the stricken target through a shower of jagged metal bits of debris, zooming beneath it in a snap roll just before we were to collide. Mueller was right behind me.

"Watch the ball turret!" he shouted with alarm. I saw tracers whizzing by me from behind as the belly gunner of *Texas Totty* made a vain attempt to clip me as I buzzed past. The tracers stopped abruptly. "Got him!" I heard Mueller call out with satisfaction.

Mueller and I pulled out of our shallow dive after making the first pass and climbed back to altitude while at the same time executing a wide arching turn towards the now disorganized bomber stream. My squadron followed. We would soon catch up to the Boeings and race in front of the lead element, then turn and come at their noses one more time.

From my high vantage point I took in the first images of the destruction we'd just visited upon our unwelcome guests. The blinding sun shined down upon a five-mile-high panorama of flashes, black smoke, and wounded bombers trying desperately to maintain their tight "combat box" formations. I could see several of the large aircraft drop out of the pack with engines belching flames and trailing thick streamers of smoke, their propellers feathered or shot off completely. One of them abruptly peeled up vertically, stalled, and then fell back on itself to commence the horrifying death spiral towards the earth hidden somewhere twenty-five thousand feet beneath the undercast. Panicked airmen were bailing out of their doomed planes and taking to their parachutes. Little cream circles, like floating jellyfish, dotted the sky. One chute was snagged on the stabilizer of the spinning bomber—the poor fellow being whipped around like a stone in a sling. Another of the bombers simply exploded in midair, one moment a large war machine, the next a flaming ball of bright orange streamers raining down to the ground.

"Captain Becker!" The boyish chirping of an excited Kluge crackled through my earphones. "I think I got one!"

"Keep the airwaves clear of chatter, boy," I said.

We leveled off at our original altitude with the bomber phalanx to our three o'clock. We were flying a parallel course to them, careful to stay just out of range of their fifty-caliber guns, and gaining on them.

Black puffs of smoke began to burst around us, presenting a new hazard of deadly clouds of jagged steel that buffeted bombers and fighters alike. The concussion of the blasts bounced us all over the sky.

"Keep yourselves intact and stay in formation," I commanded, trying to settle the younger pilots.

"What's happening?" begged Kluge. His voice wasn't so cocksure now.

"Flak," explained Mueller. "Eighty-eight millimeters."

"But they're our own guns!"

"They don't care," I informed him bluntly. "Alright. We'll come around and make one more pass at the high squadron. Sound off."

My headset filled with young, ghostly voices. Each name represented a life abruptly spun off its axis and thrown into the air war over Europe.

"Mueller here."

"Borner here."

"Gaetjens here."

"Zeller here."

"Von Mauer here."

"Kluge he—" *BAM*! Kluge's plane disintegrated from a direct hit by a friendly shell fired from eight thousand yards below. I turned away as my stomach wrenched. A promising and enthusiastic boy from Füssen dead on his first mission. Another letter for me to write.

"Dammit!" I heard Mueller scream in frustration. "Why can't those fat asses hit the enemy so well?"

"Who controls the flak batteries anyway?" I heard Borner chime in.

"Churchill?" added Gaetjens.

"That's enough," I shouted. "We're almost ahead of them. Continue."

"Grislawski here."

"Buchholz here."

"Osterkamp here."

"Schmidt here."

"Wittneburg here."

"Hoth here."

"Speigel here."

"Von Freitag here."

Then silence. We'd started off with sixteen in the squadron that morning. We were short one.

"What of Edelmann?"

Borner chimed in. "He collided with a heavy. I watched him bail out but didn't see a parachute."

Two losses so far. I shook my mind of them for the moment. There was still work to be done. The bombers were now behind us at our five o'clock. Their ranks were noticeably thinner and their formations more haggard. Some had engines blazing and were struggling just to keep up. They would be easy prey. Without the interlocking fields of f ire from their ten machine guns provided by their tight combat box, a lone B-17 had no more chance in a sky filled with butcher birds than did a wounded deer in a field of ravenous wolves. As we were running low on fuel, I would leave them to Two Group winging in to relieve us.

"Indians!" Borner suddenly called out over the radio. Enemy fighters.

A wave of adrenaline surged through me. Dammit! I spun my head left and right. Where? Where? "Mueller, do you see them?"

"Not yet. Borner, where are they?" Mueller demanded, annoyance and strain coming through his voice. Then: "Three o'clock. Thunderbolts."

I whipped my head to the right to spy what looked like twenty of the heavy fighters winging in to hit Two Group. They were also painted olive with bright red cowlings around their huge radial engines. At almost twice the weight of our nimble aircraft, the American P-47 Thunderbolt had a clumsy appearance, like a fat milk jug. But it was very fast and deceptively agile.

"After them!" I heard a young voice call out. A 190A roared past me, with another on its heels.

"Who the hell was that?" I demanded.

"God dammit, Von Mauer, you young turd, get back here!" screamed Gaetjens. He was in the plane chasing after the spirited young man who was heading straight for the formation of P-47s. Four of them banked off and rolled in to intercept him.

"Von Mauer, get out of there!" I ordered him.

"*Jawohl*," said the young voice. He'd lost some of his bravado upon seeing the radial-engine monsters with eight wing-mounted heavy machine guns spraying bullets at him and closing in fast.

"You get yourself killed and I'll kill you!" shouted Gaetjens, who zoomed in around him and set up to engage the Americans. Only later at the *Offizierkasino*, the officer's mess, would we laugh at that phrase. But right now one of my junior pilots was in a fix, and I debated whether to lose the squadron to save him. But it all happened so fast that the decision was made for me. Von Mauer dived away, headed for the clouds with the *Jabos*, "hunters," as we called them, quickly gaining on him.

The squadron didn't break formation and join the melee, which was a testament to their discipline. We needed the fuel to get home, and a dogfight would have quickly burned it away.

"Von Mauer, don't dive!" Gaetjens cautioned him. "Pull up and corkscrew."

I saw one of the *Jabos* throttle up hard and quickly close the range. He managed to lay a well-placed burst square into Von Mauer's wing roots, effectively sheering off the boy's right wing and sending him spinning into the misty layer of clouds.

"They got him, sir," reported a distraught Gaetjens.

The Amis made a vain attempt to jump Gaetjens, but the veteran pilot knew better than to make Von Mauer's mistake. He pulled his fighter up and corkscrewed to altitude. The heavier Thunderbolts soon gave up the chase.

I shook my head and roared at the rest of the squadron. "Listen to me, all of you! Never dive away from the Amis. They'll chase you down and kill you over the treetops where you can't bail out. Am I clear?"

"*Jawohl*," answered a smattering of voices, humbled by what they'd just seen.

Apparently the rest of my squadron went unnoticed by the prowling P-47s, who had fuel problems of their own. We saw them breaking off and heading west for England—leaving their bomber crews to fend for themselves during the last leg of their hazardous trip into Germany. Two Group then swung in for the hunt. This was our last chance to do some damage. We made one more attack, as we had to break through the bombers to get back to our base in Belgium. I spied my original prey, *Texas Totty*, chugging along in an erratic flight path. It had dropped out of the lead bomber position. Mueller and I bore in for the kill. As we dove, I felt myself floating in the cockpit, the straps holding me over my seat.

On this day, the B-17 *Texas Totty*, having survived fourteen of its required twenty-five missions, would not return from this trip over

Germany. With one more pass, Mueller and I raked the stricken bird with explosive twenty-millimeter shells until she broke into smoking pieces and fell from the sky. As we sped off, I caught a glimpse of the port wing fluttering to the earth like a falling leaf. I didn't see any parachutes.

I was credited with one B-17 destroyed when I called "Horrido!" to ground control, in our token salute to fighter pilots' patron saint, Horridus. "*Sieg Heil*," I then continued more officially. "Nebel-One to Bodo. One Fortress bomber destroyed."

I glanced at my fuel gauge and realized it was time to head for home. I called in the squadron, and we plotted a course away from the air battle still raging and back to Belgium. If we were lucky, we might be able to re-fuel and intercept the bombers on their way back to England, assuming we could find them again in this sea of clouds.

As we made our way home, our ranks thinner by three, my pilots began calling in their kills. Despite our losses, there was a sense of exuberance among the men. The ground below us was littered with flaming, twisted hulks of destroyed B-17s—and dead crews. The American commanders across the channel had to know this was a black day for them. Some of the more naive men in my command, at ease now for having survived another row with the dreaded heavies, even speculated over the radio whether the Yanks would just give up and go back to the United States. I knew better. They'd be back. That was the only thing about our lives that was not uncertain. The Amis would always come back. And no matter the odds, we would always be there to meet them, come what may.

"*O Tannenbaum, o Tannenbaum / Wie treu sind Deine Blätter / Du grünst nicht nur zur Sommerzeit / Nein auch im Winter wenn es schneit…*" Mueller's boisterous crooning filled our headsets, and some of the men joined the chorus as we made our way back to Andeville.

I was too sullen over the three pilots I'd lost to sing. There would be letters to write that evening to the families, which I would include with the standard "black note." Such was my officer's custom when men under my direct command were killed. Curiously, I didn't give any thought to the ten young men aboard *Texas Totty*—or for that matter any of the lost

American crews that were signified by the kill bars on my oil-streaked tail rudder. They, too, had families back home—wherever home was. Each boy whose life I'd cut short mattered to someone somewhere. And that someone's life was forever darkened by the simple act of my squeezing a trigger. Such is war.

9

I was the last to touch down. I taxied the fighter off the snow-dusted runway and onto the frozen ground near the hangar. My ground crew rushed onto the tarmac with arms waving and hats twirling. Martial music blared from the loudspeakers that bordered the runway.

My plane slowed to a halt, and I cut the engine. The slowing propeller swished to a rest. I slid open the canopy and removed my gloves and leather cap, rubbing my fingers over my itching scalp and tousling my golden hair. As the crew surrounded my craft, I ran my hands down my face in a gesture of utter exhaustion. The adrenaline rush that gave me the essential emotional turbo boost in combat had worn off on the flight home somewhere over Krefeld, leaving me drained.

I glanced around at a jubilant scene. The ground crews rejoiced in their pilots' successes. Other members of the squadron with jostling mechanics in tow made their way to my little fighter like a mob of vigilantes converging on a hanging. Broad smiles as they approached me. I weakly hoisted myself out of the cockpit—from somewhere I heard the pop of a flashbulb—climbed onto the left wing, and leapt to the frozen ground with my boots making a muffled thud.

Standing up straight, I found myself staring at the collar of Sergeant Ohler. Kurt, a native of Polzin, was a bare-knuckle brawler who sported a shaved pate and bushy handlebar mustache in a throwback to the days of Ludendorff and Bismarck. He looked older than his twenty-one years. This mountain of a man was a true tinkerer, having learned auto mechanics in his father's shop. His was the linear outlook of the Prussian man. Ohler's devotion was to the Fatherland and the Luftwaffe aircraft he serviced.

He stood over me twirling his kaiser-like mustache with one hand and carrying a "victory stick," a gaudily decorated baton symbolizing a significant score, in the other. "Herr Captain," he began as other members of the squadron gathered around for the informal ceremony on the frozen airstrip. "On behalf of the squadron, I salute you on your one hundredth victory." He handed me the wand. The men gave a quick cheer, and then the pilots dispersed while the maintenance men descended upon their aircraft like termites. " I'll decorate your rudder, sir."

"Sergeant," I said in a low voice. "Did my letter go out?"

He nodded. "I took care of it personally."

I pulled my yellow inflatable life vest over my head and handed it to him. "Can we get turnaround in time to catch them on their return leg?"

Ohler shook his bullet head, turned candy pink in the icy wind. "No sir. There's more snow bearing down on us from the northwest. I'm surprised the Yank even tried his luck today. We need to get the birds into the hangars."

I nodded in disappointed resignation. "Carry on then." He saluted and turned towards his crew. "Please check that fuel line," I told him. "I think I heard it rattling again."

"*Jawohl.*" He headed around to the still-cooking engine cowling and began to bark orders to his crew to manhandle the plane into the camouflaged hangar and out of the way of the approaching snowstorm.

I stood for a moment watching the maintenance men in their soft field caps haul my aircraft out of the open and into the protection of the hangar. Already I could feel the wind slicing at my face with noticeably more fury than before. I stared up at the lowering mantle of granite clouds bearing down on us and knew this day's work was over. I'd survived another battle to defend the Reich. At least one, and maybe three, of my men hadn't been so lucky.

"Well, well!" I turned to see a beaming Mueller strutting towards me, an unopened bottle of wine in his hand. "So you made centurion. Congratulations." He playfully patted me on the shoulder with the bottle. "I see you have your victory stick," he observed.

I glanced down at it, having forgotten I was even holding it. It was a yard-long finely polished piece of mahogany carved into a snake coiling up a branch. The number 100 and the emblem of JG 32 were crudely carved into the bulbous handle. "I kill ten more men and they give me this?"

"They do those things from time to time. Good for morale." He grabbed it in his hand and began flailing it around like a fencing sword. "You should come to the *Kasino* and drink with us."

I grabbed it back and gave him a reproachful glare. "I'm not in a mood to celebrate, Josef. Kluge, Edelmann, and Von Mauer were just boys. Barely even learned to shave."

I tried to push past him, but he gently blocked me with his arm. I turned to face his disarming brown eyes. "But *we* still live, Harmon," he reminded me poignantly.

I nodded and managed a faint grin. I took hold of the wine bottle in my free hand and read the label.

"I don't know which you like more, French wine or Walloon women."

"Can't I have both?" he said, laughing and jerking the bottle away from me. Then, looking past me, he groaned. "Ach! Here comes our fearless leader."

I pivoted around and a blast of frigid air mixed with ice crystals sliced anew at my fair skin. Trailing behind the wind, as if it were a trumpeter heralding his approach, I saw the object of Mueller's disdain.

"Oh Christ, I do hate politics," I muttered.

Major Hans Seebeck, our commander of Three Group, strode towards us with a slight hobble. A black leather patch hid an empty socket where his left eye had once been. His flying days were over, courtesy of a friendly-fire incident. I knew fighter aces like Günther Specht who continued to fly quite well with one eye missing, but the major was not in his league. Yet Seebeck's wounds didn't in any way diminish his carriage. He marched towards us smartly clad in his immaculate blue uniform and greatcoat. His braided visor cap stood high and straight. His long boots shined bright even in the dreary light of mid-December. A walking stick held in his gloved hand supported his uneven gait. To his face we called him Herr Major. But privately we called him "Berlin's bitch."

And he hated me.

10

"Well, maybe we'll see you later then?" said Mueller as he saluted me. The snow was now starting to fall in earnest, painting our shoulders a virgin white. The aircraft were by now safely under cover. I could hear the echo of Ohler barking orders to the men over the metallic ringing of their tools.

"Maybe," I answered noncommittally. The lieutenant turned on his heels and retreated as the commander advanced towards me. My wingman couldn't abide Seebeck. Perhaps it was because he knew of the animosity between us. My enemies were his, I imagine. Plus, he too thought Seebeck a poor pilot.

"Captain!" beamed the major as he limped over to me through the mounting carpet of white powder. "There you are." His tone was too friendly, as it always was after a successful mission. As much as I threatened him, he was smart enough to know that the group's victories would put him in good standing with Berlin. I stood at attention and saluted.

"Herr Major."

Seebeck returned the salute, and we stood facing each other on the windswept field.

"I'm hearing good things about the mission. And the men seem happy. What is the tally?"

I did the math in my head, recounting the men's animated young voices on the way back to base. "Unofficially five heavies destroyed. Three probables. All from my squadron. We left them for Two Group to finish, as we were running low on petrol."

He ecstatically whacked his gloved hand on his thigh. "That's splendid!"

I smirked. "We couldn't have done it without you, Herr Major."

He gave me a sharp glare but otherwise ignored the slight. He'd been wary of me ever since I came here, on his orders, to breathe life back into his demoralized command. He knew he needed me. With him grounded, I commanded the group in the air. But his mark was still on the reports.

"I must make another request for the replacement belly tanks," he said, more to himself.

"Do you want to know our losses?" I asked grimly.

His smile faded some. "Berlin is more concerned with what we do to them, Becker. Not the other—"

"One confirmed dead, two missing," I snapped.

He heaved an annoyed sigh. "A terrible thing for a man to die. But, it may provide some comfort to remember that he died for the New Germany."

"Comforting to you perhaps."

He raised the tip of his wooden stick to my chest and leaned into me ever so slightly. "It should be to you as well since you are an officer of that new nation. Or do you doubt our Führer's cause?"

I gently eased the stick to one side, not taking the bait. "I couldn't fly for a cause I don't believe in."

He studied me with his remaining eye. "What else is troubling you, Captain?" I hesitated. "Come on, man, out with it."

"Very well," I said. "We lost a man to fighter escorts."

He shook his head. "That's not possible. I understand you hit them on our side of the border. Over the Ruhr. Well beyond their range, no?"

"Tell that to Von Mauer," I said coldly.

The major's face was blank. "Von Mauer?"

"The boy your non-existent American fighters blew out of the sky today."

"Oh." He thought a moment, as if working out an equation in his head. "Well, I won't mention them to Berlin. No need for us to be the bearers of bad news to the Führer. Besides, if they were so far out I'm sure they ran out of petrol and crashed. We could even record them as enemy destroyed."

I said nothing. This was a man who did not wish to face reality. I, on the other hand, didn't have that luxury. But he was my superior officer, so I held my tongue and nodded.

"I have nothing more to say on this," the major concluded. "I expect your report by tonight."

"You'll have it after I finish the letters…sir." I made a motion to salute.

"Letters," he said quizzically. Then he realized. "Oh yes. Of course."

Two armorers suddenly appeared out of the snow with belts of twenty-millimeter shells draped over their shoulders, rescuing us from the awkward moment.

"Well done, Herr Captain," offered one of them as they passed.

"Congratulations, sir!"

I acknowledged them with a slight bow while raising my victory wand. Then I turned back to Seebeck, who was covetously taking stock of my new prop. He was not amused. His eye followed the two privates until they disappeared in the shadows of the hangar.

"The men like you," he observed bitterly without facing me directly. "More so than they do me." I remained silent, studying the jagged lines of his scarred face. "Remember, Becker. This is still my group."

I suddenly grew very tired. It was time to bring this little conference to an abrupt end. "How can I forget, Herr Major? You remind me every day." Then I added: "I don't want your command. *Heil* Hitler," I said, throwing my arm up straight.

He turned without answering my salute, leaving my arm floating in the air. I could hear him muttering under his breath as he hobbled away: "Good. Because you can't have it."

So I lowered my arm and traipsed off the field, baton in hand. As I made my way to my little cottage just beyond the barracks, I passed by LeClaire, the abandoned château that served as both the *Kasino* and general mess as well as housed most of the pilots. The concrete airstrip was constructed around this elegant stone manor, as the acreage provided a broad, flat field for a runway, as well as various other estate buildings to serve a variety of functions, from administrative to senior officer housing to hospital.

As I passed by the main entrance to LeClaire at the crest of a circular gravel drive, I could hear the boisterous sounds of music and laughter within. Fighter pilots led a life of extremes. Compared to our foot-sore *Landsers*, the foot soldiers, suffering on the windswept steppes of Russia or in the stifling heat of North Africa, we lived in luxury. Hot food, fine wine, warm beds, staff cars, women, dry socks. Life on the ground was ideal. It had to be, for we would eventually count our life expectancy in the air in weeks. My younger pilots were especially vulnerable, as many were now being sent to us with inadequate training due to lack of flying time. Fuel shortages were to blame. You cannot train pilots in planes that don't fly. The Allied bombings were having an effect.

I was, in fact, heading to my cottage to write letters to several of those young pilots' families now. My men were in the château eating, drinking, and smoking cigars. They would party the night away and, if only for a fleeting moment, try to put the battles to come out of their young minds. I didn't join them yet, as I had other thoughts to gather. Perhaps Mueller was right. Maybe I should have celebrated my life more. But I couldn't. Not when I had to pen the final chapter in the lives of so many others.

11

Frau Kluge:

It is with deep regret that I must write to you of the death of your son, Heinz. He flew under my personal command and I can tell you that he died fulfilling his duty to the Fatherland. Perhaps you can take some comfort in this…

I leaned back in my chair and stared up at the grimy lightbulb hanging over my battered wooden desk. I couldn't write another line. Three letters sat fanned out before me. Each one said the same. Your son or husband is dead. Be proud. *Deutschland Über Alles*.

A wave of frustration coursed through me. I closed my eyes and could hear the sound of Kluge's boyish voice: "*Herr Captain, I think I got one*!" I opened them again and considered the pen in my cramped hand. With one motion I whipped the instrument at the wall. It careened off the stone and spun to the floor like a ricocheting bullet.

"Damn," I muttered aloud. I gazed through the dark square of my cottage window and saw the snow had finally stopped. It was pitch black outside. All was eerily silent. I could close my mind to the war and think about Amelia, who sat in her dirndl seated on a piano stool smiling playfully in the portrait on my desk. The memories of lying in her arms on stormy winter nights in the Alps were so much a contrast to the violence of my days now that if I dwelled on them for too long, they might drive me to madness.

By 1943 Germany knew no such peaceful nights. The setting sun meant only that the Americans stationed on the unsinkable aircraft carrier of Britain passed the bombing baton to the Royal Air Force (RAF), who preferred to raid my country under the protective shroud of darkness. Unlike their optimistic Yankee allies, who believed in daylight precision bombing, the British subscribed to the philosophy of carpet-bombing the general vicinity of a target and hoping in the darkness that they hit something of value. They brought to Germany a whirlwind of fire. As I stared into the ink of the night sky, I knew that, at other bases, the night fighters were scrambling. And now it would be my nocturnal comrades' turns to parade in the death pageant. Another batch of letters would go out in the morning to unsuspecting family members.

There was a light tapping on my door, and I swiveled in my chair to face the noise.

"Come," I said.

The door creaked open and a haggard young pilot in a filthy and torn flight suit, his face pelted by bruises, stepped in with his head bowed in embarrassment. He swallowed hard and then slapped his heels to attention. "*Heil* Hitler!" he barked with his arm raised.

I returned the salute and stood up to face him. A warm feeling of satisfaction eclipsed my sour mood, drowning it like water douses a smoldering ember. "Von Mauer," I said, putting my arm on his shoulder. He winced, and I realized he must have been banged up all over from his ordeal. "Welcome back. I'm glad you're alive."

His eyes flitted nervously, not making contact with my own. "I managed to bail out in the clouds. A farmer found me. He gave me a lift on his cart back here." I nodded as he continued in the tone of a Sunday confession. "I'm sorry, sir. I lost a good fighter today. I guess I got a little ahead of myself."

"Yes, you did, Sergeant."

He closed his eyes. "I just wanted to do my duty to the Fatherland."

"By getting yourself shredded by Thunderbolts?" I admonished him in a fatherly tone.

"It won't happen again, sir. I promise."

"Well," I said, pinching the bridge of my nose in exhaustion. "I think you've been punished enough. It isn't often we get to commit suicide and live to tell about it." I smiled at that. "Besides. It's one less letter for me to write." With an exaggerated motion I grabbed the letter to his father from my desk (his mother had died of typhus when he was five) and tore the paper in two as a broad grin traced across his bruised but otherwise intact face. This was a happy ending to a difficult day. I should relish it. So I donned my visor cap and leather American flying jacket. "Now. I hear there's a party in my honor at the *Kasino*."

"There is," he said, relaxing some. Von Mauer could tell that I was too happy to see him to bring the disciplinary hammer down.

"It would be impolite not to attend, don't you think, Sergeant?"

His smile widened across his purple cheeks. "It would, sir."

"Then let's go," I said. "Only pigs drink alone." And we left my cottage together, leaving the two unfinished letters on the desk while we joined our comrades for a celebration of the gift of one more night alive. Tomorrow could wait.

That night the squadron gave young Von Mauer his " birthday party," which we called the receptions we gave to downed fliers who had lived through the ordeal and were, in a sense, re-born. They doused him with beer while taking him in their arms and swaying back and forth to drinking songs that were reflective of a simpler, happier time. We all yearned for the pre-war days when we stumbled about blindly from beer hall to beer hall, with no looming shadow of death to subdue our celebrations. But now the reminders of our peril were everywhere. Tacked up on the far wall of the mess was a collage of photographs of young boys in their flier's uniforms. Each one a beloved comrade who never returned. An obituary of the flower of German youth. The wall was now covered with so many faces that the photographs were starting to overlap in a macabre competition for a space in which to be remembered, like vines groping for sunlight. While the men puffed cigars and sang songs to their women back home, I ducked away from the crowd and sullenly pinned the photograph of Sergeant Heinz Kluge up on the board. After that, my dour mood returned and I had no desire to re-join the party.

It was just as well. The bookish Lieutenant Thomson, Seebeck's polished adjutant, approached me deferentially. "Beg your pardon, Herr Captain, but Major Seebeck wishes you to report to his office."

"Now?" I said, taking a final gulp of beer.

"Yes, sir. Sorry to disturb you."

I sighed. "It's okay, Lieutenant. I won't kill the messenger. Take a drink before you return to your desk. It's been a long day."

He smiled gratefully. "Thank you, sir."

I patted him on the arm and slipped unnoticed out the back into the dark night.

12

"You wanted to see me, Herr Major?"

Seebeck sat at his desk, his nose buried in paperwork. A cigarette smoldered in his ashtray, the blue smoke curling into the stale air of his dank office. His expression turned when he heard me enter, as if he'd bitten a lemon. He glanced up at me. "You have special orders on the desk."

I looked down. There was a piece of official-looking stationery lying on the mahogany desktop decked out in Gothic lettering with an emblem of the Knight's Cross as its letterhead. I grabbed it and quickly scanned the document. "Special Jagdgeschwader (Day Fighter Wing) Order of the Day." My knees grew weak. It announced that I was to be personally awarded the Knight's Cross of the Iron Cross…by Adolf Hitler himself.

"I'm to meet the Führer?" I asked incredulously.

"Apparently so," grunted Seebeck, the envy seeping through his gritting teeth. "It seems that you've been awarded the Knight's Cross of the Iron Cross. You go to Berchtesgaden the day after tomorrow. You are to then proceed to the Führer's villa, where you, along with other Wehrmacht personnel, will have an audience with him and the high command."

I was dumbstruck. The Knight's Cross and its higher levels of oak leaves, swords, and diamonds was Germany's highest award. It was the equivalent of the coveted Prussian decoration Pour le Mérite or "Blue Max" from the Great War. Usually the Knight's Cross was awarded only after receiving the Iron Cross. Then one was incrementally awarded the oak leaves, then swords, then diamonds. Although since it was Hitler's medal, he could issue it as he pleased. This put me in an elite company of our most celebrated fliers. Men like Werner Mölders, Adolf Galland,

and Hans-Joachim Marseille. Legends in my mind. And now I was to be among them. I could feel the ghost of Manfred von Richthofen, the "Red Baron," staring down at me.

I'd be a liar if I claimed not to be thrilled at the prospect. Still, at that moment I was thinking mainly of how I could possibly manage to get home to Stauffenberg before my meeting. The town was the halfway point between here and Salzburg, which was right near Berchtesgaden. I began computing flight schedules in my mind. It could be done.

"May I go home then tomorrow, sir?" I asked. I tried to appeal to his soft side. But when it came to me, it was a side that didn't exist. "It's been a long time since I've seen my family. And Amelia."

He looked up at me. "You're grounded, Captain. No more flying for you until then. We wouldn't want our little star to get inconveniently killed." His contempt was palpable. But I was used to his petty jealousy. He and I had never seen matters from geopolitics to the running of the air group through the same lens.

I was in the Wehrmacht because I was compelled to serve, as were all German boys. I joined the Luftwaffe because if I had to fight, I would fight on my own terms. I would do it alone and high above the mud and the shelling and the flames. Although I admired some of Hitler's accomplishments—it is indeed true that the trains always ran on time—I had no zeal for National Socialism. I'd seen the movement transform the friends of my youth from frolicking, silly boys into fanatics, razors. But I was a member of the New Order. I did my duty, as my victory baton grimly testified.

And so, I thought, was it too much for me, a German officer and patriot who'd been singled out for special honors, to ask leave to see a woman who, after we had spent two years apart, utterly consumed my peaceful thoughts? A woman whose vision sustained me in the air as I carried out the Führer's bidding by massacring handfuls of boys like me over and over again until they came to me in my nightmares? My intellect told me the apparitions were not their true visages, as I never saw those I killed. But my mind cruelly substituted the faces of my own friends from home, and this made the crime so very real to me. Air combat was supposed to be an impersonal duel of machines wherein their human drivers are forgotten in the melee. A convenient moral shield permitting me to squeeze the trigger. When my hapless victims remained in my gunsights, unable to shake my pursuit despite all the violent, body-slamming maneuvers, I was immune to their panic and terror and desperation and even cries to a mother far away, carried in the air as I zeroed in and ripped them apart. But later, when I was alone, their terrifying ordeals at my hands would come to me. Phantasms of shame.

The major could not understand this. When he was wounded, ironically on his first mission by friendly anti-aircraft fire mistaking his ME-109 for a British Hurricane fighter, he'd had enough. Using his Nazi Party connections, Seebeck managed to secure a permanent ground station, a promotion, and command of Three Group of JG 32 here in Andeville. That he had me and three comrades transferred here from the Russian front was evidence of his family's influence in Berlin. That it was me, Mueller, Gaetjens, and Borner who turned his mediocre command into a fierce fighting unit was a secret that he jealously guarded from the high command. I could take liberties with him because my coming to Andeville was the best thing to have happened to him—and the worst. I made him feel so very small.

Which is why I was curious about one thing that didn't add up in the least.

"You recommended me for this honor?" I asked skeptically. The nomination had to come from a commander at Wing level or higher.

His answer was succinct, but uncharacteristically honest. "No. Your former group commander. Before you ever got here."

"Trautloft," I said with a satisfied grin. Major Hannes Trautloft had been my commander in Russia before I came west. He was a good man, that one.

"I suppose Germany needs its heroes these days," Seebeck said. Then he glared up at me. "Stay out of the air. Do I make myself clear, Captain?"

I drew myself to attention. "Clear, Herr Major. *Heil* Hitler!"

"*Heil* Hitler," he replied. I donned my visor cap and turned to leave.

"You will mention me to him, won't you?" he said, belatedly realizing the opportunity to advance his own career.

I looked back over my shoulder and smirked. Without saying another word, I blew through his outer office past the now returned and somewhat tipsy Lieutenant Thomson, and into the frigid night air.

Mueller was waiting for me. A half-drained wine bottle in his hand. He danced back and forth as if he had to piss in the worst way.

"Did you follow me?" I said.

He smiled wryly. "Maybe."

"Are you my mother or something?"

"I knew you couldn't have fun for too long." He motioned unsteadily towards the door to Seebeck's office. "Besides, as your wingman I don't like you going into combat alone." He took a swig of wine. "Well?" he said with chattering teeth.

"Seems that I'm to meet the Führer. In Berchtesgaden. To receive my Ritterkreuz."

"Knight's Cross!" Mueller beamed. "Congratulations!" He staggered and shook my hand vigorously. "Bavaria, eh? So you'll get to see that girl of yours finally?" My heart drained, and the look of disappointment betrayed my attempt to seem pleased. Mueller frowned. "What? No Amelia?"

I shook my head. "Just straight there and back."

"I swear if he wasn't group commander..." His sympathetic voice faded into the cold air. "Oh well. This war can't last forever. Can it?"

I thought about home and Amelia, and the stirring in me was like a maddening itch that had but one soft and supple five-foot-three, one hundred fifteen-pound cure. The surge of desire sent a crazy idea racing through my young mind. "There's an overnight train that heads to the Oberfranken from here at midnight, yes?"

He nodded. "They run by night, to avoid the *Jabos*...why?"

I knew that train ran right through Stauffenberg. Maybe I could actually see Amelia, despite what that political officer had said. After all, I was being summoned by Adolf Hitler himself, wasn't I? Oh yes, I had my orders. But technically he'd only grounded me. Stay out of the air, he'd said. He'd not actually quarantined me to base. Not in so many words at least. German soldiers were trained to obey orders, not interpret them. I could go to Oberbayern right from the Oberfranken. Seebeck might not even know I'd gone, though that was unlikely. I weighed in the balance the cachet of being one of the Führer's chosen warriors with the wrath of a bureaucrat Luftwaffe commander who'd requested his own wings be clipped.

"Meet me by my quarters with the staff car in ten minutes," I said.

"Harmon," cautioned Mueller, his sobriety suddenly returned to him, "whatever you're thinking, stop."

"What?" I said with feigned innocence. "He said 'no flying.'" Years of training and indoctrination would have prevented me from leaving had he specifically ordered me to stay on the base. But he'd unwittingly left a loophole I intended to slip through. I simply could not be so close to Amelia and not see her. Not after two years apart. Little did I know what she had in store for me.

"You know what he meant," Mueller said gravely.

I suddenly grew annoyed. "No. I don't know, Josef. And neither do you. Now get the car. That's a very clear order, Lieutenant."

"What if I refuse?" he said guardedly. "What if I say I'm too drunk to drive…sir?"

"Then I say that would be a first." I softened. He was just looking out for me, as he always did. And I didn't want him to get in any trouble. I put a comforting hand on his shoulder. "Josef, I know you'd never disobey a command."

He nodded. "Well, it's your hide. And an order's an order…sir."

Even in pitch dark with just slits for headlights, the slurring Lieutenant Mueller managed to avoid wrapping the '39 Horch around any trees on the drive to train depot. I was on the train and heading south to Stauffenberg through the blacked-out countryside by midnight.

13

I can still see my teenaged brother's face beaming with pride and excited curiosity. Paul was almost eighteen, but his baby face made him younger in my eyes.

I was standing in the car door as the train hissed to a stop at the little Stauffenberg station. Before my arrival I'd changed into the freshly issued field blue with pleated pockets and black epaulettes with gold insignia, a long mantel greatcoat, and topped off with a new visor cap. Clean *Gamaschen* were stretched above my pristine low boots. A Luger sidearm at my waist. I must have made an impression on Paul, because he gazed at me with awe as I stepped off the train. I was happy to see him at the station. It meant Mueller had gotten through to Papa at the police station, as per my orders after the train pulled out of Andeville.

"Harmon!" He hugged me with a force that nearly knocked me back into the car. Then he stepped back and tried to compose himself. "*Heil* Hitler!" he said with a salute.

I squinted at him, mildly amused. "What are you doing?"

He slowly withdrew his hand to his side, staring at his palm as if it had dirt on it.

"Oh. I figured with you soon to be a decorated hero, I'd make you feel at home."

"I felt at home when you hugged me, you silly sniper!" I laughed and ruffled his hair.

He returned the smile. "So good to see you, Brother."

"And you, Pauli," I said, using my term of affection for him.

"Can I take your bag?" he offered.

"You can take me home."

We made our way down the platform steps and into the station house. It was a charming stone building befitting the ambiance of the little Bavarian hamlet. Grizzled old Herr Grossmann, with his speckled skin and piercing blue eyes, still manned the ticket counter. He grimly stared as I walked past his booth. He still carried with him the images of boys in gray tunics and *Pickelhauben* (spiked helmets) pressed into service, like cattle led to the slaughter, in the Great War. His presence gave me pause, for he reminded me that Germany had known nothing but one conflict after another. A national grievance without end. Each generation of boys prodded forward to stand in the firing line and decimated. Who was I to him but more grist for the mill?

We exited the building and stepped onto the cobbled lane. I paused for a moment just to take it all in. The depot was situated at the north end of an arched stone bridge built by the Romans to span the sluggish Main River. The waters swirled and tumbled over a weir that diverted part of the flow to provide power for the munitions factory in Adelstatz three miles downstream. The river was devoid of traffic now, due to the growing threat of Allied bombing, but I remembered when tugs battled against the currents, towing heavily loaded barges, while unwieldy rafts and pleasure boats drifted down the valley, passing long quays and tidy promenades on the riverbank. But today not even a toy sailboat disturbed its indifferent waters.

At the far end of the bridge stood the old brownstone Rathaus watchtower, seven stories high, which in medieval times had served as the point of the ramparts that defended the town from marauders. Beyond the arched gateway through the tower base was the village of Stauffenberg. It rested on the water's edge at the foot of gentle slopes and wooded heights. Off in the distance, the hills rolled to the northwest, painted sporadically with the white dust of the previous snows.

I breathed in the fresh country air, untainted by the acrid octane fumes of my airbase. It was a poignant moment for me.

As we crossed the pedestrian walkway on the bridge, Paul studied my face. I'd changed. My smile never lingered.

"How are you doing, Harmon?" he asked, with a hint of maturity in his voice.

"I'm alive," I responded.

"And you're home," he said. "The war is far from here."

Maybe that was the problem. As we left the bridge and crossed through the Rathaus gate, I realized that the town hadn't changed at all since I left it. I should have been relieved, considering the destruction being visited upon unluckier cities in the Allied bombers' paths. But instead it bothered me. I'd fallen prey to the common soldier's outlook that tends to see the world as "us" and "them." Combatant and spectator. It was not fair to the people of Stauffenberg, who'd sent many of their young men to fight and die for the Reich. But I couldn't help my sense of alienation as my brother and I entered the town.

The central thoroughfare of Wilkestrasse began at the base of the Main Bridge and ran the length of the little village like a spinal cord until it terminated at ancient farm lanes that fanned out into the hills west of town. Stauffenberg was a picture-postcard collection of thirteenth-century gingerbread buildings that housed shops, stores, little Brauhauses, and quaint cafes. To the south rose the Gothic church of Saint Gerard of Toul, built between 1215 and 1402, renowned for its twin ninety-foot-high bell towers and the twenty-foot-diameter indented rose window on the western facade. Rows of attached three- and four-story homes formed the alabaster stucco boundaries of the narrow lanes of the residential neighborhood that enclosed the Von Himmel Marketplatz, or just the Himmelplatz for short. The white or yellow pastel facades were accented by heavy wooden shutters painted in vibrant colors. From every sill, charming window boxes spilled over with arrangements of spruce, fir, and holly, interspersed with winter flowers and Christmas roses. The low-pitched overhang roofs were capped by terra-cotta tile shingles. It could have been Christmas season in any year here, with the many displays of holly wreaths and the colorful *Tannenbaum* at the north end of the square. Even the fountain erected to honor Charlemagne was still spitting water as if the world was as it had always been. Although the air was chilled and patches of snow were still visible on the cobblestone streets, the sun was strong enough to prompt beer hall owners to set up tables along the Wilkestrasse.

The wide lane itself was sparsely populated by puttering trucks, horse carts, a few men in uniform (armed SS among them), occasional amputees, and small groups of civilians in fine clothes on leisurely walks enjoying the break in the weather. As we continued our stroll into the square, I asked Paul about our parents.

"They'll be relieved to see you looking so fit," he said. "And they're very proud."

"Parents are always proud."

"But you've achieved something great, Harmon. I envy you."

I looked at him. "Don't envy me."

"Why shouldn't I?" he protested. Then he paused to collect his thoughts, as if he were girding himself to say something important, which he was. "In fact, I intend to follow your example."

When I heard that, I wheeled around and grabbed him hard by the biceps as if by reflex. The visceral panic of my reaction surprised me.

"What? What on earth are you saying, Pauli? Tell me."

My brother looked around, embarrassed. "Harmon!" I took a breath and let him go. Rubbing his arm, he looked at me with subtle defiance. "I'm joining the Luftwaffe. I'm old enough now. I want to be a pilot like you."

"Are you crazy?" I said through clenched teeth.

"Are *you*?" he retorted.

"Do you understand what the hell goes on up there?" I said, cocking a finger to the sky for emphasis. "Death, Pauli. In its most loathsome forms. Falling from great heights, being riddled with bullets the size of your thumb…or fire. Have you ever heard the screams of a man burning alive, trapped in his cockpit?"

He was unfazed. "You look alive enough to me."

"My number's coming," I said. "If this war goes on much longer, I won't survive it. And a new pilot now has almost no chance. Petrol's in short supply. You'll get minimal training at best. Don't do this, Pauli."

"But it's my duty."

"Your duty is to Mama and Papa."

He looked at me with consternation. "I can't believe I'm hearing this from a Ritterkreuzer. No, Brother. My duty's to the Fatherland. To the Führer. What would you rather have me do? Join the infantry? Maybe drive a Panzer? Ah, how about a U-boat? Now there's a guaranteed black note."

I shook my head. "There must be some rear echelon post for you. I've written too many letters to too many parents. Don't have me write yours as well." I took a deep breath. "We'll talk more of this later," I said.

"No, Brother. We won't." As far as Paul was concerned, this matter was closed.

"Deluded boy," I said.

In chilly silence we moved on through the center of town in the direction of a narrow lane called the Lieslestrasse. I stared down the road towards a quaint three-story rococo house of soft yellow and stained wood trim surrounding windows framed by forest-green shutters. My anger over Paul's death wish suddenly evaporated in a wave of giddy excitement. My brother looked at the house, then to me, then at the house again.

"I suppose a soldier has immediate needs. I'll take your holdall and tell Mother you'll be home for supper. I have a meeting this evening, but we'll catch up in time. Harmon, hello?" He laughed and waved his hand in front of my face. Then he adjusted my uniform and visor cap, wiping off the dust like a manservant. "Let's have a look at you." He smiled as I stared straight at the house. "Atrocious. I still don't get what she sees in you. Perhaps she's blind."

I tore my eyes away from the house and smiled at him. "I'll see you later, Pauli."

"Try not to lose track of time," he commanded. "Your parents ache for you." He gave me another hug and patted me on the arm. "Don't be nervous, Harmon. She'll be happy to see you." Then he disappeared down the lane with my bag in hand.

My heart was hammering. I felt off-balance as I slowly stepped towards the house, as if walking on a soft mattress. I paused in front of the window and tried to peer inside. A shadowy figure moved in the far room, which I knew to be the kitchen. I could draw her silhouette from memory. Every line, every curve of her frame. Her motions were unique to her. Always of a purpose, arms akimbo, hands resting on the band of her wool apron. Through the wavy glass pane I heard her muffled humming. It was what she did when performing a mind-numbing task. *She must be preparing her supper*, I thought.

And there I stood gazing at her like a child does a favorite toy in a shop window. The love of my life had no idea I was standing outside her house. I slid over to the threshold, took a deep breath, removed my cap, and gently rapped on the wooden door.

The singing stopped. Silence. A few dainty steps to the doorway, and I suddenly realized that she was on the other side. I could barely stand.

The door creaked open. A thin band of light fell across her face. Her eyes, light gray with a ring of blue, opened wide at the sight of me. We could say nothing for what seemed like an age. Finally, in a weak voice, I broke the spell.

"Hello, Amelia."

She stood frozen, her gray eyes wide as searchlights, trying to process what she was seeing. Then she threw her arms around me, buried her head in my chest, and began to sob. "Please tell me this isn't a cruel dream!" she said.

"No," I said whispering in her ear. "I'm home."

I held her tight, pressing her so hard to me that I thought she might suffocate. I never wanted to let go.

PART 2

14

I have warm memories of my youth. I was blessed with good parents, loving yet austere. My father, Karl Becker, was the police captain of the town. During the First World War, he was a sergeant in the infantry. He was an imposing man, built block by block, and a fine soldier. He was captured at Saint-Mihiel in September 1918 and spent a long year as a prisoner of war in the island camp on Elle Ile in the Bay of Biscay. A decorated hero, he returned in 1919 to a country in disarray, reeling under the draconian impositions of the Treaty of Versailles. With support from the *Burgermeister*, who as sheer luck would have it had served in the same unit as my father, he was appointed the chief of the Stadtpolizei Stauffenberg after the sitting chief suffered a coronary. With his position secure, he sought out his childhood sweetheart, Greta Vogel, and won her heart. A baker's daughter, she was as warm and filled with humor as her husband was stoic. Karl and Greta were married in 1921. It was a good match. I can still see my parents caught in each other's gaze across the table, their eyes suggesting intimate secrets. And I'll always hold dear the memories of my mother's face, round, unlined, and fair, even as age crept up on her.

My brother, Paul, was younger by four years. He always pestered me, but I loved him just the same. I recall winter nights as our happy family sat facing the comforting yellow glow of a blazing fire. The thick aroma of my mother's roast practically dripped off the walls. Somehow much of the terrible economic catastrophe that befell Germany in the 1920s passed Stauffenberg by. My father was a practical man and, like many in our little town, he distrusted paper money; thus did he convert most of his marks to gold before hyper-inflation rampaged like a wildfire through the country. I was too young to pay attention to such things, though. Perhaps that's why I was caught off-guard by the speed and force with which the Nazis rose to power.

In my mind's eye I see torchlight rallies and pledges to fealty and absolute devotion to National Socialism. The mysterious disappearances of beloved schoolmasters. They were replaced by Nazi propagandists who no longer taught that ten minus two equals eight, but rather if you have ten Berliners and eight are of pure Aryan blood, and two are Jews, how many true Germans do you have? In 1932 there were but one hundred thousand members of the Hitler Youth. By 1936 there were 3.5 million. I see my friends in brown shirts and caps marching along the Wilkestrasse. Egon and Werner Meissner. Alfons Kraft. Paul Genth. "Little Edu" Joppien. I see them tramp-tramping on cobbles in the neat files with red banners held high, and I hear Hitler's voice declaring with sinister resolve: "*When my opponents say, 'I won't join you,' I just say your children are mine already. What are you? In time you'll die. But your sons and daughters will stand forever in my new camp. And in a short time they'll know nothing else but this new community.*" For any child desperate for a sense of belonging, this was a powerful seduction. But it was a temptress that, thanks to my music and solitary nature, I resisted…for a while at least.

One spring day when I was thirteen, I was riding my bike through the streets of Stauffenberg when I braked in front of a store window along the edge of the Himmelplatz. I heard piano music wafting from an open window in Krupinski's Music Shop. Mozart's Sonata no. 15 in C Major. I stood transfixed as something inside of me burst open. Oh, I'd heard music all my life. My mother sang in the church choir every Sunday and even was the cantor on Christmas and Easter. Our radio was always tuned to classical music. But peering through the window and seeing the person actually playing with his own hands somehow made it accessible to me. This was what I wanted to do. It was one of the missing components of my otherwise happy life. Only later would I discover the other was flying. So I pushed open the door and strutted inside.

The cramped shop featured shelves lined with sheet music on one side. An assortment of instruments, from violins and cellos to accordions and horns, adorned the other. And in the center, beyond the counter in the very back of the space sat a weathered baby grand piano. A man in his late forties, thin as a fence post, sporting wire-rimmed spectacles and a graying beard and mustache, swayed behind the keys, his eyes closed, completely absorbed in this wonderful moment. When he finished, he noticed that I was practically standing on top of him. We looked at each other for an awkward moment. His breathing was heavy, as if he'd suffered from consumption in the past. He looked much older than his years.

"Well?" he finally said, coughing. "Are you just going to stand there or perhaps tell me what it is you want, young man?"

I shook myself out of the funk and clasped my hands together. "That was beautiful."

His face warmed, and he slapped his trousers in appreciation. "Yes, well that was Herr Mozart's brainchild. Not mine I'm afraid. No matter. What is it that you want?"

"I want that," I uttered in a hushed voice.

"The sheet music?" he said. "Oh, I'm afraid this is my personal copy. I'll have to order it for you." He pushed his glasses up on the bridge of his nose and hoisted himself off the piano bench. He began shuffling over to his counter. "Now if you want a leather-bound copy, that will take three weeks. However, I happen to know a fellow in Salzburg, if he is still there, who can get the standard booklet in—"

"Can you teach me to play?" I interrupted.

He pivoted to face me. "I haven't had pupils in over a year." Then his eyes grew distant. "What with the new decrees about to be put in place, I am afraid *Meisters* of my…ilk…are not approved." He reached into his breast pocket and produced a folded pamphlet announcing the new anti-Semitic Nuremburg Laws. He offered it to me. "You see?" he said wanly. "Soon I will not even be German anymore." I skimmed the paper, which said that Jews could no longer be German citizens, marry Aryans, or even fly German flags. I handed it back to him. I didn't care about politics—as that's all it was to me then. "Can you teach me?" I asked again.

He pursed his lips, pinching them with his thick fingers. He put his hand on my shoulder and studied my eyes for a long time as if trying to look inside and see what was really going on in my adolescent brain. Then he wheezed and broke out into a grin I found instantly endearing. "You're a brave lad. I just hope we both do not come to regret this. Come here next week at this time, master…what is your name anyway?"

As I walked towards the door, I said: "Harmon Becker. And yours, Herr Musikmeister?"

"I am Leopold Krupinski. And I intend to make you a great musician."

I took to the piano eagerly. Throughout the rest of my teens, I became too engrossed in my music to get entwined in the activities of the Hitlerites outside my very window. Although membership in the Hitler Youth was supposed to be mandatory, I was never pressed into the organization. After the Nazis gained control of the government, Father found police authority slipping out of local hands and into those of the state-controlled Geheime Staatspolizei, the Gestapo, headed by Hermann Göring. Father knew which way the winds blew, and so made it a point to feign cooperation with this menacing secret police force that was able to operate outside the law with impunity. He kept his job enforcing local ordinances. The Gestapo men understood that a beloved police chief meant a stable town and one less nest of traitors to deal with. I suspect his cooperation was at the heart of that exemption from the Hitler Youth. Maybe he just bribed them.

As the economy rebounded, the war clouds grew more ominous. While my schoolmates were learning to love the Führer and hate the Jews, I was learning Mozart, Bach, Chopin, and Beethoven. By the time I was sixteen, Krup, as I affectionately called him, had taken to calling me Harmon van Beethoven, so devoted was I to my music. I'd even managed to make some marks playing for parties and halls, and now had an upright piano of my own jammed into an empty space of our already cramped living room. Towards the end, Krup started to come to my house at night to tutor me.

15

The lessons at home would come later. From age thirteen on, I spent much of my time in Krup's store. First as his pupil and eventually as an intern of sorts. I hoped one day to run a music store of my own, and he accepted my work as payment for his tutelage. When the lesson of the day was done, we would share a loaf of brown bread and a wedge of cheese and sit across from each other on rickety stools by the front window. As we took in the bustle of the little village, Leo enjoyed chatting about his life as a boy in this town. He also told me about the days when he lived in Leipzig and studied under Max Reger. I listened politely. The large storefront window with the words "Krupinski's Fine Instruments & Music Accessories" stenciled on its smooth surface was like a picture frame for a living mosaic of Stauffenberg. Among the kinetic figures roaming past us on the cobbles was a girl I'd often spied carrying a basket to market. Every time I saw her, the same thought raced through my mind: she was the most beautiful creature I'd ever set my eyes upon.

"Who is she?" I finally asked Krup after a month or so of cataloguing her daily movements.

Krup replied: "Walter Engel's daughter, Amelia. She's a wonderful girl, if a bit headstrong." I didn't mind a little spirit…even though it would one day put me in unimaginable danger.

Like so many in the Oberfranken, she had golden hair, broad shoulders, and a full chest that I could only imagine heaved as she slept. I came to learn that Fraülein Amelia was older than me by two years. An only child of sickly parents, sometimes she would catch me in the act of ogling and grin back at me playfully over her bare shoulder, her dimples imprinted on her cheek, setting my insides whirring.

Krup was acutely aware of my growing feelings for Amelia. Two people can learn a lot about each other when sharing a piano bench for years on end. My *Musikmeister* was a keen judge of the human condition, mine most of all. Although when it came to taking the measure of nations, this trait would tragically desert him.

Through the looking glass of Krup's store window, I contemplated the people of Stauffenberg. They seemed different to me now. Less citizens than cogs in a great machine of state run by the powers of faraway Berlin. I wondered how I fit into this New Order. Krup would often sidle up beside me and put a caring hand on my shoulder. We watched Amelia making her way through the streets, lazily swinging her toned arms as if in cadence with a gavotte running through her head.

"She really is beautiful isn't she, Leo?"

"I have only thoughts for my Constanze," he said. "But I notice she comes to Koppel's almost every other day at this time." He motioned to the storefront directly across the street.

I chuckled. "Voyeur."

Krup gave a dismissive gesture. "I have eyes and a window. She shops for her mother. Poor woman isn't much better off than Walter Engel, her father. God rest his soul."

"How well do you know her?" I asked.

"She's come in here searching for sheet music. Her father played piano, like you…though not as well. And when she was a little girl she used to come in and listen to me play. The same way you did when you first entered my life. I kept the door unlocked then." He ran his hand unconsciously over his Star of David patch. "These days not so much. In fact, I don't think it's wise for you to come here anymore."

I shook my head. "It hasn't come to that yet." If I was trying to reassure him, my words fell flat.

"*Yet*," he repeated ominously, as if running that word over and over in his mind. Amelia exited the store with an armful of wrapped parcels. "There, you see?" he said, happy to change the subject.

"She always comes alone?" I asked.

"She was supposedly engaged to Johann Keitel." Johann was a spoiled schoolmate of mine whose wealthy family owned the Keitelgesellshaft armaments factory. He was also a devout Nazi and Hitler Youth leader. Leo understandably despised him. He observed: "I haven't seen her with that brownshirt spider since Walter passed. It's for the best anyway. I cannot see her with a boy like him. Now, you on the other hand…"

I turned away from the window and approached the piano. "Ach. You're just a crazy old man."

"That's not fair, my boy," he said, smiling. "I'm not that old."

"Then come on, you crazy kid." I laughed. "Teach me something."

"You need no more lessons from me," he observed.

I shook my head. "I think I still have much to learn from you, Leo." He nodded at that. His eyes showed a distant look that reached out through the shop window, well past the Wilkestrasse, beyond the Main and the Oberfranken, out into the wide, hostile world. Then he began to play.

On a chilly late afternoon in early November 1938, Amelia walked into the music store just before closing time. Krup stayed home that day, as he was ill, which would soon prove to be fortunate, so I was alone behind the register. Daylight was rapidly fading as the sun slipped behind the foothills to the west. The overhanging bells jangled when Amelia entered. Even though I was closing in on seventeen and should have been more confident, I fought off the urge to duck under the counter as she nonchalantly studied the sheet music displayed on the wall shelves, running her long fingers across the booklets as if scanning for a particular piece. Then she approached me wearing that wickedly mischievous smile.

She leaned on the counter. Even though it was cold, her low-cut sweater under her jacket revealed all I needed to see. My eyes flitted down to her cleavage, and she caught me in the act. "Up here," she instructed, and I raised my eyes to meet hers. The lightness of their gray intimidated me. One felt like they were not being looked at so much as probed by them.

I cleared my throat, trying to be casual. "Can I help you?"

"I don't see any Mendelssohn," she observed. "Are you sold out? I'd like to display something by him on our piano." Her eyes stayed on mine. "In honor of my father."

"I was sorry to hear," I said.

She nodded. "He so loved Mendelssohn's music."

"So do I!" I blurted out, not sure where that came from.

She put her palm to her mouth and giggled. "I bet you do, Harmon Becker."

"You know my name?" I said with genuine surprise.

"As you must know mine by now," she said. "I like to know the names of boys who undress me with their eyes. I swear you'll make me catch a cold."

My face grew fire-truck red. "I don't understand," I said.

She gave me a dismissive wave. "You're a poor liar. I see you looking from that window." She pointed to her own eyes. "These work quite well you know."

So there was no avoiding it. "It doesn't mean anything…I mean, well, it does mean something. What I'm trying to say is…" I looked over to a bust of Beethoven on the shelf by the register. "Help me, Ludwig."

She laughed. "Please don't tell me that man's your social muse. He was far more offensive than you, Harmon."

"Offensive?" I said with a squeak in my voice. "Oh, please don't take—"

"It's quite alright." She cut me off with an assuring pat on my skinny forearm. "I'd be just as poor a liar if I said I'm not flattered." She placed her elbows on the countertop and cupped her jaw in her hands. "Lecherous boy."

I stared down at my feet. "I don't mean to seem predatory, Fraülein Amelia. It's just hard to look away when you look like, well…" I glanced back up to catch her gaze and gestured to her form with open palms. There was a thick pause as we just stared at each other. Now it was her turn to blush.

"I've asked Leo about you, you know," she confessed, breaking the spell.

"You have?"

She nodded earnestly. "He tells me you're a wonderful pianist. At least that's what I think he means when he calls you his young Beethoven. Although now I'm not so sure." I flashed a self-deprecating smile. "And he calls you a friend."

I'd never thought of Leo as a friend. But I guess he was, yes.

"You'll have to play for me one day," she said, and touched my hand. An electric charge ran through me and there was movement within my trousers that fortunately was hidden from view by the counter, sparing me severe embarrassment. "But right now what you can do for me, Harmon, is help me find my Mendelssohn."

"I'm afraid I can't," I said.

"What do you mean?"

"Well, Mendelssohn was a Jew. It's forbidden to sell his music here." Her eyes narrowed, and I suddenly felt very small.

"That's absurd," she hissed. "His father converted and he was baptized at seven and he took the Christian name Bartholdy. And, oh for God's sake, what would it matter if he was bloody Abraham! He was German, was he not? Has this whole country gone mad? Have you?"

She shot me a fiery glare, and I raised my hands in innocence:

"It's not my law, Amelia."

She was about to say something more when suddenly a jagged rock smashed through the window from the darkening street like a rogue meteorite! She screamed in shock and whirled around. I barely had time to register the act when there came another projectile, shattering more glass and sending razor-sharp slivers flying through the air like twirling knives. "What the hell!" I shouted. "Amelia, get down and come around here!" I said, crouching low behind the counter and covering my head with my hands. Another crash. More plate glass panes exploded around us. She fell to her knees and crawled on all fours as best she could in her thick skirt until she was tucked up next to me behind the relative safety of the counter. I noticed there was a smear of crimson on the floral pattern of her dress. Another volley of stones came hurtling in from the street. I could make out the faint flicker of torchlights competing with the fading illumination of a setting sun. The rocks shattered more windows and ricocheted off instruments and sheet music hanging on the walls, making an awful clatter. A pair of cymbals were knocked off their hooks and fell to the floor with an ear-splitting crash.

We found ourselves in each other's arms, crouched in a ball on the floor behind the counter as a fountain of glass and sheaves of music rained down. I was doing my best to shield her from the razor-sharp splinters.

When the final salvo of stones careened through the store, landing amidst the patina of glass debris on the floorboards, we heard teenaged voices outside: "Fucking Jews! Get out! Get out!"

Amelia's eyes widened as she picked out one familiar inflection. "That's Johann," she seethed. She went to stand up to see, but I pulled her back to the ground beside me for safety.

The murmur of the youthful mob and dancing torches moved on into the fading light of the city streets, and we rose from behind the counter to survey the damage. "Are you okay?" I held up her left hand and examined her palm, which was wet with blood. "You're bleeding," I said, as I whipped out a handkerchief from my shirt pocket.

She glanced down indifferently at her injured hand. "I must have cut it on a piece of glass as I crawled."

"Does it hurt?" I asked.

"Not really," she said. She winced as I gently pressed the cloth to the half-inch slice to stem the bleeding.

"It doesn't look like there's any glass in your hand. Just make a fist to keep the pressure on until it stops."

We rose off the floor together. I took her by her undamaged right hand as we stepped around the counter, the jagged shards of glass crunching under the soles of our shoes. I counted no fewer than twenty rocks the size of a man's fist lying on the debris-strewn hardwood floor in mute testimony to the savagery of what were Stauffenberg's opening shots of the cruel nationwide assault on Jewish-owned businesses and homes we would call Kristallnacht...Crystal Night. Or, as was most apropos to our experience, The Night of Broken Glass.

"That Johann Keitel is a bully bastard," she said. Indignation pulsed through her veins, giving her milky pallor a fiery glow. I found her zeal alluring.

"I heard you're to be his wife," I reminded her.

She glared at me as she brushed herself off and looked around at the cruel vandalism. "I'll be who I wish to be." She straightened her hair and then looked coolly at me. "Thank you for caring about my safety. And for this." She held up her clenched left hand with my kerchief. The tiny laceration was already closing. "You really are a good man, aren't you, Harmon Becker?"

I shrugged as I surveyed the destruction. "I try to be."

Amelia abruptly kissed me on the cheek and then, as if to prevent her passions from getting the better of her, she stormed off into the darkness of the street. I noticed she was smart enough to walk away in the opposite direction of the roving band of torchlit brownshirts. I stood motionless, stunned by her kiss. Then I snapped out of my bewilderment and looked over the scene around me; my heart sank as I stood all alone in the twilight and appraised the damage to Krup's store. The cold air was pouring through the now blasted-out picture window, and sheet music was dancing and fluttering in the swirling November wind. Krup would be closed for some time, I thought. There was nothing more to do but catch my breath and grab a broom. As I commenced my robotic sweeping, I was relieved that the Krupinskis lived out in the countryside, away from the violent streets of a once friendly village now wrapped in the blackening shadow of the New Order.

16

On Christmas Eve 1938 my father and family were invited to a grand ball at the Keitel estate just outside of town. It was a splendid affair complete with orchestra, waltzes, tuxedos, and Bavarian cuisine. All of Stauffenberg was there, as were a few Nazi Party members of some import all the way from Berlin. The ball was, in essence, a symbolic gesture by beneficiaries of the New Order. Johann's family's factory had been pumping out machine gun bullets around the clock to fill orders for Hitler's powerful Wehrmacht. The Keitels were growing fat off the bounty of war contracts for a war not yet begun, but one that was inevitable. They were not the traditional German barons but rather, new wealth—a cabal that owed its good fortune to the Nazis and would repay them with blind loyalty and support. This was the last peacetime Christmas of a beloved Germany that I would later see turned to dust.

I'd put Kristallnacht behind me. I hadn't seen Krup since the day after the vandals struck, when I helped him board up his windows. "I will re-open in the spring," he declared in naive defiance. But I wasn't thinking of him now. I was instead enjoying the spectacle even as I held up the wall in my evening best. I can still see my mother in her dinner gown, my father in his most formal dark blue constable's uniform, twelve-year-old Pauli running about the snowy courtyard outside the ballroom making mischief with the younger boys of the town. Over the main entrance to the house, a giant red Nazi flag was draped from the second-floor window and fluttered in the frigid air. Inside, an ornately baubled *Tannenbaum* greeted arriving guests in the great foyer embraced by two marble staircases. Crowning the tree was a brightly lit swastika.

The New Germany encapsulated. We are your new shining star. Your north, your south, your east, your west. A beacon of hope. A covenant between the Führer and the *Volksdeutsche.* With one body and one soul we will build a Reich to last for a thousand years.

An introvert by nature, I found myself gravitating towards the musicians near the ballroom windows, a glass of champagne in my hand. They weren't very good, and my pitch-perfect ear recoiled as they hacked through *Die Fledermaus* just a hair to the sharp side.

"Not exactly the Berlin Philharmonic, are they?" A girl's voice.

I turned and found myself a yard apart from Amelia. I blushed and, unable to speak at first, furiously guzzled my champagne.

"You have a lovely ear," I stammered. "I mean you have a *good* ear. For music." This bit of Freudian clumsiness came out in a voice I did not recognize. My cheeks were on fire.

I looked around for a waiter with a tray and more champagne, but none were nearby.

"How's your hand?" I asked.

She smiled and held up her palm. "You do good work, Herr Doctor." A thin, pink dash crossing the heart line was the only physical evidence she carried from that night. She sidled closer to me. "I bought you this," she said, handing me a little square box. I gave her a quizzical look and opened it. Inside was a brand-new handkerchief with "*HBN*" embroidered in the silk. "The one you gave me was too bloodstained."

I felt its softness before tucking it into my pocket. "I love it. But you really didn't have to do that."

"I wanted to," she said. "I even had the tailor initial it for you. Your middle name is Nantwein?" I raised a questioning brow. She grinned impishly. "I asked Paul."

"That kid's mouth runs like a stream," I said. "Not the best of names. But my parents meant well. Saint Nantovinus was burnt at the stake. His skull is in a museum in Münich."

"Lovely," she said. Then she lowered her voice to a near whisper. "I was hoping you would visit my home to check up on me so I could give you this in private. But you never came. Should I be hurt?"

"It was a frightening experience. I figured I'd just remind you of that, I guess."

She looked around, as if to see if Johann was near.

"Well, you'd be wrong. I told you. You have a good heart. That's rare for the men of Germany these days. They're all Hitler's little robots."

"Shh!" I admonished her as I instinctively glanced around.

Amelia moved even closer to me. Her hand brushed against my thigh, sending an electric charge through my waist. My good heart started a drumbeat inside that I thought was loud enough to throw the band off.

"Play for me tonight, Harmon."

Then she disappeared into the crowd of dancers in tuxedos and elegant ball gowns, leaving me stunned.

I soon regained my composure enough to try my clumsy hand at mingling. Herr Wechsler, the new *Burgermeister* appointed by Reichsführer-SS Heinrich Himmler, who was now also in charge of the Gestapo as well, was engaged in a discussion with another local Nazi party apparatchik. The latter was flanked by fiercely patriotic young men of the SS in their menacing black dress uniforms and visor caps brandishing the silver-skull-and-crossbones *Totenkopf*, the "death's head." I hoped never to cross such men.

I searched for Paul, as he was the only one here who seemed more socially uncouth than I, but he was off roaming the grounds. Instead Johann Keitel himself bounded over to me with palms out and a warm smile. He was curiously decked out in his black Hitler Youth winter uniform.

"Becker! I haven't seen you since secondary school. You're enjoying yourself I hope?"

I took his hand and bowed. "Yes, thank you, Johann. The house is just grand."

"It keeps the snows off Father's head. Is your family here?"

"They're knocking about somewhere. I'm sure constable Becker is being his usual garrulous self."

Johann chuckled at my gentle sarcasm. "Like father, like son."

"Mother talks enough for us all."

He looked me over. "No uniform yet?" he said.

I shook my head. "No. I'm hoping things don't come to that. I'd make a terrible soldier."

"You may soon have no choice," he said seriously. "There will be a war, Harmon. Soon I think. And we both know that we must do our duty to the Fatherland."

Johann said he would join the SS on the first of the year. For a boy whose devotion to his Führer was absolute, who threw rocks through Jewish windows, only Hitler's personal army rather than the Wehrmacht would do.

"If a war starts," I said without emotion, "then I'll do my duty and trust the Führer has it all in hand."

Johann nodded thoughtfully. "Well put, my friend. And that world will rue the day it stands in our way. Versailles will be avenged. With single-minded ruthlessness. We are a hail of ninety million bullets. It must be so, Harmon. National honor demands it."

"That sounds more like revenge than honor," I observed.

He fixed me with his steely granite-black eyes. "They are often one and the same."

We turned and gazed out at the crowded ballroom. Swirling bodies spun past us in the thralls of a lively Bavarian folk dance.

"I noticed you were having a kind word with Fräulein Engel," he said, trying to sound indifferent.

"Who?" I asked. I knew who.

"Amelia."

"Oh, her. Yes, well I…"

"Isn't she exquisite?" he exclaimed with a boyish squeal. "Am I not the luckiest man in the Reich? God bless Walter Engel…it was his dying wish that she be my wife."

I nodded robotically. "I imagine she's excited to marry the richest boy in town."

He hesitated before answering. "She'll come around."

I felt like saying, "No she won't," but held my tongue. I had the feeling that something momentous was going to happen this night. I could feel its approach like the rise in humidity before the rain falls.

Johann put his hand on my shoulder and beckoned for a waiter. He handed me a flute of champagne and took one for himself. "This is living, eh Becker? A good friend, a bright future as we march for the Führer, and a beautiful woman to call my own." He laughed. "My God, Harmon, will you listen to me! Tell me. Have you ever been in love?"

I gazed at Amelia, and for the briefest second our eyes locked before she turned and disappeared. "Yes," I said. "I have."

"Then a toast! To love."

"To love," I said. I downed the glass in one forlorn gulp.

I spent most of the evening orbiting the hall and eavesdropping on conversations among the local townsfolk. A common theme was that the chief threats to Germany were international Jewry and Bolshevism, and their declared nexus. Between glasses of champagne, the notion was put forth that a positive first step would be to rid the country of all the Jews and their Communist lapdogs. I heard not one opinion uttered in disagreement. "*Irgendwann mal*," they said. "Someday." I shied away from such serious matters, as they were not my concern. So I said nothing.

Instead I tried to absorb the gaiety of the night. The splendor of the Keitels' columned grand hall lined with more red, white, and black flags of the Nazis. A giant portrait of the Führer hung from the dining room wall, his penetrating eyes like sapphires casting a covetous gaze towards some distant conquerable land just beyond our imaginations. Happy waltzes, laughter, clinking of never-empty glasses, courtesy of a purveyor of bullets in Hitler's New Germany.

Eventually my need for solitude welled up in me, and I found myself alone in a quiet drawing room set aside from the rest of the house. I shut the high, whitewashed doors behind me with a loud echo and strode across the marble floor to the shiny black concert grand piano that was the centerpiece of the elegant room. I slid onto the bench and faced the freshly polished keys. With all the gentle touch my tipsy fingers could muster, I thought of Amelia's late father and entered into the soft octaves of the *verboten* Felix Mendelssohn's Rondo Capriccioso. It's easy to be brave when you're alone.

So engrossed was I, as I am always oblivious to the outside world when I play, that I didn't notice when Amelia opened the door and quietly slipped into the room. The piece transitioned from the softness of the two-page introduction to the true rondo section, whose bouncing sixteenth notes, staccato taps, and trills gave the impression of sprites darting through moonlit woods on gossamer wings. The song climaxed with a downpour of octaves and a series of ta-da chords.

There followed a pronounced silence, as if the room required a moment to digest the torrent of notes. But then the quiet was broken by Amelia's cracking voice.

"My God, Harmon. That was magnificent."

I turned on the bench and found her standing over me in tears.

"Oh," I said softly. "I didn't know anyone was listening."

She beamed. "You really do love Mendelssohn."

"Where's Johann?" I asked, reflexively scanning the empty room.

"I don't know," she sighed, still staring down at me. "Nor do I care."

She sat herself beside me on the bench. "Now why would you say such a thing?" I asked her with intense interest. "I thought you two are to be married."

She shook her head as if clearing away a bad memory. "That was my father's notion," she offered. "I didn't want to refuse him. Not as he was dying. But now that he's gone…" A look of pain swept over her, then passed.

"And your mother?" I asked. "How is she?"

"Cantankerous as always."

Amelia leaned forward and brushed her lips to my ear. I saw the fine white hairs of her forearm standing on end. "Enough sad talk," she whispered. "My life is mine. I've already decided…when Johann threw that first stone and you went to protect me. Play something else for me."

The door suddenly creaked open, and we both whipped around on the bench as if caught naked. Johann Keitel marched into the room as though he'd been following her. If earlier he was bursting with affection for us both, now Johann was cold in his demeanor with deeply set eyes and a chiseled jaw. Amelia stiffened at his approach. For his part, Keitel said not a word but coolly clenched his teeth until his jowls pulsed, and surveyed a scene that could not have appeared so innocent to Amelia's groom. His calculating mind quickly came to its own conclusion.

"This is cozy," he said, swallowing hard.

I stood up and tried to put on an innocent front. "Johann. It got too noisy out there." But then Amelia rested her palm on my shoulder and sat me back down. Her hand was shaking.

Keitel's expression remained fixed. "You best get up, Becker. I don't think I like you so close to my bride." I remained seated.

Amelia then spoke: "I'm not your bride yet, Johann Keitel. And I do not appreciate you following me as your SS friends do Gypsies and Jews."

"Then don't associate with them," he responded without a beat. His black eyes flitted to me, then back to her. "Or their friends."

He was referring to Krup. A chill ran through me. I knew my fraternization was calling attention to me...and my family. I suddenly felt the need to explain my association with a Jew to this soon-to-be SS man with the most powerful family in town. "Is there anyone else in Stauffenberg who can teach me to play?" I asked him.

"I don't have time to learn such frivolous parlor tricks."

"Oh yes," Amelia sneered. "That's right, Johann. You're going to be a big man in the Nazi party. I forgot. Maybe when you're done breaking more defenseless shopkeeper's windows, you can shove your nose far enough into Heydrich's crotch. I hear he likes boys like you."

Keitel's body went rigid as if touched by a live wire. His eyes narrowed to hyphens and his fists clenched. He suddenly looked foolish in his Hitler Youth garb. Like a patsy. But he soon set this brash woman straight: "I could have you arrested right now for saying such a thing. You too, Becker. You better be very careful what you say next...Fräulein Amelia." He was reaching for his whistle that hung around his long neck.

"You'd have your own fiancée arrested?" I asked in astonishment.

"Watch me," he said with a coldness in his voice that told me he was serious. *Who is this?* I thought. *Where's the boy I was just drinking with in the grand hall?*

"What the hell's gotten into you, Johann?" I said, diffusing the situation and returning the subject to the more benign music. "Since when is music of German masters like Bach or Beethoven frivolous? Don't I see you marching through the streets singing martial tunes?"

That disarmed him. He was still just a boy like me, despite his haughty bravado. "That's not what I meant. I love all things German. And the New Germany will not have the patience for vermin like your piano instructor. Or with that one, if she's not careful," he said while aiming a finger at the defiant Amelia. The change in personality, as if I were confronted by his dark twin, was both unnerving and fascinating. Was he stable?

I condescended to chuckle at his little tirade, which just disarmed him more.

Amelia shook her head, as if she'd heard his cautions before. "What do you want, Johann?"

"To check on you," he replied.

"You mean to check up on me."

Keitel looked at me, then her, then me again. "No…but should I?"

I exhaled and rolled my eyes. "Come on, Johann. We're just taking a break from the noise of the party." I turned to Amelia, and her look betrayed to us both that I was lying. My heart was thumping. Then I did something foolish. The champagne was clouding my judgment, and I forgot who was standing before me. "Here, let me play a wedding march in your honor. It's by Bach. Then you tell me what's frivolous."

He placed his hands behind his back, like a drill sergeant. "Very well, Becker. Maybe I'm being silly. Let me hear it."

Amelia watched me quizzically. I played a wonderful march in C major that I'd recently adapted for piano. It was only three pages, but the melody was familiar. I could see by the end through the corner of my eye that even Keitel was able to crack a thin smile. Amelia, however, was sitting next to me and staring with a mixture of confusion and then the slowly broadening grin of one in on a joke. Which she was. But for the Hitlerite in our midst, I know she would have put her arms around me.

When I finished, I turned to Johann. "Well?" I said.

He smiled. "Bach. How could one not enjoy such music? It's as the Führer says; the German way is the true way. With the arts as well. You've proven that point."

I started laughing. "That was 'The Wedding March,' by Felix Mendelssohn."

Amelia suddenly burst into boisterous laughter.

"What sort of nonsense is this?" demanded Keitel, his face turning deep crimson.

"You just praised the work of a Jew. One whose music our Führer has *banned*." I sat there eyeing him in contemptuous silence.

Amelia was not so contained. "Watch out, Johann. Perhaps you should blow your little whistle on yourself?"

Keitel stammered, feeling every bit the fool I'd just revealed him to be.

"You're a bastard, Becker!" he screamed. Then he turned his frenzied gaze upon Amelia. "And you, you slut, I won't tolerate your flirtations! I can assure you of that!"

I was stunned at his acidic vehemence, which had me soon questioning whether mocking Johann Keitel to win the affections of Amelia Engel was such a good trade. Obviously, I'd crossed the line. And something inside the boy must have snapped.

But Amelia didn't take kindly to his insult, and in one phrase sowed a seed of hatred this future SS officer would cultivate over the course of many years that would eventually bear tragic fruit.

"Slut?" she fired at him. "Why, you Nazi troll! I am no one's whore… least of all yours!" And then she pointed her shaking finger squarely in my direction and laid waste to my relationship with Johann Keitel. "If anything I'll be his bride!"

His face went from red to ashen, as if someone had pulled out a stopper in his throat. He opened his mouth to speak but nothing was forthcoming. As he turned on his heels and stormed away, Amelia leapt off the bench and walked briskly after him. She stopped at the opened doorway and shouted at his back as he marched down the hallway back towards the ballroom and his guests. “Do you want an encore, you small-minded boy?”

She slammed the doors violently and strode back with clenched fists to sit back down on the bench with a huff. She leaned against me, catching her breath. This woman was nobody’s handmaiden. I turned and whispered into her ear.

“You’re a remarkable woman, do you know that?”

Her anger fading, she looked at me with profound feelings and took my cheeks in both of her delicate hands. “And you’re a sweet boy.”

“This will be hard on Johann,” I said.

“I know,” she said dreamily, resting her head on my shoulder.

“And there’s a war coming.”

“I know.”

“I’ll have to do my duty.”

“I know.”

“You won’t have many friends tomorrow.”

“I know.”

As the festive intonations of Germany’s apogee continued just beyond the parlor doors, I took her chin under my forefinger and eased her lips onto mine. How often had I dreamt of this since I first felt her bosom press up against me as we took shelter under the malevolent shower of Nazi glass. Her lips, like sweet strawberries, took mine in kind and a shiver ran through me.

“I’ve wanted to do this for a long time,” I confessed.

“I know,” she said breathlessly. Her exhalations blew against my tingling ears. “I want you too.”

I pulled my head back. “Here?” I looked over to the door. “Is the door locked?” I asked as I ran my lips down the side of her swan-like neck and inhaled her feminine scent. My entire body felt as if it were being jolted with a mildly pleasant electric charge.

“I don’t care,” she cooed. “Let them see I’m free.”

She moaned and gasped as I slipped one hand up the folds of her dress to caress her bare thighs, while the other moved behind her and methodically began to undo the laces on the back of her dress one by one.

17

Stauffenberg lay dormant under a heavy quilt of thick, wet snow when word finally pushed its way through town that the much-anticipated wedding between Amelia Engel, the daughter of the widow Hanna, and Johann Keitel, son of George and Lila of the Keitelgesellschaft armaments fortune and Hitler Youth leader, had been cancelled. There was some local chatter about what—or who—was the cause of the rift, including speculation about the young prodigy Harmon Becker, who played pianoforte under the tutelage of the town's remaining Jew. But the short-lived gossip storm soon subsided, buried like everything else under three feet of Bavarian powder.

Johann and I wouldn't speak for five years. And when we did, the tone of our meeting was quite the opposite of our once cordial interactions. At the end of March 1939, the Keitels had their annual gala in celebration of Hitler's assumption of power six years before. As was the custom of the richest family in town, every citizen of Stauffenberg received an invitation to ski and take in sleigh rides on their estate grounds. Everyone, that is, except for three families: the Krupinskis, the Engels, and the Beckers. And so it was made clear that SS man Johann Keitel counted me as an enemy…the equivalent of the Jewry he despised and the woman who had rejected him. I would have to be careful.

I spent the cold winter days with my time divided between my house and Amelia's. There was talk of war commencing when the spring thaws ushered in Europe's traditional campaigning season. To my father's dismay, Paul's zeal for the Nazi cause was growing as the local schoolmaster drummed into the children the purity of the Aryan race rather than the multiplication tables. I would often come into the house to find him crouched before the wireless, listening with his mouth wrenched into a satisfied smile and his eyes alit with the fire of patriotism while our Führer spoke to the youth of his nation:

"*We do not want this nation to become soft*," his guttural, speechified voice exhorted the boys of my country. "*Instead, it should be hard and you will have to harden yourselves while you are young. You must learn to accept deprivations without ever collapsing. Regardless of whatever we create and do, we shall pass away, but in you, Germany will live on and when nothing is left of us you will have to hold up the banner which some time ago we lifted out of nothingness [applause]. And I know it cannot be otherwise because you are flesh of our flesh, blood of our blood, and your young minds are filled with the same will that dominates us [applause]. You cannot be but united with us. And when the great columns of our movement march victoriously through Germany today I know that you will join these columns. And we know [wild applause] that Germany is before us, within us, and behind us.*"

Time rolled on. Winter stubbornly surrendered to spring. The white cloak on the hillsides receded, revealing the patchworks of lime green that rolled away to blue mists under the watchful eye of the Alps to the southeast. Germany in 1939 was full of promise and excitement about the future. Amidst talk of imminent war, the people of Stauffenberg went about their daily routines. Anyone who paid attention to the *Wochenschau* newsreels offered at the local cinema could see that the Führer, through his mouthpiece Goebbels, was steeling the nation for a fight. But where would the first blow fall? And against whom? Those were the unanswered questions during those last fleeting hours before the lamps of Europe went out again. The second hand of destiny was ticking ever louder in our collective ears.

Summer brought clear skies and dry roads. One fine morning, I stood on the sidewalk and observed a battalion of young, as-yet-untested *Landsers* as they wound their way in two lines through the narrow streets. These were battle columns. Infantrymen with their summer green tunics and calf-hugging jackboots tramp-tramped on the cobbles through the

Himmelplatz and out of town, passing under the Rathaus tower and then crossing the Main Bridge. They sang martial hymns to the Reich as they marched. The town's women, in their colorful embroidered dirndls indigenous to the Oberfranken, lined the streets waving, cheering, and tossing bouquets at the smiling troops. It all looked so clean, so *German*. National pride swelled in me at the sight of these handsome, disciplined centurions of the Fatherland…regardless of what was happening to Krup and his family.

But I wasn't blind to the realities of a foot soldier's life. I could not see myself in their ranks as a human packhorse. A typical Wehrmacht infantryman carried thirty pounds of equipment slung over the shoulder. The leather harness would hold together pouches for sixty rifle rounds and a spade, gas mask, water bottle, breadbasket containing some bread and meat or sausage, small fat tin, and bayonet. The infantrymen were being toughened for a field campaign. I did not envy these dusty, weary men on the move, their Mauser rifles (another eight pounds) slung casually from one aching shoulder to the other to alternate the weight for comfort. Their bell-shaped steel helmets were not worn while marching but rather attached by the chinstrap to the harness equipment. The hands idly played with the helmet straps, revealing the tedium of a long march. Aluminum identity disks dangled on light chains about the necks. Pressed in halves, they could be snapped in two should the fellow die, one half going to the unit chaplain or to the administrative office, the other sent home. I wondered how many discs would be bisected before this impending war was over.

As I gazed at these young boys, many my age, I was reminded of my duty. That night at supper, I informed my family of my intention to join the Luftwaffe if they would have me. My father said nothing. My mother disappeared upstairs and wept. Paul begged to go with me. "Not yet," I said to him with a pat on the head, and he scurried off.

It was just me and Father sitting across from one another. He stared into his buttermilk. "You are decided then?"

"Yes, Papa," I said. "I have no choice anyway. I'm conscription age."

He took a deep breath. "Damn that...*Austrian corporal* and his fascist brown wood ticks."

I was shocked. It was the first time in my life I had ever heard him utter a political thought. "You can't mean that," I protested.

He just looked up at me. "You're doing what you must, Son. I understand and respect that. Since it's unavoidable, I'd rather see you up in the air anyway. A smart move, but you always were the smart one. Smarter than Paul." He lowered his voice. "Little fool and his Hitler Youth goon squad. They're taking him to a camp next week."

"Why'd you let him join? I managed to escape service...thanks to you."

He hesitated a moment. "They came to the door. Keitel at their head. First time I've seen that cocksure hector since Christmas. He's fully ensconced in the SS now. He informed me that all youths between the ages of twelve and seventeen were 'asked' to join. If I refused to allow it, then I would lose my position as constable." He waved his hand. "Oh hell, the little Nazi pest wanted to join anyway. So what do I care, right?"

I looked at him. "Papa," I said soothingly. "Everything will be okay."

"Do you know what that Keitel said to me?" I shook my head no. "He said, 'We may not have you, Herr Becker, or even Harmon. But Paul will be one of us. We have your youth. Your future. That's all that matters now.'" He pounded his fist on the table, spilling the milk on the faded wood surface. Through clenched teeth he growled: "I'm losing my boys to the Nazis."

"No you're not," I assured him, wiping the milk up with my sleeve. "You're just lending them to the Fatherland for a spell. You must have more faith, Papa."

He pulled out his rosary from his breast pocket and stared down at it, fingering the beads. "My faith is all I have left."

Amelia and I spent the last of our carefree days sitting in the Himmelplatz or taking care of her mother, who'd suffered what appeared to be a series of mini-strokes and was now slightly disabled. Hanna Engel, diminutive and white-haired, took a liking to me. "So much more earthy than Johann," she would say as we pushed her in a wheelchair under the vermillion light of the gloaming along the Wilkestrasse. "That boy frightened me, my dear. But Harmon here is a doll."

"Mother, you'll embarrass him!" Amelia would giggle, noting that I was indeed blushing.

"He may blush, but does he ever speak?" she would observe with a hearty laugh that belied her condition. I adored Hanna Engel. But she would pay dearly for loving me.

When we could get away alone, Amelia and I would spend lazy afternoons strolling along the banks of the sleepy Main under a blanket of sunshine. Even in the mountains it was often warm enough to remove my shirt and let the sun ink a golden bronze on my back and shoulders. Amelia, so much a creature of the hills, remained milky fair and freckled. She would pick edelweiss as we walked through flowered cloisters of the old Wurtzenberg monastery or took in twilight chamber music concerts in the park.

Having officially applied as an officer candidate, I was slated to report for my first physical at the end of August. "Why do you wish to fly, Harmon?" she asked me once as we sat on the river bank with our bare feet splashing in the water.

For the first time I admitted to her my fears.

"Although he never speaks of it to me, I've heard my father in the *Brauhaus* with his old comrades telling stories of the Great War. The gassings, the maiming, the blood, and the stench of feces, urine, and decaying flesh all about him. Shells constantly warbling overhead. So utterly helpless." I pointed to the heavens. "Up there is none of that. Besides," I offered on a lighter note, "I was never one for crowds."

She took my hand and turned my head away from the water to face her. Her crystal eyes could hold me in a trance. "I don't want you going off to war at all, Harmon."

"I have no choice," I said quietly, trying to beat away thoughts of what fate had in store for me. I drew from my school lessons to garner strength in my ingrained love of country. I admit even I was infected with the disease of National Socialism. Amelia was the only one my age I knew who seemed immune. So my speech fell on skeptical ears. "There are forces at work greater than the self. We are a united hail of bullets now. I'm tied to the fate of this country, and the Führer…as are you," I said, echoing the thoughts of ninety million German patriots.

She brushed her dress with her palm. "I wonder sometimes. This man may bring us to ruin."

I instinctively looked around to make sure no one had heard that. Fortunately we were alone on the grassy bank. "It's not wise to second-guess the Führer."

She shot me a look. "Please don't tell me you've fallen under the spell too. I don't want to lose you."

"What are you talking about?" I chuckled. She was not smiling.

"Do you know how much you sound like Johann lately?" she said.

"I sound like me," I retorted, more insulted than I would have expected. "I sound like a true German."

"How could you ever defend this Third Reich? Can you not see it's built on a foundation of lies?" she said, holding her ground.

I reminded her of the dark years. "You remember how miserable our country was not so long ago? I was only a boy when my father took me to Münich, but I can still see the sallow, anxious faces. The abject despair. Men wandering the streets in tattered clothes. Most shameful were the beggars in Wehrmacht uniform. Some even had medals attesting to their courage on behalf of a fat kaiser and then a Weimar fraud that abandoned them to the alleyways. To see our people reduced to rags. Thanks to the Allies and their damned reparations bleeding our nation dry. As if they were so noble. Well, Hitler changed all that. I don't follow him blindly, Amelia. I'm not Keitel or my kid brother. But I do admire his accomplishments. He gave men work, security, and above all self-esteem. Aren't you grateful for this?"

I think that was how many of us felt at the time. Though not a member of his party, I'd been impressed by his achievements.

She just stared at me gravely. "And what of the hatred?"

I shrugged. "I can't tell if it's hatred or just renewed national pride. A pride stifled at Versailles, but since then come into its own as—"

"Oh enough!" Amelia could take no more as rage struck her with all the expectation of a cruel surprise. She leapt to her bare feet and turned away from me, storming several yards down along the riverbank to stand with her arms at her side, gazing out to the far shore as if hoping to glimpse some happier promised land. "If I need to hear the Nazi party line, I'll turn on the radio and get an earful of Goebbels." She shielded her eyes from the bright sunlight gleaming off the moving water. Botticelli's *The Birth of Venus* in the flesh. "I've grown tired of excuses. The Long Knives, Nuremberg Laws, Kristallnacht. They weren't brought about by Versailles. This blot on our soul that is National Socialism comes from some corruption of our own national self." She cast her eyes to the blued folds of the faraway mountains in the mist. "This is not the Germany of my childhood."

"There's only one Germany," I reminded her as I rose to a stand and walked towards her. "And I'm a part of it."

She turned to me. "What about the way the Nazis terrorize Leopold? He's your friend, for God's sake. What about all the Jews?"

I stiffened. I'd actually gone to see Krup just the week before at his house in the country, where he now spent his days, far removed from the tormentors who were once his townsfolk. It was the first time since November '38. When the pogroms began. I'd kept my visit clandestine because I didn't want Amelia to follow me; I knew my movements were being watched. Nor did I want her to hear what I had to say to him. That I needed to forget about him. For my family's sake. It was a painful last meeting I tried to forget. But it would come back to me in vivid detail when my world suddenly was knocked off its axis right in the middle of a war…courtesy of the woman who now stood in judgment before me.

"Well," I said, clearing my throat. "I don't completely understand the Führer's animosity towards the Jews. But then again," I added dutifully, "my only experience with them has been with Krup and his family. I don't know, Amelia. Maybe things really are different in the big cities. Perhaps what they taught us in school, about how the Jews were behind our capitulation in the Great War just so they could wrest control of the businesses and finance away from German Christians, is true."

Amelia's look shifted from anger to sweet despair. "Will you listen to yourself? What happened to that boy who held me when the glass was raining down? That young musician who knows right from wrong? This is not you talking. I know you, Harmon Becker."

"I'm not saying I agree with everything about the New Order. But I must accept it. War is coming," I warned her. "The fact that my call was accelerated tells me fighting will start any day now."

Her eyes reddened. "This is why I hate Hitler so. He will kill your soul, if the war doesn't kill you in the flesh. You have an extraordinary gift that will be wasted in the Wehrmacht. You just turned eighteen. So much life to live. So much talent! To throw it all away to march for a spiteful bully."

"I have a duty to the Fatherland."

"Duty!" she snorted. "Duty to who? Hitler and his thugs?"

"To the people of Germany," I said. "To you."

"Don't you dare turn this back on me!" And she slapped me on the face! I was more startled than hurt. My cheek stung, and marks stood out like red exclamation points on my face, but I was no worse for the wear. I'd never seen her so passionate…so reckless with her own safety. I shuddered to think what fate might befall her had anyone heard her traitorous rants. This should have been a clue as to what lay ahead of me.

The little blonde demon looked up at me wide-eyed, as much in shock over her primordial spasm of violence as her target. "I hope you didn't re-open that old wound," I said with a coy I-deserved-it grin.

She shook her head at her folly and with a hint of shame said: "I made sure I clocked you with my right hand."

"Christ, I hope whoever we fight doesn't hit us like that," I said, rubbing my cheek while I flashed her a come-hither smirk. "It'll be 1918 all over again."

She stepped in close. "I'm sorry. I just get so frustrated when I see my two years of age on you are a chasm at times. Can you not see the signs, Harmon? I see apocalypse. Don't fall under that man Hitler's wicked spell. Promise me."

I opened my arms out to her. She smiled contritely and moved in to hug me. We stood together as one on the edge of the Main. "You worry too much. Everything will be fine."

She squeezed me tighter. "Fine for us. But for the world at large, I'm not so sure." I could still hear Johann's prediction that the world would hold its breath when Germany finally went on the march.

We both peered down into the running waters at our toes, searching for our future. It was such a beautiful day, the sky so deep, the fragrant smell of pine, the *cree-cree* of grasshoppers leaping about in the tall grass of the meadows creating a chorus that surrounded us.

"Harmon, tell me you'll come home safe after this war everyone's predicting is over."

That I could not do. And she knew that. I could only continue to embrace her quavering form in silence as we awaited the advent of wartime, once more, on all the Angeluses of the world. It was the first time I ever saw Amelia Engel angry. And it was the first time I ever saw her cry.

18

"A part of me still found it hard to imagine that the Führer would lead us to war," I confide to my reporter guest. She scribbles this down.

"But the war came," Rachael says.

I sigh at the stupidity of it all. "At 5:40 a.m. on September 1, 1939, our armies smashed into Poland. And so ended the last summer of my boyhood."

"What part did you play in the beginning?"

"I attended the Kriegshule, the military academy, as an NCO. Flight training, drill parades, studies, indoctrination. A year after I left home I was commissioned a lieutenant in the Luftwaffe. It was a very proud day for me, as you can imagine."

Rachael shakes her head admonishingly. "No, Mr. Becker. I can't."

I close my eyes. "They were confusing times, my dear. We stood in the rain on the parade grounds of the school, in our fitted uniforms, with shiny helmets dripping water on our mud-soaked boots. We raised our right hands, with index and middle finger pointed to the gray clouds, and we took the Führereid."

"The Führ-er-eid?" She struggles to pronounce it.

"Our sacred oath of allegiance to Hitler. It may help you understand our mindset at the time. Perhaps it's beyond anyone now."

I can still recite it by heart:

"*I swear by almighty God this sacred oath that I shall render unconditional obedience to Adolf Hitler, the Führer of the German Reich, supreme commander of the Wehrmacht, and that I shall at all times be prepared, as a brave soldier, to give my life for this oath.*"

"That's a little too convenient. I'm not buying it. The oath made you do it?"

"No," I reply vigorously. "It's just an explanation, not an exoneration."

"Did you see Amelia in all that time? Your family?"

"I saw them briefly, before my first assignment in Yugoslavia in spring 1941. By that time," I continued, "we Germans were masters of all Europe. Poland, Holland, Denmark, Belgium, Norway, even the mighty France with her million-man army was crushed by our swiftly moving armored columns in just thirty days. Crete, Greece, North Africa. Only the island nation of Britain held out. This was the time of the *Blumenkrieg*. The War of Flowers. When the men would return to Germany to march in triumphant parades while ladies showered us in bouquets."

"And then?"

"And then came Russia," I say. "And the series of events that brought me back to the West and put me on the path of treason."

19

The vast emptiness of the Russian steppe, a mustard-yellow ocean of wheat, sunflowers, and shoulder-high grasses, stretched out to the distant horizon, where the edge of the earth touched the wide-open sky. Warm breezes whipped up from the south and rippled across the plains, heralding the end of the excruciating cold. Although it was only mid-April, already the second horrible winter I'd endured there had ended and was receding into the shadows of my mind. The thaw caused me to wonder whether the dirge of titanic battles with the Red Army that rolled eastward in 1941 for 600 miles from the River Bug to the very suburbs of Moscow—only to be beaten back by the massive Russian counter-attack supported by their insidious ally, the brutal winter—and then the catastrophe of Stalingrad in the second half of '42, had all been just a terrible dream. But for the families of the half million German dead and many times that wounded and maimed, Hitler's foray into Stalin's Russia was no dream. It was an agony. It was also showing all the hallmarks of being one of the greatest blunders in military history, although we in the Luftwaffe were too preoccupied with flying missions and staying alive to think too much on that.

Now it was the springtime again, 1943. Sitting out in the open, the sun drenching us in its warm glow, our little group of pilots were hunched in our folding chairs around card tables enjoying the fine weather. We appeared but specks on the surface of a sea of waist-high grass. Out here one could easily grow disoriented, as the topography had no discernable features against which you could figure out where you were or which direction you were even facing. No matter which way you turned, you confronted a land spread out for miles in front of you, only to abruptly terminate at the false crests of the horizon that were illusions created by the curvature of the earth. You really did come to suspect that you were at the farthest end of the world.

Our ground crews were taking advantage of the warm spell along with the relative quiet in our sector to give our aircraft a much-needed re-tooling. While they worked hard to keep us flying, we pilots had not much to do but smoke cigarettes and play cards in impromptu games of Skat set up in the shadows of our parked fighters. I was losing money in one such game with three other members of my squadron.

I'd made some good friends in the past two years of combat. Lieutenants Gerhard Borner, a Clark Gable clone, and the portly "Big Werner" Gaetjens, seated at opposite ends at my elbows, were two of them; but my closest friend was my cigar-chomping wingman, Josef Mueller, who was sitting next to me analyzing my hand. He and I had been paired up upon our assignment to Jagdgeschwader 54, an air group known as the Greenhearts, and it was an uneasy match in the beginning. He thought me cold and aloof and had no qualms about telling me so. I thought he drank too much and talked more so. But our differences melted away when in combat together with the Red Air Force. To our mutual delight we soon discovered that we had an uncanny feel for each other's movements in the sky and covered each other with textbook fluidity. On the ground we came to understand that our differences were at first tolerable and then, as the crucible of war formed a deep soldiers' bond between us, we eventually grew fond of each other's quirks.

Josef was a lithe twenty-one-year-old from Saxony, and as such his tastes for the finer things were more discriminating than mine. Discussions about our lives before the war were rare though. It was as if we wished not to dwell on home should we grow too melancholy. His devil-may-care bearing prompted me to imagine I was flying with the spoiled son of a wealthy baron who was too embarrassed to say so. When the mood would turn serious, if the squadron suffered losses, he would be the one to lift our sagging spirits with a practical joke or two—often at my expense. His favorite was to cover the earpiece of my phone with boot polish. Childish and cliché, I admit. But when you're under the chronic stress of combat, even the silliest prank can be more valuable to the psyche than a box of medals from the Führer himself.

Major Johannes Trautloft's staff car, a weathered BMW convertible, skidded over to us in a cloud of dust. I hadn't noticed our wing commander's approach, as I was contemplating not so much my losing hand as the thunderstorm several miles distant along the horizon. A great blackened mass of cumulonimbus clouds, its anvil top swollen with moisture, towering fifty thousand feet over the steppe. The rain falling from its flat base resembled wispy brushstrokes of gray mist pulled down to the ground.

My daydreaming was interrupted by Borner, who leapt to his feet and called out: "*Achtung!*" We all jumped stiffly to attention, my cards fluttering down to my dust-covered boots.

Major Trautloft stepped out of his car onto the grass, the Ritterkreuz under his collar gleaming in the sunshine. He was a svelte and handsome man. He was thirty-one, and I looked to him as a mentor. He was a skilled fighter pilot and excellent leader destined for advancement. I would find out later that as *Inspekteur der Tagjäger,* inspector of all German day fighters, in late 1944 he personally intervened to save the lives of one hundred sixty Allied aircrews just days before their scheduled executions. When compared to Major Seebeck, Trautloft was a god to me.

"As you were," he said.

We returned to our chairs, and I collected my losing hand from the dirt. "Trouble, Herr Major?" inquired Mueller through clenched teeth as he puffed his cigar.

Gaetjens studied his cards. "We ain't flying today, are we, sir?"

"No, nothing like that," replied Trautloft. I noticed he was clutching some official-looking documents in his gloved hand.

I looked up at him, shielding my eyes from the sun. "What do you have there, Herr Major?" They seemed to be the reason for his visit.

He uttered a disgruntled sigh. "These, Lieutenant Becker, are transfer orders. To the Western Front."

Our eyes lit up.

"Whose?" I pressed. "I hope they're not yours, sir?"

"No," said the major. "They're yours, Becker."

"Hah!" I guffawed while frowns formed on my comrades' faces. Then Trautloft looked at the other three men. "And Lieutenants Mueller's, Gaetjens', and Borner's. The full swarm. Pack up your things, report to the duty officer for processing, and be on the next transport out. I must say I'm not happy about this. I'm losing four good pilots."

Mueller and I glanced at each other. Smiles wormed across our young faces. Any place was better than this sullen, dismal land of Stalinist oppression and its wretched hordes. A wasteland of endless steppe where the new spring grasses were spouting over the thawing graves so many German youths. We were getting away from this campaign of annihilation and hatred; a crusade without honor. This *Keineblumenkrieg*: war without garlands.

Trautloft caught our joyous expressions and tried to temper our moods. "Don't look so thrilled, gentlemen," he cautioned. "You're being transferred to a base in Belgium to replace comrades lost by the score. The Tommies are a tougher foe than Russian women in biplanes. And now with the Americans jumping in with both feet, the bomber offensive will only grow more intense. Quite frankly, I don't expect more than maybe one of you to survive."

Mueller grinned and looked at the rest of us. "You poor, doomed bastards."

"We'll take our chances, sir," I said. I was already thinking of Amelia and home.

I was rather mystified that our swarm was being transferred on the eve of the summer offensive, which we all suspected would be against the Russian salient, like a bulge into our lines, centered around the village of Kursk. I figured that Luftwaffe support would be in high demand, thus requiring every man and machine available to be on the line.

"Makes no sense to me," commented the major. "Why I should have to give you up now. And you, Becker, a sixty-bagger. I envy your new commander."

"Who is he, by the way?" I asked.

Trautloft held up his papers. "Another major, since you boys love me so much. Major Hans Seebeck. I remember him." I got the feeling Trautloft did not care for this other major. Although I'd have been upset too at losing my best swarm. "Very well then," concluded the major. "The duty office will process you. You are hereby relieved from the Greenhearts. And may I say it's been a pleasure."

Borner spoke for us all: "And we've been honored to serve under you, Herr Major."

"Thank you, Lieutenant," the major replied with a cracked voice. "Pack your things, gentlemen, and bid farewell to the worker's paradise. Good hunting and Godspeed. *Heil* Hitler."

"*Heil* Hitler!" we all replied in unison as we leapt to our feet.

Trautloft walked back to the idling staff car. We immediately dismantled our game.

"Herr Major," I called to him.

He turned. "Yes, Lieutenant?"

"How did these orders come about?"

He gave me a puzzled look. "I believe you were requested," he said.

"By this Major Seebeck?" I pressed.

"Who else? Someone in Berlin's been following you, Lieutenant."

"Very strange," I offered to the horizon with a shrug.

Trautloft asked me: "You know Seebeck?"

"No, Herr Major. But you do?"

"We were cadets together. Bit tightly wound for all his money. But that was a long time ago." Then he added: "He must really need help. You be careful, Harmon. And watch over these brave lads. It's getting dangerous up there." With that he hopped in his car. "Back to my hut," he commanded the corporal behind the wheel. The enlisted man hit the accelerator, kicking up a cloud of yellow dirt in their wake as they sped off towards the main compound.

I took in the vista of the hated steppe for the last time in my life. I had no love for Russia, and it certainly did not love me. But I'd honed my air combat skills here. And survived, so far. It would be good to leave—even though I had deep reservations about this whole transfer.

Mueller looked at me as the dust blew away. "Now why would a man you've never met request you?"

"I have no clue," I admitted. I picked up my playing cards and replaced them in their box. Borner and Gaetjens were already walking to their tents. They were as elated as schoolboys before a dance. I didn't know what to feel. And so I chose to feel nothing at all. And then let the cards fall where they may.

20

"I ordered you here, Lieutenant, because I need a man like you and your swarm."

Major Hans Seebeck peered up at me from his desk and let that phrase ferment in the air. I was standing like a wooden beam at attention as I reported for duty to him. My visor cap tucked in my armpit, my eyes focused on the portrait of the Führer hanging on the otherwise bare wall just above the major's head. "I have your service record here. Quite impressive. I'm glad I could use my influence in Berlin to secure you."

"Why's that, sir?" I could already tell, within minutes of meeting this broken man, that he was no Trautloft. He was a wounded predator, one to be wary of. My eyes flashed down to him. His wounds carved out deep canals on his face. A black patch covered the socket of his gouged-out left eye. He was lanky and frail, and he tottered around the base with the aid of a walking stick, which he played with mindlessly at his side while he spoke to me.

"Very well. I will tell you. We've suffered cruelly at the hands of the Allies. The new men are coming in ill-prepared because petrol shortages are keeping their training hours down. We need experienced pilots to lead in the air. My group especially." He leaned forward, bringing the stick up to lie across the pristine mahogany desk. "And I will be even more frank. The men are afraid. They see the Allies grow stronger by the day. The Amis even have the temerity to attack us in lumbering bombers in broad daylight—and with no fighter umbrella over them! And when we do see their fighters near the channel, they are superb machines. But even with drop tanks they can only go so far before they must abandon their charges. I think they're insane to even try these raids. But the men unfortunately do not." He heaved a deep sigh and ran his gloved hand over his scar. "I cannot lead them in the air anymore. I'm grounded, Becker. And now Berlin is threatening to remove me from command. Your name was mentioned as my replacement."

"My name?" I said with genuine surprise. So that was it.

He paused, sizing up my ambitions. I had none other than to serve my country and make it home alive, but of course a man like Seebeck couldn't understand that.

"Yes, Captain. Which is your new rank now. I guess congratulations are in order." He didn't offer his new captain his hand.

"Thank you, sir."

THWACK! I blinked as he smacked his cane on the desk like a whip. "Dammit all, Becker! How can they want to replace me?" He pointed emphatically at his eye patch. "After all I've given to them!"

"I know nothing of this, Herr Major."

He waved me off. "It was that golden boy Trautloft's idea. If he had to lose you, then he insisted that you be considered for a command of your own. Your promotion is, shall we say, our compromise."

Seebeck hoisted himself to a stand and hobbled around the desk to get in my face. He was slightly taller, but I could tell there was little meat under his sagging uniform.

His breath reeked of stale cigarette smoke and schnapps. "You're a good pilot, Becker. But I'll be damned if you take my command. That's why I brought you here before Berlin could—on my terms." I didn't flinch but continued to stare straight past him.

"My only ambition here is to serve, Herr Major." He gawked at me, studying my face like a confused doctor. Outside I could hear the hum of engines throbbing overhead. "But am I to understand that you've manipulated the lives of me and my swarm over your insecurities?"

"How dare you!" he roared. He raised his cane in an abrupt gesture of command. "This is about rebuilding the group." Then he added candidly: "Still, if it also allows me to keep you out of this desk, so much the better. And who knows? Anything could happen to you. Your chances are not so good here against well-trained crews in bomber formations bristling with machine guns as they were against Slavic *Untermenschen* in kites."

His implications were not lost on me. "I'll try not to get killed, sir. For the good of your wing."

He shook his head. "Facts are facts." He pointed to his collar. "You see this insignia, Becker? I am a major. You, a captain. You'll remember that, *ja*? I have a powerful family with many friends in the party."

"So I gather…sir."

He ignored my snarky remark, as he was too caught up in his bona fides. "I'm in a position to either help you or harm you, Captain. The choice is yours. Help me. Work with my men. And I'll protect your family—and Fräulein Engel."

My heart tripped. "Beg pardon, sir?"

He gave me a smile that said much yet revealed little. "I know many things about you. This is the New Order, Captain. Remember that."

I stepped back. If I stayed where I was I might have choked this mercurial sot where he stood. In his debilitated state I could have. But I reined in my anger and swallowed my pride down hard. Facts were facts. In this case Seebeck had me. Because he somehow had my family. He had Amelia. I guess I really didn't know all there was to know about this New Germany. Obviously though, raw power, and the protection of that power, was one virtue of the Nazi regime that the major had adopted for himself.

"Will that be all, Herr Major?"

"For now, Captain." He reached for his phone and put the receiver to his ear. "Come in here," he barked. Within ten seconds a bright-eyed Lieutenant Thomson stepped into the office.

"*Heil* Hitler!" the polished young Prussian snapped at both of us while he raised his arm and clicked his heels in a fashion that I could only imagine Paul was being taught this very day…wherever he was.

"*Heil* Hitler," Seebeck and I answered in unison.

"Lieutenant Thomson is the duty officer on base here. Thomson," he said while motioning to me, "this is our newest squadron leader, Captain Becker. He comes from Russia, so we need to get him used to the idea that Western skies are not target practice. Please show him the base and see to it that his men are billeted in the château."

"*Jawohl*, Herr Major. Follow me please, sir."

I donned my visor cap. "Lead the way, Lieutenant."

He ushered me outside. The air buzzed with the activity of a full-blown fighter base in wartime. Men busily walking to and fro. Mechanics cursing over the metallic dinging of tools to engines. A staff car whizzing by. The tower with its windsock manned by helmeted men scanning the heavens with binoculars. Anti-aircraft emplacements disbursed about the perimeter. The revving and releasing of engines being fine-tuned beneath camouflaged hangars. And, of course, the ubiquitous odor of ripe gasoline filling the air.

As if keeping an omniscient watch over the base, the red banner of Nazi Germany fluttered in the spring breeze atop the high flagpole planted near the château-turned-*Kasino*. Below it, in a brusque symbol of subjugation, drooped the black, yellow, and red bars of the Belgian flag...its primacy denied it by the Teutonic invaders now ensconced in its occupied country.

I could see peeking, just visible, over the distant treetops not cleared away by our sappers, the ancient church spires of the little village of Andeville.

I followed Thomson in silence until we were well out of earshot of Seebeck's open window. Then to my surprise the young spit-and-polish adjutant spoke in a hushed tone. "I'm sorry, sir."

"Excuse me, Lieutenant?"

"The door is thin. I heard your conversation. The major likes to demonstrate his authority over new officers. I don't think it's personal. If I may say so, sir. Let me know if I can ever help you. We're not all like Seebeck here."

I winked at him. "Thank you, Thomson. I may take you up on that one day."

And with that I made my way over to my new quarters where I could sit in silence, undisturbed by anyone, and wonder what I'd gotten myself into.

21

That night I wrote to Amelia for the first time in many weeks. It started as the others did. But it was more mechanical in tone, which was reflective of my own diminished spirits. Still, I had to stay in touch with her. She needed to know I was okay, and I her. I tried to craft a correspondence that would pass muster of the state censors.

April 23, 1943

My Dearest Amelia,

I hope the spring finds you well. You will be relieved to know that I am no longer on the Eastern Front. I have been transferred to Belgium for Defense of the Reich duties. I cannot speak in depth of my assignment, but know that I am in good health and improved spirits. I am satisfied in knowing that soon we will be in combat with those who attack our homes, instead of merely defending theirs. It is so good to be away from Russia. I feel like I am among the civilized world again.

Do not fret for my safety. We fly good machines, and the Greenhearts taught me well.

I am anxious for news of Stauffenberg. Please write and keep me informed. I briefly spoke with Willy Spiegel as his unit passed through our base on his way to France. You remember him from gymnasium, with the different-colored eyes? He is a mechanic with JG 1 and mentioned that, when he is not in the field, Johann Keitel is SS Kommandant of the town. I need not tell you that he is a most capable and diligent man. I hope you are working well with him. You understand what I mean. Although he must have more urgent matters to attend to than the past. I would like to know if my family is faring well without me. I fret about my parents. Paul is another matter.

And of course I worry about you and Hanna. I miss you so. I should like so badly to see you, but this matter of the war that keeps us apart must be decided first I suppose. But let us both take solace in that it cannot go on forever.

All My Love,

Harmon

It would take several weeks to get pilots into even a semblance of fighting order, but the major now had not just one but four *Experten* (aces) to show the youngsters the way. I began training the men in earnest with the aid of Mueller, Gaetjens, and Borner. Two years in Russia had aged me, and I was ready to assume the heavy mantle of command. With my swarm's help I impressed upon our pilots the value of teamwork. I was squadron leader, with Mueller on my wing forming the lead pack. Borner and Gaetjens I separated to be swarm leaders within the squadron.

They were as close friends as Mueller and I, and also as different. Just out of his teens, Borner was the epitome of the dashing knight of the air with his thin mustache, penetrating brown eyes, and haughty swagger. But for the war he most surely would have been in the movies. At twenty-eight, Big Werner was an irascible man, older than the rest, portly and unkempt, and completely without pretense. He let the kill markings on his rudder speak for him. Both were magnificent fighter pilots, and I granted them considerable latitude to take the men up at their discretion, assuming they had adequate fuel, which was rarely.

We utilized our combat experiences to ram into eager young minds all we had learned on the Eastern Front; we hoped to try and save these excellent young German boys' lives.

Seebeck was pleased. But I knew the upcoming struggle with the Western Allies would be difficult. But just how dangerous I had yet to discover. Had I known what to expect in the coming months, I may never have left Russia at all. It would be that bad. And soon I would come to understand why Seebeck had me transferred to his post. It was simple really. Yet cunning. He wanted me to train his pilots better than he could ever have. Then he wanted me to die.

22

"You really think he wanted you dead?"

I shrug. "That's what I thought at the time. I don't care anymore." I yawn and lean back in the sofa.

Rachael checks her watch and realizes that it's almost lunchtime. "Do you want to take a break for a moment?" She can see my old face sags, as if melting under a hot sun.

"I have to use the lavatory," I announce with an embarrassed smirk. "I don't think I could have flown then with my bladder as it is now."

"Are you hungry?" she asks. "I could go get us something…the *Times*' treat."

As I hoist myself to my feet I tell her that Dora usually makes me a cucumber sandwich at this time. "That used to be her mother's chore. It's a taste I acquired from living here. I'll ask her to make you one too."

Rachael respectfully declines. "Please don't bother." Her jet lag is kicking in, and she's more interested in sleeping than eating.

"No bother. Not offering to make it myself," I kid. "You must be hungry after your long flight."

"I ate on the plane."

"Your loss." Then I disappear through the kitchen to the WC.

She follows my creaking form and wonders. Nothing she's heard thus far gives her any reason to believe that there's more to me than simply what I claim to be in my book. A stellar if lovesick fighter pilot who nevertheless found himself on the wrong side of a war.

She hears muffled conversation between father and daughter in the kitchen—in German. She cringes. Remember, Rachael, she tells herself. This man fought so that you and all of your people would be wiped from the earth. Don't let your guard down. Don't be drawn into liking him. Be professional. This may not be the man.

Dora emerges from the kitchen with a tray of sandwiches and two bottles of seltzer water. She places it on the table in front of the reporter.

"Papa thought you might be hungry."

She laughs. "He doesn't take no for an answer, does he?"

"He'd be insulted if you don't at least take one bite. He's very proud. More so than he leads on." Then she pauses. "Miss Azerad—"

"Rachael."

"Very well, Rachael. May I ask you something?"

Rachael grabs a bottle and twists it open with a *pssshhht!* "Certainly."

"Why are you asking my father to re-open old wounds?" she demands. "The war was a long time ago. It took him many years to get past his experiences."

"I understand that," Rachael replies, slightly put off. "But I assure you that I'm not here to re-open wounds, as you say, but to get a story. One I think your father may still have to tell."

Dora's expression hardens. "Why don't you just leave him alone? I can see you judging him. I heard you before."

Rachael shifts in her seat. "I'm not here to judge anybody."

The woman looks to the kitchen to see if her father is listening. "You are Jewish, yes?"

The reporter raises an eyebrow. "I am."

"And yet you're here to interview one of Hitler's decorated soldiers. Why?"

"Dora," says Rachael. "How much do you know about your father's past? During the war? And that of your mother?"

"I know enough to let the past stay there, Miss Azerad. Whatever bad things he may have done, let them go. He's old and harmless." At that moment I enter the room. "My parents are good people." Her lip flutters. "I still speak of my mother in the present tense." Rachael opens her mouth to press the issue, but Dora intercepts her with: "Ah, Papa! Are you better now?"

I sigh as she helps me to my seat. "I'm not an invalid, Daughter," I remind her, shaking off her arm. "Not yet, anyway."

Then I turn to Rachael to continue my story. "Where was I? Ah, yes. The training went by quickly. And then we were thrown into the mix of an air battle that was growing more violent as the Americans weighed in with their awesome industrial might. After our first few missions against the heavies, I very quickly came to understand Major Trautloft's dire prediction about our fate. And I realized that I was right about Seebeck's wanting me to die while helping him to live. In time, he knew, the Americans would be his assassin."

"And yet you're still here," she observes with interest. "What happened?"

"That December I made my unauthorized trip to home." I look into her alluring eyes. "That was when I first learned what Amelia was up to."

PART 3

23

I held Amelia so tight I thought I might crush her up against me. I could feel her body quivering as she sobbed into my chest. So many little things about her I'd forgotten. The silky hair running through my calloused hands, the musky scent of her skin, the back of her muscular neck and shoulders. Two years! I feared I might have changed beyond recognition in that time. I'd left her as a young, idealistic air cadet. A mere boy. And I returned to her as a cold-blooded warrior who'd killed and watched others die in the violent skies around me. We'd been thrown into different worlds—neither like that in which we had both lived before the war. Would we still be what we were? Would she still love me? Or, for that matter, would I still love her? I trembled as much at those questions as from the release of the longing for her I'd carried with me from Stauffenberg to Berlin to Russia to Belgium and back again.

"My God, Harmon!" she finally said as she disengaged from our embrace and regained her ladylike composure. "I had no idea you were coming. When? How? Oh my, I must look a fright!" A strand of golden hair fell across her high forehead over her eye, and she shooed it away with her hand.

"You look perfect," I said softly, as she made a frantic attempt to brush flour off her dress and straighten her apron.

"I'm a disaster. Why didn't you tell me? Is everything alright?"

I didn't want to tell her that at least in spirit I was absent without leave, although as I was on my way to be personally decorated by the Führer, nothing would come of it short of Seebeck's increased resentment...a redundancy at this point.

"I just received my orders late yesterday. And the lines are down from the bombings." This last part wasn't true, as Mueller had managed to follow another order by getting word to Papa at the police station about my visit. Hence Paul's meeting me at the station. He'd also let news of my Knight's Cross slip. "Everything is fine," I said. "I'm just passing through for a night. I had to see you."

Her face radiated relief. "Let me look at you!" she said, and she sized me up. The uniform, the boots, the coat. But her battleship-gray eyes rested on mine and peered inside me, as they always could. Then her face morphed from glee to pity. The war was forcing itself out through my cool facade, like grim light through a translucent shade.

I stood erect and tried to usher all my steel to shield me from this vulnerable moment. I forced a smile. "I'm home," I said with my hands out. "And I'm safe."

But she just waved the words away. Her eyes swelled and her nose turned crimson. It was as if she had so much to say and didn't know where to begin. Her lip began to tremble.

"Oh you poor man!" was all she could cry out before breaking down and weeping into her cupped hands. She saw what I'd become. A seasoned veteran. A killer. And she would never call me a boy again.

I wiped her eyes and took her by the hands. Our emotions had subsided enough for us to grasp the wonder of seeing each other again, and happiness soon returned to our red faces.

"I'm hungry," I said in an attempt to introduce normalcy to our meeting. "You must be too." She had, in fact, lost considerable weight from the stress of the war and taking care of her stricken mother. Stauffenberg as a whole remained a well-fed little town, with steady supplies of wheat and meats coming up and down the Main. The lack of bombing damage meant that the cafés and *Brauhauses* were intact.

"I was going to bake some bread. But now I'm too excited to eat." She laughed.

"Then show me the town," I said. "It's been a while."

She nodded. "Let me straighten up this mess and get my coat. I have much to tell you."

We were soon strolling in the low-hanging winter sun along the Wilkestrasse. When I told her about my impending decoration, the news seemed to agitate more than excite her, so I changed the subject of our conversation. I pelted her with questions about families that I once knew. Stauffenberg, I saw, was not so immune to the war after all.

"How is Ernst Geisshardt?" I asked.

Amelia shook her head. "He joined the paratroops. He died in Crete."

"And what about Karl-Heinz Freytag from my rowing team?"

"He was in a Panzer and fought in North Africa. He's back home now. Minus both arms."

With each name from my boyhood days, Amelia relayed to me a heartbreaking story. As we walked the narrow lanes, each turn of a corner brought back a memory of my younger days. We all used to jostle and chase each other through the cobblestone streets of our little village as the Nazis seized power all around us. In our teens, when the New Order came, in one degree or another we all embraced it as the dawn of a great age for Germany. We couldn't see that our youth condemned us to a collision course with the rest of the world as the spearhead of our Führer's ambitions. I could see all their smiling young faces.

"Herbert Hräbak?" Killed in Russia.

"The Meissner brothers, Egon and Werner?" Both *Landsers*. Both killed in Russia.

"Paul Genth?" His U-boat was overdue, presumed lost with all hands.

"Eduard 'Little Edu' Joppien?" Disappeared in Norway when his transport crashed.

And on it went. Name after name. An entire generation of boys, just as old Grossman had no doubt been thinking, was being ground to dust.

We passed by a burned-out shop. At first I didn't recognize it. I halted and stared at the destroyed site. Then I realized where I was, and the memories washed over me. The word "Jude" could be discerned in dried paint chips with a Star of David painted beneath it on the discolored plywood that covered the shattered store window. "Is that really Krupinski's shop?" Amelia grew solemn and nodded.

"He never returned to it after Kristallnacht," she added. "Hitler Youth did that soon after you left for training. So terrible."

I turned to her. "Was Paul one of them?"

She nodded, while coming to his defense. "He was one of many, Harmon."

"I would've pasted him," I said through gritted teeth. "Why is it still standing in the middle of town like some gaping wound?"

"SS orders. Keitel wants it to remain as it was."

"But why?" I said.

"To serve as a symbol."

"Symbol?"

Her expression was dour. "Of the end of Jewry in our town."

So Keitel had turned Krup's store into a monument. "I first met you there," I said with a sudden sharp pain in my throat. Amelia's eyes remained on the store. Then it dawned on me. In fact, my innards churned as I formed the question that a part of me did not want answered.

"Where are the Krupinskis now?"

24

Amelia and I sat outside at one of the *Hofbrauhaus* tables set up on the wet sidewalk, observing the meticulously dressed citizens of Stauffenberg pass by. It was uncommonly warm for mid-December, and the people were taking advantage of the break in the winter weather, desperately trying to re-capture a sense of the pre-war Bavaria we'd once known.

I stared into my beer and shook my head.

"I'm sorry, Harmon," she repeated. "One day they just vanished. Right after they destroyed his store."

"Maybe Krup finally came to his senses and left?" I proposed.

"No," she said with certainty. "By the time they disappeared there was no way they could have made it out."

"Did you ask Keitel about them?"

She lowered her eyes. "You know how he feels about us."

"Still?" I said. "After five years?"

"Still," she said ruefully. "Besides, what good would it have done?"

I yielded to her logic. "None I suppose."

She leaned forward to whisper, cautiously glancing around for prying ears. "It's terrible what's happened to all the Jews of the Oberfranken, Harmon. Not just here. The Katzes in Pottenstein, the Weissmans and Frankels in Bindlach. All gone. Some fled to Switzerland. But 'I, Leopold Krupinski, refuse to go,'" she said, mocking his hand gestures and scratchy voice.

I shook my head. "Stubborn man. I tried to tell him." I paused and fought back another welt in my throat. I cast a look towards the burned-down store. "Krup worked many hours with me in there." A smile broke out on my young face.

Amelia managed to return the grin. "He was very fond of you." She put her hand on my wrist. "And you him, Harmon. Don't forget that."

I leaned back in my chair and repeated: "Now he's gone."

Then I heard a shrill voice I will never forget. "Better to leave Germany to the Germans."

I looked up and shielded my eyes from the low sun. There before me stood a tall figure, very Germanic; angular and crisp. His field gray long coat was pulled taut to his narrow waist by a thick leather belt. Underneath it I could see the proudly displayed double-lightning insignia on his collar and the *Totenkopf* emblem on his visor cap, announcing to all the world that this was a proud member of Hitler's most feared combat unit: the Waffen-SS.

"Harmon Becker," he crowed. "As I live and breathe. You're still alive then."

"Sorry to disappoint you, Johann," I said stiffly. "I see you made it into a combat unit after all." I was referring to his *Wolfsangel* emblem sewn onto his coat bicep identifying his unit, the Second SS Panzer Division—*Das Reich*. I knew they'd been mauled in Russia. I also knew them to be fanatical soldiers for the New Order. That Keitel should have fallen in with them was only logical.

"Indeed," he said with a hint of a smirk. "I'm actually Hauptsturmführer Keitel now." He was proud of his rank, which was the SS equivalent of my own. He was a man who sought station in life outside of the family fortune. "*Heil* Hitler!" he saluted with raised arm.

"*Heil* Hitler," I saluted back without emotion.

His eyes flitted to Amelia, who gave me a cautionary glance. An unspoken message passed between us: *Be careful, Harmon.*

Keitel clicked his heels and bowed slightly. "Amelia." He extended his gloved hand to her. She took it dutifully. I said nothing more. He didn't move on with the other pedestrians out strolling on the Himmelplatz, but rather stood there contemplating the both of us. What did he want?

"It's warm for this time of year," he observed.

"It seems to have brought out the townspeople," Amelia answered dryly, figuring she'd better say something, as he was not leaving.

Keitel took up a chair and slid onto it. “May I sit?”

“You already are.” I nodded. “*Das Reich?* You’re a bit far from the front lines. Where’s your Panzer?”

He grinned. “I’m in reconnaissance.” He sized me up some more and then said: “I see Major Seebeck’s been kind enough to send you home before your little ceremony in Berlin. I’m envious.”

I leaned forward with a sense of vulnerability. “You know Major Seebeck?”

He ignored my query and twisted his torso as he called out to a waiter: “Beer, please.”

“Answer me,” I insisted. Amelia put her hand on my forearm to keep me composed. But I already knew that the SS through their now absorbed Gestapo liaisons probably knew the comings, goings, and associations of everyone from this little town.

“That uniform looks good on you, Harmon,” he said. “You’ve become quite the soldier. A pity you joined the Luftwaffe. You’d have made a fine SS man.”

I accepted that no answers were forthcoming. “I prefer to fly.”

“Yes, yes.” He groaned dismissively. “Always above it all. I imagine you get a distorted perspective on matters from so high.”

“Do my men not die just because they’re killed five miles high?” I shot back.

Amelia was watching in silent trepidation as the tone of the conversation grew more hostile. “Pilots are soldiers, like me. Why does the Luftwaffe act as if the loss of a pilot is somehow more tragic or heroic than that of a foot soldier or Panzer driver or SS trooper?”

I took a swig of my beer. The waiter brought Keitel his. “I don’t think that, Johann. But I take special offense when my men are jumped by Allied fighters that supposedly don’t exist because little robots like Seebeck refuse to tell Berlin the facts.”

Amelia’s eyes widened. “Harmon,” she cautioned, looking at the SS man in our midst. “You don’t mean that. His humor is lost on many, Johann.”

I turned to her. “You of all people are telling me to curb my tongue?” The beer was getting to me, I admit.

"Harmon Becker, shut up!" she sneered. "No one thinks you're funny. You're just upsetting me." She gave me a "Go along with this, you idiot" look.

Keitel drummed his fingers menacingly. He clenched his chiseled jaw. "Listen to her, Harmon. You're on dangerous ground."

I was about to say something that could have landed me in serious trouble when I was saved from myself, ironically enough, by the Americans. As if by signal, the unmistakable droning of high-altitude bombers began to grow over our heads. Like a hive of wasps in bass baritone. Everyone in the Himmelplatz craned their faces skyward and shielded their eyes from the sun. We could see the familiar white string-like contrails streaking across the sky.

Keitel stared up angrily. "More bombers. Murdering criminals. I actually interrogated one of them once. A tail gunner. You should have seen him by the time I was through with him."

I noticed that the townspeople were not exactly scrambling to get out of the streets. "Shouldn't we take shelter?" I said, slightly confused.

Amelia shook her head as if this were no longer a noteworthy occurrence. "They don't come for us. It's Adelstatz they try to destroy. But it's a hard target, so protected by mountain folds along the riverbank."

Keitel snorted. "Our munitions factory." Then he leveled his dark eyes on me. "It seems that our indispensable pilots are unable to blunt these criminal raids."

The juvenile faces of Kluge and others flashed before me, and the effect on me was galvanic. I felt like I was watching someone else lurch across the table and grab Keitel by the leather lapels of his jacket with both hands. My fiery assault startled him, and he knocked over his beer trying to fend me off. The glass stein rolled off the table and shattered on the stone sidewalk. Heads turned to watch us.

"Harmon! Stop!" Amelia cried.

Keitel turned white as I pulled his face to within a foot of my own. Gritting my teeth I fumed at him: "We've lost twenty-five pilots in three months, you snide son of a bitch! You think those losses come from hiding out in *Brauhauses* casting inane judgments?"

Curious pedestrians, civilians, and military personnel alike forgot about the bombers overhead as they stopped in their tracks to observe the curious row between the Luftwaffe captain and feared SS-*Hauptsturmführer*.

Keitel quickly regained his senses. He was still just slightly smaller than me, but years in the field had given him a wiry vigor. He was able to release himself from my grasp and shove me back so we were both standing. Amelia, too, rose from her chair.

"Enough of this lunacy!" she shouted. She wedged herself between us and cupped my face in her firm hands. "Harmon, calm yourself. Now!" Her touch diffused my temper, and my hyperventilating subsided. Still staring at Keitel, I took my seat.

The SS man straightened his long coat and replaced his hat. He glanced at the people, who quickly turned away to resume their day. He seemed more concerned with how this looked to them than with any breach of military etiquette on my part. He grabbed a napkin from an empty table next to us and wiped beer off of his sleeve.

But Amelia wasn't finished. She shot a mean leer at my antagonist. "You've seen enough here, Johann. I know what this is about. You may tell yourself that Harmon and I are very much in love." Then her tone softened. "I'm sorry you still carry such a burden. After so many years. You *must* move on."

Keitel stiffened. In a very cool manner he offered me some advice. "If I were you, Becker, I'd keep that Ritterkreuz you're about to get very close to you. It's the only thing that prevented your arrest in front of these people today."

I said nothing more. I turned away from him and stared at the fountain of Charlemagne while the bombers continued on their indifferent trek above us.

"Good day to you, Amelia." Keitel clicked his heels again. "I'm sure we'll be seeing each other again, Becker," he said to my back.

He marched off, tramping into the crowded square. People stepped back to let him pass. An angry SS officer was not an enemy to be made lightly in a small German town in 1943. Amelia made sure I knew this as well.

"Are you trying to get in trouble, Harmon? Honestly, what's gotten into you?"

"He's a swine," was all I said in reply. "What else do I need to know?"

She squeezed my forearm. "What else do you need to know? That I must live here. That the SS runs Stauffenberg and I need to be careful. It's not easy being the lover of Harmon Becker in a town run by the Keitels." Then she added chilling words I'll never forget: "Not with what I'm doing."

I put down my beer. Off in the distance I could hear the muffled thuds of faraway explosions echoing down the banks of the Main as the bombers emptied their payloads onto the general location of Adelstatz.

"And what exactly have you been doing, Amelia?"

She looked around to make sure there were no eavesdroppers. "Finish your beer. There's something at the house I think I want to show you."

"You think?"

She exhaled as she spoke. "I need to know that you love me, Harmon. That you truly and without question love me."

I tried to size up her question. "Of course."

"More than Germany itself?"

I paused. "Does that matter?"

"Yes," she said firmly. She let that curious answer sit in the air. Now I was getting concerned.

"I think you'd better tell me why you're asking such a question, my dear."

"Okay, Harmon," she finally conceded. "Come with me."

We rose from the table and strode casually through the town center arm in arm. She was taking me back to her house. What waited for me inside I could only guess. And I never would have guessed right if given all the time in the world.

25

We stood in the front parlor of Amelia's tired house. The piano I used to play during happier times sat against one wall. A burgundy velvet sofa with its solid wood frame and carved claw feet faced the instrument, beckoning visitors to sit awhile and listen. The hearth was decorated with colorful hand-painted ceramic beer steins and playful figurines, small boys and girls in traditional country garb on their way to the well or market, that celebrated a simpler Bavarian life that seemed to belong to another universe.

"Amelia?" called a defiant, if shaky, voice from behind a closed door to the side of the room. "Is someone here?"

Amelia smiled mischievously at me.

She called out: "Oh, just an old friend of ours, Mama. No one special. Come out and see."

"If she's not so damned special then she can come and see me. I have no desire to get out of bed, Daughter."

Amelia put her fingers to her lips and ushered me into Hanna's dark bedroom. Although it was a sunny day, the heavy curtains were drawn, lending a tomblike atmosphere to the chamber. Sitting up in a sleigh bed, her head and back propped up by thick pillows, Hanna waited to receive her visitor. She was knitting a scarf. I remained behind Amelia as we entered.

"My dear," Hanna said with irritation in her grating voice. "You know I loathe surprises." Amelia stepped out of the way so her mother could make out my form. "Well, I can see that our she is a he. Come closer. Is he a soldier? Not that Keitel I hope." When I stepped forward, there was enough light for her to see my face, and her eyes widened with delight. "Harmon Becker!" she gasped, clasping her hands together. "Can it really be you?"

I smiled. "It's good to see you, Hanna."

"I never thought I'd lay my eyes on you again, young man!" She placed her knitting on the end table and beckoned me with outstretched arms. "Let me look at you!"

I took her hands in mine and I kissed her on the cheek. Her hands were icy and skeletal. She trembled from either fever or some other syndrome. And she emitted that musty, dank odor of the chronically ill.

"You're still a handsome one!" she exclaimed weakly. "And so splendid in uniform!"

Amelia came up behind me and wrapped her arms around my chest. I let go of Hanna to acknowledge the hug. "Mother always asks about you," she said, resting her chin on my shoulder.

I smiled at the old woman while caressing Amelia's hand. "You look well, Hanna."

She chuckled knowingly. "You're a bigger liar than Goebbels. I know I'm in a staring contest with death."

"Oh Mama, stop such talk," chided Amelia. "You'll outlive us all."

"For your sakes I certainly hope not."

"Can I open the curtains for you?" I asked.

"No," she sighed. "I'm not too fond of the world outside my window these days."

Amelia ignored her mother and purposefully strutted over to the window and threw open the drapes. Sunlight poured into the room, revealing Hanna's drawn and deeply creviced face. Her white hair was pulled back taut. Her pallor a mottled gray. I was, in fact, shocked by her sickly appearance. Everyone in that room knew that Hanna Engel's days were numbered.

She scorned Amelia: "You may bring the outside to me, daughter, if you must. But I'll not go to it."

"The doctor said that it would do you good to get up and out."

She looked at me. "I don't know whose droning annoys me more. The doctors' or those awful bombers'. Actually they both take a distant second to the Nazis." She laughed. If her body was failing, her wits were still robust.

Amelia picked up Hanna's crumpled robe off a side chair and re-folded it before laying it back down. She moved a glass of water on the end table next to the knitting and, like a doting nurse, asked her if she needed anything.

"Yes. I would like this damned war to end."

"I'm working on that," I assured her.

"I know you are. The soldier prays for peace most of all. You are the ones that must bear the scars of war for the rest of us." Her face grew forlorn as she turned to the window. "At least that's how it is supposed to be. The Americans bombed the kindergarten outside of Ebensfeld last week. Twenty children died. To what end? There's nothing there." I nodded my head in assent.

"Such talk is senseless, mother," said Amelia, fluffing up her mother's pillows. "I have parcels coming to the house. I'll boil some soup and you will eat. Is that clear?"

Hanna coughed. Even this brief interaction seemed to have drained her reserve of energy. "What is clear, Daughter, is that I am not your child. You are, in fact, mine. I will decide when and what I eat."

Amelia shook her head. "Stubborn old *Brauhaus* maiden."

Hanna chortled as she settled in to nap. "In my day I was. Oh Harmon, you should have known me in my youth. But I am so tired now."

"Then you should rest," Amelia said.

"Can you do something for me?" Hanna looked up at me as she pulled a blanket to her chest. "Can you play a song that I might sleep? It's been so long since we've had piano music in this house."

"Of course." I'd forgotten how much she enjoyed my playing.

"Now do as your daughter says and rest," I told her.

Hanna nodded and closed her eyes. She breathed deep. "It's good to see you again. Please promise you'll stay alive. For my little girl."

"I'm afraid that's up to the Allies," was the only assurance I could give her. We backed out of the room and closed the door behind us. While Hanna drifted off to sleep, I sat down at the dusty old spinet piano and began to play Beethoven's Moonlight Sonata. It was always Hanna's favorite. So soothing and melancholy. Soon I grew too engrossed in the music to notice that Amelia had closed all the shades and darkness now cloaked the parlor as it had Hanna's room before. Then she disappeared up the stairs.

26

I was just walking my fingers down the keys, retarding to the last haunting C-sharp minor chord of the Moonlight Sonata's first movement, when I detected not one but two distinct footfalls creaking down the steps behind me. Deep in concentration, I barely noticed when the shadows of a pair of individuals fell over the piano. One of them sidled up to me and sat uneasily next to me on the long bench.

My hands lay flat on the keys, preparing to enter into the sonata's allegretto second movement. I closed my eyes, took a breath, and to my astonishment before I could begin I heard not Beethoven, but Chopin's "Gota de Lluvia" prelude. The music was full of longing and made me think of staring through a rain-pelted window out at a stygian morning. It was the most moving piano music I'd ever heard. And in my heart, despite what my mind told me could not be so, I knew who was playing.

I opened my eyes with trepidation and turned to face the man who'd been the most important force in my young life, outside of my own family and Amelia. His appearance shocked me. He looked so much older than I remembered. In his emaciated face was abject despair. As if all he'd once believed in had been proven a grand farce. And in a sense, it all had been.

"Leo?" I said softly. He continued on with his somber melody as if I was not there. It must have been so utterly satisfying for him to play again.

I twisted in my seat to face Amelia. Her hands trembled as she tried to gauge my reaction. Harmon Becker, the man she loved, was also an officer in the Führer's Luftwaffe. And now he sat side by side with a Jew in hiding, deep in the heart of Nazi Germany. It was too much for me at first, and the effect of that first realization was mind-blowing. I abruptly retreated from the bench as if my former *Musikmeister* were a leper. But the old man played on.

Amelia's eyes widened, and a look of disquiet flushed across her pale face. Standing in between them I darted glances back and forth from her to Krup and back again. Then I shook my head in utter disbelief. Amelia made a furtive move to take my arm, but I backed away from her, only increasing her unease.

When the final notes drifted away, the old man remained seated on the bench, hunched over the keys, and I could see that he was fighting back tears. It had been too long for him. Too much of his life had spiraled down into a nightmare for him to contain himself. His gnarled hands leapt off the keys to cover his face as he broke down and wept in front of the two German gentiles he needed most. One to give him succor, and the other to forget his duty and the Führer to whom he'd sworn absolute fealty.

Amelia stepped forward and put her hands on my broken teacher's shoulders, which bounced up and down as his uncontrolled sobbing went unabated. She gazed at me again, her doubts about me growing with each passing moment that I said nothing.

Amelia had to know that for me to ignore what I'd just seen would send me down a path fraught with the unseen twists and turns of high crimes against the Reich as an accomplice to hiding Jews. It meant, in all probability, a death sentence for me and my family if I didn't report this. And with a man like Johann Keitel about, I knew it would only be a matter of time before this mad charade was discovered. Had I known how little time we really had, I might have chosen the safe course. I do not pretend to be a hero after all. And if I told you I don't struggle with my decision, especially given how many paid the price, I would be a liar. For only one who was in the Wehrmacht in that time could understand how ingrained in us was the notion of devotion to the state, and to Hitler above all else. Above friends, family, above decency. As we had been told in Russia: "*Officers will be required to sacrifice their personal scruples.*"

As I stood paralyzed with shock, the memory of the last time I'd seen Leopold Krupinski raced through my mind in a torrent of acidic reflections.

On the day before I was to leave my home and report for duty at Number 22 Flying Training Regiment in Shonwalde, just outside of Berlin, I went to see Krup at his home on the outskirts of town.

A thick morning mist hung over the still sleeping town as I made my way through the deserted Himmelplatz and into the outlying country houses sprinkled amidst the rolling forest several miles to the west.

The Krupinskis lived in a whitewashed stucco cottage with dark brown trim and emerald shutters that sat alone, set back from a dirt lane under a shady canopy of blue coniferous trees that shimmered in the humid breeze of late summer. As I approached their house I could see that the family was already awake, tidying up and going about their morning chores as if all was right with the world. But it wasn't, of course. Not for them.

Frau Constanze Krupinski, a delicate woman ten years her husband's junior, was beating out a rug with a straw broom while their little curly-haired toddler, Elsa, played with her dolls at the threshold of the open door. Jakob, their dark firebrand boy of twelve, had half his small body buried under the hood of a 1922 Ford. He was gifted with machinery and would have had a bright career with Heinkel, BMW, or Daimler-Benz but for being a Jew.

As if to add an appropriate backdrop to this peaceful homestead, the tranquil notes of Chopin's Waltz no. 2 in C Minor floated through the open windows of the master's study. I paused at the edge of the lane, my morning shadow stretched out in front of me, just listening and wondering how this could be a civilization on the brink of war.

Frau Krupinski saw me coming and waved excitedly before disappearing into the house. To my disappointment the music abruptly stopped, and both Frau and Herr Krupinski emerged from the doorway, stepping over Elsa, who was too busy dressing her dolls to notice their visitor.

Jakob poked his head up from the Ford's engine as I followed the dusty walkway to the house, his face streaked with motor oil. With accusatory and embittered eyes he watched me pass but said nothing. Jakob was an angry boy. Years of being spat on, ostracized, then banned from school because of his Judaism had turned him resentful of Germany and suspicious of the world.

"Is that my young Beethoven?" called out Krup as I approached. He coughed and wheezed and then extended his hand in greeting. We shook, I bowed to Constanze, patted Elsa on her head, and turned in time to see Jakob sneer and disappear under his hood once more. "Come in, my boy. I haven't seen you since the winter. You've grown."

"Would you care for some tea?" offered Constanze, who seemed thrilled to have a visitor who came without taunts or insults.

"I'm sorry but I can't stay for long," I said.

"No," said Krup with a sigh. "I suppose that would be dangerous for you now." He bade me come in. I remember little now but the menorah resting on the open hearth, which stuck out in my mind. Family photos hung on the walls or adorned cabinets and end tables draped in alabaster knits. He motioned for me to enter the study, in which the dominant piece of furniture was his weathered grand piano. Streamers of light streaked through the room, shining rays of dust across his tired face.

"Leopold," I said. "I've come to say goodbye. I'm leaving Stauffenberg. I was accepted into the Luftwaffe."

"I see," he said with disappointment while lowering himself uneasily onto the piano bench.

I paused. Then I gave him a gentle squeeze on his weak shoulder. I could see his lip quivering under his bushy white mustache. "Try to understand. I'm not a Jew. I'm a German."

He looked up at me. "*Et tu*, Harmon? Am I no longer German to you?"

"All I meant was my life is not your life. You've taught me to play wonderfully, and for that I'm most grateful."

"No," he protested, waving his hands. "That was you, my boy. I just held a mirror up for you to discover the gift you always had."

"However you wish to view it, I'll not forget you, Leo. I want you to know that."

He turned to face the piano keys. "And I want you to know that I meant it when I said you have the makings of a great pianist. Another Paderewski perhaps."

I sat down next to him. "Move over," I said softly.

He eased himself off the bench and moved over to settle into a leather chair whose cracked skin complemented the piano. As he reclined with a humph, legs crossed to reveal veined calves, he pressed his fingertips to his forehead with eyes closed. I played for him more Chopin, who was his personal favorite composer. The ballad *Air*. At first as I played, he quizzed me on my life and the world outside his study, his redoubt of sanity, as he called it. "Are you finished with school?"

"It took me two days of work but I passed my senior matriculation."

"And what will you fly?"

"I'm hoping for fighters. Our Messerschmitt 109s are the best in the world."

"War," he said. "So senseless. Like the vandalizing of my store. For what purpose? To what end?"

"No reason at all, other than who you are, I suppose."

It seemed as if my life was headed along two divergent paths. Here I was playing piano for a Jew who, despite years of Nazi indoctrination, I tried to consider a friend. And yet I was about to join the Luftwaffe as a flight cadet. I was to fly under the banner of the very regime that I knew wanted to see Krup and his kind gone from Germany.

As I played I noticed that Krup suddenly closed his eyes and slipped deep into thought. I raised my hands off the keys, abruptly filling his study with an oppressive silence.

"You stopped playing," he said. He raised his head and fixed his eyes on me. They were pink and swollen with tears.

"Leo, why are crying?"

He shook his head. "I'm sad about the world, and my place in it."

I pivoted and sat on the edge of the bench, facing him directly, my palms cupping my knees. "Why have you stayed in Germany?" I asked bluntly. "Wouldn't you prefer to live someplace where you're wanted?"

"No one wants us," he replied with a hushed voice. "Besides, Stauffenberg is my home. My life was built here. My wife had family here. My children have friends."

"I dare say those friends no longer speak to them," I reminded him.

"That may change." His tone was unconvincing.

"No it won't," I said.

"Harmon," he said more sternly now. "I tell you this. You will rue the day you ever donned the uniform. You are not meant to kill. And certainly not in the name of Adolf Hitler."

"In the name of Germany's honor, I am," I retorted by reflex.

"They are now one and the same," he said.

"Maybe so," I conceded. "But my place is with my countrymen. Not here playing ballads for Jews." That seemed to come from another's mouth. Even with a wary sort like me, the indoctrination through osmosis could be insidiously effective.

Krup went silent. A sullen look flashed across his tired face, accented by veined hands running down his cheeks to tug at his bushy mustache. "Why so much hatred in this land that has managed to turn even you into a warrior?"

He looked to me with the pain of a man watching his loved one slowly dying in his arms and powerless to intervene.

"Harmon," he pleaded. "Can you not see that Hitler is like a slipshod surgeon mutilating the body of a people who gave the world Beethoven, Bach, Handel, Mendelssohn, Brahms, and so many others? I refuse to accept that the same people who produced *Ode to Joy* can also produce the Nazis. I refuse! You want to know why Leopold Krupinski does not flee? Because he still believes in the old Germany."

"Then he's a fool," I shot back at him. I looked him square in the eye and repeated: "I'm sorry but you're a fool, Leo. There's only the New Germany now. And you're not a part of it. That's the reality you have to face."

I rose from the piano bench just as Constanze came in to join us. Her disappointment was palpable when she realized I would stay no longer.

Krup remained pinned deep in his chair, staring at an invisible spot on the wall. I wonder if at that moment he even recognized me. But I was who I was. I understood then that I was Cadet Harmon Becker of the German Luftwaffe. I had to close the door on this part of my life, step in line with my Wehrmacht comrades, and follow the Führer, although I knew not where we were going.

"Thank you for your tutelage." I extended my hand to him. But he refused to say another word. My outstretched limb hung in the air until I slowly returned it to my hip. "You should leave this place while you still can." I turned to Constanze, who stood perplexed by what she'd just witnessed. "I'll show myself out."

I straightened up, retrieved my hat from the top of the piano, and marched from the study, through the front hall, and out the door into the bright sunshine. I could feel Krup's eyes boring through my back as I left. But he remained silent. I patted little Elsa once more on her curly black locks as she combed her dolly's hair, and strode down the pathway to the roadside. Jakob leaned against the car and observed my passing while wiping off a greasy carburetor with a filthy rag. His bright hazel eyes, accented more so by the oily grime that darkened his young face, followed me to the end of the property. He carried himself in a way that made him seem far older than his twelve years.

"You're not nice anymore," he called to me. And then he went back to the comfort of his tinkering.

As I began walking down the dirt road, retracing my steps back to town, something struck me as odd. The master's window was open, but there was no more music. A mournful silence had descended upon his house. And I wondered if it would eventually spread to cover the whole of my nation that Krupinski still so forlornly believed in…even if it had renounced him a long time ago.

That same man was now sitting warily beside me on a piano bench. He was, in fact, quaking with fear. He knew he was staking the lives of his entire family on that goodness he suspected still resided under my gray uniform and swastika. What to do? This was treason with a capital *T.* The camps were filled with gentiles who'd been caught harboring Jews and mercilessly tortured to reveal all their secrets. My mind raced. But then I gazed up at Amelia, and it was as if a dam holding back all my sense of decency and Christian charity I'd bottled up since taking the Führereid first cracked and then burst to drench my heart with a sense of humanity I'd forsaken in the moral rot of war.

I took a hesitant step forward and then, shaking any residual clouds of doubt from my head, I put my hand on Krup's as it trembled on the keys, his fit of tears spent. He turned, and in the dim light of the cloistered parlor I saw a face I'd come to love over the years…and I nodded reassuringly. He smiled wanly up at me, and then in a voice that cracked from the unbearable strain of the moment, he simply said: "Thank you, my boy."

27

When his nerves finally allowed, Krup hoisted himself uneasily off the bench and gave me a weak hug. I could feel his bones through the sweater that draped over him like a canvas sack. Holes were beginning to open through the elbows. It was evident by his stale odor that he wore the same clothes day after day. It was also plain enough that his health was failing.

"Come see the family," he begged in a feeble, rasping voice.

"I'm not sure that's a good idea," I cautioned him, though I aimed my comments at Amelia. As the emotion of the moment began to fade, the dangerous reality of my situation began to sink in. Suddenly I saw SS men everywhere…on the streets, atop the roof, behind the draperies, under Hanna's bed.

Amelia, too, was fearful. "Leo, you must go back upstairs. I took a terrible chance with this already."

He grudgingly nodded, and turned towards the stairs, beckoning me to go with him. I paused and then followed him. At the foot of the steps he stared up as a man would returning to his prison cell after a brief parole. And then he weakly ascended to the top with the difficulty of an oxygen-starved mountain climber, grabbing on to the banister like a life rope. He had to pause once, after only a few risers, to hack and wheeze, and then he managed to make it to the top.

Amelia remained downstairs while I nervously followed Krup up the creaking staircase. Once on the second floor, he led me to the end of the corridor, where a ladder hung from a small trap door. I knew of this garret from my times with Amelia before the war, and I remembered the space to be cold, dank, and dark, suitable only for storage. That a family of four could be living up there gave me pause. But I could hear whispers coming from the ceiling above me.

The old man mounted the ladder and with considerable effort struggled up into the hatch. I stood beneath him craning my neck to stare up at the little opening in the ceiling. "Come up," he whispered. I looked around pensively and then hauled myself, uniform and all, up into the darkness that had been the home of Leopold Krupinski and his family for two long, unimaginably cruel years.

I could hear Frau Krupinski's agitated voice. "What are you doing, Leopold? Who is coming?"

"It's alright, my dear," he said in a soothing tone. "He's an old friend."

I poked my head above the floor level and surveyed the attic, which had been converted into a cramped makeshift flat. The narrow windows on each end had blankets hanging over them to prevent anyone from seeing inside. A little table covered in books and orbited by rickety chairs was set up. Arranged in neat stacks against the exposed studs were rusting pots and some non-perishable supplies, like canned peaches, jerked beef, and a bucket of water. Off to the side were several quilts laid out on the bare floorboards. This is where they slept. A lone dresser sat up against one wall with a wash basin and towel. Another bucket sat in the far corner. Even with the windows blocked, there was still sufficient light for reading.

I twisted around to see Constanze standing behind her husband in a guarded fashion. Like him, she was haggard and had aged considerably since the time I'd last seen her. She had many more gray hairs than before, and they fell in front of her face in frizzy strands.

At first she recoiled from the sight of my uniform as I rose up through the trap door entrance. But she very quickly recognized me. "Harmon!" she gasped. When I hoisted myself to stand before her, she went around her husband and embraced me. "I'm so happy you're still alive," she said. I held her emaciated body in my arms. As she'd been a portly woman most of her life, her weight loss was especially unsettling. "I'm sorry I have no tea to offer you this time."

Then two smaller forms appeared from shadows in the corner of the garret, one shorter than the other. Jakob and little Elsa, still carrying her ragged doll, stood silent. They were trying to make sense of the bizarre scene of their mother embracing a man who wore the uniform of the people who wanted them dead. Though two years older than when they first went into hiding, Elsa was still unable to fully grasp what was happening, and to her it must have seemed all a great game. But I could see Jakob's look had only grown more acutely hostile since he insulted me from behind the hood of his Ford a lifetime ago.

And there I stood beholding the huddled and hunted Krupinski family, now reduced to hiding in an attic to survive. "Oh Leo," I said. "That you should have to live like this."

Jakob sneered: "This is not living." Of the four he was in the best health. Spry and with a mind like a razor, he was a teenager now. He'd grown almost a foot while he stewed in his prison, wondering if he would ever see his way into manhood.

I made a conciliatory move towards him. "Jakob."

"You go to hell!" he spat. Then to Krup: "Papa, you must be insane, bringing him here—"

"That's enough, Jake!" said his mother. "This is Harmon Becker."

But the boy was adamant. "I don't care if he's Elijah in the flesh. He's wearing a Luftwaffe uniform! When he leaves here he'll go straight to the SS!"

I was hurt by this, but I couldn't blame the boy. His father stepped between us. "Finish your studies, Jake." He looked down at Elsa and smiled. "You too, little one," he said as he patted her head. There was a wire strung across the length of the garret, bisecting the room. The trap door was located in the middle. Constanze took them both and led them to the table. Then she draped a bed sheet over the wire and thus were two rooms made in a fashion, each private from the other. Krup and I at least had the illusion of being alone together.

While Amelia paced downstairs, the old man led me to the far corner of the attic. I had to stoop at points so my head wouldn't hit the ceiling joists.

He peeked from behind a blanket at the gathering dusk. "Ah," he finally said. "It grows dark. We cannot light any lamps. We've hidden in the shadows for two years."

I felt a swell of emotion rise in me. "Oh Krup," I said. "What can I say?"

He turned to face me. "There is nothing to say. This is the new world." Then he considered my uniform. "And you seem to fit well in it. You are the big German hero now?" He motioned around him. "Well, behold. This is what you fly for. What you kill for."

I shook my head. "I joined the Luftwaffe to defend my country. You know that. Not to fight for this."

"But you do nonetheless." A knowing look passed over him. "I can read your thoughts, eh? You consider yourself above all this? This is the work of the Nazis, yes? You are just a soldier. An officer and a gentleman?"

I nodded grimly.

"My country, right or wrong?" he pressed.

I grew annoyed. "The Allies bomb us. I try to stop them. What more is there to understand?"

Krup shook his head in exasperation. "That is the mind of the soldier. But the mind of the rational man asks, why do they come in the first place?"

I had no answer. Then he peered into my eyes. I could see he was on the verge of breaking down in sobs again.

"Look at me," he demanded. "I have lost everything! Can you imagine what that is like? To see streets you walked, or cafés you visited…a certain corner that once housed your music shop. A meadow just beyond town that once embraced your home. To have done no harm to the world but try to give the beauty of music—a gift I gave you—and still only be allowed to dream of the treasures you once knew from an attic window? And why? Because I am a Jew? What does that matter? I am as German as you or that dog Keitel. But I must hide. And yet my family and I are the lucky ones. You know what is happening, of course? All across Europe, I fear?"

I stared at a dark smudge on the far wall. "I don't read the papers," I said weakly.

"Stop it, Harmon! You are too intelligent to let your station blind you to the truth. A truth that I can see from way up here, isolated as I am. The darkness has descended. It's all around us, penetrating to the very core. It is like a wet fog, sticking to the pale skin of all Germans who plead ignorance to the slaughter!

"All of the Jews are dead," he continued. "If I step one foot out of this house I am dead. And I tell you there will come a time when this black shroud lifts and the light of justice shines again. And then all the good little Nazis will scatter from the light like roaches. They will disappear and rearrange their banal masks into those of grief, despair, and, of course, shock. You will not find a Nazi among them. But none will be without guilt. Because this is exactly what the Third Reich promised. There was no subterfuge. Hitler spoke and delivered, and the people rejoiced. Harmon, don't you see? You have never harmed a Jew in your life. Think hard. Be true to who you are."

I was growing more uncomfortable by the second.

"What do you mean, who I am?"

He closed his eyes in frustration at my pigheadedness and between wheezes and coughs loosed his anger upon me.

"Imagine putting a bullet through my brain, thrusting a bayonet through my wife's belly, smashing my children's skulls. So long as you fly under the swastika, you fly for that." He let that rest with me. Then he concluded with: "You think you are brave? The courage that Amelia has shown in hiding us is far more profound than any your uniform implies. What you do next will show just how brave you really are."

I stood silent, trying not to look too hard into him. Though I towered over him by a full foot, I felt small in his presence.

"Krup," I finally said. "I promise you I will tell no one of what I've seen here."

At that he grew less coiled and managed to even let a slit of a smile crack through his leathery face. I'd just vowed to commit treason on his behalf, as failure to report Jews to the authorities was a crime. But he also knew that, as an officer, my sense of duty was strong—ingrained in me through years of indoctrination in a blend of ancient Teutonic military code and modern National Socialist zeal. And so he cautioned me: "I hope you're true to your word. But only time will tell."

It was growing dark, and I was anxious to leave. Leo ushered me to the trap door opening. "Now you must go," he said. "Fear is the life-blood of us all these days. You take care of yourself, my boy."

I patted him on the shoulder and climbed down the ladder. He was about to close the trap door above me when he offered me some advice: "I believe you are a good man, Harmon. What you choose to do with that goodness is entirely up to you."

Then he folded up the ladder and retracted it with the door until it was flush with the ceiling.

I stood weak-kneed in the dark hallway and tried to make sense of all I'd seen. The only sound I could hear was the hammering of my own heart. I would like to say it was thumping so hard from a sense of renewed love for my old master, or an awakening of conscience deep within me. But it was much simpler than that. I was scared out of my wits.

28

"You foolish girl!" I said to Amelia in a severe yet hushed tone so as not to wake Hanna, who was sleeping in the next room. "Are you trying to get yourself hanged?"

"Calm down, Harmon."

"I will not calm down." I paced back and forth, wiping the sweat from my palms on my new uniform trousers while she stood with her hands defiantly on her hips. "Do you know what you've done? You have to get them out of here."

"Get them out of here?" she shot back. "To where?"

"Will no church take them?"

"The priests must live here too," she replied. "The ones who did try to help in the beginning were taken away. You don't know what it's been like. Keitel's people are all around. Everyone watches everyone. Neighbors spy on neighbors. Children turn in their parents. You don't know who will report who."

I stopped pacing and exhaled, glancing up at the wooden beams in the living room ceiling. "Well, I know what Keitel is like," I said with foreboding. "He'll eventually become wise to this."

"What would you have me do? Throw them out on the street?"

She came up close to me and took my hands. "If you love me," she declared, "then you must embrace that I cannot accept things as they are. I have to help them."

I ran my cheek against hers. Her skin was so soft, like a newborn babe's. It belied her grit. "You can help no one by dangling from Keitel's rope," I whispered.

"Nor can I help them by doing nothing." Then she dropped the bomb. "But *you* can."

I took a step back. "What do you mean?"

"You can get them out of here." I giggled nervously. But she remained adamant. "I'm serious, Harmon."

"You're crazy." I laughed. When I saw her eyes narrow and her jaw clench, my laughter faded. "Me?" I challenged her. "How?"

"You can fly them out." She said that in so matter-of-fact a way, I thought for a moment she had no clue as to what she was asking of me. "You're a pilot. Isn't that what that uniform is all about?"

My God, she was serious! Too stunned to even reply at first, I turned my back on her, my frustration growing. I stepped to the window that faced the street and the land of the Nazis beyond. If only those in the Himmelplatz knew what we were talking about in here. Finally I turned to her. "You really are insane. You want me to commit treason. To betray my own people for—"

"These are your people!"

I ran my fingers through my hair. "The Führer thinks otherwise," I reminded her. "They're Jews. By not reporting you I'm already committing a serious crime."

"Such a brave man," she said sarcastically.

Terrified anger popped in me. I advanced and grabbed her rather sternly by the shoulders. "No. A stupid man! As it stands now I could lose everything."

She looked down to my clenched hands but remained unfazed. "They have lost everything."

"That's not my fault."

My grip softened as I saw her brave facade start to crumble. Her nose grew red and her eyes welled with tears. "It *is* your fault. It's my fault. It's all our faults."

"Shh," I said, trying to soothe her. "Such a stubborn girl. Look at me." She would not. "Look at me," I demanded. She did this time. To drive home my next point, I produced for her my identity book, complete with photograph and eagle and swastika emblem. "My country is at war. And I am Captain Harmon Becker. Acting group commander of Three Group, Jagdgeschwader Thirty-Two of my country's Luftwaffe. That's all I can be at this point."

"You can be so much more than that."

My head swam as I returned the booklet to my pocket. "I'm sorry," I said with an air of finality. "What possessed you to do this?"

"They came to me for help," was her simple reply. Then she added what could have been her epitaph: "Sometimes the right choices are the hardest choices."

I pulled her up against me and held her tight. "Woman," I whispered with a mixture of admiration for what she'd done and resentment over the position she'd put me in. "What am I to do with you?"

Then there was a knock on the door.

29

The rapping on the door continued with insistence. My first instinct was to reach for my pistol. She saw the motion of my hand and looked at me quizzically. I followed her to the threshold.

"Who is it?" she said.

"Um, it's me, Stefan, Fräulein Amelia. From Koppel's store?" She looked at me before opening the door. I holstered my sidearm and nodded.

The door creaked open and there stood a teenaged boy in rumpled pants and a brown frock coat, carrying a parcel wrapped in brown paper and secured by frayed twine.

"Oh hello, Stefan," Amelia said with a relieved smile. "I'd forgotten about you. Come in while I get your money."

"Thank you," the boy said, and he stepped inside, removing his hat.

Then he almost leapt back out onto the street when he saw me standing there. He didn't expect to come face-to-face with a Luftwaffe officer, and the look of awe was readily apparent. Boys who came of age after Hitler's rise to power had been drilled to worship authority and my uniform.

He tucked the parcel under one arm and drew himself stiffly to attention. "*Heil* Hitler!" he blurted with a squeak. I returned the salute casually. Were there not a family of four with death sentences two stories above my head, I should have laughed at the sight. Instead I stared coolly at him. An awkward silence followed while Amelia rummaged in the next room for her purse. The lad was eyeing me curiously, as if cataloguing me, when Amelia returned with some *Reichsmarks* jingling in her palm.

"Stefan Rosner," she said in as natural a voice as she could summon, "this is my friend, Captain Becker. He grew up here in Stauffenberg. The captain is on leave from the front."

"Hello, sir," he offered politely. Still he seemed to be taking mental notes about me, which made me uneasy in my heightened stage of paranoia. The younger children had been programmed by Nazi indoctrination to be on the constant lookout for enemies of the Reich—even among their own families.

Nevertheless, I tried to be nonchalant as I took the parcel, which contained canned goods, eggs, and powdered milk, from his hand. Amelia replaced it with the coins. "Tell Herr Koppel thank you and I hope he feels better."

"I will, Fräulein." He counted out the money with his finger. He nodded respectfully to my chest. "Herr Captain." Then he clicked his heels and once more threw up an enthusiastic Nazi salute. "*Heil* Hitler!" I returned it in the same manner, and he retreated back onto the cobblestone street.

After Amelia shut the door, she stepped over and peered through the curtains, following Stefan's retreat.

"Nazis," she snorted. "And he could be such a nice boy. He reminds me of you when you were a young sprout."

"I can't remember ever being so young," I said.

"It wasn't that long ago." Amelia smiled. "Koppel lets him work there. His father was killed in North Africa. He was a captain, like yourself."

"No wonder he was gawking at me." I sighed with relief. "He was making me nervous."

"He was enamored with your uniform," she said.

Carrying the groceries, I followed her into the kitchen.

"He seems more enamored with Hitler," I observed.

"He's not alone," she said. "Even now as our cities burn and our young men die by the thousands, he still holds a wicked spell over us." I handed her the items one by one, and she placed them in the cupboard. Then she wrapped me in her arms once more. "And now our pilots risk their lives every day to protect us."

Although I held her close, as she closed her watery eyes and buried her face into my chest, my own eyes, dry and clear, uneasily drifted to the ceiling as if pulled skyward by a sinister magnet. *This pilot is risking much more than that*, I thought. And I shuddered at my future.

30

Supper at my home, my first in years, should have been filled with gaiety and celebration of my survival. But this was war, and even though I was far from the immediate dangers of the front, the shadow of the reaper by my side, waiting for his moment, was an unspoken presence in the house.

Outside my door, a clamoring parade of Hitler Youth, their unlined faces illuminated by bobbing torchlights, marched proudly through the streets of Stauffenberg like a brown-and-red striped serpent, singing and chanting. *"Ein Volk! Ein Reich! Ein Führer!"* Paul was among their standard-bearers, so it was just three of us, as Amelia thought my parents might want some time alone with their boy. While my mother circled the kitchen table ladling out portions of stew into our bowls, Father and I sat in the little parlor at the front of the house, our chiseled faces outlined by the familiar glow of a comforting fire. We sipped schnapps as I brought him up to date on what I'd been doing for the past two years.

Papa smiled in the direction of the kitchen. "You've made Mama happy tonight." From the wireless on the counter by the stove drifted the Berlin Festival Orchestra's performance of *The Marriage of Figaro*. Frau Becker knew every word in Italian, and her accompanying voice was pleasant to the ear. I could see where my own musicality originated. But the man responsible for my understanding the logic and mathematics of it all sat across from me as we soaked up the warmth from the fire—and the bottle. Two Becker men in uniform. He was a constable, and I, a fighter pilot. One soldier from the first Great War, one from the second. Through this common bond we'd paradoxically grown closer by my absence.

He was, of course, relieved that I'd survived thus far, but he was clearly unnerved by my tales from the front—unfettered by the omnipresent threat of censors and Nazi informants. I first hesitated to relate to him too much so as not to worry him, but he knew better. And as the alcohol unshackled us both, he grew more interested in the war and I more willing to tell him my tales. I recounted for him my part in the Russian campaign and how the first winter had almost wiped out the Ostheer, the Eastern Army. How only fanatical devotion to Hitler had saved it from annihilation. He reveled in my colorful escapades with the Greenhearts and was intrigued by the science of air combat. Finally I told him of my curious transfer to the West and my subordination to a paranoid major.

"And now a political lapdog is your commanding officer," he said, sighing and peering into his glass. "How typical. New Order indeed. Like the barons of old. Only now it's who drops his pants for those criminals in Berlin."

"Papa," I begged in a hushed voice. "It's dangerous to say such things."

"Bah! Who will report me?" he said dismissively. "Greta? You?" I noticed he didn't say Paul. He knew better than to speak his mind in my kid brother's presence these days. His eyes gleamed in the fire as he spoke. "Son, I do hope you're being careful. On the ground as well as in the air. I heard you had a little row with our local SS worm Keitel." I raised my eyebrows. "I know the owner of the *Brauhaus* where you two, shall we say, conversed with some animation. That boy is developing a reputation that will see him answering to Saint Peter for many things in the next life. Please tread lightly."

"I know," I said. "I acted stupidly." Desperate to change the subject from the SS, considering what I now knew about Amelia's undocumented guests, I smiled while reminding him of my pending meeting with the Führer and my medal. "Well, at least when I fly I don't tread too lightly, eh Papa? But," I added somberly, "I don't know how much longer I can continue against such odds. The Allies grow stronger while we grow weaker." I lowered my voice so Frau Becker couldn't hear me from the kitchen. "You and Mama have to be prepared for my black note one day."

He turned his reticent gaze towards my mother. "I wish you wouldn't say such things, Harmon. I've lost one son already." I saw a resignation that all would be lost reflected in his kind eyes.

"You mean Pauli?" I asked. "Oh, he's just a boy. He'll come to his senses in time."

The old constable traced his finger in a circle on the rim of his glass, as he often did when deep in thought. "He thinks we're winning, the little imbecile." Father looked at me in helpless frustration. "He's joining the Luftwaffe. Does he have a death wish?"

I put my hand on Father's knee. "I tried to tell him, Papa. He won't listen to me."

"The only way he'd listen is if it came out of Goebbels' sewer of a mouth."

A deep silence but for the crackling of the flames enveloped us. Then my father said with a pleading gaze: "Try to protect him, Harmon. He's not like you. He has too much of his mother in him. She is an unbearable optimist. But you are my son. You know as I do that, win or lose, only those with fighting skill and common sense will be left standing when this is all over. That or dumb luck. I fear Paul has neither."

I shook my head. "I'll try to get him assigned to my unit. Other than that, there's not much I can do."

He leaned back in his leather chair and exhaled deeply. "I suppose there's nothing any of us can do for him."

My mother broke the mood by calling us to supper. Father and I made our tipsy way into the kitchen. The sweet aroma from simmering beef stew, my mother humming along to the wireless, and the familiar sights from the happy days of my youth brought to me a sense of security within the plaster walls of my little home. For the rest of the evening we ate in peace and, for a brief time, the war was out there, in some other dimension apart from this toasty-warm cocoon deep in the Bavarian winter.

But then my thoughts would travel to the Krupinskis. Their gaunt faces staring at me with bewildered and frightened eyes reminded me that my life could not remain as such. And I could sense that even after two years of air combat, and one hundred kills on my rudder, my real war was just beginning.

Although it was well past midnight, I laid on my back in my old bed with my hands behind my head, staring through the darkness at the ceiling. My uniform hung neatly in the armoire; my visor cap rested on the end table next to a copy of *Mein Kampf* that I found on Paul's dresser. I actually thumbed through it by the soft glow of a lamp. A heavy quilt, suspended by nails driven into the pane, was draped over the window to keep the light contained in the room. With air raids on German towns growing more common despite our fliers' efforts, every little village of any consequence observed blackout conditions. As today's raid on Adelstatz showed, being nestled in a remote river valley of the Oberfranken did not guarantee safety from Allied bombs.

Reading while in my bed was a simple pleasure I'd forgotten once in the Wehrmacht. Too few idle moments of relaxation presented themselves during wartime. But now I was home, in my familiar bed in the old room I shared with my brother, actually wearing warm flannel pajamas instead of my uniform, in which I often slept. Unfortunately there was nothing to read but Hitler's memoir from prison. We had all been required to read it in gymnasium, our high-level secondary school, yet I never paid much attention to it then. But that was when I lived in another world. Now, with my country in its fourth year of war, with millions buried in countless holes dug into the continent or at the bottom of the sea, the words took on new significance to me:

"*The personification of the devil as the symbol of all evil assumes the living shape of the Jew.*"

When I read such passages, I understood now the reality of those words. I saw the Krupinski family huddled in Amelia's attic while sadists like Keitel patrolled the streets. *Mein Kampf* had ceased to be Hitler's "struggle" a long time ago. It was now a blueprint for the New Order.

"*Hence today I believe that I am acting in accordance with the will of the Almighty Creator. By defending myself against the Jew, I am fighting for the work of the Lord.*"

And I was doing my part to construct his vision of a New Europe, devoid of all but pure Aryan blood. Most of my countrymen, even if they had not become criminals, had easily donned the robes of accomplices. And I was among them. Krup was right.

All this was running through my mind when I heard the door to my room creak open. A line of light appeared in the door jam and widened until a lithe figure in a Hitler Youth uniform and cap revealed itself to me.

"Harmon," he whispered. "Are you in here, Brother?"

I sat up, squinting until my eyes adjusted to the hallway light shining behind Paul like an aura.

"I am."

"I hope I didn't wake you," he said, entering the room and tossing his hat on his bed.

"I can't sleep," I said, leaning on my elbow. "It's too quiet for me."

Paul sat on his bed facing me. He slid off his high boots. "I'm surprised you're not staying with Amelia." He had a lecherous grin on his young face.

"We're not yet married." I smiled back. He crinkled his brow with doubt. "Fine," I said, laughing. "Hanna would have me castrated if she thought I was having her daughter under her roof." That was a lie. Amelia and I knew it would not bode well for my family if the Jews were discovered while I was staying at her house. The SS penchant for making the parents pay for the sins of the children, and vice versa, was legion by this time.

"She's too frail to care," Paul declared, removing his shirt. He looked so pale and thin to me. So much a boy still.

"Hardly," I replied. "She's quite aware of the world around her." Then it hit me. Hanna must have known what was going on two stories above her head. Amelia never would have continued to house them without her mother's approval. The apple, as they say, does not fall far from the tree. I was coming to appreciate what exceptional women the Engel ladies were.

"How was your rally?" I asked Paul, clicking on the lamp on the end table.

"Splendid!" replied my kid brother as he removed the rest of his brown uniform and donned his sleeping thermals. The transformation from fierce Nazi to innocent boy was startling.

Paul went on to tell me about the rally. How his troop was organizing a trip to Berlin to help clear rubble from British raids, but he was soon to report for duty in flight training. (I cringed but held my tongue, as it was pointless.) He went on about how well the war was going. How it was only a matter of time before the Russians had had enough. That the Allies were taking a pounding in Italy. And those making any attempt to cross the English Channel to breach Hitler's "Atlantic Wall" would suffer the same fate as the slaughtered Canadians in Dieppe the year before. But most of all he waxed poetic on how proud he was to be German and how he could not wait to finally join the fight. "Now don't try to change my mind again, Harmon," he cautioned me.

"I'm through with that discussion," I assured him wearily.

"Glad to hear it. In fact you're lucky I didn't report you for what you said to me."

I shot him a frown. "Report me? For what? For trying to save my brother's life?"

Paul shrugged and crawled into bed. "For trying to stop me from doing my duty to the Fatherland," he replied. "Others have been arrested for less," he added indifferently.

I shifted to sit up on the edge of the bed and glared at him while he seemed to pay me no mind at all. "I should give you a good thrashing."

Paul smiled wryly. "I hardly think that would stop the SS from coming for you, don't you think, Brother?" He understood better than I the ways of the New World, it seemed. Without a cockpit or an airbase, I was out of my element. "Good night, Harmon. I'm tired."

"And I'm sick," I said as I laid back down on the bed. "What's happened to you?"

Paul hoisted himself up on his side. I can still see the boyish face with hazel eyes grinning in the orange glow of the lamplight. "I saw the truth. That's what has happened to me. You and Papa are from other worlds. Papa's an old fart and will never change. But I still don't understand why you don't fully embrace the New Germany."

"Perhaps because I have blood on my hands, Little Brother. As does Papa. Can you say as much?"

"I hope to soon," was the last thing he said before curling up and falling asleep, as if he didn't have a care in the world. I just stared at him as his breathing grew deeper and dreams of the glories of a Reich that would last a thousand years filled his unconscious mind.

The weather turned increasingly foul during the night. December returned and brought damp snows and frozen clouds to Stauffenberg. The next day I spent the time before my train for Berchtesgaden was to depart in the company of Amelia in her home. We stayed inside this time. That was fine with me, as out there in those once friendly streets strutted Keitel and his SS minions like gamecocks. Despite the risks of the SS kicking down the door at any minute and whisking us all away, I wanted to be with her. I'd never realized the steel girders that held up her soft facade. This was a woman who would give a man nothing but grief until the end of his days should he marry her. And that was exactly what I intended to do. But not until the war was over and I'd made it through. I had no intention of inflicting the status of war widow on anyone.

My desire to be alone with Amelia had been so strong leading up to this moment that I even parsed an order from a superior officer to grant myself leave to see her. Yet now that we were finally together after so much time apart, I wondered whether I could put the intense anxiety I was feeling out of my mind enough to be intimate, even with one so beautiful. Given the gut-wrenching secrets I now knew were living in this house, I could have been forgiven for not rising to the occasion, so to speak. But two years of abstinence creates so much pent-up desire in a soldier in love that even the shadow of an SS firing squad cannot suppress it. And so, as Hanna slept deeply in her room and the Krupinskis somehow stayed alive in their clandestine cage above us in the unheated attic, we made love as quietly as we could by the fireside. "Shh. Softly, my love."

As we lay naked afterwards, she read me poetry, Schiller, Goethe, Eichendorff, while I sat back draining a glass of wine, just waiting for the time when the evening train's whistle would pull me away from here, out into the cold, and deposit me first to the Führer's lair and then cast back into the whirlwind.

"Oh, Harmon," she sighed morosely. "Why were we condemned to live now, in wartime?" Her eyes flitted to the ceiling.

"I don't know," I said, kissing her sweat-shined forehead. "It's God's will I suppose. Perhaps you were meant to be here, in this place, for them."

"Harmon," she said. "You and I are not meant for this world. A world I believe God has abandoned. We're both of another time and place. Far from my fear of what I've let into this house. Far from Johann's probing eyes. From Hitler and bombs and black notes and hollowed-out survivors hobbling the streets with amputated limbs and dead hearts."

I poured myself another glass. "This is our world. I don't know when and where I'm destined to be. But I know it's with you, Amelia. Come what may."

She smiled and took a sip from my glass before resting it on the hardwood, and climbed on top of me, pulling the blanket over us. "Come what may."

Once thoroughly drained and rested, we dressed and I played piano for her, knowing that my audience was not limited to the Engels. Occasionally a distant bump or a sudden shuffle from the planks two floors above would remind me of the unearthly burden Amelia had taken upon herself.

When it was time to leave, I slipped back into my full dress uniform and we strolled through the snowy streets to my house to say goodbye to my parents at their doorstep. My mother gave me a kiss on the cheek and tried to say something but broke down into soft sobs. "I know, Mama." I tried to comfort her with a hug. "I'll be careful. I promise." She quickly disappeared despairingly into the house.

My father's eyes followed his wife with helpless concern, and then he turned his gaze on me. "I'm going to whip Paul within an inch of his life when I see him. To not bid you farewell. He could have missed one damned Hitler Youth meeting. Especially since you're off to meet his demigod."

I shook my head. "Let it go, Papa. His mind is elsewhere these days."

My father snorted, but I could tell he knew it would make no sense to berate his younger boy. And so he concentrated his feelings upon the Luftwaffe captain standing before him. "Son," he said in the tone of an order, "you come back to us."

I gave him a resigned smile. "I'll try, Papa. That's all I can ever say." He pulled me to him and gave me a powerful hug followed by a sharp slap on the back. He kissed Amelia on the cheek. "I'm glad Harmon found you," he said to her with an uncharacteristically warm smile I figured he'd always kept in storage for the daughter he never had.

"We found each other," said Amelia. He nodded approvingly and then followed after his sobbing wife, closing the door behind him.

Amelia and I walked arm in arm to the station while my holdall swung from my free hand. Our path wound through the town center, and then we exited through the Rathaus tower archway and down to the bridge spanning the partially frozen Main. Snow was falling heavily now, and we both plodded through the streets avoiding the brown piles of steaming horse manure that sat atop the white powder. She was bundled up against the cold in a woolen jacket, flannel dress, shawl, and hat. I cut a fine figure in my tapered uniform greatcoat, leather gloves, and smart visor cap.

I couldn't wait for the weather to turn warm so Amelia's charms as a woman could be released from the prison of her heavy winter garb.

The stifling cold was the least of Amelia's concerns at the moment. I saw she was frightened. Perhaps my little speech had caused the reality of her crime and the full consequences should she—we—be discovered to come crashing down upon her like a pile of stones. As we stumbled through the drifting snow, she occasionally glanced around furtively as if to check if we were being followed. I read her concerns and I addressed them frankly.

"You know, this can't continue indefinitely," I said as we neared the far side of the bridge. "Even if you're obsessively careful, it's only a matter of time before some event betrays you."

She stared straight ahead, releasing my hand and hoisting her shawl further over her broad peasant shoulders against the falling snow. "I can't undo what's done. Not now. I'd rather be dead."

I shook my head. "The SS would be happy to arrange that."

She stopped and turned away from me to stare back at the Rathaus tower looming in the distance like a sinister doorway to a frightening world. So much had Stauffenberg changed in her mind from when she was a girl chasing butterflies in the meadows.

"My God," she whispered softly.

"What?" I said, looking around with a start. "What is it?"

The snow was collecting on her head and shoulders. I couldn't see her face. "You're going back to the killing."

"Well," I said, trying to lighten her mood. "The Berghof first. Then I—"

"Oh to hell with that man!" she said sharply. "You'll soon be getting shot at again while he'll still be playing with his damned puppies in his mountain hall."

I closed my eyes. "Amelia."

"This may be the last time we ever see each other," she said, still facing away from me to the tower.

"Yes," I admitted. I felt as if I was abandoning her to face her dangers alone.

She said nothing more. Tears welled up in her gray eyes. I laid my bag in the snow and pulled her close to me.

"I wish they'd never come to me!" she suddenly confided.

My heart melted. "Hey," I whispered. "Krup came to you because he knew you would help them even if you didn't want to. Only fools tempt danger willingly. I tell you, Amelia Engel, I've seen men act heroically on the battlefield. They do extraordinary things and are rewarded with shiny medals. But you are the bravest person I've ever known."

"Really?" she said, composing herself.

"Really," I assured her. I produced a cloth from my breast pocket. She took it and dabbed her swollen eyes. Then she examined the embroidery; "*HBN.*"

"You still have this?" she said, handing it back to me.

"I keep it with me always." Now I felt the welt in my throat. "I do love you. I hope someday you'll do me the honor of loving me half so much."

As if on cue, the train whistle sounded. I looked in its direction with dread. I did not want to go back to the fighting. But my uniform made the choice for me.

"Harmon," she said. "You've got to help them."

"I can't," I said firmly. "Come, I'll miss my train."

We kept our farewell brief and silent. We'd said all that we could by the time we reached the snow-covered tracks. She gave me one last kiss and, as if trying to indelibly imprint the picture onto my eyes, I took in one last image of her face made pink by the cold. I followed Amelia as she retreated from the platform, gripping herself as if she were shivering.

"Amelia," I called to her. She turned, and I could see that her eyes were covered in a glaze. "This war can't last forever."

She nodded and then turned away once more, back to town and her home. Back to her potential death sentence.

I didn't notice Keitel's approach until I heard his shrill voice over the hissing of the idle steam locomotive mixed with the din of passengers chatting as they waited to board the train. I always seemed to hear him before I saw him.

"She's still quite beautiful." I whipped around and found him at my side, beneath his death's head visor cap, tracking Amelia like a hunter as she disappeared down the concrete steps to the street below the platform. "If only she were more practical. What's she still doing with you, Harmon?"

"What do you want with me, Johann?" I said warily.

It was then that I noticed that he was dressed in the combat fatigues and full kit of the Waffen-SS. His steel helmet strapped to his side. Across the platform about thirty feet was a small band of SS foot soldiers in field dress with rifles or sub-machine guns slung over their youthful shoulders.

He grinned coldly with his hands behind his back. "Captain Becker, I want nothing but to see you leave Stauffenberg."

"Well, as you can see I'm leaving. So you've done your duty."

He fixed his black eyes on me before finishing his thought. They never seemed to move. "Don't worry, Harmon. I don't have time for old rivalries. Not today at least."

A heavy silence fell over us. I could feel my heart beating faster. "You're off to the front?" I finally asked. "Russia again?"

He shook his head no. "You'd like that, I bet. No, we're taking the other train heading west. My field unit's stationed in France now. In preparation for an expected invasion. But there's no rest for my squad. We go to the back country where the resistance makes its home in the dirt. One of my functions is to oversee the pacification of certain French regions."

"Pacification?" I asked innocently.

"Never mind. It's something a pilot couldn't possibly understand. But I'll still be in Stauffenberg most of the time. You just never know who to watch these days."

He gripped my wrist as I moved away from him.

"Becker. I offer you a warning."

"What are you doing?" I said, suppressing the chill in my veins.

"You've indeed fought bravely. Even I'm forced to admit that. But it doesn't make you immune to my reach. I'll be watching you. I sense something about you. Something that makes me wonder."

I pushed his arm away. "You say this to me as I'm about to report to the Führer for a decoration? You might order around my brother if you wish while you concoct petty schemes to win back a woman you never had in the first place. I have more serious matters to attend to. I'm going back to do battle with Thunderbolts and Boeings so that your precious factory keeps your daddy in his big house on the hill as men die!"

His face grew flustered. "The SS does more for the greater good of Germany than you know. Someday you'll realize this. Or you will not. In such a case, I shudder for your fate. And that little Bolshevik tart of yours."

Once again my temper was getting ahead of my senses. What was it about this sot? "Amelia a Bolshevik?" I chuckled. "That's the best you can do?"

"That charge alone is enough to end up before a firing squad."

I sneered. "You should know." Then something occurred to me. "Although Johann, when you think of it, the Führer claims that there are no more Bolsheviks left in Germany. Are you calling him a liar? Or have you failed in your duties?" I leaned in, jabbing my finger at his shoulder. "Either way, you may want to be careful that it's not I who ends up reporting *you.*"

He stammered. I relished the moment, even if I was just making myself more of a target in his eyes.

Before he could respond, the train pulled up to the station, huffing as it groaned and hissed to a stop. The conductor called "all aboard" and I gripped my holdall. I fell in line behind a small band of mostly military passengers who emerged from the warmth of the station waiting room. They all stepped into the first car. "*Auf Wiedersehen*, Johann," I said. "Let your wounds heal."

I climbed aboard, leaving him to mull this over. I was glad my train was headed in the opposite direction of Keitel and his goons. Once again, my temper, my great betrayer, had made me foolish, and I silently cursed myself for my insult to Keitel while he had such a reach in my loved one's backyard.

Once onboard, I sidled up to a window, pressing my sweaty cheek against the cool, moist glass. No one sat in the empty four-passenger compartment, which gratified me, as I wasn't in a chatting mood. I contemplated my steamy breath on the glass as the train lurched with a jolt out of the station and sounded its high-pitched whistle announcing that the sons of the Third Reich were once again bound for war.

I left Stauffenberg behind, but not the smells, the sounds, and the faces. The faces especially stayed with me, for I saw a commonality among them all. The people of my town tried so hard to go about their usual routines as if the war beyond the hills were somehow not real. But written on all their faces was distracted unease, as if they were trying to remember if they'd left the boilers on their stoves lighted, which no cheery mask could erase.

31

The lumbering overnight train from the Oberfranken rolled on across the Berchtesgadener Land district and then pulled into the town station itself at midmorning. A shiny black Mercedes sedan driven by an SS-*Rottenführer* (corporal) was waiting to whisk me to the rendezvous of other Ritterkreuzers before making our way to the Führer's villa perched high in the mountains. I was one of a group of six who were to be decorated; we were divided up evenly among two pilots, two tank commanders, and two infantrymen. Having either ridden trains or flown in from various points of conflict, we all met at an airfield outside of town, where a small fleet of yet more black cars patiently waited. Each of us had our own chauffeured vehicle. I kept the one that picked me up at the station, but now I was accompanied by a heavily armed SS-*Untersharführer* (sergeant), who sat beside me in the back seat. The soldier remained stone-faced throughout the entire awkward last leg of my trek.

We sped across the rolling terrain through the picturesque village of Berchtesgaden, nestled in a remote corner of the Bavarian Alps. From there a winding roadway snaked higher and higher to the Obersalzberg plateau on the mist-shrouded mountain. After passing through the stone and mortar SS guardhouse gate at the base of the hill, from which we could see the Führer's chalet towering above us, the driver took us in a series of climbing twists and turns and, after a sharp right, eventually pulled to a halt in front of the main steps to the Berghof. News footage often showed a smiling Hitler descending to warmly greet his guests and escort them back up the stairs and through the arches that led into the Great Hall. But today there was no one there except more SS guards, who instructed me to follow them.

The Berghof, or Mountain Court, was Hitler's private hilltop villa and conference center. It was originally called Haus Wachenfeld. Built by a German businessman in 1916, it became Hitler's favorite retreat, which he rented for several years. After becoming chancellor in 1933, the Führer purchased the villa with proceeds from his bestselling *Mein Kampf*, renamed it Berghof, and began expansion and renovation two years later.

The entrance hall was lined with an odd display of potted cactus plants, which seemed quite out of place high in the Bavarian Alps. The color scheme throughout this airy chalet was jade green. In the outside rooms, the sun-parlor chairs were made of white, woven cane. Soft linen curtains in light hues framed high windows that peered out into the sprawling valley below. The cheerfulness of the home was accented more so by the trilling of Harz Roller mountain canaries, which sang from gilded cages that hung or stood in some of the rooms. I took particular interest in the curious little watercolors of Viennese street life no wider than eight inches that adorned many of the mahogany walls. The signature "A. Hitler" was scratched into the bottom corners. They served as a reminder of his humble beginnings as a penniless Viennese artist, which made my Führer's rise to mastery of all of Europe even more astonishing. The Great Hall was furnished with expensive Teutonic furniture, as well as featuring a red marble fireplace mantel and a large globe. Expensive artworks, including paintings by Panini and enormous Gobelins tapestries, adorned the walls, abundantly lit in the evening by two chandeliers hung from the wood-beamed ceiling. I was, of course, drawn to the Bechstein grand piano, on which sat a bust of Richard Wagner. But the most striking feature was an enormous picture window made from ninety individual panes of glass; at one hundred square feet it offered a stunning view of the Untersberg mountain in Austria, his home country.

My first impression being up so high was that the war didn't seem to be hindering the Führer's comfort at all. I tried to imagine him indifferently reading casualty reports from Russia while sipping tea by a warm fire to keep out the cold that was laying waste to his armies a thousand miles to the east.

A uniformed staff offered us our choice of beverages and invited us to take them on the stone terrace over the garage. Cigars and cigarettes were available in abundance—even though Hitler himself never smoked and rarely drank alcohol.

We stepped outside into the crisp December air and let out a collective gasp at the stunning view below us over the stone rail. You really did feel on top of the world gazing down upon the little alpine hamlets below, tucked away in emerald-green mountain folds and capped by snow-covered peaks that jutted into a rich blue sky. One could envision Hitler and his young, mercurial lover, Eva Braun, strolling a secluded path even higher up on the mountain to take sanctuary at the little secluded tearoom, or "Eagle's Nest," perched at the very edge of the summit. It must have been grand days in the first phase of the war, when victory after victory lay before the Führer like the misty blue mountain folds that stretched out below him.

And yet, it again dawned on me that, from here, the seat of a power waging campaigns across two continents against forty nations, the war was the furthest thing from these people's minds. Oh to be sure, they had maps and reports and communiqués. But the actual life-and-death struggle being waged on their behalf by men at their wit's end was beyond their understanding at this point. They knew nothing of the soldier's lot: scared to the point of madness, hungry, exhausted, filthy and in pain, suffering in the harshest of climates from the stifling heat of the African desert to the vicious cold of the Russian steppe, fighting in a brutal fashion with demoniacal fury just to make it through another day alive. The battlefields of the Wehrmacht were as alien to the men atop this mountain retreat as the surface of the moon.

As if to underscore that sentiment, a haughty voice greeted us and we turned to see Hermann Göring. He strutted over in his powder-blue uniform and heavily braided visor cap, with his massive gut protruding over his leather pistol belt. His high riding boots *clop-clopped* on the slate. We extended our arms in "*Heil* Hitler," and then he took each of our hands and offered his personal congratulations. I looked into his blue eyes and saw a vacuous glint as if he were under the effects of a dreamy narcotic. His skin was pale and clay-like, prompting us to conclude that the air marshal wore make-up.

One of his adjutants introduced me to him.

"Ah!" he crowed. "Captain Becker! At last we meet in person."

I clicked my heels. "An honor, Herr Reischmarschall."

"Ach," he chortled. "The honor is mine, lad. I understand you've racked up one hundred air victories? Half of them in the west. And an impressive thirty-two heavies?"

I nodded, slightly embarrassed to be lauded in front of the others. But Göring was unrelenting.

"Now this is the kind of spirit we need if we're to turn back the criminal raids against the Fatherland. It's refreshing to see that the British do not hold a monopoly on guts in the air." He was referring to the Tommies' brave stance against the Luftwaffe in 1940 during the Battle of Britain. We fliers had heard this unfair comparison before and resented it, as we knew it was the blundering high command more than German fliers who lost that fight.

An odd man, Göring. Vain, pompous, completely isolated from the growing strain the constant combat with the bombers was inflicting upon the Luftwaffe. My verdict: although he genuinely cared about his pilots, he simply did not understand what we were up against.

"Well done, Becker," he concluded with a pat on my shoulder. He was about to turn away when something occurred to him, almost as an afterthought. "By the way, I understand you qualified for this honor months ago. When I checked, your commander Seebeck claimed that the paperwork was misplaced. Yet I saw Hanny Trautloft's signature. What do think of that, eh?"

I drew myself to attention and stared ahead, showing my displeasure. "If that is what Major Seebeck says, then it must be so, Herr Reichsmarschall. But I'm grateful to Major Trautloft for the double honor, sir."

"Well said, Becker," he said with a cunning grin. "Very politic. You know I'm dear friends with Hans Seebeck's parents. They have more money than God. It was a shame what happened to the young man's eye. He was never quite himself after. Always trying to prove himself." Then under his breath Göring added cryptically: "It's easy to make enemies in this game...on both sides of the channel. If you're successful enough. Keep it up, lad." Then he lumbered off, disappearing inside.

After a half hour more of fine wine, fresh mountain air, and lively banter, a high-command colonel appeared and led us inside to the Führer's study. On the wall hung a huge map of Europe with arrows indicating the momentum of the conflict. I could see Göring staring up at it, his arms locked behind his wide back. He seemed fixated. And no wonder. From Italy in the south to Russia in the east, the arrows were all pointed towards Germany. I caught just a glimpse before several SS men hastily drew a curtain over it.

Then the Führer himself, with a small band of aides and his chief of high command, Field Marshal Jodl, in tow, entered the room. We immediately drew to attention, arms straight out, angled up to the heavens. "*Heil* Hitler!"

And there he was. The epicenter of my world. The man to whom I had sworn final loyalty. And I was disconcerted by what I saw.

This was not the robust, heroic figure with the steely gaze of the propaganda posters or newsreels. That man, I quickly realized, was a myth. Like so much else here on this Mount Olympus, the disconnect from reality was unsettling.

I sized him up as he returned our salutes with his unique palm flip. He was stooped, with a slight hunch to his back. His left hand trembled. His face was drawn and haggard, like a wax mask sagging in the heat of the sun. Dark circles swooped under his pale blue eyes. His gray uniform coat fell loosely about his frail figure. The man actually looked physically weighed down by the pressure of managing a world war. And yet he seemed animated enough, flashing his slit smile beneath the square mustache.

Our arms fell to our sides, and we continued to stand at attention like chess pieces. He clasped his hands and rubbed them together as he moved about the room. He paused in front of us and in his French horn voice exclaimed: "So here are the great knights of the Reich! I welcome you to my home as recognition of your outstanding bravery in upholding the true ideals of that greatest of God's creations: the German soldier. At ease, my comrades." We shifted to parade rest as he launched into a stream of rhetoric which, judging by the bored look of the general staff, he'd given many times before along the same lines.

"This war," he continued, pacing and staring down at the wooden floor, "was launched to create an ideal Europe in which the superior Germanic race can live in peace, security and homogeny, its progress unfettered by the inertia of the *Untermensch*. And it was started because the honor of our people demanded it. The world laughed at us in 1919, humiliating us at Versailles. But after we entered Austria, annexed Czechoslovakia, rolled over Poland, swept through the Low Countries and, most satisfying, utterly annihilated the arrogant French in less than a lunar cycle, it was they who trembled.

"The British will soon come to their senses, of this I am sure. The Russians are on the brink of collapse. The Americans are corrupt and soft. As we speak we are clearing living space for our people, ridding Europe of the pestilence of international Jewry and its bastard child Bolshevism. A great light shines upon us. This, my dear soldiers, is your moment!"

The fawning staff bellowed a loud "Hear! Hear!"

The Führer then turned to an adjutant who was carrying six elongated black leatherette cases, each containing a Knight's Cross. The officer opened them and handed the decorations to him as he made his way down the line of us. As flashbulbs popped, he draped the medal over each of our heads so it hung down over our chests suspended by a ribbon of black, red, and white. Each man clicked his heels and gave the Nazi salute. Hitler returned the gesture and then shook each man's hand, offering a quiet "well done" or "congratulations." When I and a fellow pilot were presented, Göring made it a point to stand just behind the Führer, so as to be in the photos.

When I looked Hitler in his eyes, it was then that I understood how the man could take such hold over my country. His gaze was intense, hypnotic, and unwavering. I cannot honestly say that, had I met him earlier, when Germany was in happier times and the Wehrmacht was conqueror of all Europe, I would not have willingly followed him to whatever end he chose. I'm therefore glad I met him when I did.

I dutifully saluted my Führer with outstretched palm, clicked my heels smartly, and shook his soft hand.

And then, just like that, the bizarre ceremony was over. Hitler disappeared alone into the bowels of the Berghof, and we were left to mingle with the high command. One of the staffers took us on a brief tour of the kennels, where the Führer bred magnificent Alsatians. A few of these pedigreed pets roamed the grounds. It gave one the impression of wolves lurking about to keep the guests in line.

We strolled the half-mile up to the "Eagle's Nest" and took in the spectacular scene. Considering we'd come so far, several traveling much greater distances than I, it all seemed a rather pointlessly quick affair. Although it did confirm what I already knew. Seebeck was very well-placed in Berlin. He had the ear of the air marshal himself. I'd better just grit my teeth and take my lumps when I returned from my unauthorized, though not forbidden, trip home.

Back at the Berghof, more photos were taken. By now I was anxious for my driver to take me to the Berchtesgaden station, where an overnight train would send me back to Andeville. But there was still some time to kill. I tried to mingle, discussing tactics with my Luftwaffe comrade, or lending an ear to the Panzer commander's tale of the enormous Kursk battle that featured the largest tank-versus-tank fight in history. (Reading between the lines, it sounded like a major defeat.) But small talk was never my strong suit. The other RK recipients seemed so old, so battle-hardened. Did the war show on my face so much as well?

In a moment of quiet reflection I withdrew from the little cocktail party and stepped back out onto the balcony. It seemed as if all of Oberbayern stretched out in the valley below me. Beyond it, Hitler's native Austria. From this viewpoint I spied a chain of slumbering lakes, with ancient shrine-chapels hidden within folds of towering rocks and sylvan gullies. Such a beautiful country, I thought. One worth fighting for. But were the leaders I'd just met doing their best to bring this fight to a close and spare my home the ravages of conflict? I wondered. Had they lost control?

I kept glancing down at my new decoration. A black Maltese Cross inlaid over a silver frame. Inscribed on the medal itself was the swastika; underneath, it read “1939,” the year it was instituted by Hitler. I should have felt elation. But I knew better. For a soldier, such an award meant that death was always near. And when I considered my Führer, a question jelled in my mind. I remembered all the men I’d seen die violently over the past two and a half years. All the future potential wasted, robbed from Germany by an unending war against the world. And I thought: this Hitler whom I’ve just met face-to-face. Whose eyes I saw up close. He’s just a man. And a frail one at that. Could this be the same man to whom I’d sworn my life? For the first time I wrestled with the nagging feeling that I was not ready to die for the Third Reich anymore. Even if my Knight’s Cross testified to the contrary.

Perhaps I really didn’t deserve such an award, no matter how many enemy planes I destroyed. Maybe, in his jealous and petty desire to prevent me from wearing the medal, Seebeck had been right all along.

32

I tried to sleep on the eight-hour train ride to Belgium, but it was impossible. The momentousness of my meeting with Hitler was fading in my mind, being crowded out by a more sinister encounter. I kept running Keitel's warning through my head and then rewinding it again. Did he already know about the Krupinskis? And now my complicity in Amelia's madness? I dismissed this troubling notion; he would have never allowed me to leave Stauffenberg had he known. Instead, I concluded that he could detect a hairline fissure in my patriotic armor. Indeed, to a man like him, I was as great a danger to my country as the bombers I would soon be knocking down again.

I spent the entire day barely moving from my seat, my forehead against the window watching the greater part of southwestern Germany pass by my line of sight. White-capped mountains jutted up defiantly against the steady snowfall that inked the ground like a watercolor in alabaster. The fresh coating may have hidden many scars upon the earth from the escalating war that was rolling ever closer to the German border. But it could hide only so much. For above the blanket of white, as if protruding through a layer of clouds, were the signs of things to come: burned-out homes, obliterated towns, felled bridges, and the occasional dead horse lying beside a shattered ammunition cart blown to pieces by Allied bombs.

A jostling train ride gives a young man in the midst of a world war more time to think than he would like. Especially if he's coming to suspect his side is losing. I reflected on Hitler, Göring, and the rest so high up in the mountains, isolated, like some Nazi coven. So oblivious. It all seemed so surreal. The wall map I was not meant to see, with its red arrows pointing from east to west, like spears aimed at the heart of Germany, kept appearing before me. There it was. I believed that, whatever his past greatness had brought us, my Führer lived in a fantasy now. But the boys like me he'd sent to war lived a brutal reality. Only those still fighting—and Hitler was not—could understand what he'd put his armies through.

33

I stood shivering in the cold, leaning against the outside wall of the hangar nearest the runway with my shoulders hunched up to my ears. The fur lining of an American flying jacket caressed my stinging cheeks. I heard myself saying as if in a dream, "*Leo, I will tell no one of this.*" Damn that woman.

I'd arrived back in Andeville that evening and was given a ride to the base by a generous Belgian shopkeeper. The men were in the *Kasino* but I stayed away. It was just after 11 p.m., and blackout conditions were in effect. Still, I could discern the ghostly silhouettes of our night fighters as they hummed high above me in the black sky en route to meet the incoming RAF. Just faint echoes reverberating off the low clouds.

Reflecting on the fading drone of distant engines and the insistent howling of a fierce wind sending silver wisps of loose snow across the deserted runway, I didn't notice Mueller's approach. Instead I detected a faint whiff of alcohol mingling with the sour aroma of petrol fumes and engine oi that constantly laced the air. I turned to find him leaning back against the wall by my side, staring up at the night sky. He gripped a half-drained bottle of Chablis in one hand and an extinguished cigar in the other.

"It's good to have you back, Harmon," he said.

"Seebeck say anything to you?" I asked with a knot in my stomach.

"Not a word." A pause. "So how is the Führer?"

"Optimistic," I said. I peered up to the northwest. I could make out faint white lines of searchlights crisscrossing the sky. "Do the Allies ever rest?"

"No," he said. "At least not yet." Mueller gulped a swig of wine straight from the bottle and wiped his mouth with his sleeve. He was in his garrison blue uniform, his flight cap jammed over his tight auburn hair. "Why don't you come inside and join us? It's cold."

I shrugged. "No thank you, Lieutenant. I'm fine out here. These American jackets are warm. You should get one." I was wearing the bomber jacket of a Yank whose body I'd stumbled across while inspecting the twisted wreckage of kill number eighty-two: a B-24 called the *Mary Lee* that crash-landed after my head-on attack near the little village of Bastogne. I wondered who Mary Lee was. His wife? Lover? Now grieving mother perhaps? It didn't matter anymore. And he certainly had no more use for his jacket, which was more practical for daily wear than our wool knee-length greatcoats.

"I suppose you've had too much to drink to feel anything?" I said to my wingman.

"Eat, drink, and be merry," he exhorted, "for tomorrow we die."

He offered me his bottle and I willingly gulped a mouthful of the dry white wine. "I'd offer you some cheese, but the only kind I have on me is from the crack of my arse!" He howled at that, and I tried to maintain a stoic front. I handed him back his bottle as a grin slowly cut through my frozen cheeks. I took a deep breath and leaned my head back, staring up at the busy night sky. Flak batteries—like the ones that killed had Kluge—began to flash in the distance, rumbling like faraway lightning.

I exhaled deeply, watching the fog of my breath curl away. I turned to my wingman. "Any word on Edelmann?"

Mueller nodded. "They found his body yesterday."

I stole another mouthful before surrendering the bottle back to him.

"Oh Josef," I finally said. "It gets so hard now. What do I say to the families?"

The drunken lieutenant swallowed and wiped his mouth. "You tell them that they died defending their Fatherland." I thought he was being sarcastic, but his earnest expression told me he was serious. He offered me the bottle again. "Take another swallow," he ordered. "You think too much, my friend."

"And you, not enough," I said. Another mouthful.

He chuckled at that. "I think when I have to. Harmon, this may be my last night alive. If I survive this war, then I shall return to thinking proper. But for now give me a fine wine, a good cigar, a buxom blonde and I will smack my heels, shout '*Jawohl!*' and do my duty to my Führer and my country."

I thought of the Krupinskis and how the country had so turned on them. I thought of the Führer I'd just met with his trembling hand and fantasy war. "I hope you're right."

"Of course I'm right."

Then I added: "Whatever right is these days."

Mueller gently removed the bottle from my hand. I felt a need to lean on the wall now to steady myself. But for the distant thumping of the flak beating back some RAF raid far away and the occasional muffled sounds of carousing from the officer's *Kasino*, all was still. And that was when Lieutenant Mueller got a sublime look in his glazed eyes. He touched me on the arm as if to say, *Look at me if you want the secret.*

"What's right," he began, "is what's best for Germany. I grew up in Dresden. Have you ever been?" I shook my head no. "Oh it's a beautiful city, Harmon, right on the Elbe. The baroque architecture of the Zwinger, the royal palace, the equestrian statues of Frederick, the opera house, and Frauenkirche. I would like to return to it intact when this whole business is decided. Those Allied bastards are trying to level my country. That, my friend, is all a soldier needs to know."

But that was not all that this soldier needed to know. "But why do they attack us? Especially the United States? Why should they care what goes on in another continent?"

Mueller took a swig. "You'll have to ask the Amis that. Now," he said, pointing to the air, "I'm no political scientist, mind you, but I suspect that the Führer declaring war on them may have something to do with it. He didn't tell you why? I thought you were friends now."

I finally let out my suppressed laugh. Once again, Mueller was able to snap me out of my moroseness. "And when this war is over and you return to thinking, what will you do, Josef? Go back to Dresden?"

Mueller grinned sheepishly. "I haven't thought about it."

I pressed him. "Come now. You've brightened my mood. You win. So allow me this. I want to know. Seriously."

"Oh, I don't know, Harmon. I'm a barrel maker by trade. As was my father and his father."

In all the time we'd flown together, he'd never revealed much to me about his pre-war years. It's a defense mechanism soldiers learn. Especially one like him. Too much intimacy with a comrade today means an extra hard death to bear in the morrow. Best to keep things superficial. So much for his being the son and heir to riches.

"You?" I said. "A cooper?"

He nodded. "Seems a bit dull now, I admit. After all this. I do love flying. Perhaps I'll be a commercial pilot. Or maybe go to America and be a, how do they say, crop duster?"

I looked at him. "You don't find irony to that?"

He shrugged. "It's just a thought. And what about you? What does the great Harmon Becker do after the shooting stops?"

I knew the answer with absolute certainty. The war had diverted me away from my true passion. And yet, based on my killing prowess in the air, I may have been a better fighter pilot than pianist. I hated that thought. "I'll return to Stauffenberg and enter the little conservatory there. I intend to be a concert pianist."

"The next Paderewski, eh?"

"If I'm lucky. My old master, Leo Krupinski, called me his young Beethoven. He'd be pleased to see me blossom into a great musician."

Mueller nodded. "Would it please you?"

I took a deep breath of frigid air. "More than you know."

He slapped me on the thigh and raised the bottle to the heavens. "To a pleasing future then."

I grabbed the bottle as well. "The future."

PART 4

34

The next day my war resumed. I sat in the cockpit awaiting takeoff, strapped into the harness and parachute, hunched against the icy winds. The temperature was thirty-two degrees Fahrenheit and the canopy was open, yet beads of sweat popped on my forehead. Seebeck wanted me to see him later about my visit to the Berghof—and no doubt my trip home—but his retribution would have to wait until I finished with the Americans.

I looked left and right to see a crooked line of FW-190 fighters, painted in colorful schemes on the cowlings, aimed at an angle to the sky, stretched across the snowy field. Way in the distance at the command hut, I could see the ungainly figure of Major Seebeck standing in his door well, leaning on his cane and smoking a cigarette as we prepared to take off.

The target today was a gaggle of heavy bombers, coming in fast and heading straight for a railroad junction on the Belgian border. Intercept would be quick. We noticed that the Allies had begun attacking tactical targets, like railway junctions, bridges, ammo dumps, and less strategic targets of the major inland cities. This new phase pulled us farther west towards the channel, and sometimes within the range of their escorts. Just when I thought my world was as dangerous as it could get, this cruel twist of fate made it even a little more so.

With my leather cap covering my ears, all was quiet. The usual thoughts filled my mind. Is this the last of earth for me? What will my family say when they receive the black note? At least my war will be over then. During training we lost one pilot when his fighter rolled on takeoff from the torque of the propeller and burst into flames as he hit the ground. He lived for two days in agony with horribly disfiguring burns over most of his body. That was what I feared most. Not dying, but surviving a grotesque wound only to live the rest of my life as a cripple or a deformed freak show exhibit. I looked up to the clear sky above me and whispered a soft prayer. "Please God, I ask that you let me live through this day. But if it is thy will that I should die, let it be swift."

Another question: What is Amelia doing right now? I looked to her portrait on the instrument panel. I thought about Krup and his family, and my stomach churned and I felt lightheaded. The Amis weren't all I had to fear now.

And then the green flare shot up from the operations building. Sergeant Ohler, who was sitting on the port wing lost in his own thoughts, got up and closed and locked the canopy over me.

"Good hunting, Herr Captain," he shouted through the glass with an encouraging thumbs-up.

I slowly increased the throttle to taxi. Another crewman sat on the wing to guide me, as I couldn't see in front of me over the steeply angled nose. He directed me to the takeoff point. When I hit the brakes he leapt to the ground. It was time to fly.

Takeoff was always exhilarating to me, and today it served to snap me from my anxieties. I throttled smoothly and the BMW radial engine roared. Then I slammed a bootful of hard right rudder to hold straight against the propeller's torque. With a release of the breaks, I was pushed back into my seat as the plane bounced down the runway. Picking up speed I edged the stick forward to raise the tail—being careful not to flip myself over—and then after reaching enough airspeed I eased it back as the little fighter swooped into the sky, trailing white powder in its wake. Gear up, flaps up, and we were off to do battle.

I craned my neck left and right to see that my squadron was following me in good order. The FW-190 was a fast climber at over three thousand feet per minute. Tuning my radio, I awaited the ground controller's instructions.

We soon leveled off at twenty thousand feet and followed a north-by-northwest heading, leaving the clear blue skies to the east behind us and straight into a storm front. The clouds were getting thick, so I commanded the squadron to form up into swarms and climb to twenty-five thousand feet to get above the layer.

"I can't see anything in this soup," observed Mueller, who'd pulled up to form our pack.

I called to the squadron: "Is everyone with us?"

Borner called back in consternation. "I'm having engine troubles. Damn this bird."

"Can you make it back to base?" I asked.

"I'll try." I dipped my wing and glanced down to have a look at his airplane. It was sputtering smoke and losing altitude. "Good luck, fellows," he said and then disappeared into the fog below.

Cursing silently to myself I called out: "Who's his wingman?"

"Lieutenant Stahl," came a jittery reply. At just nineteen, he'd been with the squadron for three months but hadn't yet scored a victory.

"Very well, Stahl," I said. "Form up with my pack. Mueller you're in the lead with Stahl as your wing. I'll fly solo on this one."

"You sure that's wise?" cautioned Mueller. "There could be Indians, sir."

"I'll be careful." Actually I was quite uneasy about being caught in a dogfight with no wingman to cover me. I didn't have time to think anyway.

"Attention, Nebel-One, this is Bodo."

"Victor," I said. "Go ahead, Bodo."

"Heavy babies in sector Dora-Dora. Go to Hanni nine zero."

"Victor, victor. Message understood."

We climbed higher still and then leveled out. Way up here, above the clouds, the golden sunlight burst forth from the west and blinded us. This was late for a Yank attack. After twenty more minutes of mundane flying, with the ground controller calling in adjustments to the enemy position and guiding us ever closer towards them, I noticed my fuel nearing the halfway point. We were quite far from base to the southeast.

Then Mueller spotted them. At first I thought they were blotches on my windscreen, and the blazing sun only added to my confusion. But as they got closer I made out the shapes of heavy, twin-tailed bombers. Below us and tightly boxed. They looked like American Liberators, and I figured there were at least two hundred of them.

"Do you see them, Nebel-One?" inquired the controller.

"Victor," I called back. "Fat cars directly at our twelve o'clock low." Then I called out my usual instructions to the squadron. "Attack en echelon. Mark your target. Get in quick bursts towards the cockpit. Use your machine guns to get the range and then open with cannon."

"*Jawohl*," chimed some of the younger men.

"Be careful flying solo," warned Mueller. "You've got no cover."

"I know," I answered him with agitation. I knew better than to fly with no wingman, even if it was only against what I thought were unescorted bombers. Anything could happen.

We dipped our noses and started to make our run towards the bomber formation. As they grew in size at an exponential rate, I breathed deep and zeroed in on the lead plane. I switched on my gunsight and lined him up for a head-on attack.

It was always intimidating to new blood how quickly these encounters happened. At such high speeds it took less than fifteen seconds to close from two miles out. One minute you're flying towards what looks like nothing more than a dot on your windshield. Then you make out the thin shape. Then the shape grows to a fuselage and wings. Then a plane. Then a four-engine monster bearing down on you with hundreds more behind it! Your heart hammers and suddenly you're firing your weapons. The guns in its turrets blinking like Christmas lights firing back at you. A *POP!* if you're hit. Then your own *thump! thump! thump!* of cannons. Your plane shuddering. The white flashes as your rounds strike home near the cockpit. The screech of engines in your ear. Slam the stick forward. More rattling of machine guns and wailing of engines. More shapes flitting past you. Glowing tracer rounds crisscrossing as you slice through the bomber formation. That last buffet as you punch though the prop wash. And then you're below the stream of aircraft and behind it. And now all is eerily quiet again but for the humming of your engine and the chatter on the radio. It all takes but a few seconds. You pull up abruptly and perform a chandelle—a sudden, steep climbing turn—to get a look at what destruction you've just visited upon your target.

I leveled off at a ninety-degree angle to the bomber stream and scanned across the open sky to see several trails of smoke spewing from a few Liberators in the pack. One I saw spinning out of control to the ground. My gut told me that one was mine, although I'd have to wait to see what verdict my gun cameras returned.

And this is where I got sloppy.

I was too busy watching the air combat one mile below to scan the sky around me. If I had I might have noticed high, thin contrails above me, moving wickedly fast across the sky. The white streaks weren't Liberators, as they showed only two engines per plane. And they were swooping around to enter the fray—right above my head.

Once again it was Mueller calling from somewhere nearby to warn me. "Indians! Watch out behind you, Becker!"

"What?" I shouted.

I instinctively snap-rolled hard to the right, and just in time. Tracers zipped under my fuselage and would have ripped my little fighter to pieces had I been in their path.

I heard the distinct wasp-like hum of inline engines zoom past, and got my first glimpse of a strange-looking machine. A futuristic fighter plane, sleek lines, with two engines, each in a thin boom with the twin tails and the pilot and clustered guns housed in a center nacelle between them. The Yank had brought an escort of P-38 Lightnings. As I'd feared, we were in escort range. And now I was caught up in a melee with high-performance fighters and no wingman.

"Get out of here, Captain!" called out Gaetjens. I still had no idea where half the squadron was. We'd been caught by surprise. Now it was every man for himself and "see you back at base."

A Focke-Wulf zoomed in front of me from out of nowhere with two Lightnings right behind him. It was Stahl.

"Stahl!" I commanded. "Don't dive. You can out-turn them. I'll come in behind them."

"*Jawohl*," he replied with surprising poise. *You may survive yet*, I thought.

"I'm on them too!" called out Mueller.

I managed to pull the little Focke-Wulf in behind one of the twin-tailed machines whose pilot was too fixated on his own prey to watch his back. "No, no my friend," I uttered as I squeezed the trigger.

My tracers sliced through the Lightning's right boom, and the whole section sheared off. The plane broke in two and fell tumbling towards the gray layer of clouds below. The other P-38 immediately dove for the clouds and cover, all thoughts of dispatching young Stahl forgotten.

"*Abschuss!*" shouted Mueller. "The captain just saved your ass, Stahl!"

"Thank you, sir," he said with relief.

But there was still a swarm of Lightnings out there. The fact was brought home to me by the desperate calls of my surprised squadron on the radio. "I'm in trouble here!" A terrified voice: "I can't shake them!" Another called: "Blast! Where'd they come from?" Resignation from this one: "Bailing out! See you home, boys." Frustration: "Get out of there, Von Mauer!"

POP! POP! POP! What the hell? *BANG!*

Behind me. Two more Lightnings with guns blazing! Their concentrated fire from four fifty-caliber machine guns and one 20-millimeter cannon all bunched together in the cockpit nacelle had the effect of a massive shotgun blast. They punched a great hole in my left wing, and then I saw flames start to belch from the engine at my feet.

Oh, Becker. This is not good, I thought.

POP! POP! POP! Again. Unrelenting, they sent more hot metal and explosive charges into my plane, and now I felt a hammer blow followed by a searing pain spread over my shoulder. "Mueller!" I called out. "Those bastards just shot me!"

"Hang on," he said frantically. "I'm on them."

But it was already too late. I could feel the engine seizing. Thick black smoke was filling the cockpit, and my legs were starting to cook as the fire spread. Then suddenly the world started to flash faster and faster before my eyes, and I realized I was in a spin. My control surfaces were useless. I couldn't move the stick. Spinning, falling. My stomach whipping all around. I floated in my chair as my plane tumbled end over end through the air.

Suddenly all was light gray out my canopy. I was in the clouds. Still spinning. Altimeter bleeding. *Oh hell, I'm falling out of the damned sky!*

"Becker, what are you waiting for?" Mueller was shouting. "Get out of that plane, do you hear me?"

"I'm trying, dammit!" But I was having a hard time blowing the cockpit open.

Oh Christ! I darted my eyes to the left wing and saw that it was gone. *I MUST GET OUT OF THIS FALLING COFFIN!* Still falling. My legs starting to burn.

Now it was no longer gray. I could see white and drab browns spinning past me. The ground! *Do something now, Becker, or you've had it!* I frantically unbuckled my straps and then I leaned back in the cockpit, fighting the centripetal forces suddenly whipping me this way and that. With both feet I tucked my knees up to my chest to escape the rising heat and then kicked up at the glass as hard as I could. *Whooosh!* The canopy flew off and the whipping of the wind blasted my face. I was too scared to notice the cold—or my injured shoulder. My legs cooled, thank God.

I struggled to hoist myself out of the spinning, flaming airplane. Then as the fighter somersaulted end over end, I was literally tossed out into the air and sent tumbling with my legs flailing as if on a bicycle. Suddenly I felt a blinding pain slice through the back of my head, and I immediately saw white spots. A dreamy sensation came upon me, as if I were outside myself. It was so peaceful and falling was such a pleasant sensation that I figured I could sleep the rest of the way to the ground.

I was so tired. *Just close your eyes and it will be over.* My hand dreamily reached down and tugged on what I thought was the rip cord of my parachute. But I didn't really care. I was fading. Not even my head hurt anymore. I smiled as I drifted off to sleep. *Dying's not so bad.*

And then all went black.

35

It wasn't light but sound that pulled me out of my sleep. "Captain?" said a voice in the distance. "Can you hear me?"

I swam up out of sleep and managed to force my eyes open. I found myself looking up at the colorless sky, outlined by a border of snow-covered evergreens fingering into the air. I was lying on my back, half swaddled in the silk of my parachute, which lay spread out on the snow next to me like a bridal train. My eyes struggled to focus, and through the haze I caught the silhouette of a German helmet. It grew larger in my field of vision until I saw the young soldier's face with his inquisitive eyes gazing down at me.

I must have groaned something incoherent, because he backed off and turned to call for someone.

"He's alive!"

Another voice, this one deeper, shouted back. "He's a damned lucky bugger to miss those trees." Then a larger man, who owned the voice, appeared and stood over me as well. He displayed the twin diamonds and double-lightning insignia of an SS *Untersharführer*. "He's moving. His back must be good. Nasty cut on his forehead." He knelt down close and began prodding me for broken bones.

"Is he alright?" asked the younger man who found me.

The *Untersharführer* tapped me gently on the cheek. "You best get up now, sir. You've been lying in the snow long enough to keep you from spoiling, but any longer and you'll be in a bad way." Then to the boyish soldier. "Come on, Loos. Make yourself useful and grab his arm. Careful."

As the dizziness subsided I felt myself being hoisted to my feet, a bolt of pain shooting through my shoulder. I gritted my teeth but kept silent.

"Can you stand, sir?" asked Loos. He couldn't have been more than eighteen.

Fighting to regain my balance, I glanced down to see my boots buried in a foot of snow. I motioned the two soldiers away with a nod and another groan. Then another wave of pain ripped through my forehead, as if an animal trap had clamped down on my skull. I waded through the anguish and unharnessed my parachute.

Well, it had finally happened. The Yanks got me. And, through some sort of miracle, I'd survived.

"That's quite a thrashing you got, sir," said the *Untersharführer* with a comforting smile. He still held on loosely to my arm until I was stable, while brushing the snow off me with the other. "You should see your plane. It was wise to jump out of it."

"My plane?" I uttered through the throbbing in my head. I took a step out of the straps of my chute and bent over with my hands at my knees.

"Your one-ninety went down about a half mile east of here," said Loos. "We followed your chute."

"You'd have died of the cold soon," added the older man. "But it probably slowed the bleeding some. Whatever the reason, you're lucky to be alive. And you're doubly charmed we found you before the damned French got to you."

"Where am I?" I asked.

The men looked at each other.

"France, sir," Loos answered.

"France," I said, more to myself. I looked around and found that I was in the far corner of a field with fir trees boxing it in on three sides. The clear side was bordered by a stone fence, which followed an iced-over back road. Brittle shoots of wheat stuck up sporadically through the snow. "I have to get back to my unit."

"In time, sir," said the *Untersharführer*. "You've had a busy day." He looked me over again. "I'm more concerned about that blow to your head than the clipped shoulder." He went for my cap and goggles. "May I?"

I nodded. He then took off his glove and ran his bare hand over the wound. I grimaced as he probed the laceration. "I can't feel a skull bone, which is a never a bad thing. You've got a nice lump too. But that beats a cranial hematoma. You'll live. Which is convenient, since our search for you upset our timetable. Can you walk?"

"I think so," I said. I took a few wobbly steps. And then nodded.

"Very good," said the *Untersharführer*. "Loos, take him to see the *Hauptsturmführer* while I collect the men."

"*Jawohl*," barked Loos.

The boy slung his rifle over his narrow shoulder and led me towards two Opel trucks parked by the side of the frozen dirt road. A handful of SS men clad in greatcoats loitered by the idling vehicles. Another group was huddled around the hood of the lead truck, studying a map.

"Herr Hauptsturmführer," announced Loos. "We found the pilot."

The man Loos was addressing had his back towards us, hunched over the map with his bare finger tracing a route over a line on the parchment. "And is he in one piece?" he asked, still facing the hood.

"Here he is, sir."

The group looked up at me. The *Hauptsturmführer* turned slowly, tugging his gloves back on to his hands, and I went numb. I knew who it was before I even got a full look at his cold face. All I needed to see were the black eyes growing wider in astonishment as they stared back at me from beneath the *Totenkopf* of his visor cap.

There was a tense silence. Then he burst out laughing at the sheer chance of it all. His men exchanged confused glances.

"Oh my! This is a small world indeed. Wouldn't you agree, Becker?" He waved his hand in the air and marched over to get in my face. "So good of you to drop in on us."

The men chuckled at the pun.

For the third time in a week, I found myself in the presence of Johann Keitel. Only this time we weren't in a public square or train station with civilians all around. We were instead in occupied territory among a group of heavily armed fanatics who would follow any order he gave them.

"Yes, it's me again, Harmon." Then he leaned in and whispered under his breath. "Today is your lucky day." Then to Loos, "See to his wounds and help him into your truck."

"*Jawohl!*"

"We've wasted enough time already."

The noisy Opel troop transport bounced me and eight soldiers over the frozen dirt road of an obscure back corner of France. Despite the canvas flaps over the metal frame of the cabin like a tent, the bitter cold still infiltrated through to our bare faces. I made a pitiful sight with my crude bandage wrapped around my head. The throbbing in my skull grew steadily more pronounced as I fully regained my senses, and my shoulder felt as if someone had taken a mallet to it.

The men in the truck examined me with unnerving curiosity, as if I was some exotic zoo attraction. Most were younger than I, and by the fresh looks on their boyish faces, many had missed the combat in Russia that earned *Das Reich*, and Keitel, such a fearsome reputation.

The soldier who discovered me lying in the snow, Oberschütze Loos, seemed most curious of all. As I leaned back, trying not to think about the pain in my head and shoulder, the SS private equivalent peppered me with questions.

"Where are you stationed, sir?" The men leaned in, grateful that someone had broken the silence.

I answered flatly. "JG 32. Andeville in Belgium."

"Who shot you down?"

"Alright, Loos," the *Untersharführer* interrupted him. "He's had enough for one day without you interrogating him." Then he winked at me. "Sorry, sir."

I waved him off and cracked a smile at Loos' inquisitiveness. "Lightnings jumped me. Americans. Somewhere near the coast."

Loos' eyes lit up. "Yanks!" he said, oddly excited. "So you've fought Americans?"

"Seems like they're all we fight these days," I informed him. "Why so interested, Loos?"

Another SS man rubbed the boy's disheveled hair and laughed. "Oh stop it, Emil. You must pardon young Loos, Herr Captain. He wants to see America after the war. America! That's all we hear from him."

I found that odd, but then again nothing about the war seemed to have any rhyme or reason these days. All I could do was offer him a warning. "Be careful what you wish for. You may be seeing more Amis than you know what to do with soon enough."

The *Untersharführer* let out a grunt. "Bah! Why would anyone want to go to America anyway? I hear the vile place is crawling with Jews. Like roaches everywhere."

Loos was unfazed. "Don't fret over them. I'm sure when we conquer America, the Führer will know what to do with them, eh fellows?"

The band nodded its assent with the satisfaction of those absolutely convinced of the righteousness of their cause.

Another man nudged Loos, whom I soon came to recognize as the kid brother figure of the squad. "Hah! Your helmet was probably made by a pretty Jewish girl in Poland with curly black locks and a heaving bosom."

Loos blushed and they chided him affectionately. I grew uncomfortable at the thought, and the Krupinskis, as they had so often since my return from home, flashed through my mind.

The *Untersharführer* changed the subject. "You and Herr Keitel know each other?"

"We grew up together."

"Ah, so you're old friends?"

"We grew up together," I repeated.

A pregnant pause followed as the men saw there was no love lost between me and their squad leader. I leaned back and closed my eyes, effectively shutting down all conversation for the remainder of the torturously uncomfortable ride.

Through my pain, I cursed my bad luck. I couldn't believe that this morning I had been an expert with over one hundred victories on my rudder, and now I was a broken wreck, stuck in a frigid troop carrier in the French hinterland with a group of crazed Nazi boys and Johann Keitel of all people as my guide. But I was not entirely ungrateful. After all, it may not have been good living, but it surely was not dying, and I felt that perhaps there was a reason for my survival beyond dumb luck. Had I been killed, I wouldn't have been a witness to what was to follow.

36

It was near dusk when we approached the sleepy village of Sainte Laurie-Olmer. It was an unassuming little town nestled in a thick woodlot with a stone chapel that had stood for five hundred years in the main square. Ringing the church were barns and modest cottages of country peasants who'd known simple lives of quiet contentment before the war. Before the Germans came. Amidst a heavy snowfall the trucks entered the town and stirred the civilian population, bundled up and just settling in for the night, to peer at us through their windows in trepidation. They had ample reason to fear us, for Keitel had a message to deliver this evening.

I can still hear the screeching of the brakes as the trucks pulled up next to a small graveyard at the side of the church. Only the very tips of the stone crosses and tombstones poked above the blanket of snow. Our truck came to a halt by a little stone gate, and that was when these boys suddenly changed before my eyes into a band of demons.

"Alright, let's move," commanded the *Untersharführer*, and the men poured out of the back of the truck. With my injuries I had to cautiously lower myself onto the film of ice that covered the lane leading through the gate. I held on to the truck to steady myself as my boots almost slipped out from under me. Then I began to stiffly make my way over to the scene being played out in the village square.

I could see the SS men shattering windows with their rifle butts and kicking down doors, screaming like hyenas at the terrified civilians. "*Raus! Raus!* You French pigs! *Raus!*" they shouted as mostly old men, women, and little children were herded or dragged out of their warm homes into the frigid air of the windswept common. Some children were still in their nightgowns and bare feet and were shivering violently as their dismayed parents pulled them close in a vain effort to protect them from the cold, and from us.

As I wandered through the scene, like an invisible ghost, SS men continued to clear out all the houses and kick, shove, and prod the French townsfolk into a crude huddle against the far wall of the church. I saw only one man of fighting age, and as he took in the situation his expression showed his fears. Even Loos, who seemed so much like a kid to me, transformed into a hector herding an old woman at gunpoint into the square with the rest. Although his expression betrayed a hint of disquiet that made me think there was some sliver of humanity in this boy.

All the while, Keitel sat in his *Kübelwagen*, like a Roman procurator, calmly waiting until the entire village of some eighty frightened souls was assembled before him. He yawned and checked his wristwatch.

The squad formed a single file facing the uneven line of hapless civilians. Things began to calm down now. I stood on the perimeter, leaning against a tombstone, absorbing the scene.

The *Untersharführer* breathlessly reported to Keitel: "Herr Hauptsturmführer. That's all we can find."

Keitel stepped into the ankle-deep snow. He straightened his long coat, adjusted his visor cap, and calmly paced over to the huddled townsfolk.

All was silent but for the whistling of the winds through the bare treetops and the occasional whimper of the little ones slowly freezing to death in the steady snowfall. I hobbled over to Loos, who was standing near the gate as a sentinel. He watched the scene with little expression. As I considered the helpless group, I asked Loos why there were no able-bodied men to be found.

"They're in the Maquis," he explained in a whisper.

"Maquis?" I asked.

"French resistance."

Still unsure why we were here, I watched as Keitel strode from his *Kübelwagen* to the square, kicking up white puffs of snow.

The *Hauptsturmführer* passed between the line of soldiers and civilians. His breath poured out in a fog. He approached a little boy in a nightgown and wet socks. He must have been nine. "What's your name, little man?"

The boy's mother shivered with fear and pulled him close to her. The child stared blankly at the menacing figure in uniform, teeth chattering, clearly not understanding German. Keitel took him by the shoulder and roughly yanked him from his mother's grasp, marching him five paces out and in between the townspeople and the rank of SS men. The woman made a move but an older man with a bushy mustache, whom I assumed was her father, held her back. By this time the boy was turning blue and shivering so violently that I thought he would come apart. Keitel put his hand reassuringly on the child's head, which was no higher than his tormentor's holster. While the child stood petrified at his side, and the SS squad stood immobile, Keitel began to speak.

"Yesterday the railroad marshaling yard at Château-Benoit was sabotaged. Two Wehrmacht soldiers were killed. Ten more wounded. We've traced the resistance bandits responsible to this village."

There was an eerie silence as he let those words sink in. By their sudden expressions of fear I could tell most of the villagers knew enough German to realize their dire circumstance.

Then Keitel called out: "*Untersharführer!*"

The big man who had tended my wounds ran over to him. "*Jawohl.*"

Keitel released the boy from his grip. He took a step back and pointed to the shivering and utterly confused child. "Shoot him."

"*Jawohl.*" The sergeant equivalent took the boy by the shoulder to lead him away.

"*Laissez nous tranquile bêtes!*" cried the mother. She lunged towards her son, only to be intercepted by two SS men and knocked violently to the snow. She remained on her knees, sobbing and pounding her fists deep into the powder.

Keitel ignored her. "No," he commanded. "Let them see." The *Untersharführer* shrugged indifferently and whipped out his Luger pistol and cocked it. He lowered the barrel to the cowering boy's temple.

The mother, seeing her child's impending execution, grew mad with maternal rage and stormed forward again. She attempted to tackle the man holding the pistol to her son's head. "*Fuis, mon fils! Fuis!*" she cried to the boy, who stared wide-eyed at the pistol aimed right at his head. Somehow she reached the sergeant before the SS men could grab her again, and she bit down like a rabid dog hard on the soldier's bare hand. He yelped in pain. The boy looked to her and, finally comprehending what was happening, made a pathetic dash for the nearest cottage, his little legs struggling through the thick powder. But Keitel himself was on the boy in two bounds and collared him, upending him and tossing him down into the snow.

"You bitch!" shouted the bleeding *Untersharführer*, who pried her off of him and dropped his pistol. In a swift motion he swung his rifle around off his shoulders and raised it high in the air, the butt aimed squarely at the young mother's nose. With a powerful motion driven by his fury, he slammed the wooden stock down on her face. I couldn't help but cringe upon hearing the sickening crunch of broken bones and seeing the blood spray in all directions before she collapsed into the snow. A crimson stain spread out from her crushed nose and cheeks but that was not enough. The rifle butt came whistling down again and again upon her skull until her head resembled a gelatinous mass oozing crimson that seeped through the white powder.

The crowd howled and the father broke into a fit of weeping. "Murdering bastards!" he shouted in German above the din.

"Mama!" the boy cried and extended his blue arms to her, but he was held firmly in his place by the heel of Keitel's boot as if nailed down.

Keitel addressed the crowd again, his voice never becoming any louder than necessary to be heard above the wind. "You can take some comfort that from your example others will learn. And then future scenes like this will be prevented as your countrymen think twice before taking up the arms again. The choice is theirs. Yours, I'm afraid to say, has already been made."

Then he closed his eyes, as if mildly irritated with his sergeant for the sloppy scene just witnessed, produced his own Luger and aimed it straight down at the back of the boy's head.

"No, Johann!" I shouted, unsure where my strength came from.

Keitel looked over to me and then back down at the little boy at his feet. *BANG!* The child's head jerked then he lay still, as if peacefully asleep on his stomach, while a pool of blood spread out into the snow.

"You cannot do this!" shouted the young Frenchman I'd observed in the horrified crowd. "These people have done nothing wrong." Then he changed his tone to appeal to Johann's humanity. "Please, *mon capitaine*. In the name of decency, I beg you!"

Without saying a word, Keitel stepped over to the brave man and shot him between the eyes. A red cloud burst behind his head, and he fell as if his legs turned to rope. Keitel then commanded to his squad, "*Achtung!*" The soldiers drew themselves in a line at attention. "Aim." They lowered their rifles and assault weapons at the huddling crowd. The older men closed their eyes, while crying women in futile attempts to shield their freezing children stood in front of them or crouched down and held them tight.

I doubt they noticed the wounded Luftwaffe captain who was hobbling over to the menacing SS commander while screaming at him in German.

"Johann!" I cried. "This is madness."

When I got to his side he stared at me coldly. "Correction, Becker. This is policy."

Then, while still facing me to add effect to his defiance, he shouted: "Fire!"

The quiet of the frozen countryside was shattered by the ear-splitting crackle of rifles and *rat-tat-tat* of submachine guns unloading a sheet of bullets into the crowd. The frigid air first held then echoed the gunfire from the stone walls to the treetops to the chapel spire. I could hear above the din of gunfire shrieks and cries of pain while the squealing of little children added high harmony to the gruesome symphony. I watched in despair as the last of the civilians fell onto a pile of twisted, mangled corpses. In less than ten seconds the population of Sainte Laurie-Olmer was erased from the human register.

That such power could be in the hands of a man like Keitel sickened me. But I realized that as a warrior I, too, possessed the same power to knock airplanes filled with men out of the sky with the mere pull of a trigger. But it seemed so much different in the air. So much less... *criminal.*

Keitel read my mind. "I suppose you're not privy to such a view of the war from five miles high?"

I was too revolted to speak. Instead I watched as the squad produced torches and set fire to buildings, from the church to the barns to every one of the little dwellings that lined the main road. Glass shattered as men smashed rifle butts through window panes and tossed in their fire. Soon the flames licked out of the charred frames and black smoke filled the darkening sky. I heard a woman scream and saw her dash out the doorway of a burning cottage with a little girl in tow. She'd hidden herself and her daughter in the house upon our arrival, only to be flushed out like game birds by the flames. Keitel lowered his pistol and took careful aim.

I whacked his arm down. "Johann, that's enough!"

This startled him, and he turned on me with a sense of outrage that had escaped him while slaughtering civilians a few moments before.

"How dare you give me orders!" he roared.

"I'm a captain!" I responded, trying to buy the woman and girl time.

"In the Luftwaffe, not the SS," he reminded me. "This is my world, Becker. And I will carry out my orders."

"Your orders are to slaughter women and children?" I challenged. They were still fleeing as we spoke.

"My orders are to pacify this region as I see fit. When I have the impertinence to climb into your cockpit, then you can tell me my duty."

He turned and drew a bead on the mother and little girl, who were not yet far enough, as plodding through the deep snow was slowing them down. Had this been summertime and dry they might have made it to the relative safety of the surrounding forests. But in the undisturbed layer of knee-high powder barring the way, they had no chance. Keitel calmly dispatched them each with a single shot to the back as if in target practice. They fell forward into the snow, first the mother, then her bewildered little girl.

I shook my head in dismay. "Since when is a German's duty to commit murder?"

Keitel's face flushed crimson. He'd had all he could take from the man bedding his onetime fiancée. My face must have drained of all color when he turned his pistol on me and placed the cold circle of the barrel up to my forehead. "The only 'murder' here," he said through gritting teeth, "will be me finishing the work the Amis started today if you do not stand down! And that, Captain, is something that I *will* have to explain to Berlin."

Then to my horror I heard a click as he pulled the trigger. My knees buckled and I fell into the snow. He looked down on me with bemused contempt, a pall of black smoke shrouding his form in a sinister backdrop. He let the empty clip slide out of the stock of his pistol onto my chest before producing a fresh magazine from his belt and locking it into place.

His work here finished, Keitel strutted away, disappearing from my field of vision. I lay back in the snow and tried to process all I'd just seen. It was growing dark, and the maroon glow from the spreading flames flickered in the eyes of the milling-about SS men as they methodically fired bullets into the heads of any in the pile of bodies they suspected might still be breathing.

Then a hand reached down to me. "You need help, sir?"

It was Loos. His baby face outlined in the radiance of the conflagration that was once Sainte Laurie-Olmer. I took his hand and he heaved me out of the snow and onto my feet.

"How old are you, Loos?" I asked as we stood contemplating the grisly scene.

"Sir?"

I shook my head. "Never mind."

But then, after another moment of silence between us, Loos mumbled something; I couldn't tell if it was directed at me or just to himself.

"Say again?" I asked.

He looked at me: "Try not to think about it too hard. It's better that way."

I'd always been curious how Paul could have been indoctrinated so quickly. Apparently Loos was proof that it didn't take much at all to turn an innocent boy into an instrument of mass murder. What would become of my brother, then?

Still separated from my unit, I was obliged to move on with them into the night. While I sat in silence, the men casually chatted in the back of the jostling truck while the village continued to blaze. The bodies were left as they had fallen. As we rounded the corner, the burning town disappeared behind the woods. But the sky glowed above the treetops to serve as a reminder of what had just been done.

If you look at a map of France today you will not find Sainte Laurie-Olmer. It was never rebuilt.

37

It was about nine o'clock in the evening when we pulled into another village, Carontein, which was more contemporary and developed than the ancient Sainte Laurie-Olmer, including a small downtown of shops and cafes. The squad was billeted here for the night by a wary, bespectacled priest who also served as a hotel manager. He wore the thick brown robe of the Franciscan order. He wanted no trouble with the band of SS men seeking refuge from the snow.

The squad descended upon his little inn and demanded he produce whatever spirits he may have stored away. He did so obediently, disappearing into a cellar behind the crude bar and returning with a case of aged port wine. He also produced from his pantry a wheel of cheese and some bread. The soldiers fell upon his offering eagerly without a nod of thanks. Then the old man retreated from the scene, leaving his hotel and adjacent café at the mercy of the German invaders while they tried to figure out how a Franciscan priest would come to run an inn in rural France.

Keitel was nowhere to be found. He must have turned in to one of the rooms for the night. I hadn't spoken to him since he pointed his pistol in my face, and I wished to never speak to him again. Amelia was right. Johann Keitel was a dangerous fellow indeed.

I followed the little monk into the hotel lobby. He didn't notice me behind him until I called out, in German, "You there, priest."

He stiffened and turned furtively to face me. In German he replied: "Yes? Is something wrong?"

"No," I said. I looked down, contemplating the dusty floorboards. It was difficult to face a man of God after what I'd seen. "I just don't wish to be with those men."

He looked me over and relaxed some. My bruised and bandaged appearance prompted pity rather than fear. He approached me and in a hushed tone inquired: "You are not SS."

"No," I said. "Luftwaffe. I'm a pilot. I was shot down. They found me."

"Ah," he replied in an understanding tone. "Are you okay, my son?"

I shrugged. "Do I look okay?" My head, in fact, was still pounding and my shoulder had now grown painfully stiff.

"I've seen worse. I would offer to change your dirty bandages but I have none here. Is your base in France?"

"Belgium," I said. "Andeville."

He nodded. "I know it. You are in the fighter base there. In the gardens of the Château LeClaire."

I nodded. "Is it close by? I'm not sure where I am."

He pinched his lips with his fingers. Then a chorus of drunken singing and back-slapping erupted from the adjacent café. I heard a glass shatter, followed by a roar of belly laughter. The priest stared at the door as if he could see through it before returning his attention to me.

He checked his watch. "It's after curfew," he said. "But I do not want to stay near those men either. I know what they have been doing." I lowered my head again. He could read my thoughts. "God will punish you all for this. Do you know that?"

I stiffened. "All I know at the moment, Father, is that I need to get back to my base."

He sighed. "It is three hours' drive in this weather. There's a car out back. It belonged to the owner of this place. I am just the caretaker." A sadness crossed his face. "I am fulfilling a promise to an old friend."

"Where is he now?" I asked.

"*She* is dead." The monk didn't care to elaborate. I didn't want to know any more.

"I can't take someone's car," I told him. "Even if she's…it's not mine."

"Why not? You Germans have taken everything else," he said. Then he smiled. "Is there actually a decent one among you Boche horde? God be praised."

I leaned against the front desk, growing slightly faint. He pulled up a little stool, its legs scraping along the wooden floor. "Sit. You should see a real doctor. I can take you to Andeville, but you must secure my safe passage back here."

I lowered myself uneasily onto the stool. Gesturing to the other room with the singing and carousing, I asked: "What about them?"

"What about them?" he replied. "I suppose they will have the run of the place. I just hope they treat this village better than they have others. There are no partisans here. Your people killed them all a long time ago."

From the back room he retrieved his thick overcoat and tossed another to me. "Take this. This was left by a guest a while back. It is a cold night and you have lost blood."

"Where's that guest now?" I asked.

"You Germans executed him along with the owner," he said matter-of-factly.

He helped me to my feet and covered my shoulders with the long coat. I didn't realize how cold I was until I wrapped myself in its fur liner.

As he walked me to the back door, I asked him: "How did you learn to speak fluent German?"

"I was once the priest in a parish in Alsace. I used to like Germany, you know."

Me too, I wanted to say. But I kept silent.

In the back of the inn was a dark plaza and carport where an old Amilcar sat protected from the heavy snow.

The priest helped me into the dead woman's car. It was odd seeing him in a cape, a friar's robe, and thick rubber boots. He depressed the starter, and the vehicle struggled to turn over against the cold. "This old thing," he muttered. But then the engine rattled to life. It sounded like hammers banging around in an oil drum. He slammed it into gear and my neck wrenched back as we sped out into the cold. I thought for sure we'd get lodged in a drift within a half mile into the countryside. But the roads were passable and we made good headway through the darkness.

I curled up my aching body against the door. "German, are you okay?" he asked again.

"It's been a hard day," I answered him.

"It's a hard war," he sighed.

We passed most of the drive in silence. I saw no sentries posted along the route, but it really was the back country, tucked away in a small corner of occupied France in which Arras was the nearest town of any consequence. By midnight we were across the Belgian border without incident and soon, even in the darkness, I began to get a sense of familiarity, which buoyed my spirits enough for me to sit up and take notice.

I occasionally looked over to this kindly priest in quiet fascination. This man would surely have hidden Krup and his family had they come knocking on his door. To say no one in Stauffenberg could help them was untrue. The fact was that, other than the Engels, no one wanted to help them. They were Jews, and as per the Führer's directives, they needed to be eradicated. How could things have gotten to this point?

"What's your name, Father?" I asked.

"Peter," he replied.

"Well, Father Peter," I said. "I'd like to thank you."

"You may thank God," he said, staring straight at the road. "Your people will need His forgiveness for what you have done."

At that moment we turned a corner and were confronted by the first line of security to the Andeville base. A blockhouse painted in diagonal red, black, and white stripes, manned by four gray-uniformed Luftwaffe guards toting Mausers.

When we pulled up to the gate, they surrounded the car and eyed Father Peter with suspicion until he pointed out that he was bringing back a wounded Luftwaffe pilot. One of them peeked in to see me and smiled.

"It's Captain Becker," he announced with relief. "Proceed," he said, waving us through.

"I am not so comfortable around so many Boche," Father Peter confided.

"You'll be alright," I assured him. "I'll tell them of your kindness."

As we pulled up to a lighted hangar, he asked me: "Will you tell them everything you witnessed today?"

I looked at him. "Those men in the SS. I have nothing to do with them."

He gave me a look of reproach. "Keep telling yourself that, German, and you may believe it someday."

With that thought floating in the air, I heard the familiar voice of my burly crew chief call out to me from beneath the hangar. The man never slept.

"Herr Captain," said Sergeant Ohler. "We were wondering when you'd decide to come back!" He was up to his elbows in the exposed radial engine of a Focke-Wulf fighter. His genuine delight upon seeing me was touching. How could a man like Ohler be from the same country as Keitel?

Regardless, it was good to be back. And so it was with great relief that I was able to come to the close of a terrible day that I would rather put out of my mind—but I never would forget it for the rest of my life.

38

The largest building other than the main house of LeClaire was the stone hall that must have been used in happier days for balls, recitals, and the like. It was a fifty-pace walk from the *Kasino* along a narrow pathway under a canopy of sycamore trees.

Now it served as the JG 32 base hospital. The dimly lit hall was lined with cots along each of the windowed walls, with a nurse's station at the end on watch. Helena, our head nurse, whose braids, square frame, and chiseled features were lifted straight from a Wagner opera, sat with her face buried in paperwork. Most of the patients were sleeping. Some were pilots recovering from battle injuries. Many were wounded men from different wings who'd made emergency landings at the nearest airfield they could find, and ours, situated as it was between the French and German borders, was a common haven. One fellow was terribly burned when his plane cartwheeled and burst into flames upon landing, and he wasn't expected to live. Others were in various stages of recovery. Many sported casts on their arms, legs, across their torsos. Most had either bailed out like me or tried to bring their wounded birds down intact only to end up bellying in.

I noticed that tonight the nurse was accompanied by an armed private, seated in a chair behind her barring the door. I eased up onto my elbows and scanned the room. My eyes quickly rested upon the reason for the soldier's presence. Sitting up in a bed in the corner, staring at the ceiling, was a boy who seemed out of place here. His face was bruised, one eye was swollen shut, and his black-and-blue arm was in a crude sling. He still sported his hat, which was like our Luftwaffe visor cap, but it was muddy brown rather than blue-gray and crushed on the top.

It too bore the golden emblem of an eagle, although it didn't clutch the swastika in its talons but rather arrows in one and an olive branch in the other. On the chair next to him lay his signature leather jacket with the fur-lined collar and wrists.

So this is the enemy? I thought. I sat up in my cot and studied him.

He caught my eye, then turned his gaze to stare straight up at nothing. I was struck by how much like the rest of my pilots he looked. Sandy blond hair. Hazel eyes. A handsome lad despite his bruises and swollen face. He could have been any of my boyhood chums. This unsettled me. He was the first Ami I'd ever seen alive and up close. I was hoping for something, anything, that betrayed a sinister nature. One worth shooting out of the sky. But I saw just a boy like myself. And he was frightened, as I would be.

I wanted to ask him questions. How many planes do you have? What do you want with us? But then I felt the vice grip of nurse Helena's beer hall hand on my good shoulder.

"Why aren't you lying down, Captain?" she demanded like a scolding aunt.

"I'm fine," I protested.

"You need rest," she insisted while prodding my legs back onto the mattress. The Yank looked over in mild amusement, even though he couldn't understand what we were saying.

"I need to get back to my own quarters, Helena."

She shook her head. "Out of the question, Captain. Tonight you stay for observation. Doctor Kraus' orders."

"I outrank him," I protested.

"Not in here," she said sternly.

I looked over at the Yank and rolled my eyes. "Women," I said in English. He grinned. Then he closed his eyes and leaned his head back against the pillow.

"Now you stay put please, sir," said Nurse Helena as she covered me with a blanket.

I looked back to the American flier. In a way, I envied him. Whatever future as a POW lay ahead, at least his war was over.

"What will happen to him?" I asked.

"I have no idea," she said with indifference. "All I do know is what will happen to you if you get a fever. Now please try to get some rest."

She retreated back to her station to resume her paperwork, her hard face illuminated by her solitary desk lamp. All was now quiet again.

I closed my eyes and drifted off to sleep.

"Fuis, mon fils! Fuis!" I reared up in my cot, breathless. My shirt was soaked through with sweat. Looking around me, panting hard, I struggled to get oriented in my surroundings. Quickly my dreams reliving the last moments of Sainte Laurie-Olmer faded and I lay back on the wet sheets, embracing the comfort of the dark hospital ward. I stared up at the cracked ceiling, barely visible in the dim light of the nurse's station lamp, and cursed my mind for forcing me to relive the horrors of yesterday. My breathing returned to normal. I rolled onto my good side, trying not to open the stitches in my scalp or agitate my bruised and stiff shoulder. Glancing over to the Ami's cot, I saw they must have taken him away while I slept.

Despite my fears of what nightmares waited for me on the other side, I knew I needed rest, so I forced myself to sleep by employing an old trick. I closed my eyes and soon I was sitting before a piano, on a great stage, with a mesmerized crowd shrouded in darkness as all the lights fell upon me. But then Krup's bearded face invaded the soothing imagery. Now it was him playing and gazing with fear up from the piano bench as I ran towards him, but I kept slipping farther away as if pulled by a powerful undertow. The stage grew dark and the music stopped and suddenly the lights burst wide and bright. Now I saw his family, hanging by their necks from scaffolds, and there too was Amelia with her blackened face and lolling tongue. Mama, Papa, even Paul twisted and writhed in the air with them. Only I remained. "This I need not explain to Berlin," cackled Johann Keitel somewhere out of my line of sight. And then I too felt the abrasive rope around my neck and my throat contracting…

Suddenly I couldn't breathe! I snapped open my eyes only to see more blackness, and in my hysteria I panicked, fearing my head wound had somehow blinded me! Then I realized a pillowcase was stuffed over my head, and I could hear men giggling like naughty schoolboys. I struggled and fought, but they laughed all the louder. Pain fired through my shoulder and I went still. Through the black and the heat of my sticky breath I smelled beer and stale cigarettes. My assailants lifted me up like a carpet roll and carried me away, ignoring my muffled protests. I heard Nurse Helena's rasping Prussian voice: "Doctor Kraus would not approve of this!" But there were more mischievous guffaws in response. I relaxed, figuring out that this was Mueller, Borner, Gaetjens, and others who were up to no good.

After feeling a blast of cold and then warmth again, I heard their boots clopping along on hardwood while my prone body bounced roughly in their drunken arms.

Suddenly I was hoisted upright onto my stockinged feet, and they released me. I immediately whipped off the pillowcase and gulped in air heavily saturated with cigarette smoke. When my eyes adjusted, I saw I was in the *Kasino*, facing my entire squadron standing at attention with beers in hand. Some of the men were so drunk they swayed on their feet, their eyes mere slits. Their uniforms were disheveled. I'd missed quite a party.

"Squadron, *Achtung!*" belched a red-faced Mueller.

"Now!" shouted Borner, and the men fell upon me pouring what felt like a full keg of thick beer and sticky foam over my head. I screamed and then laughed as an unrelenting train of my comrades doused me. They all roared and I could do nothing but be a good sport about it.

Mueller leapt up on a table while Gaetjens held him steady. Someone handed him a full stein.

"Friends! Squadron mates! Comrades! I welcome you to Captain Harmon Becker's birthday party!" They all cheered. "I say 'birthday' for yesterday he was as good as dead. And now he is born again!"

They clinked their glasses and put their arms around each other in a gesture of physical support and camaraderie that comes only with men who have experienced battle together.

"A toast!" shouted Borner. "To you, Captain! Happy birthday! Do not do that to us again!"

I bowed my head in gratitude and put a fist over my heart. It was a touching tribute. Young Lieutenant Stahl, who'd carried himself so well in the melee with the Amis the day before, handed me a glass. There was laughter followed by cries of "Speech! Speech!" Then the hall grew quiet as the men gathered around. Mueller extended his hand and with Big Werner's help pulled me up next to him on the rickety wooden table.

I fought off a wave of dizziness. "Well." I cleared my throat. "That's one way to get Nurse Helena to give me a sponge bath." They all roared. I thought about Krup…about Hitler…and Keitel. Then I grew somber: "Seriously. There was a time when I thought I knew what this war was about. Now? I don't know anymore. So all I can say is it will be my sublime duty to look after you, my men, and try to shield you as much as I can from the coming tempest. And I see all the signs here. The world often presents a bill for the havoc we wreak. I sincerely hope that you men, my beloved fliers, do not pay the price for our nation led astray. So I say drink up, for tonight we toast the Germany that we all know and love. That good nation of our youths…and long may she endure in our hearts. Come what may."

The men stood before me and raised their steins in uneasy silence. Was I doubting the Führer's cause? I wondered the same myself.

From the back of the hall Mueller spied a figure leaning against the door well with his cane at his side.

"*Achtung!*" my wingman shouted, drawing himself to attention and giving the Nazi salute.

The men all turned and went straight, smacking their heels in unison; the spit and polish of the moment was lost as we pilots stood with one palm outstretched in a salute while the other hand grasped a mug of ale. That I was still in my socks added to the silliness of the matter.

"At ease," said the major. The squadron relaxed and parted as our group commander hobbled towards the table upon which I was standing with Mueller by my side. With his good eye Seebeck surveyed the men, who looked back at him with unease. The tension rose with each limping step he made towards me.

I looked down on him as he stared at my stockinged feet. "Well spoken, Captain." He made a motion to Stahl, who quickly handed him a beer. "Yes, let us raise our steins to the Fatherland." The men did so. "And toast our beloved Führer, who has led our people so far out of the oppression of Versailles and the Weimar stain."

"Hear! Hear!" shouted my squadron mates, relieved that Seebeck sought only to join in the revelry. But I sensed there was more to his appearance than camaraderie, and though I put the mug dutifully to my lips, I saw over the rim his eye fixed upon me.

The group spontaneously entered into a rousing chorus of "*So Leben Wir.*" We drank to life. To love. To friends still among us and those whose images lived only as fading photographs on the wall.

Borner helped me down and I stood soaked in stale beer, facing the major. The men swaying arm in arm were so boisterous and loud that no one heard what Seebeck said to me under his breath.

"You're lucky I need you, Becker. A year ago I'd have had you arrested for what you just said."

I returned his steely glint with my own in a moment of clarity that had eluded me until that moment. "A year ago I wouldn't have said it."

PART 5

39

The tempest came at last.

Although my near-death experience at the hands of the P-38s in late December should have been a harbinger, the new war, in my mind, began on March 6, 1944. It began like any other day. Clear with the heatless sun of late winter low in the western sky. The alarm sounded, and we scrambled to our fighters and leapt into the air.

When we were vectored by ground control, the significance of the bombers' path became clear. For the first time in broad daylight, the Americans were headed to Berlin. Over six hundred bombers filled the sky. And the Luftwaffe threw at them every fighter we had from the English Channel to Poznan.

We were well over Germany by the time we caught up to the formation of Boeings and, I thought, out of escort range. As usual, Mueller, now a first lieutenant, spotted them first. I'd never seen so many enemy planes before. Like the fabled Persian cloud of arrows thick enough to blot out the sun. And as we lined up and swooped into the olive phalanx of determined Yanks, I spied multi-colored aircraft moving very fast and banking in to take us head on. These weren't the twin-boom Lightnings, but rather shark-like single-engine fighters. At first I thought they were a flight of BF-109s turned around in confusion with so many aircraft jockeying for space in the crowded sky. But when they approached us I heard Mueller shout with genuine surprise: "Indians!" This was followed by Borner to Gaetjens: "Oh shit. Come on, Werner," he said to his paunchy wingman. "We're going to earn our *Reichsmarks* today."

The enemy fighters jettisoned their drop tanks with gasoline to spare, and I realized that these fellows weren't leaving like the big P-47s had back in '43. All we had to do then was stalk the bombers from a safe distance until the escorts, low on fuel, peeled off for home. Then the Yank smorgasbord would commence. Not today. The bombers would never again be without fighter protection. The devil himself had sent the Americans P-51 Mustangs. It was a remarkable aircraft. Not only could it do what the dreaded Thunderbolt could do, it could do it anywhere over Germany. Mustangs would eventually appear in enormous quantities, and be flown by well-trained pilots. We had nothing to combat this threat. And our war would never be the same again.

That winter and into the spring of 1944, the Allies effectively took control of the skies over my country. Göring, ever the fat, pompous, hopped-up fool—and rapidly losing favor with Hitler as the capital city thundered and rocked and burned under the merciless pounding of Allied bombers—railed about pilot "cowardice." Even when Seebeck privately pleaded with his family friend for more fuel and better-trained pilots, the air marshal's only answer was, "You must fight harder!" After the war I read that Göring admitted to his American captors: "When I saw Mustangs flying over Berlin, I knew the jig was up." But no one ever told us that.

Meanwhile, our good men were being chewed up in the meat grinder that was the air war over Western Europe. It became grimly apparent that these unrelenting deep penetration raids, which would grow to over a thousand bombers strong and accompanied by clouds of Mustangs, ranging far ahead of the bombers to break up our formations before we could mount coordinated attacks, had only one strategic purpose: to draw the Luftwaffe up to battle and with their overwhelming numbers kill us off in a war of attrition. So dangerous now had the skies become, it was said that every Luftwaffe pilot was destined to be awarded either the Iron Cross or the "wooden cross." Still, we flew on.

And so, I began to lose old comrades whom I'd thought were invincible. The dashing Lieutenant Gerhard Borner was killed on April 6 when he was jumped by P-51s over Aachen. No one saw him go down in the melee, but I saw three Mustangs on his tail as his smoking plane was diving away. His charred body was eventually found in an orchard among the burnt wreckage. Gaetjens burst into tears when told the news. I'd never seen the big man, barely able to squeeze into a cockpit, so unglued. "I couldn't save him," he lamented bitterly. "There were just too many." That night we had a raucous party in Borner's honor with Big Werner stumbling like a mule, challenging anyone foolhardy enough to pass near him to a fistfight. The next morning I found Gaetjens sitting alone in the *Kasino*, staring up at his best friend's photo as the newest addition tacked to the wall. He'd been drinking most of the night and was in no condition to fly. "Too many. I'm so sorry, Gerhard. Too many…" he repeated again and again. He asked to write the letter with the black note, and I had no objection. By the time it reached Borner's devastated family, the man who penned the letter would be a ghost. Just two weeks later a ball turret gunner raked Big Werner's FW-190 as he passed underneath it, and his bird blew to pieces. I wrote that letter. Still, we flew on.

It was now June and though all hell was breaking loose on the French coast, our sector farther inland finally experienced a period of relative quiet. Although we welcomed the respite, the eerie peace unnerved us for two reasons. First of all, it told us that the Allies were concentrating their efforts around tactical bombing, isolating the French beach heads. Secondly, that the high command didn't want us up to the front to challenge Allied airpower, as it would have been futile. So we bided our time and waited for the final chapter of the war to play out. France would decide the issue in the West. If we didn't win there, we had no chance of holding back both the Russians hordes and Anglo-Americans. A blind man could see that. But I vowed, like many of my countrymen, to fight on. In that time I tried to put the Krupinskis out of my mind. But they would soon come roaring back to me.

Debate in the squadron raged about whether the recent landings in Normandy represented the much-anticipated invasion or were a mere diversion for the real landings yet to come farther up the coast at

Calais. We engaged in these lively military punditries while sitting in folding chairs, sweating in full flight gear, our planes at the ready on the runway. Myself, Mueller, Stahl (who by now had racked up twenty kills), and Ohler were seated around the flimsy card table playing Skat and waiting for the alarm. I was just watching the three-hand game, while contemplating the unusually empty skies. We'd each allowed ourselves the luxury of one glass of beer. The glasses sat warming in the sweltering summer sun.

Mueller slapped his cards down in frustration at the hand he was dealt as much as at our situation. "Five-minute alert!" he said, taking a swig. "How many hands can we play? The heavies haven't hit us in weeks."

"Where'd they go?" asked Ohler as he rearranged his cards and smiled conspicuously.

I shrugged. "Normandy I guess. That's where the invasion is."

Stahl was skeptical. "Not Normandy."

"You don't agree?" I said.

"No, sir. My cousin's in an SS *Panzertruppe* in Calais, and I know for a fact they haven't moved from that spot. The Führer certainly wouldn't keep them there throwing pebbles into the English Channel if the real show's farther south."

"Who the hell knows?" I said, studying Mueller's hand.

Ohler offered his thoughts: "I hear that gangster Patton ain't even in charge of the landings. Why would they use that pansy Montgomery instead of him? Unless the real blow hasn't fallen yet."

Mueller chimed in. "I heard he slapped a soldier. They say he's going home."

"Doubtful," I said. "He's their best general. It'd take more than a slap to send him home."

"I heard it's true. No one's seen that arrogant bastard in weeks." Ohler grinned. "The fools."

My wingman's face brightened naughtily. Then he turned around and suddenly hauled off and whacked Stahl, open palmed, across his young face. A red handprint swelled on his freckled cheek. Stahl leapt to his feet, furious. "What the hell!"

Mueller mused. "You all saw it. I confess. I slapped this little turd. I deserve nothing short of being shipped home as punishment. Fair's fair."

After the initial stunned silence, Ohler and I burst out laughing. Even Stahl calmed down after I ordered him to take it in stride and play out his hand.

"You think it's all a diversion then?" asked Stahl as he rubbed his stung cheek, giving Mueller the evil eye.

"This whole goddamned war is a diversion…from my life," I said.

"You seem pretty good at what you do for this to be a diversion," Mueller reminded me, fanning his cards in his hand.

"I'm good at flying, First Lieutenant. Not killing."

Mueller looked up. "I fancy there's a lot of Allied families who disagree."

That comment struck hard, completely missing the levity intended. I stood up, insulted. "You go to hell, Josef." Then I stormed off to my waiting aircraft in a huff.

Mueller looked around at the others. "What'd I say?"

"Don't ask me," shrugged Ohler, who filled me in later on what followed. "That's an officer's fight." He looked up from his hand and spied a young sergeant wearing a field cap over his cropped hair and an unsullied holdall slung over his shoulder approaching the table hesitantly. The three remaining men looked up at him coldly.

"Excuse me, sirs," he said. Although eighteen, he spoke with an almost feminine voice that sounded just barely out of puberty.

"I ain't no officer," said Ohler scornfully. "But these men are. I think a proper salute is in order."

The young sergeant's face lost what little color there was; the oozing pimple on his cheek glowed a contrasting ruby red. He dropped his bag and clicked his heels, staring blankly ahead. "*Heil* Hitler!" he shouted.

Mueller raised up his fanned cards. "*Heil* Hitler." He cupped his hand over his forehead to block the sun. "Move over. As much as I would love to get out of here, I prefer not to let blindness be the reason."

"What do you want, Sergeant?" asked Stahl, returning his attentions back to his hand, already losing interest in the latest walking dead man.

"If you're looking for the adjutant, Lieutenant Thomson's in that hut over there."

"No, sir. I've been processed already. Thank you, sir."

"Well?" said Mueller, taking a swig of warm beer and belching loudly. "Can't you see we have a very important strategy session going on here?"

"Beg your pardon, First Lieutenant. I was hoping to find Captain Becker."

Mueller gestured with his beer to my plane. "This probably isn't the best time to introduce fresh meat to him, Sergeant. Who are you anyway?"

When the young replacement pilot introduced himself, the three men just sat there, mouths agape. Finally Mueller exclaimed: "You don't say! Well then come with me, young pilot." The first lieutenant abruptly stood up, chomped an unlit cigar between his teeth, and briskly took the boy by the shoulder.

"Herr First Lieutenant, where are you going?" said Ohler. "I'm winning this hand!" Resigned that the game was over, the mechanic showed his cards to Stahl. "I am, see?"

Stahl just lit up a cigarette and moved himself over to a deck chair. He reclined, covered his eyes with his visor cap, and enjoyed a calm smoke on a summer day.

I stood leaning against the wing of my fighter, my armpit supported by the twenty-millimeter cannon protruding from the leading edge. I was thinking of all the men I'd killed, as I have every day since. I found myself missing the company of such fine men as Borner and Gaetjens. Even those with whom my life had only briefly intersected, boys like Kluge or Edelmann who, but for their photos on the wall, I couldn't even visualize. I felt tired and stretched inside. I didn't even care who won the war anymore. It just had to end soon or I would die. Either at the hands of the Allies or, worse, swinging from Keitel's noose alongside Amelia. What was I to do about Leo? That thought eclipsed all others as I leaned against my aircraft contemplating what value were four lives against millions? *Against mine?*

"Well, Herr Sourpuss," Mueller's chipper voice called to me. "Still feeling sorry for yourself?"

"What now, Josef?" I said deadpan as I stared out to the row of fighters lined up on the airfield at the ready.

He backhanded me on the arm. "Maybe this new addition to the squadron will cheer you up."

I sighed and turned my head. "Let's see the new tombstone." That was all I could say, as I was stunned into silence.

The sergeant stood at attention, beaming at me under his ill-fitting field cap: "Hello, Brother."

Paul was taller and lankier, but still showed that familiar grin. A frailer, darker version of me. He seemed too much a child to be sporting the uniform of a Luftwaffe sergeant. But here he was in the flesh. And my life had just gotten even more complicated. But I remembered my father's words. And I would do my best to protect Paul Becker from the Allies. But only he could protect him from himself.

40

My brother and I stood alone in the hangar. A stripped-down FW-190 sat quietly underneath the tin roof. Ohler's people used it to cannibalize parts. Paul circled the menacing craft, running his hands across the control surfaces. I stood quietly and watched him. My plane sat not more than thirty yards away should the alarm sound. But Paul was curious about the fighter, and so I obliged him. It would give us a moment together.

"So this is the 'Butcher Bird.'" He whistled with boyish admiration. "Does it fly as good as it looks?"

"Better," I said. "They send us good planes all the time. What they don't send us are trained pilots." I rubbed my eyes wearily. "I'm afraid to ask this, but how many hours do you have?"

"Twenty-five," he answered while still giving the fighter plane his attention.

My heart sank. "Bastards," I groaned, more to myself. "Even the greenest Americans have ten times that by the time they send them up."

Paul stopped and looked over to me as if personally insulted. "The schools were low on petrol from the bombings," he said. "They did the best they could."

I grinned sarcastically. "I'm sure the first Ami that gets on your tail will give you a break for that." There was a wrenching silence. Finally I said: "Dammit, Pauli, why did you sign up to fly of all things? Why now?"

Paul stood up straight and answered: "Because there's a war on, Harmon. And I intend to do my part for the glory of the Reich."

I let that seep in for a moment and then couldn't help but chuckle at his blind, pitiful zeal. "You have no idea what you've gotten yourself into, do you?" He didn't know how to respond. So he walked up to me, put his hands on my shoulders, and smiled warmly.

"I know that I'm with family, Harmon. Of all the great coincidences."

"It was no coincidence," I said.

His eyes narrowed. "What do you mean?"

"I brought you here," I confessed. "Well, actually Lieutenant Thomson made sure you were assigned here. I took him up on an offer he made a while back."

"Why would you do that?"

I looked past him, thinking of the warmth of a winter night's fire that seemed a lifetime ago. "I told Father I'd look after you as best I could."

He laughed. "But who'll look after you?"

"I'm fine on my own," I said. But of course, I really didn't know.

"Admit it," he quipped. "You're happy to see me."

"I am." I ran my fingers over my drawn face. I needed a shave. "So what's the latest from Stauffenberg?" I asked. "Have the Allies flattened it yet?"

Paul stared at me. "That's not funny, Harmon."

"I wasn't trying to be." Another pause. "Have you lost weight?" I patted him playfully on his hard stomach.

He smiled. "Flight training will do that, as you know."

"And how are Mother and Father?"

He shrugged. "As well as can be expected. They worry about you."

"As they should," I said.

"But you know Father," he added. "He'll never show his true feelings."

I smiled. "A stubborn old constable, that one. And Mother? Does she still sing?"

Paul shook his head. "Not often."

I inquired guardedly about Amelia too. He said he rarely saw her. Although admittedly he'd been away at flight training for most of the time.

I grew uneasy as his answer brought back to my mind what she was doing. I had no doubt that Paul would have reported her if he knew she was hiding Jews. In fact, who knows if he'd have forgiven my complicity in her crimes? I honestly couldn't say.

"Hanna's very sick," I said offhandedly.

"I know," Paul piped up. "The *Sturmbahnführer* sends his men look in on her, but Amelia shoos them away. You're in love with a headstrong girl."

"Don't I know that," I agreed. Then it hit me. "The *Sturmbahnführer*? SS? Who's that?"

Paul smiled. "Keitel of course."

My heart sank. Keitel was now an SS major. His sniffing around Amelia's house wasn't an act of neighborly kindness. He was looking for something. Or someone. But why not just storm in? The SS needed no invitation. Strange.

Paul crouched down, inspecting the swivel tailwheel of the machine. "She really is beautiful, Harmon. I can understand why Keitel hates you."

"To hell with him." I snorted. "Anyone else visiting her?"

"There's a boy from Koppel's who delivers her food. But fear not. He's too young. She mostly keeps indoors."

"She has little money. War's hard on civilians," I observed.

"We all must make sacrifices to the Fatherland. We are a hail of—"

"Ninety million bullets, I know," I cut him off with impatience. Then I added: "It'll be eighty million if this shitshow keeps going."

Paul glared at me. "Don't say that. The Führer has it all in hand."

"So I hear. Anything else about home?"

"Oh!" he said as if I had jarred his memory. "Amelia asked me to give you this."

He stood and retrieved a crumpled envelope from his breast pocket. I eagerly grabbed it from his hand and inspected it to see that it hadn't been opened, but my brother read my mind.

"It's sealed, Harmon." He laughed. "Do you take me for a voyeur?"

He was telling the truth. Still, if she had written anything about Krup then she was foolhardy to entrust such an incriminating note to this Nazi brat. She must've really needed to tell me something to recruit Paul as an unwitting accomplice to avoid the censors.

I slipped the envelope into my pocket. "I'll have Lieutenant Thomson show you around."

"You're welcome," he said with irritation.

"For what?"

"For bringing you the letter."

"You should be thanking me for bringing you here," I said. "The other groups near the coast have been decimated. And we've had no picnic."

"Well, maybe we can win this war together then," he said, slapping me on the back as we walked out of the hangar.

"Maybe."

The order to stand down came a half hour after I left my brother with Thomson. If the Allies hadn't come by now, they wouldn't. That suited me fine. My urgency to read Amelia's letter was unbearable.

When I got to my quarters I closed and locked the door behind me. Examining the tattered envelope more forensically in my quarters, I could see that it was indeed the original seal. But Amelia, showing more caution than I gave her credit for, still knew to write cryptically. *Good girl*, I thought. The meaning behind her words, however, rang clear to me:

June 10, 1944

Dearest Harmon:

I miss you more than words can say. Little has changed since we saw each other last. My life here continues as it has, although I do not know how long I can go on like this. Each day that goes by, with no end of the fighting in sight, I ask myself: Is this the day?

There is more activity in Stauffenberg lately. The SS keep us safe. They watch over us. Checking to see that we are alright, yet respectful of our privacy for we are all in this war as one people. They root out the criminal elements with arrests of Bolsheviks and spies. They watch my house to protect me from enemies of the Reich. Although I feel safe under Herr Keitel's ever-surveilling eye, I wish you were here to protect me as well. I cannot see myself lasting another summer in this state. Please return home to me safe, won't you? There is so much you can do here.

The SS watch over your family too, so do not fear. Although they are kind enough not to interfere in their daily affairs, I know that should anything happen to your parents, Keitel's men will be there. They are all the New Germany has promised. A sight to see.

(I believe she inserted this following paragraph, so I could tell if our correspondence had probing eyes. Censors would have redacted it.)

We hear little of the war, other than what we see on the Wochenschau. But I wonder sometimes. We hear whispers of invasion in France. Heavy losses in the east. Yet I am confused as all of the news we get is of victory, heroism, the glory of the Reich. I see more boys coming home, legless, armless, or whole in body but with a ghostlike quality that makes me fear what they have seen. Do you too possess such darkness? Are you indeed well, my love? I hear nothing from you, yet no black notes come so I comfort myself with the passing of each day that you are still with me.

I wish I could write more, but I have said what I need to say. I know this war will end someday. I only pray that it will end before time runs out for those we care about. In many ways, that is as much in your hands as mine.

Do be careful. I miss you so much that the weight of your absence physically presses down on me. I must go now.

All My Love,

Amelia

I folded the letter and stuffed it in my drawer. A terrible sense of foreboding came over me. She was telling me that Keitel suspected her of something. Time was indeed her enemy—and the Krupinskis'. But for now I had a war to fight, although my heart began to tug me in a different direction.

And all the while I grew more despondent, more reclusive, and angrier at the world and all things that tied me to this life of the walking dead that Amelia so astutely described in her letter. Every day I dodged the scythe. And I was coming to abhor all who made this my reality.

I was angry at the Allies for their invasion, the merciless bombing, and now their hosts of fighter planes and well-trained crews. I resented their alliance with the Bolsheviks to the east against us. I fumed at Hitler for bringing this whole bloody mess crashing down upon Germany when we—when *I*—had once trusted him without question. "The Führer has it all in hand," as Paul still recited like some pull-string doll. That seemed an alien notion to me now as I recounted his growing madness before my very eyes. I hated Keitel for who he was, Seebeck for what he represented. I was even annoyed with Krupinski for being a stubborn old man and not getting his family out when he could. I was furious with Amelia for dragging me into her idealistic folly. And most of all, I was livid with myself for caring about Leopold and Constanze, little Elsa, and even the bitter Jakob. I was angry for being in love.

I didn't have long to gnash my teeth, as I heard a gentle tapping on my door and Paul's voice calling to me. "Harmon, are you in there? Let's go for a beer, shall we? I'm parched."

I exhaled and donned my visor cap. Reality was what it was, and I had a brother with twenty-five hours of flying who had to very quickly be taught the dos and don'ts of his high-performance FW-190 if he was going to survive.

I opened the door and stepped into the sunlit air. One thing did bother me. "While you wear that uniform, you will address me as Captain Becker, is that understood, *Sergeant*?"

Paul clicked his heels, grinning. "*Jawohl!*"

"Come," I said, "let's go look at your crate first."

He followed me across the airfield past several pilots taking catnaps on the grass with their caps over their faces. We approached his lone aircraft, which sat in the field next to the dispersal area. It had grayish green mottled camouflage with the blue-and-white-striped spiral pattern painted on the cone-like propeller cowling as our squadron marking. It looked quite ferocious, and the thought of this little boy climbing into that buzz saw of a flying machine gave me pause.

"Are you familiar with the 190A?" I asked, fearing the answer.

He didn't disappoint me. "I only flew the Messerschmitt. Two hours total. It was a tricky bastard to land."

I nodded. "This plane's landing gear is wider and more forgiving."

Sweat trickled down my back as I took him through a walk-around of the machine. I pointed out many technical aspects of the aircraft that I knew were most relevant to his combat survival. After ten minutes of one instruction after another, I turned to him and asked doubtfully: "You think you can remember all that?"

He nodded without much confidence.

Then I heard a shrill voice. "What's this? Another Becker in our midst?" bellowed Major Seebeck, hobbling over to take a look at the two of us. Paul's uniform was much more regulation than my flight suit. "Like Manfred and Lothar of old," he said, likening us to the "Red Baron" and his brother.

Paul immediately drew himself to attention and threw his palm to the sky. "*Heil* Hitler!" I saluted lazily. I was too damned tired to care.

"Are you settled in, Sergeant?"

"Yes, Herr Major," he said beaming.

Seebeck stood with his infernal cane supporting him. "Well, I'll not disturb you two further. I just found it quite coincidental to have two Beckers on the base. Lieutenant Thomson might shed some light on this. Still, I wasn't sure what to expect, but Sergeant Becker here seems to be the New Germany incarnate." He looked at me mockingly. "You could learn from his example, Captain."

I tried to stay cool. "I think right now I'm the one who has much to teach here in lieu of our training schools, Herr Major."

He didn't miss a beat. "Then you can both learn from each other."

"Herr Major," I pressed. "Sergeant Becker is not ready for combat yet."

"Hey!" Paul objected, but I ignored him and instead looked at Seebeck.

"His training I'm sure is adequate. Besides, Captain, he'll have plenty of experience this far from the coast before seeing any serious action."

"Oh, is that so?" I said sarcastically.

Seebeck cleared his throat and stood straight. "That is so."

"Please tell the Mustangs this."

Seebeck ignored the jibe. "I expect you to have all of our new pilots combat ready. I have the utmost confidence in Sergeant Becker. Look at him. He is the model German soldier. How can such a superior figure be defeated?"

My brother beamed at that, swallowing it whole. "Thank you, Herr Major."

"Carry on, Becker." Then he bowed in a cute gesture. "I mean *Beckers*."

"*Heil* Hitler!" the little runt blurted out again.

Seebeck was clearly impressed with the contrast. "*Heil* Hitler." Kindred spirits, I thought.

After Seebeck was out of earshot, I said to him, "You still swallow that snake oil?"

"I'm not going to apologize for being a Nazi," he said defiantly.

I rolled my eyes dismissively. "If I were you I'd put down *Mein Kampf* and start learning the turning radius of a Mustang or the blind spots of a Boeing."

"You don't object to the Führer's philosophies, I hope." This was the Paul I remembered. That little Hitler Youth machine who'd forgotten that being a German patriot didn't mean surrendering your humanity. Perhaps Karl Becker was right. Maybe he had lost his son to Hitler. Nazi or not, it didn't stop me from trying to throttle some sense into that brainwashed head of his.

"Listen, boy!" I snapped, grabbing him by his collar. "When you're up in the air and tracers scream past you and you look back to see three, four, hell *ten* Indians on your tail, I goddamn guarantee you that the sinister role of the Jewish bankers in the Versailles Treaty had better be the last thing on your mind! You study the politics of this chaos on your own time. But up there you belong to me!"

He shook me off of him, and then stood his ground. "I belong to the Reich! I swore my oath to the Führer, not you."

But I wouldn't leave it at that. "No, my little plebe. Your mind is Hitler's, and your heart is Germany's. But your ass is mine! Father issued it to me, and I intend to return it to him in one piece. Do you understand, *Sergeant* Becker?"

Paul went rigid, all warmth between us extinguished. He saluted properly and said, "*Jawohl, Herr Captain.*"

I calmed down, and the enmity in me fizzled out. "Very good. Now come, let's get that beer."

He stared straight ahead. "I'd rather not…sir."

Now I felt deflated. "Please," I said. He stood silent. I think I even saw his lip quiver. The tough Nazi wasn't made of the same material as his father and me, it seemed. So I tipped the balance with a smile and said: "That's an order."

He finally relaxed, and that sheepish grin spread across his face. "Well, I can't disobey an order."

I grinned widely as I took him by the arm and led him to the *Kasino*, where I knew Mueller would be waiting.

We had a wonderful evening. The beer flowed and the wine was poured as a thick haze of smoke clung to the ceiling of the noisy hall. Music played on the phonograph, and we sang along to songs of love, of loss, of country and a general longing to have this damned war be over. It was good to have family with me. The squadron subjected Paul to the usual initiation of beer over the head. They poured it on extra heavy, as they knew he was my brother. In a way, their jovial mistreatment of him was a token of their affection for me. We pilots lived an odd life.

Paul, his eyes half closed, weaved up to me at the bar at one point and asked: "Say, Harmon. Whatever happened to that old Jew who used to teach you piano?"

An electric charge ran up my spine. I paused and wiped my mouth. "Krupinski?" I said, trying to sound deadpan. I swigged my beer for effect but I was quaking inside.

"Yes, that's the one."

I shrugged. "I guess he went where all the others went."

Paul actually grinned. "Then we won't see him anymore." And he even drew a finger across his throat to emphasize his satisfaction. "Good riddance to them all, I say."

I stared at him, my fear shifting to disgust. "Why do you say that?"

He swallowed a shot handed him by Lieutenant Stahl, who was behind the bar. Slurring his words, Paul prodded my chest with his finger. "They are a plague. Like lice. Even that old man. I know you had a fondness for him, Harmon. I mean, Herr Captain. Sorry. It was something I never understood. Although I'm not a musician. But no matter how this war ends, whether we just declare a truce or achieve ultimate victory, I do know yet another thing that the Führer has done for our national good."

"Oh?" I said. "And what's that?

"He rid our country of Jews once and for all. For that alone he'll go down as one of the great men of history. He is in a pantheon with Frederick the Great, Hannibal, Attila, Caesar, indeed, even Jesus Christ."

"Hear! Hear!" echoed young Stahl. "I'll drink to that!" I looked at them both in disbelief as they clinked shot glasses. But I said nothing as Stahl poured a refill.

Paul finished with a blurry-eyed pronouncement. "We are blessed to have seen such times!" Before I could utter another word, he was pulled into a circle of dancing pilots. Spouts of beer, like from the blow holes of a pod of whales, flew into the air. I for one didn't feel so blessed as my dear brother. And although I'd seen hatred in the men fester and grow as we suffered more and more losses in the desperate fighting since the new year, I felt none—and that was for men trying to kill me. How Paul, young Stahl, and the rest of my nation's youth could harbor such animosities against people like Krup who had never done them any harm, I just couldn't comprehend. I buried my face in my beer.

At one point during the festivities, Mueller and I caught each other's eye. Both of us had grown old in our time at the front together. I noticed deep lines on his once-smooth face, and a general hard look to him that betrayed years of fighting. I knew what he was thinking. It wasn't the same without Borner and Gaetjens. Trautloft's dire prediction was coming true. But we still lived, as Mueller was fond of reminding me. We stood tall amidst the rows of the slain who had fallen under the reaper's blade. Mueller raised his bottle of wine to me in a gesture of warm-hearted friendship. From across the room I toasted him back with my beer. He seemed gratified that tonight at least I was taking his advice. I took another swallow and with my kid brother at my side, I lived for the moment as we swayed arm in arm singing martial songs. All of the rest, the madness, the death, the constant tension of my two lives—one as a fighter pilot, the other as the keeper of Amelia's traitorous secret—gave way to gaiety and cheer. But for Paul's commentary, the forlorn family hidden away in a small corner of Stauffenberg was out of my mind. It was good to feel human again.

41

Much of what I'm going to tell you going forward I did not witness with my own eyes. How could I? But after many years of profound reflection, and tying together the strands of what I've learned since, I believe I paint an accurate picture of the events that followed, including how the players behaved, and what were their motivations. I knew these men and women. Some more than I would have liked. Others not enough. This is their story as much as mine.

In the sleepy town of Stauffenberg, a Jewish family in hiding sweltered in Amelia's sauna of an attic while the June sun beat down on the tile roof directly over them.

The family sat, motionless, shades drawn. Sweat rolled down their faces, filling the sticky folds of their necks, their armpits, running down their backs. This was their third summer in these hellish conditions. Had Amelia not brought them a daily supply of water, and removed their rancid waste from old bedpans, they would have died in days. Yet they persevered through frigid winters and roasting summers. But they were reaching the end of their endurance. Their confinement combined with the heat was having a maddening effect upon them. And it was only June.

Constanze looked to her husband in despair. "How long are we to live like this?" she moaned.

Krupinski, his breathing growing more labored by the day, could only sit in his wet shirt clinging to his itchy skin, and shake his head.

"Mommy," breathed Elsa, fanning herself with a towel in the corner. "It's so warm. May we please open the window?"

"No, Elsa," answered her father. "It's too dangerous in daylight." The little girl slumped in disappointment.

"Try to sit still, bug," her mother offered, using her pet name to reassure her.

Krup looked at his wife, and a silent message passed between them. "Have you not seen all the SS men out there lately? They might see," he protested, annoyed that he needed to justify his caution.

"Perhaps the children can at least wash off in one of Amelia's basins downstairs?"

Krup shook his head. "Out of the question. It's the middle of the day."

Constanze begged off, toweling off her high forehead. "Sometimes I think it would have been better to go with the soldiers when they came for us. It could not be a worse existence than this."

Her husband ignored that. He knew it could be much worse. He often pressed Amelia as she handed him up food and water to relay what she knew about the Jews of Europe. A whisper here. A rumor from over there. Drunken boasts by SS men. Stories of trainloads of Jews transported east, stuffed to overflowing in cattle cars, never to be seen again. No food trains ever spotted on the same rail lines. Just people. Endless shipments of human cargo. Talk of camps where signage with the evil slogan *Arbeit Macht Frei* (Work Will Set You Free) offering hope where there was none greeting the new arrivals at the gate. Hitler's ravings in *Mein Kampf.* Goebbels' anti-Semitic vitriol. The "war of annihilation" being waged in Russia against the *Untermenschen.* It all created a sinister tapestry from which Leopold Krupinski, a musical man with an eye for patterns, could draw only one logical conclusion. The Jews were being systematically exterminated. Luck had preserved him long enough to see the truth.

Leopold recalled the day the SS had finally come for them. They pulled up in an Opel truck and leapt out screaming "*Raus! Raus, Juden!*" A young Obersturmführer Keitel, now a decorated SS lieutenant just returned from Russia, directed the men with single-minded purpose to search the grounds in a gesture of newly commissioned authority. They kicked in the door and tore through the house.

But the Jews weren't there. Only by chance had they been off in the forest bordering their home enjoying the fine weather, picnicking in the sun, desperate to recapture a fleeting sense of the good life they once knew. Until this moment—despite the yellow Star of David patches he and his wife and son were now forced to wear in public—Krup had clung to the hope that it could get no worse for the Jews. But when he watched Keitel from afar, while hunkered down among the brush in the wooded hills overlooking the house, he saw that all was lost. The SS was determined to take his family away. It was a chilling moment of clarity, and as he surveyed his confused, frightened clan, they in turn looking at him to make sense of it all, he realized he'd made a terrible mistake in believing in a Germany that was long dead.

The SS troopers camped outside the house for the rest of the day, waiting in vain for the Jews to return. The Krupinskis hid until nightfall before returning to their ransacked home. Standing in the dark, surrounded by cracked picture frames, upended furniture, and scattered papers, Leopold realized that his world was over. But now it was too late to leave Germany. They would never get through. And through to where? All of Europe had fallen under the Nazi banner.

The SS would come back for them tomorrow, of that much he was certain. Perhaps even during the night. They couldn't stay here a moment longer. In desperation, Leopold thought hard and long. Who could help them? Who *would* help them? Who would risk execution to save a family of Jews? There was only one person he could trust. But she lived in the heart of town.

In the dead of night, when all was quiet and the village windows blacked out as a precaution against British air raids, Leopold led his family like stealthy commandos across the bridge spanning the black ribbon of the Main. They crept under the forbidding Rathaus tower and through the deserted streets of Stauffenberg to the home of Amelia Engel.

"Please God," he whispered to himself as they slunk along the Leiselstrasse, hugging the walls of the little homes that backed up to the lane. "Please."

Constanze and Elsa clung to him as he gently tapped on the front door. Jakob stood with his back to the wall scanning the block, but the cobblestone street was deserted. It was fortunate the two Engel women lived on a dead-end lane.

A quick flash of light glowed from the second-floor window as a corner of the night shade was briefly drawn back and Amelia's silhouette appeared like an apparition and then moved away. They could make out just the dimmest hint of lamplight through the shades, lighting up in rapid succession, following her as she made her way from her room down the steps to the front of the little house. The door cracked open, and Amelia, in her nightgown, groggy from being awakened from a deep sleep, peered out to see her lover's *Musikmeister* and his family staring back at her with the vacant eyes of the condemned.

Amelia stood in stunned silence and processed the scene rapidly; she knew exactly why they were here.

"Please," said Leo, shamefully regretting his own intransigence that had brought them to such a desperate state. "We have nowhere else to go."

Amelia hesitated. The SS had made it quite clear what the penalties were for harboring Jews. And yet, this was her chance to do something. To strike, even in a small way, a blow at the Nazis. Even if it meant her own death at their hands. Who she was defined the moment, which in turn defined her. She carefully looked around to make absolutely sure that no one was watching from behind shadows or drawn curtains. All was clear. With a beckoning hand she ushered them in. "Come inside. Quickly."

They did, and the doors to the outside world closed behind the family of my master and friend.

"Papa," a young man's voice was saying. "Papa?" Krup snapped out of his daydream. Jakob was standing over him. A wiry, intense boy, well on his way to strapping manhood. "I opened the window. I'm sorry but the heat was unbearable."

Leo sat up and processed what he'd just heard. Too late an alarm rang within him. "You did what?!" he said in a panic. "I said no! It's dangerous!"

"As is heatstroke," countered his teenaged son.

Krup gave his son a severe look and quickly moved past him to the window, which was indeed opened wide. A refreshing breeze poured through and the temperature was noticeably cooler, but that meant nothing when sized up against the risks of being discovered. He suspected people were watching this house. Amelia had told him how Keitel loathed Harmon Becker, and how he'd like nothing more than to exact revenge upon them both for the insult of stealing Amelia's hand. Krup drew one last wonderful breath of fresh summer air and then slammed the window shut, drawing the shades and letting a shadow fall back onto their world.

Constanze and Elsa, lulled to sleep by the heat, rubbed their eyes and inquired what all the fuss was about.

"Your son is trying to get us killed!" Krup hissed to his wife.

"What?" Constanze looked at Jakob, who rolled his eyes.

"I only opened the window, Mama," he said, dismissing his father's histrionics.

She considered them both but took no sides. "Do you think anyone noticed?" she said to her furious husband.

He looked sternly at his unrepentant son. "For our sakes we'd better hope not."

Stefan Rosner stood on the cobblestone Leiselstrasse by a lamppost and continued to study the window. He'd been spying on the Engels' little yellow house with the pretty flower boxes for several weeks now, as per Sturmbahnführer Keitel's instructions. But he wasn't even sure what he was looking for.

"Anything out of the ordinary," was the SS officer's curt reply, whenever he asked. He wondered if it had to do with the famous pilot he'd met here this winter. There did seem to be a tense air about the place, what with the sick mother and all. Who knew? All he cared about was that he was doing his duty by helping the SS watch those suspected of disloyalty. Perhaps they were engaging in criminal acts, conspiring against the Reich in there. Maybe they were even Bolsheviks, although Herr Hitler said there were no more Jews, Gypsies, or Communists left in the New Germany, so to think otherwise was to call the Führer a liar—an awful crime. He shrugged; who was he to say? He was bored and just wanted to go home. But duty kept him watching the house. And no one in the Hitler Youth would call him a shirker.

Then he saw the human form in the attic window. He appeared briefly, and the window slid open. Stefan continued to watch, paying close attention. Five minutes later another figure, bearded and frail, showed himself for a brief second and shut it. Then the shades were drawn, leaving a tiny, dark shuttered rectangle under the A-frame that supported the terra cotta roof.

After standing there for twenty more minutes, Stefan decided that he'd observed whatever was going to happen. Should he report this? It was strange that people would be up in an attic on a summer day. And keeping the window shut rather than opening it wide to beat the stifling heat? He concluded this was, indeed, out of the ordinary enough that it was worth mentioning to Herr Keitel.

So he left the Engels' home behind and made his way to the center of town, where people were out in the Himmelplatz enjoying the sunny weather. He would find Herr Keitel and do his duty to the Fatherland. The Führer would be very proud of him. And that was all he cared about in the whole world.

Sturmbahnführer Keitel and two other SS officers sat at one of the tables arranged along the Wilkestrasse under the shade of an umbrella, sipping tea and watching the town pass by while discussing the Normandy invasion.

"Oh yes," Keitel was saying to the two other men in uniform. "We'll be on our way to the front in a day or two."

Stefan approached him sheepishly, his hands folded behind him, not wanting to interrupt the *Sturmbahnführer* while he was speaking.

"What's the status anyway?" inquired one of the soldiers.

"We'll drive the Anglo-American mob into the channel, of course," declared Keitel. "Just as we did at Dieppe." He leaned back in his chair, casually put his cup to his lips, and crossed his jackbooted legs. "Or we'll all die trying." Then he noticed Stefan, standing at attention in front of him. "What is it, boy?" asked Keitel, looking up from his seat.

"*Heil* Hitler!" shouted Stefan with an extended palm.

"*Heil* Hitler," the Sturmbahnführer answered.

Stefan clicked his heels. "I wish to report odd activity at the house, sir."

Keitel sat up straight and put his cup back on the saucer. "Oh? What kind of odd activity?"

"Movement in the attic. At least two people. Although I can't be certain. They looked like men. I thought it best to report it to you."

"And what of Fräulein Amelia?"

"I watched her leave ten minutes before. She'd not yet returned."

Keitel considered the officers with him. If there were any men at the Engel home, a house supposedly occupied only by an invalid granny and a whore, he would want to investigate them personally. "We'll discuss this later at my office. Now run along."

"Yes, Herr Sturmbahnführer," he chirped obediently. And then he ran along.

"Trouble, Johann?" one of his companions asked while ripping a bread roll in two.

"I'm not sure," the SS commander said, as wheels inside his head lurched into motion. "But I'll find out in due time."

Keitel would come to regret not investigating sooner. But who could have predicted what was to happen next? Certainly not me.

42

The sun, a blood-red disk in the sky, was just peeking over the woods to the east. Robins caroled from poplar branches above a heavy mist that shrouded the airbase like a translucent quilt.

The NCOs slept in a barracks in the east wing of a château that had once served as a library. It was strange to see two lines of cots, lockers, coat racks, boots, and uniforms piled into a room with rows of leather-bound books lining the high walls. The men were asleep, snoring loudly. They sounded like a petting zoo.

Paul lay in his cot curled up securely in his sheets, unaware of the jolt about to come crashing down on him. Mueller and I stood above his sleeping form. It was 0500 hours, and we were already in full flight gear. I held a full bucket of ice water. Both of us reeked of booze from the night before and were fighting off mind-crushing hangovers. At one point Paul rolled over on his side and mumbled, but then retreated back into his dreams. My wingman and I fought off an attack of the giggles.

Mueller looked at me and nodded. One, two, three! *SPLASH!* A wall of water cascaded down upon my unsuspecting brother, who lurched upright and thrashed his arms with a frenzied gasp. "What the bloody hell!"

I waited for him to get oriented and recover from the shock. He shook his head, flinging water off his matted hair. He patted his soaked uniform. "Oh great," he snarled, leaping out of his soggy cot. "Just wonderful!"

I dropped the bucket and tossed him his field cap.

"Let's go, Sergeant Becker," I commanded. "Your training begins now. Meet us at the dispersal point in ten minutes."

Startled junior pilots sat up in their cots to watch us pass. A wave of guffaws swept through the room when they saw what we'd just done to the new recruit. Paul, on the other hand, was not so amused. I didn't care if he hated me for life. If I was going to bring him home to Mother and Father in one piece, then he'd need at least rudimentary training from experienced fighter pilots. And an early-morning flight, hopefully before Allied patrols swept in from the channel, would be a good beginning.

Mueller and I strutted to the airstrip, where Ohler had three FW-190s armed and ready.

Our purring aircraft brought us to ten thousand feet, and I gazed east towards Germany and a glorious dawn. The morning sun cast knife-like shadows on the fertile ground below. I'd been flying for several years, over terrain varying from the flat yellow Russian steppe to the jagged North Sea coastline to the snow-capped Alps, but still the views never ceased to astonish me. The interwoven tapestries of emeralds and ochers, the spider veins of sun-dazzled rivers, the little clusters of houses, each representing a separate life with a story to tell. There were worse ways to fight a war.

But there were better ways to fight an air war. And being properly schooled to battle a highly skilled foe who vastly outnumbered you and flew superb aircraft was one way to start. With his inadequate training Paul couldn't survive for long. And so he flew at the apex of a *V* in his little Focke-Wulf, with two experts with a combined one hundred seventy-eight air victories flanking him.

Even though the American fighters had such a long range, I assumed they wouldn't be on this leg of their sorties from bases in England so early. Believing we had a window of safety, I vectored us east into clear airspace.

"Alright," I said over the radio. "We're two miles up. Time to make a fighter pilot out of you, Sergeant Becker."

"Fine," said Paul. "What now?"

"First some basics you learned in flight school to see your form. Lieutenant Mueller will act as leader. You're his pack wingman. Follow him through a split *S*."

The first lieutenant's voice crackled over the radio. "Let's go, boy. Cover my ass."

Mueller's plane suddenly banked hard into a half roll and promptly disappeared towards the ground in a screaming half loop. The other 190 whipped over and wobbled after him. I could only cringe. Paul had no chance of following him, and quickly fought off a stall. When he recovered control, he was over a mile in the opposite direction of his leader.

Mueller made a chandelle and throttled up to regain altitude as I circled over them both and banked slightly to peer down on the pathetic spectacle.

"Congratulations, Sergeant Becker," barked Mueller acerbically. "You've just left me an easy mark."

"Sorry, Herr First Lieutenant," Paul mumbled weakly.

"Where the hell are you, Sergeant?" I called to him.

"At your four o'clock low. I'm trying to get back up to you." He sounded like a frightened child now, all bravado stripped by the knowledge of his perilous position as an untrained fighter pilot in a violent air war.

"Good God, boy," said Mueller as he leveled off at my three o'clock. "What the hell'd they teach you besides takeoff and landing?" He waved to me. "Let's go around again."

"Any day now, Sergeant, you can come back and join us," I said snidely.

His plane eventually leveled off with ours. I made mental notes. The first thing I noticed was that Paul had a hard time keeping formation, and his plane bounced and weaved as if caught in a typhoon. He was having difficulty handling his crate in general, which I knew to be a forgiving plane to fly. At lower airspeed he tended to bank too hard and slip into a stall due to the high wing loading. The little plane recovered well though.

"So much to learn," I mumbled to myself. "I don't need this shit." He kept his wobbly machine about two hundred yards away. "Let's go," I said. "That's all I need to see."

"I'm sorry," Paul said again. "I'm doing the best I can."

"That's what scares me," I said coldly.

I observed him encased in that cockpit, bobbing along as he concentrated on the most elemental of tasks. To a passive observer he looked like the typical fighter pilot with his scarf and goggles. A fearsome knight of the air. But to me he was not Sergeant Becker of the Luftwaffe. He was Pauli, my kid brother. Vulnerable, impressionable, completely out of his element in a cruel world that had abducted him too soon. I couldn't accept him as a warrior, even in his sun-drenched fighter plane, cloaked in camouflage, bristling with cannons and machine guns ready to do battle. I saw only a boy who tipped my hat off my head when he scampered past me on the Wilkestrasse. The little nuisance who spilled milk on my sheet music. Who climbed trees and fell out of them. He should have been skipping school to splash in the Main on a warm spring day. I yearned for the Paul I had grown up with. His Hitler Youth days still ahead of him. An innocent mind unencumbered by the weight of Nazi dogma that taught him to hate that which he did not understand. But as Karl Becker had lamented to me over a drink by the fire, that boy was gone. Those days, like Germany's former goodness, had passed. He was an archetype of my country. So instead he and I flew as warriors in a lost war. As I looked at him I thought: *You should never have come here.*

No one saw them this time. Not the hawk-eyed Mueller. And not the hyper-cautious captain who swiveled his head so much scanning the sky, his muscles ached after each mission. And certainly not the boy pilot with just twenty-five flying hours to his credit who was too preoccupied with keeping his powerful aircraft level to watch for any threats.

At fifteen thousand feet, a squadron of Mustangs, an abundance of gasoline sloshing in their wing tanks, was stalking us. Patiently maneuvering into the perfect attack position at our six o'clock high with the sun at their backs.

I didn't see them jettison their tanks and wing over to scream down upon us. What first even alerted me to their presence was the familiar *POP! POP! POP!* of fifty-caliber rounds slamming into my fuselage. They hit Mueller at the same time.

"Jesus Christ!" shouted my stunned wingman. "Where in bloody hell did they come from?"

He and I immediately broke right and instinctively went full throttle to gain altitude. Our sudden leap skyward bled off our airspeed while putting us in a steep climb. This must have caught the Ami pilots by surprise, as they had built up so much momentum in their power dives that half of them blew right past us. Both of our planes had been hit, but neither seriously. Ironically the Mustang's blazing speed had been our savior in this case. They closed too fast to get in well-placed shots.

Four of the silver P-51s ripped past me, and I could make out their sleek lines with the conical snout propeller hubs and the black-and-white bands on the wings. Through the Mustang's Plexiglas teardrop canopy I saw one of the Amis eying me with frustration as he passed. Four more aircraft banked into the engagement as Mueller and I corkscrewed higher, and I realized that we'd have to use every trick in the book to get out of this scrape alive. Swiveling my head I spied yet two more climbing up after me. My adrenaline went into overdrive as I saw the white blinking on their wings, which meant they were firing their six heavy machine guns at me. But I made an elusive target as I pulled back hard on the stick and looped over towards the ground. Twisting and turning as I fell, I lost contact with Mueller as I threw my FW-190 across the sky. I looked back and now, briefly, my six was clear.

Then a cold shudder ran though me. "Josef!" I shouted above the din of my straining engine. "Where's Paul?"

Mueller's voice crackled through my headset. "I can't see him. But I see you. Four Indians on your tail. Break left. I'll get in behind them." Somehow, they were on me again!

"Shit!" I yelled, and slammed the stick hard left with full left rudder as well. It was everything I could do not to spin, but the rugged plane stayed true. Tracers zipped over my right wing. And then in my mirror I saw the Mustangs. They effortlessly followed me this time, making sure not to accelerate too fast. They were glued to me, firing away. Then I saw one burst into flames and drop like a stone. "Horrido!" shouted Mueller over the radio.

The other three scattered to get out from behind Mueller's guns. We'd been doing this long enough that no thanks were needed. My main concern was, where was Paul?

"Do you see him?" I asked again.

Mueller pulled up next to me and we banked up again to regain altitude. Several of the Mustangs actually passed between us, as we had them confused enough to be going down as we went up. They had reckoned on three easy marks before breakfast. They didn't expect two *Experten* to be among their prey. But that left a third who was indeed an easy kill. I had to get to my kid brother before the Americans.

Paul's voice suddenly burst through the airwaves, panic resonating in his high pitch. "Harmon! Where are you? They're coming after me!"

"I see him," reported Mueller. "Eight o'clock low."

I whipped my head down and to the left and kicked over into a dive. There he was, plummeting away in a vain dash for home while hugging the treetops at full throttle. I'd given him stern orders before takeoff that if we ran into any trouble he was to get to altitude or find a cloud and then head for home. And now with a gaggle of Mustangs in the area, his one plane couldn't have tipped the balance in our favor but rather hindered my wingman and me from taking proper evasive action.

He tried desperately to get escape the dogfight. He didn't make it. The Amis apparently tagged him as the least threatening of the three marks and purposefully concentrated on me and Mueller first, hoping to dispatch us in an ambush. But now all was chaos, and a lone enemy plunging away desperate to disengage was too tempting a target. With their powerful in-line Merlin engines, those Mustangs could fly over thirty miles per hour faster in level flight than Paul's Focke-Wulf.

And now Paul was doing the exact thing that I always cautioned my new pilots against. The very foolish maneuver that had gotten young Von Mauer shredded by P-47s last winter. He was acting on a primal instinct that said: gain airspeed. Go faster. Dive away and head home. Many a German pilot would end up a charred patch of earth as a result of this tactic.

"Paul, come around one hundred eighty degrees," I commanded him, trying to maintain my cool so as not rattle him further. "You won't get away like that."

But my brother, probably frozen in terror, didn't respond. I saw four Mustangs bearing down on the lone 190, which was still doing nothing but gunning full throttle for home. "Dammit, Pauli!" I now said with animation. "Pull up and come around. They're all over you!"

Realizing the trouble he was in, I called out to Mueller, whom I had left in the sky behind me.

"Josef, can you get to him?"

"I'm bailing out actually," said Mueller in a resigned voice.

"What?" I pulled up slightly to peer at the sky a half mile above my head and witnessed a disheartening sight. An FW-190 spinning towards the ground flaming from nose to tail. Mueller's lone parachute floated down gingerly as silver P-51s circled overhead like agitated sharks following a feeding frenzy.

In my zeal to save my brother, I'd left my wingman alone to face the Amis. But he'd stayed up there, risking his own hide to act as a decoy luring them away from our young apprentice.

I was frantic to get to Paul before it was too late. I gunned full throttle, risking overtaxing the BMW engine. There were bullet holes all over the fuselage, I could hear a cylinder rattling in an engine that could have seized at any moment, and I wasn't high enough to bail out safely. But the fighter ran smoothly, and I was making some progress. I leveled off at less than two hundred feet. The ground below me sped by in a blur of olives and browns. An invisible hand forced me back against my seat, and I groaned to fight the g-forces as my airspeed indicator hit four hundred miles per hour and the Mustangs in front of me grew larger in my windscreen. I was gaining on them. And more important, they didn't see me.

The trees whizzed underneath me now as I just cleared the highest branches. "Hang in there, little brother," I called out to him again. The familiar tone seemed to shake him out of his dread.

"Please hurry!" he begged.

"Listen to me," I instructed him calmly. "Slowly ease back on the stick. I'm almost there."

He did as I said and pulled up slightly. The relentless Mustangs edged up with him, which in turn closed the gap between them and their hidden Luftwaffe pursuer creeping up behind them. The one in the rear of the chase suddenly fell into the yellow circle of my gunsight, and I opened fire. The Focke-Wulf buffeted as my four-wing cannon pumped out explosive rounds while the machine guns directly in front of me flashed and rattled as they fired through the propeller arc right into my brother's tormentor. White flashes riddled the silver machine in my crosshairs and it instantly caught fire, broke apart, and spun into the trees.

"That's one!" I called to Paul.

"Hurry!" he pleaded again.

I flew through a large fireball as I continued to follow my brother's tormentors in this odd three-way chase. The Americans stayed focused, however, either oblivious to or unfazed by their squadron mate's death.

I quickly learned why. *POP! POP! POP!* Dammit! I looked up in my mirror to see three of them right up on my tail. Their intercooler intake slot under the red propeller nose gave the impression of demoniac grinning faces. As if they knew they had me. Now it was them chasing me chasing them chasing Paul. My plane began to shudder violently under the hammer blows of the heavy machine guns. Between the P-51s and the undulations in the hilly terrain, I had many a peril to contend with. But I tried to stay on Paul's hunters.

Then my heart sank. I saw puffs of smoke from the leading edges on the wings of the three Mustangs in front of me, which meant that they were all firing on my brother. The sparks on his unevenly ascending aircraft told me they were scoring hits too. Black smoke began to belch from Paul's engine and cockpit.

I dreaded what would come next over my headset.

"Oh God, Harmon!" he was screaming "I'm taking hits. I'm burning! I'm burning! It hurts!"

POP! POP! My stick grew sluggish, and I knew my plane could take no more pounding. "Pauli," I cried out. "Get up to altitude and bail out! Do you hear me?"

My fighter, though riddled with bullet holes by this point, still gave me good manifold pressure, but I had to face the diabolical mathematics of war. Paul was going down no matter what I did at this point. If I didn't take evasive action within seconds, then two black notes would be arriving for my parents, who were unaware of what was happening to their children at this very moment.

In an agony of frustration I fired a long burst towards Paul's pursuers in a forlorn attempt to spook them off. But they were still too far out of range and my spent rounds fell harmlessly behind them. The Amis must have been talking to each other, and I'm sure the planes to my rear told them that I was no threat at this point.

"Get the hell off him, you bastards!" I raged and pounded my fists against the glass, but my protests fell only upon my dying kid brother's ears.

"I'm sorry, Harmon," he coughed. More rounds slammed into the burning Focke-Wulf, and his screams filled my ears. Then I wrenched my stick to my groin with both hands and soared away from the ground. The force slammed me back against the seat as I made for a lone cloud that could shelter me until I figured out what next. Climbing hard up to get away from the fighters behind me, I looked back one last time and watched in anguish as Paul's bullet-riddled plane rolled over and spiraled towards the trees, a thick trail of dense smoke and flames behind it. "I'm so sorry," I heard Paul gasp one last time as his plane became an inferno.

"I'm sorry too," I said back, as the tears clouded my vision.

The radio went silent and Paul Becker, my only sibling, slammed into the trees of some nameless woodlot on the German border, and his plane burst into flames.

The Mustangs, fairly pleased with their work, immediately climbed to altitude. I still faced a flock of enemy fighters, and through my sobs I forced myself to concentrate. I disappeared into the cloud and used it to shield me. The Amis' blood was up, having shot down two of us in as many minutes, and they were on the prowl for more kills.

I used my instruments to navigate in the blinding fog. Turning a one eighty and leveling off, I burst out of the cloud where they least expected—exactly where I'd disappeared into it. They waited for me on the other side, circling in futility. I gave one last look back at the silver devils and gently opened as much throttle as I thought my crate could handle. I prayed that my limping machine, shot half to pieces but trailing no smoke, wouldn't break apart on me. Gently descending to one five hundred feet to blend into the terrain, I could clearly make out below Mueller's cream-colored parachute, flattened out on the green grass like a deflated balloon. I thought I saw him sitting down, probably in shock. I would send a recovery team to get him the moment I landed.

Four planes, two German, two American, were ablaze in the rolling fields, gouging deep black scars in the ground as testaments to the force of the impacts. Plumes of oily black smoke fingered up into the morning air.

I grew physically ill as I passed over the last crash site containing the almost unrecognizable remains of Paul's fighter. My little brother was in that mess. Half my parents' legacy erased, and with him all generations of Beckers from his line, forever more. His first combat mission, not even a real mission, had been his last. The Americans had made fast work of him as they had so many of the other novices. My dear brother was just the latest chapter in the lengthening tragedy that was the story of the Luftwaffe in 1944.

Finally out of danger, I felt my heartbeat begin to slow, and as the adrenaline rush faded I contemplated what had just happened. The deep heartache of the moment all came rushing at me like the trees just below my wings. The flood of pent-up emotions that the levies constructed by duty, honor, country, love of Fatherland, even belief in the Nazi cause had kept in check finally broke through and drowned me in overwhelming grief. As Paul's final moments burning alive as his plane hurtled towards the ground ran through my mind, I ripped off my mask and bawled aloud. But beneath my anguish, a resolve began to rise in me. In a moment of lucidity that often comes on the heels of trauma, I realized that I'd had enough of this war. I vowed to turn my back on a country that so willingly sent untrained boys like my brother before the guns of the Allies to be picked off like small game. I thought about Amelia. She'd been right all along about this New Order. She'd been right about me. Right about everything. And then I knew….

It was time to make a difference.

43

I touched down to find the base in a state of pandemonium. Upended aircraft smoldered on the dispersal field, their landing gear groping up into the air. Fires blazed in one of the hangars near the château, sending a river of smoke into the otherwise clear morning sky. Ground crews and other personnel raced back and forth, while fire control technicians operated hoses that fed from water trucks. Medical staff were loading wounded men, some unconscious, others covered in blood and writhing in pain, into ambulances and carting them off to Doctor Kraus' hall. The château itself was pockmarked with fresh bullet holes. Blood-spattered horse carcasses littered the circular drive that looped in front of the main entrance to the *Kasino*.

My wounded fighter bounced along the runway and slowly came to a standstill near my still intact hangar, the spinning propeller swishing to a stop. When I slid open the canopy, I was overwhelmed by the din of men barking at one another in confusion and the choking smoke and smell of cooking metal and burning wood and gasoline. Few even noticed me, so frenzied was the scene. I could guess what had happened but called out to Ohler, who was trotting up to me.

"What happened here, Sergeant?"

"Captain!" he cried. "Thank God you're okay." I leapt down from the wing and leaned against the shot-up fuselage. "You just missed them. Mustangs came down on us. They shot us up pretty bad."

"I didn't miss them," I said grimly.

Ohler looked the plane over again. Bullet holes covered it like a mass of freckles. "No, I guess not. This crate should have broken apart."

I looked around for the rest of the squadron. There were no aircraft other than those destroyed by strafing.

"Where is everyone?"

Cooking ammunition inside the hangar suddenly exploded in an ear-splitting blast, and we both ducked. An angry fireball curled up into the sky. Some of the firefighters were knocked off their feet but looked okay. They stood back up and resumed spraying the inferno to keep the flames from spreading beyond the obliterated structure.

"The survivors took off after them," he told me as we rose to stand upright again.

"Did we lose any people on the ground?"

He pointed to an upended 190 sprawled on its back, engulfed in flames just beyond the lip of the runway. Its landing gear was still extended as if caught on takeoff. It crackled and hissed like a broiling roast. Only one of its charred wings with the black cross still defiantly visible on its surface was recognizable. Occasionally overheated rounds from its guns would pop like firecrackers.

"Lieutenant Stahl, sir," Ohler said quietly.

I nodded. I'd grieved all I could today.

"Where are the other two?" asked my crew chief.

I removed my flying cap and gloves and handed them to him. "Lieutenant Mueller bailed out somewhere in sector R-N. See to it that Thomson sends a party for him."

Ohler shook his head. "I'm afraid Lieutenant Thomson's dead, sir. Caught out in the open when they dove in on us."

"Oh," I said. I felt nothing by this point. "Well, whoever then."

I started towards Seebeck's hut, which was still intact but for a few superficial bullet holes. "Herr Captain," called out Ohler. "Where's Sergeant Becker?" I turned to face him. His voice trailed off when he saw my eyes. "I'm sorry."

It pained me too much to speak of my brother. "See to it that someone gets Mueller. He bailed out but he may be wounded."

"Are you okay, sir?" Ohler said.

I just turned and walked away. I didn't want him to see me cry.

Through the haze of my tears, even as chaos reigned outside, I saw my trembling hands perform a ritual that up to now I'd only observed from a distance in the past. In a way, I still felt as if I were a spectator watching a stranger performing this ghoulish ritual. An image. His wide eyes and goofy, if naive, grin. A young sergeant in his fresh Luftwaffe uniform, so blissfully unaware that burning to death while spiraling helplessly to the ground awaited him in a fortnight.

"Goodbye, Pauli," I muttered as my whole body weight shoved the tack holding his photo through the wall, plastered with so many images of the slain before him. At that point I broke down and fell to my knees, no longer giving a damn who saw me.

I soon composed myself and stepped out of the *Kasino* and into the open, where the chaotic scene of our demolished airbase was still playing itself out.

I ran into Seebeck as he was strutting aimlessly in front of his quarters, hobbling along on his cane, unable to grasp all that had just happened to his shattered command. The war, which he thought he'd left behind along with his eye, had returned to find him. His face was ashen. But I felt no pity for this man, for he'd come to represent all that I despised about the war. Men were fighting and dying for the "New Germany." Yet, though some of the players had changed, my country was still governed by the same old rules of hierarchy and privilege and old money. An unholy alliance between monocled Prussian generals, fat *Burgermeisters*, and wealthy barons desperate to hold on to the past on one side…and Nazi gangsters determined to erase it while growing rich through mass murder and plunder on the other. And in between stood the businessmen and profiteers like the Keitels, as grease in the machine, willfully ignoring the savagery of Hitler's assault against the world, so long as the lucrative orders from the front for bullets and ball bearings and grenades and helmets and uniforms and pots and pans rolled in. Major Hans

Seebeck was to me like that band of delusional henchmen I'd seen high on the mountaintop at the Berghof. Detached, aloof, ready to believe anything the Führer said, regardless of what that map told him. I blamed my group commander for obsequiously genuflecting before Berlin, and fielding pilots completely ill-prepared for what they faced, only to be sacrificed on the altar of the Third Reich.

But for me it was a personal animosity as well. I had enough of his petty jealousy and his threats while brave men died before my eyes. And I saw in him the personification of what killed my brother: arrogance, delusion, a fanatical belief in a state that followed a madman to its destruction. In my mind the Americans did not kill Paul Becker. The Nazis did. And one of my least favorite Nazis of all stood ten feet in front of me.

"You!" I shouted aiming an accusatory finger in his direction like a gun. "Do you still say that there are no Allied fighters out here? Do you still believe your puppeteers' bullshit? Did you ever?"

Seebeck stood straight, shocked at my tone. "Obviously there are American fighters, Becker."

I stepped to within an arm's length of him. "Do you know that my brother is dead! You killed him, you son of a bitch!"

He smirked. "*I* killed him?" Even amidst all the mayhem, he could still find it within himself to act smug.

"You and all your Nazi thugs who send boys up to fight your war."

Men dropped what they were doing to gawk at this curious scene. This was the Wehrmacht. It wasn't too often that a captain shook his finger in the face of a major. There I was, sweat-stained and haggard in my flight suit, confronting a perfectly groomed major in his blue-gray uniform, visor cap, and shined boots.

"That's quite enough, Captain Becker!"

I gritted my teeth. "I'm only beginning."

Seebeck grew uncomfortable at his authority being challenged so blatantly in front of the men. Especially by an officer so established on his airbase.

"You will hold your tongue!" he commanded with less inflection than he'd aimed for. Though the fires still raged, and screaming wounded were still being carted away, several corporals dropped what they were doing to observe our little theater. One of them was sitting in the driver's seat of an open *Kübelwagen*, temporarily distracted from the turmoil all around him.

"I will not!" I said. "You've had your last free ride to glory on my coattails. On the blood of my men."

"Your men?" he said, repeating an old line.

"Yes. My men!" I shot back. "I'm the one who takes them into battle while you sit back here twirling your cane and writing reports and speechifying on the glory of the Third Reich. Look around you, Major. *This* is your Reich!"

Your Reich. Not mine. Amelia had tried to warn me that day we sat together on the edge of the Main. She feared for the future…and the future had arrived with a vengeance.

Seebeck cocked his head. Suddenly there was silence between us. Only the ambient noise of the shattered base trying to recover. The onlookers waited to hear what their group commander would say next.

"Well, Captain," he said. "Perhaps next time you'll not be so careless in taking one of your new fliers into the teeth of Allied fighters on his first flight then, eh? So clever you were sending him here. Who do you think you are, Saint Horridus? A lot of good you did him by bringing him under your wing. I'm sure your parents will be grateful."

The corporals gasped. And I just stood dumbfounded. Seebeck seemed pleased with that and he smirked. Amidst all the bedlam and destruction, despite the fact that his out-gunned and out-trained squadron was off chasing after Mustangs minus two of its most experienced pilots, what mattered most to him was putting me in my place.

I stepped towards him until our noses practically touched, and looked with darkness into his good eye. "You'd better be very careful what you say next…*Herr Major.*"

"Becker," he stammered while taking a step back. "You're relieved of your command. I'm placing you under arrest."

I didn't really care anymore. "Very well," I said. "You can find me at home." I turned my back on him and approached the stunned corporal in the *Kübelwagen*.

"Step away," I barked. The startled enlisted man obeyed immediately, and I slid into the driver's seat.

The major's eye widened. "Becker, don't you dare!"

I ignored him and started the engine. Seebeck shouted: "Stop that man!"

I didn't even look back. I threw the car into gear and sped off in the direction of sector R-N, leaving nothing but a cloud of dust and defiance in my wake.

Before anyone could really process what just happened, I left the grounds of the wrecked aerodrome behind me. After a few twists and turns on the country lane heading east away from the château grounds, it was as if the base no longer existed. Only the high columns of smoke rising from beyond the trees into the sky and the soft thud of distant secondary explosions offered even the slightest hint of the violence just visited upon Andeville.

As far as I was concerned, my war was over. All I wanted was to get my little brother, what was left of him, and bring him back home for a proper burial. It would have broken my parents' hearts to know their son's final resting place was a charred metal hulk imbedded in a field of the country he'd loved so much and died for, because in the end it cared so little for him.

The dumbfounded corporal I'd left standing in the dust of his commandeered *Kübelwagen* looked over to his furious commandant. "Shall I call the Feldgendarmerie, sir?"

Seebeck shook his head no. He wanted to leave the military police out of this. "I'll take care of it." He limped into his office and closed the door, smothering the din of the devastated airbase behind him. He needed to make a phone call.

44

It took me two hours to find the crash site. Bouncing along dirt lanes, my flight suit soaked with sweat from the midday sun drilling down on me, I homed in on the last wisps of smoke floating just above the crest of a grassy ridge. The ground undulated like waves on the ocean, and I marveled that I'd been able to fly so close to it without slamming into the side of one of these deceptively high ridges.

My heart tightened as I pulled up to the mangled wreckage. The fire had all but spent itself. Not much of the broiled FW-190 was recognizable beyond a bent wing root, the twisted propeller, and the tail plane with the swastika on its gray-green surface as if to taunt me.

I stopped the car about thirty yards from the blackened mess of twisted steel and aluminum. I cringed as I slowly approached the plane, afraid I wouldn't be able to bear the site of my brother's charred remains. I expected to find what I can only describe from past experience as a charcoal briquette suggestion, with any true resemblance of the person seared away to reveal nothing but a humanoid form in ash. It was a queer relief then when I found Paul's body, not strapped and broiled black in his cockpit, but lying in the grass some fifty paces away. He'd been thrown clear of the wreckage from the force of impact.

Still, his body was contorted in an unnatural pose, twisted like a discarded rag doll as he'd smashed into the ground. With a churning stomach, I walked up to him and gazed down. I'd seen dead men before. But he wasn't a faceless combatant. Nor was he even a passing comrade-in-arms whose image would adorn the wall of honor in the *Kasino* and fade in time to be just another on the list. He was my baby brother. His lifeless, half-closed eyes stared sightlessly at the blue sky from whence he'd come hurtling down. Dried blood was smeared across his face like brick-red clay. His flight suit was soaked in fluid from the fire extinguisher he'd frantically sprayed in a futile attempt to snuff the flames gnawing through his blackened legs…the only real desecration of his otherwise well-preserved form.

I knelt down in the grass and laid my hand over his face. Even then I thought he might only be wounded. It's funny how you cling to hope when there is none. My brother was dead. I gently closed his eyes and tried to wipe the blood from his young face, but it had hardened. Then I removed his flying cap. With his tufts of dark brown hair, matted and still parted on the side as if ready for church, all semblance of a warrior drained away from him. He was just a boy.

"Come on, Pauli," I said softly, as if he were merely resting. "Let's take you home."

I scooped up his body, limp as a blanket roll, and hoisted him in my arms. With a huff, I carried him back to the *Kübelwagen*. I tried to lay him gingerly in the back seat, but I lost my grip and he fell into it with a sickening thud, his blackened legs dangling over the door as if he were a drunkard. I cursed my clumsiness for inflicting such ignominy on him. It didn't dawn on me that I hadn't eaten anything but a roll and a cup of black coffee before taking off this morning and was probably weaker than usual. I heaved his damaged legs into the car and rearranged his body until he lay curled up on his side. Looking him over, I was struck by how peaceful he appeared. But for the caked blood on his face, it was as if he'd merely crawled into the back seat to steal a quick nap. I wondered if death was like sleep. And then I pondered why I'd been so fortunate to never learn the answer for myself, considering that for three years I'd been in the midst of a most dangerous enterprise. Perhaps I was meant to live? But then that would mean that Paul was meant to die. I couldn't accept that. I hoped that all things would reveal themselves in good time.

But what mattered most to me now wasn't pondering the questions of life and death but rather getting out of this place before patrols came.

Still, I granted myself enough time to do a quick search for Mueller, who'd gone down nearby. I drove in widening circles around the area for about fifteen minutes before coming upon another crash site in a patch of woods. In the underbrush were scattered the silver pieces of the Mustang I'd shot down. The fuselage that housed the cockpit and pilot, the engine, and the red propeller hub were intact. Below the cockpit were three little black crosses denoting kills. Painted over the engine mount in black script was the sobriquet "*BAD ASS II*." The pieces of the striped wings and tail were spread about in the thickets and branches above. The pilot, a young man with red hair sticking out from his cap, was still strapped in his seat, head slumped with his chin on his chest, mouth agape. As with the Yank prisoner, I was struck by how much like us he looked.

Back out in the open I came upon Mueller's parachute lying in a tussled heap on the ground. The harness straps had been unhooked, and my friend was nowhere to be seen, which was as a good sign. I feared coming across him either having died from wounds suffered in the fight or badly broken in an agony of pain and thirst. There was a dairy farm about a quarter mile from where I was, so I assumed they had come to help him. Satisfied that he was at least not dead, I knew that I couldn't afford to tarry any longer.

I calculated that I had roughly two hundred miles from this sector to Stauffenberg. That would be a long drive to make with Allied fighter-bombers patrolling the clear skies. I would stick to the wooded routes I knew, trying to conceal my movements until I found a good spot to hide and wait for darkness to fall. I would make the long drive through the night. Out in the open as I was, I made an inviting target for prowling *Jabos*. They were hunting us now. All over Germany. But it was not the Allies that I feared most at the moment. It was the Germans.

I knew that I'd be branded a deserter by Seebeck. And in a moment of blind folly, I had told him exactly where I was going. Yet I had no choice but to proceed, taking care to avoid population centers like Frankfurt and Mannheim. Paul needed to go home. My family had a burial plot under a tree on Cemetery Hill just north of town looking down on a bend in the Main. My brother deserved to rest there.

As I pulled away from the debris field, I gave myself short odds of even making it to Stauffenberg. I figured there were soldiers after me by now. And even if I got through, surely Seebeck would have people waiting to arrest me. What I didn't know was that the Allies had already handed me my first break. It would not be the last.

First Lieutenant Josef Mueller stood stiffly at attention before Major Seebeck's desk. The group commander sat behind it, furiously puffing away on a cigarette, lost in his own thoughts. Deep lines ran down his face from the stress of the day. Five of his pilots hadn't returned from their wild hunt for the American marauders who had so audaciously shot up his base. They recorded one kill for their efforts. He was now trying to oversee the movement of the entire aerodrome into the cover of nearby woods. No longer would the base be on the pleasant manicured grounds of a fine château with a strong concrete runway and sturdy metal hangars. Rather it would be a series of tents pitched around aircraft hidden in wooded thickets with nothing but an open pasture as their landing strip. It was an ignominious admission of the tide of battle turning against his beloved Fatherland.

And now his best pilot, Captain Harmon Becker, had deserted—off on a personal quest to take his idiot brother home. It was a stain on the command structure and a personal affront. He would not escape punishment this time. Becker's days were numbered.

What was it about Becker? Seebeck thought to himself, contemplating his cigarette while Mueller looked on. Why did Becker so actively try to thwart him? He overshadowed his commander with his Knight's Cross. And while Seebeck languished on the ground nursing his wounds, he won the loyalty of the men and the accolades of the nation. That the men should usurp the major's authority and see Becker as their real leader was a slap in the face. And, most unfair of all, the man simply refused to die and get out of the way.

Well, thought the major, this is where it ends. Now, he is a deserter. And who knows what else? A traitor perhaps? That psychotic SS man from the Oberfranken who called from time to time to check up on his movements thought it very likely. What was his name? Geiger? Keitel? *Keitel.* A man who claimed to hate Becker more than the major and was just waiting for the right moment to bag him. Becker could choke on his Knight's Cross while he hanged, for all Keitel cared. And rumor had it in Berlin that this SS fellow had an uncanny nose for disloyalty. The moment he got word to Keitel, he knew the SS officer would find out once and for all.

Seebeck ripped himself from his seething revenge fantasy to stare up at the grimy, but otherwise intact, first lieutenant. "You sent for me, Herr Major?"

"Ah yes, First Lieutenant Mueller. I'm glad you're unhurt."

Mueller nodded. "Thank you, Herr Major."

"We were worried when only your wingman returned." He tried to gauge Mueller's emotions. "Rather cowardly to leave you out there alone, no?"

Mueller stiffened. "He was trying to protect Sergeant Becker, sir. I could handle myself."

Seebeck tilted his head and smiled. "Apparently not. Otherwise you would not have returned to us on the back of an ox cart. Becker, however, did make it back safe."

"I'm glad, Herr Major."

"Yes." Seebeck jammed his cigarette butt into his full ashtray. "Well, we have a problem now."

"What's that, sir?"

"Your wingman deserted."

Mueller frowned. "Beg your pardon?"

Seebeck was gratified to finally get a reaction out of Becker's lackey. "You heard me, Mueller. Captain Becker disobeyed my direct order and left the base. He is now a deserter. And not for the first time. As I'm sure you are well aware."

The first lieutenant stiffened. "Herr Major," he said. "As I understand it, he left here to find his brother. Surely you can understand that."

Seebeck angrily ground the cigarette to a nub. "I understand that he abandoned his unit while we were under attack. Anyway, it will soon be out of my hands."

Mueller raised his eyebrows. He didn't like the sound of that. "Sir?"

Seebeck leaned back in his chair and pointed his cane at the young pilot.

"What I mean, First Lieutenant, is that it's time this group accepts once and for all who commands here. Starting with you."

Mueller remained silent as Seebeck continued.

"I happen to know he's on his way to Stauffenberg if he finds that dead brother of his. A rather macabre thought actually. Anyway, the phone lines are down due to these damned Allied raids, so I cannot directly contact a certain SS major there."

Mueller leaned forward and placed his fists on the desk, a chill running through him. "SS!" he said, mystified. "Sir, you can't do that!"

"Stand at attention, you!" Seebeck shouted, and whacked his cane with a smack on the desk. Mueller backed off and smacked his heels, going rigid.

"I beg the major's pardon." He composed himself. "But this should be a Luftwaffe matter, don't you think, sir? If I may, I don't believe it's right for you to turn him over to the SS for this."

Seebeck just sat there, looking up at Becker's wingman with haughty contempt.

"I am not going to turn him in to the SS," Seebeck said quietly.

Mueller, though confused, breathed a sigh of relief. Even if Harmon had technically deserted, his record and the circumstances involved would get a sympathetic ear from the Luftwaffe high command, including Göring himself, who by all accounts had taken a liking to him at the Berghof. Maybe the major was even bluffing.

But then Seebeck dropped the bomb: "I'm not going to turn him in to the SS, because you are."

45

The same sun that shined down upon my brother's mangled corpse also cast a warm glow over Amelia Engel as she strolled along the Leiselstrasse. It'd been days since she left the house, and she was starting to feel like a pent-up animal. How the Krupinskis could live so confined for as many years was beyond her. But, she reminded herself, she wouldn't be sent to the camps if she ventured outside. That was a powerful incentive to endure the unendurable.

She turned onto the cobblestone street that ran past her house and saw him. The lithe, ghostly figure of Keitel in his trimmed gray uniform, unaffected by the sweltering heat. She paused, hoping she could slip back around the corner before he saw her, but it was too late. He pivoted his gleaming boots, as if able to sense her presence, and caught her eye.

A broad, emotionless smile spread across his pale face. She resumed walking towards her house, and as much as she wished to turn her nose up at him, that would be unwise considering who resided with her.

"Fräulein Amelia," he said formally, bowing and raising his gloved hand to the tip of his visor.

She stopped by her door. "Johann, what a surprise."

He let her pass. "I hope it's a pleasant one."

"I've no interest in holding grudges," she said. "Especially on such a beautiful day."

He made an exaggerated motion to gaze up at the attic window on the third floor. Amelia followed his line of sight with unease. "A little hot for my liking. It would be terrible to be cooped up inside all day." He lowered his eyes back to Amelia. "Russia was much colder."

Amelia smiled nervously. Why was he looking up at the attic? Her mind raced. Yet she knew she had to appear relaxed. "Yes, I heard it was freezing. So what brings you to my house? Just to talk about the weather?"

He put his arm on her shoulder, and her carefree facade cracked. Her stomach churned and her legs shook. "Are you feeling okay?" he asked with a probing stare. "I hope even my touch is not repulsive to you now. You never used to object. It's a shame we never even kissed. Becker, I suppose, has experienced all your charms."

Amelia ignored the provocation. She had to. He'd never come so close to the house before. So near to where she was hiding her death sentence.

She smiled softly. "I do still feel a fondness for you, Johann," she lied. "You always treated me well." He seemed unsure what to say to that. He'd expected her to be more combative with him.

"Well, I was just passing by," he said. Then he caught himself. He was here for a reason. "But…may I come in?"

"No," she said a little sharper than she'd have liked. He raised his brow. *Interesting*, he thought. "I mean, Mother's resting. Otherwise I'd gladly invite you in for some tea."

Keitel feigned a look of concern. "Still bedridden is she?"

"Yes, I'm afraid so."

"Poor Hanna. I assume while you're out, you have someone to look after her then?"

Amelia forced a smile. "You obviously don't remember Mother. She would never let anyone but me care for her. And I was only gone for a short while. As I am sure your soldiers will tell you tonight."

He chuckled and gave her a knowing smirk. "We keep track of everyone."

"Of course." She adjusted her grip on the parcels.

"You know," he said, still feigning concern "I'd be happy to send some of my men over to assist you with errands." She didn't like where this was headed, so tried to end the conversation without being overly curt.

"Thank you. That's sweet. But, as I said, Mother's very private. And stubborn." She made a move to pass him, but he kept his gloved hand on her shoulder.

He wasn't finished. "It must be difficult for her to go up and down the stairs to her bedroom each day. I could at least help you with that."

Amelia chortled nervously, uncomfortable with his touch. "Mother's bed is on the first floor now. In the sewing room. She can barely walk, let alone climb stairs."

"I see." Keitel glanced up at the attic window. His mind was moving, trying to piece it together. Then he released her from his grip and stepped out of her way.

"Oh well. Just a thought. Good day to you, Amelia."

"And to you. Thank you for your concern, Johann."

The SS officer bowed. "I'm just doing my job." And with that he turned away.

When she entered the house Amelia had to steady herself against the door. She was shaking so violently she dropped the parcels to the floor. Then she wept.

46

So without my realizing it, the Allied bombers cutting the phone lines had made it possible for me to pull into Stauffenberg at 3:00 a.m. unannounced. The drive had been difficult with my being forced to take a serpentine route along as many back roads as possible. The *Kübelwagen* bounced over pockmarked dirt lanes, and the heat was oppressive. My brother's body lay in the back seat, and as much as I hated thinking about it, I knew that he would soon start to emit a vile odor. Already his face was hardening into a swollen mask.

I briefly pulled the vehicle off to the side of a road that bordered a shallow creek bed. I searched the trunk for a canteen filled with vodka or schnapps that I knew some drivers liked to keep handy should the mood strike them. Unfortunately the corporal who had surrendered the auto was all business. I didn't want the spirits, just the container. I would have emptied any canteen and filled it with the clear creek water for later. My mouth was beyond dry from the heat and the stress of this terrible day. Plus I was dehydrating from sweating in the *Kübelwagen*, which was so warm—even though it was a convertible, with Paul in back I obviously had to drive with the canvas top up. I knelt down on the edge of the brook and greedily slurped up the refreshing water, and splashed my face and neck to wash away a layer of salt and grime. Then I took an oily rag I found in the back, rinsed it, rung it out, and submerged it in the running water until it was fully saturated. I used the dripping cloth to wipe the caked blood off Paul's face. I didn't want my parents to see him like that.

I steered clear of scattered columns of *Landsers* I encountered, and passed through villages quickly, leaving nothing but dust clouds in my wake. All around me evidence of Allied air power was visible. Demolished houses and barns, cars overturned in ditches along the side of a road, their drivers lying spread-eagle and swollen to grotesque proportions as they rotted in the June sun. On several occasions I had to make a quick turn into a patch of woods as I heard the distinctive low growling of marauding American Thunderbolts. But luck stayed with me. I came upon an abandoned fuel truck that had been shot up but miraculously failed to explode. The main drum was empty, but the vehicle's own tank was full and thus I could siphon it off to the *Kübelwagen*. I even managed to fill a replacement can, which gave me ample fuel to make the drive.

Once night fell I headed east by southeast down the autobahn, making for the Oberfranken and home. Under the gift of a new moon shrouding me in blackness, I motored though the countryside of my youth. Rolling pastoral folds and pleasant hillside vineyards gradually rose into more imposing escarpments and then into the steep foothills of the Bavarian Alps to the southeast. In the dead of night I crossed the Main Bridge and passed under the Rathaus tower and into the Himmelplatz. I was near collapse from exhaustion, and I fully expected the SS to be waiting for me. But the town was unnervingly quiet. Only a lone dog, a low-slung shadow, shuffled around in the darkness before raising its mangy leg to piss on the fountain stones.

I needed to think. Now that I was here, what next? I'd made up my mind to first find Amelia before seeking out my parents. She was close with the local priest, Father Anton, who could coordinate Paul's clandestine burial. Then I would have the horrible duty of informing Mother and Father that their baby boy was dead. That I'd failed to protect him.

I tapped softly on the door until a light appeared upstairs through the drawn-back curtain. I recognized her shapely silhouette. She was in the process of tying her robe at her waist when she peered out the window. I can't imagine her primal fear at hearing a knock in the middle of the night. I was the last person she expected to see. And in Germany in 1944, an unexpected knock on the door often spelled one's doom. But there was no other way.

When her eyes adjusted, she saw me standing by the door and her body sagged with visible relief. I motioned for her to be quiet while looking around. She'd just started making her way downstairs when the door suddenly swung open.

It wasn't Amelia but rather Hanna who heaved open the wooden door with extreme effort and stood there, diminutive and frail, with her white hair hanging loosely about her shoulders like that of a character in Greek mythology. Even though it was June and the night was still warm, she wore a shawl draped over her sloped shoulders. Her eyes, a haunting shade like her daughter's, pierced through even the moonless night. Sick as she was, she seemed determined to lay into whoever dared disturb her household at such an ungodly hour. "I swear I'll have your head for this, if this isn't the most important…." She stopped cold. "Harmon! My dear boy, what are you doing here?"

I gave her a kiss on the cheek and stepped inside briskly. Amelia stood at the bottom of the steps looking anxious. She went to her mother and supported her on her arm. She didn't need to be told that my presence here meant I was in serious trouble. My dust-caked appearance offered nothing to quell her fears. "You're wearing a flight suit," Hanna observed. "And you're filthy."

"I'll explain. But first…." I glanced up at the ceiling and then to Amelia.

She nodded. "They're still safe."

"For now," I said. "We need to talk."

Seated at the heavy wooden dining room table, it took me just five minutes to give the Engel women the abbreviated version of Paul's death. Besides wearing a heartfelt expression of condolence, Hanna sat stoically as she tried to imagine what this all meant for my future and therefore her daughter's. Amelia, for her part, openly wept. The war seemed to be creeping ever closer. Now those she truly cared about were starting to die. I was over the shock of what had happened. But another profound sadness washed over me as I asked aloud: "How am I going to tell Mother?"

"We can both tell her," said Amelia, reaching across the table.

I took her hand but dismissed her suggestion. What I needed her to do now was get to the rectory and arrange with Father Anton a *very* private burial at the cemetery just outside of town in our family plot before daybreak. I couldn't be seen in the streets, as I was a deserter and faced arrest. Amelia agreed without hesitation.

After putting a distraught and near faint Hanna back to bed and then getting dressed, Amelia followed me to the rear of the house, where a solid wooden door led to a small gravel courtyard and a vegetable patch behind it. I'd parked the *Kübelwagen* back there to keep it out of sight.

"Where is he?" she asked with a shaky voice as we approached the car. Paul's body lay crumpled in the back. Amelia peered inside and gave out a tiny shriek before catching herself. "Oh! Just look at him!" she cried. "Oh poor dear Pauli! I'm so very sorry!"

But there was no time. I needed to get to my parents' house to give them the devastating news. Then I needed to go to the church on the edge of town and wait. Amelia would take the car and my brother to the priest right now. Darkness was our only defense, for it would have been an odd sight to see her driving a vehicle with military markings, even if no one noticed a dead *Jagdflieger* in the back seat. I remembered her letter. I knew the SS were watching her. I just prayed not all the time. I desperately needed my luck, as it were, to hold.

Amelia, a faithful member of the parish, had worked with the old monsignor, Father Anton, to raise money to re-shingle the rectory. Now she would call in a favor.

We parted ways. Amelia started the engine and pulled the vehicle onto the blacked-out street and drove off. I stood like a specter in the shadows of her vegetable garden and listened. The engine faded, but there was no other sound. No one seemed to be awake at this hour. And if so, it was just an auto making its way through the streets early to avoid pedestrian traffic…and bombs. Satisfied that she was safe, I snaked my silent way down the narrow side streets to my home.

It was my father who opened the door. Gruff, in his trousers and suspenders, his shirt wrinkled and with dark circles under his eyes. A half-finished snifter of schnapps sat on the end table in the parlor by the dormant fireplace where we'd last talked so freely about the war. He'd fallen asleep in his favorite chair while listening to a phonograph of Grieg that spun and hissed on the turntable. Seeing him made me wonder what was worse in a time of war—being in the fighting yourself or having someone you love do it while you sit home, helpless and in the dark as to their fate. Your stomach sinking every time there's a knock at the door. Afraid to receive any notice from the post, as it could be a black note. But now his days of wondering about his sons were at an end. When he saw me at the threshold in my flight suit, he knew immediately.

"Papa," I stammered and stepped into the house. He closed the door and followed me inside.

When I turned to face him, he bowed his head and exhaled with a pained expression in his eyes. "When?" he asked me. I was unable to even speak. "When?!" he asked again, more forcefully.

"Yesterday morning," I said in a voice I did not recognize.

His face fell and his eyes glazed with tears. Reeling into the parlor, he collapsed back in his chair and buried his face in his hands. I saw his body quaking. So many memories must have flashed through him in an instant. Paul's birth, his first words, his first steps. The first time he kicked a football. The way my father would watch the two of us squeal with delight as we wrestled on the grass during family picnics. Those crisp autumn Sundays when we all strolled as a family to church. Snowmen and sleigh rides. Those wonderful, secure moments when we all sat huddled around the fireplace in the deepest Bavarian winters with the winds whistling through the narrow streets outside our door. We were happy then. And my father had just learned he would never preside over that happy family again. So many memories, yet no more to be made. The book on his second son was abruptly closed, with so many pages that would forever go unwritten.

He was positively weighed down with the intense grief. "How?"

"American fighters," I said, kneeling down in front of him as if in a pose of contrition. "Oh Papa, I tried! I tried but there was no way. There were just too many. We even got two of them. But there were just so many of them!"

His took me in his arms and gave me a bear hug, patting me on the back as he would when I was a boy. "I know, Son," he whispered. "I know."

He then eased me back with his hands on my shoulders and gave me a forgiving nod. "You didn't kill him. I think we both know who killed him."

I nodded, fully understanding his objections to all that was happening for the first time since the Nazis had come to power just ten short years ago. I gave him the details on how I had recovered his son's body and brought him here so he and Mama could say goodbye. At dawn, I told him, if all went as Amelia thought, Paul should be with Father Anton and Gregor and we'd have his burial.

"Such an early service?" he asked, confused. "Why so hasty? We need time for a proper viewing. People will want to pay their resp—"

"I left my base against orders," I said, cutting him off. I told him of my confrontation with Major Seebeck. His face showed concern. "I'll be okay," I assured him with a lie. He remained unconvinced. "I just need to figure out what to do next. I have friends in the Luftwaffe. My squadron. Major Trautloft. Maybe even Göring himself. My record speaks volumes. Knight's Cross. Over one hundred victories. And I left because of…Pauli. I'm too valuable to lose with the way the war's going. But I can't stay in Stauffenberg. I have to leave right after the service."

He swallowed hard. "I understand. Thank you for bringing him home, Harmon. That was the right thing to do. Orders be damned at this point. And yet why do I feel like there's more to this?" he questioned me with a knowing gaze. Karl Becker may have been the smartest man I ever knew.

I debated revealing the truth I knew of Stauffenberg's last Jews, but I decided there was no reason to put him in danger. He was a good man, but not a crusader. So I told him my tale only.

He seemed okay with that. Then he cast a sad look to the ceiling. There was a shuffling of feet. Soft, feminine. A falsetto voice drifted down the narrow staircase.

"Karl?" I heard a voice. "Who are you talking to?"

How does one tell a mother that her youngest son is dead?

My mother fell to the dusty wood floor when told the news by us both. "No! No! It cannot be true!" she protested, bordering on hysterics. "Please, God no! Oh please…my baby…" Then she curled up in a pathetic fetal position with her face buried in her fists. "Why? Why?" she kept asking no one in particular. My father knelt down and tried to hoist her up, but she shook him off. "*Schatz!*" he whispered to her, calling her by a pet name I hadn't heard him say in years. "Get up off that floor! You must be strong."

She looked up from her fists. "Damn you and your strength! My son is dead! How am I supposed to be strong?" She slammed her forehead with her palms. I stepped forward, fearing that she'd gone temporarily insane with grief.

My father comforted her by sharing her pain. "He was my son too," he said. With that she regained her self-control. This was not her burden alone. She held out her trembling hand, and he took it in his iron grip. With a tenderness I'd never seen before in a man so stolid, Karl Becker pulled his wife off the floor and smothered her in his arms. They held each other while I lingered like a voyeur. Even in such an agonizing moment as this, I saw the strength in the bond that had sustained their marriage for so many years, from the end of one war, through the turbulent times of a country reinventing itself in a more sinister form, to the horrors of sending their children off to fight the world. If I survived, I vowed to have such a marriage with Amelia. If I even made it out of

Stauffenberg, that was. And that thought quickly snapped me back to another unpleasant reality.

I gave them a few more minutes to comfort each other. But the purple light creeping through the front window told me we had to move. I could only hope Amelia had made the arrangements.

I heard the *Kübelwagen* pull up to the curb outside, its brakes making a deafening squeal that I thought for sure would wake up the entire Main valley. But it was fear heightening my senses. Amelia stayed outside in the idling vehicle.

"We must go," I said.

"To where?" sobbed my mother, confused.

"I'll explain on the way," said Papa.

I gave them a moment to get dressed. I felt so cruel doing this to them, but if they wanted their son buried properly before I was arrested, this was the only way. War is cruel. In my insubordinate state, my only hope was to get back to base before Seebeck sent the Luftwaffe authorities to find me here. What I didn't know was that Seebeck had something much more dangerous in mind for me.

47

Father Anton Hackl was a lanky, leathery man, nearing his eightieth year. He stood atop a lone hill with a crisp mountain breeze blowing his priest's robe like a luffing mainsail, scattering his few strands of white hair. From his perch he could trace a small path winding its way through the cemetery headstones and out a stone archway. The road disappeared over the crest of the hill and then re-appeared a half mile farther down as a gravel lane tracing the curves of the Main until it entered Stauffenberg. From up here the village appeared in the orange light of dawn as a collection of terra cotta and white rectangles, dominated on the far end by the towering Rathaus. As the sleepy village began to stir, little figures, early risers, moved in the stony square of the Himmelplatz, which from this distance looked small enough to fit in the palm of my hand. To our backs opposite the town, the hills undulated in waves of blue until they disappeared in the mist, only to pop up again far to the south and west as jagged, snow-capped peaks. It promised to be a beautiful summer day like those I had known so many times as a child of these hills.

Gathered around Father Anton stood an allegory of despair. Four weathered sheep come to mourn the youngest member of their flock. Dressed in black and standing over the fresh grave of their son, Karl and Greta Becker had aged ten years in one morning. Still in my grimy flight suit and boots, I stood next to them, not even registering the words of the priest as he rambled on about God and country and the better place in which my brother now resided. Amelia stood at my side, her hand cupped in my forearm, and openly wept. Gregor, the priest's giant, neckless mountain of a nephew, too mentally feeble to serve in the Wehrmacht, had dug the grave in an incredibly short time. He stood with his hat reverently over his sweaty and dirt-stained shirt, his head bowed deep in prayer.

"Harmon?" I heard in the fog far away. "Harmon, my son, you're next." *What? I'm next for what?* I snapped my head up and bore my eyes straight into the soft brown of Father Anton's, hidden behind folds of crinkled skin. He offered me a flower to lay on Paul's coffin. I came to my wits and took it from him robotically. Stepping up to the casket, which lay next to Gregor's freshly dug ditch, I tossed it unceremoniously on the pine box, which the priest had the foresight to order in bulk. Only a carved swastika disturbed its smooth, unvarnished sides.

My mother approached from the other side with her husband just behind her. She gazed in bewildered anguish at the plain coffin. She knelt down, her rosary cupped in her trembling hand, and laid her smooth cheek against the wood as if trying to hear a faint heartbeat. She rubbed the surface in small circles in one final maternal gesture of comfort, like she would often rub his back when he crawled into their bed during a particularly violent thunderstorm. Her motion probably brought one such memory reeling back to her, because she grimaced as if in physical pain and then wailed anew. In a now familiar pattern, my father took her by the shoulders and led her away from her son's grave to a little copse of trees on the crest of the hill.

Father Anton approached me. "We must leave now," he cautioned. "There may be Allied aircraft who would love nothing more than to strafe even this solemn gathering. God have mercy on them."

That's not all who may be coming, I thought, but kept that to myself. Instead I thanked the priest for his help, and gave both him and his nephew a five-*Reichsmark* note. Gregor would wait for the rest of the gravediggers to arrive before lowering the coffin into the ground.

Father Anton bowed. "I'm sorry for your loss, my son. Truly I am." He adjusted his frock, called for Gregor, and walked up to Amelia.

"I can't thank you enough, Father" she said through her sobs. He took her hand.

"I try to do God's work. Even in times like these when I wonder if He has abandoned this world."

That was that. In a moment of anti-climax, my grim quest had been fulfilled. *If only my mission to protect him in the air had been so successful*, I thought.

I watched the priest and his simple ward slowly make their way east into the rising sun towards the cemetery gatehouse, which sat just below the crest of the hill. Only the roof and chimney were visible over the edge. As they sunk behind the ridgeline, I saw to their right another figure rising up. I couldn't make out exactly who it was in the morning glare, but the uniform was unmistakable. My stomach buckled. The Luftwaffe was coming to arrest me.

I looked around and spied my parents sitting under the shade of the trees. I hoped whoever this was would give me a chance to say goodbye to them before taking me away.

Amelia took my hand and squeezed it hard. "Harmon?" she said. "Are you in so much trouble that they would come for you at your own brother's funeral?"

I looked at her anxiously. "I guess I am." Should I run? I did indeed entertain the thought as the Luftwaffe officer approached me. But if he'd come to arrest me, why was he alone? I shielded my eyes trying to get a better look at him. There was something familiar in his cocky gait. This was no adjutant pencil-pusher but a combat flier. A notion flashed through my mind, but I dismissed it as silly. Yet as he got closer to me I recognized his face, surrounded by a halo of emerging sunlight.

"Josef," I said with audible relief. Amelia looked on with curiosity that for a moment shut out her sorrow. I, too, felt a weight lifting. "I'm so glad you're in one piece."

With a deep look of concern, my wingman stopped a mere five paces from me. He slapped his heels and threw his arm up in a salute. "*Heil* Hitler," he said robotically.

His formality took me aback. I struggled to even reply and flipped up my wrist in a minimalist gesture. "Okay. *Heil* Hitler. Why so formal, Josef? And more to the point, what are you doing here?"

He stood at ease. "I've been trying to find you, Herr Captain."

"You flew down?"

"Yes. I was told this is the only cemetery."

We looked at each other for a painful moment of silence. Something had changed in him. Or so I thought. Looking back on it now, I realize that it was I who had changed. First Lieutenant Josef Mueller was still fighting the war. I wasn't.

"I'm so sorry, Harmon," he then said with compassion. "I lost your brother."

I emphatically shook my head. "No, Josef. You know that's not true. I was the one who failed him. You almost lost your own life trying to save him. What more could be asked of you?" I took him by the shoulders. "Thank you for coming."

Amelia stepped forward. "You must be Josef Mueller," she said, trying to ease the tension. "I've heard so much about you."

He bowed formally and took her hand. He kissed it and cracked the faintest smile. "Ah, the fabled Amelia. I feel like I know you already. The captain failed to tell me just how lovely you truly are." She blushed slightly, and for a spell we could forget that we were at my brother's burial or that we were at war with the world and I was running from that war. "I'm sorry this is how we finally meet," he said, bringing us back to reality.

There was nothing else to say. I nodded to her. "I'll leave you two alone," she said, and retreated to the *Kübelwagen* parked on the lane.

"How'd you get away from Seebeck?" I asked.

He avoided my glance and took in the whole scene. Then he swallowed hard and stiffened. "I didn't get away from him. I was ordered here." He could tell I was confused. "By Seebeck."

"Ordered by Seebeck? Why?"

He was having a hard time struggling through this. Which he promptly admitted to me. "Herr Captain…Harmon. I have orders to report you to the SS here. A man named Keitel."

My mouth went dry. "Keitel? Not the Luftwaffe?"

Mueller breathed deep. "That's right."

"But why did he send you personally?" I asked.

"The lines are down, and the only way to get through was for someone to come here. He picked me. I think to torment me. Or you.

Probably both. His orders are to report your desertion to the SS and let them deal with you. He washes his hands of you."

I couldn't believe it. There was no way I was ever going to let Keitel get a hold of me, or my family. And I told Mueller so.

"Look," he said, trying desperately to steer me back to what he considered to be the right path. "Maybe the bombings gave you a break. They meant I had to find you. And now that I have, I want you to know that I intend to carry out the major's order only if you won't come to your senses."

I looked at him. "My senses?"

"Good God, man," he said with a voice showing the strain of frustration in choosing duty over friendship. "You did what you had to do. Paul's where he should be. Which is more than others lying in ditches in Russia or at the bottom of the Atlantic can say." He calmed some and put a soothing hand on my shoulder. "You did an admirable thing here, Harmon. No one can fault you for that. If he were my brother, I might have done the same. But now it's time to come back to Andeville." He lowered his voice. "Seebeck's scared. Those Mustangs really spooked him. He knows he needs every good pilot. He'd be a fool to let you go."

I smiled. "I don't think you quite know the man."

"I know that he's first and foremost a soldier. He'll want his best pilot back."

I turned and faced the rising sun. A glowing peach hovering low in the humid morning air over my town along the river below us. "I'm not going back, Josef," I said quietly.

Mueller gritted his teeth. "Are you crazy? If I go to the SS, what chance have you then? If you come back with me now, then perhaps—"

"My war is over," I declared with growing conviction. I looked over to my sobbing parents standing arm in arm under the trees. What would this decision mean for them? And Amelia? Did I have a right to condemn others to the wrath of the Nazis? Still it didn't matter. It was as if something had broken inside me and I'd become paralyzed. My sense of honor forbade me from going back up in the sky to defend the men and the ideal that had put Paul Becker in his grave at eighteen. Mueller pulled at me until I turned around to face him again. In all our years together I'd never seen him look so dour. And in his uniform I realized that he was a soldier. And he reminded me of this: "Harmon. I can't bear to see the SS take you away. But I have my orders. You know that I'll carry them out. You know it!"

"Then do as you must," I said, resigned to my fate. "I've had enough."

His face grew red. "It's your duty as a German officer to return to your station and defend the Fatherland. Hitler or no Hitler, this is your country we're talking about! Your home. Doesn't that mean anything to you?"

"My country killed my brother," I reminded him.

"You mean the Americans."

"No!" I seethed. "The Amis just carried out the sentence."

"Paul is not the last," Mueller pleaded. He could see I was serious, and this unnerved him to the core. "Many more Germans will die before this game is played out."

Gazing past him, I saw an eagle soaring high above the mountains, riding the gentle currents of humid air. Circling, it seemed to be calling to me to rise above this world. Above those men of mayhem and mischief. Those men who did such harm to the world. Who took it upon themselves to decide who lives and who dies. Who were these wretched people? And why was I doing their bidding? Why should I have to climb into a flying machine and kill boys by the scores so they could have their congratulatory parties of wine and cheese high in cloud cuckooland at the Berghof? They didn't even know who Paul Becker was. He was just a number to them. An entry on the ledger that read "KIA." No more, no less. Hitler's own arch-enemy, Stalin, offered that one death is a tragedy, one million a statistic. The Nazis were no different. But people are not numbers. Gerhard Borner, Big Werner Gaetjens, and Paul Becker were not ledger entries. They'd been given the gift of life by God. And only God could take that away. But the Lord can make His will known through our hearts. And though I'm not a wholly religious man—I've seen too much death to view life through anything but a jaded lens—I do know that someone spoke to me at that moment. That eagle swooping over the hills was there to remind me that I could do a decent thing in the middle of a great indecency.

"Well," I finally said, "I know four Germans who are *not* going to die...not if I can help it."

"What are you talking about, Harmon?"

I turned to my old wingman. "Josef, you've been a good friend to me over the years. A better friend than I've been to you. It's just not in my nature to give so much of myself. But you know that every time you saved my skin, the place in my heart for you grew more solid, like bedrock that will never break. But now I must do something that you'd better stay clear of. I can't have a wingman on this mission. Take care of yourself, my friend. Perhaps we'll meet in Dresden when this is all over and it's safe for me again. Then you can show me one of those barrels you make. If you're half as good a cooper as you are a pilot—or a friend—I'm sure they're a sight to see."

And on that note I tried to leave him on the hilltop. I started towards my parents to collect them and load them into the *Kübelwagen* for the silent drive back to town. But Mueller would have none of it.

"Captain Becker!" he called to me. My parents and Amelia turned. "Don't make me do this. If you return, look for the new base in the woods, a half mile west of the château grounds."

I glanced one last time at Mueller, his fine soldierly form in his uniform outlined against the glowing promise of a new day. "You speak of duty, Josef?"

He stood straight and swallowed with his arms behind his back. "I do."

"Then allow me to do my duty. As a man." And I said nothing more to him. Instead my father and I each took my mother by the hands and led her back to the wagon. Amelia slid over and I hopped in the familiar driver's seat. Then I threw the auto into gear and the four of us headed over the hill, down the lane into the town.

I didn't hear him mutter the words, but I know what he must have said.

"And I must do my duty. As a soldier."

PART 6

48

After I left Mueller to make his solitary vow on the hilltop, we drove the *Kübelwagen* cautiously back into town. It was midmorning, and the streets were now awake and filling with people. But Amelia knew every approach and guided me through tree-covered back lanes that led into the village through routes that avoided the more conspicuous Himmelplatz approach. I was surprised by how much I'd already forgotten about my village as the data of war crowded out more peaceful memories. We made it into the narrow cobblestone backstreets of our block with little scrutiny other than the occasional horse-drawn wagon hauling a load to the market. Only the echo of the car's engine reverberating off the gingerbread facades of the cottages that lined the lane announced our presence. Fortunately, this was the day when the townspeople congregated in the square to ply their wares, and so most of the people were away from our neighborhood. There wasn't an SS man in sight. Our luck continued to hold.

When we pulled up to my little home, I took my father aside and revealed to him that Mueller had orders to report me to Keitel. His face turned pale.

"What more do you have to tell me?" he insisted. His patience was wearing thin, as he knew there was more to this. "Son, tell me, as this involves us all. What else have you been up to?"

It was then, at the step of his door, that I revealed to him Amelia's secret about the Krupinskis and that I planned to get them out. "They're still alive?" he gasped. He seemed impressed actually. "Everyone just assumed they were dead. And all this time right here under the very nose of the SS? Keitel is such an imbecile. But he's a ruthless imbecile, nonetheless." As Amelia escorted my mother past us into the house, he pulled me aside and whispered: "If you're taken by the SS, this will all come out. I don't have to tell you they are adept at getting information. And then we're all dead. Your mother and I need to leave this place."

The look of resignation on his face gave me pause. "Papa, no. This is your home. And there's a war on. Where will you go? Germany is surrounded by enemies."

He gave me a grave look. "The same place you must go."

I shook my head. "No. It's far too dangerous. We need to get you to Switzerland. Over the mountains."

My father scolded me as if I were on the football field. "Your mother would never survive the trek! Think for a moment. You cannot lose your head now!"

"Papa, now that the SS are involved I can't go back to my base and return to flying even if I wanted to."

"I figured that," he said. "So then it's to the Allied lines."

"If we try to cross the battlefield on foot we'd be dead in a day," I said. "Flying out is the only way. Over the channel. And that runs risks I don't even want to think about."

He closed his eyes and cringed as if hit with a stick. "England? Is it even possible?"

So great was the tension that I actually broke into a chuckle. "Sure. Assuming we can get you, Mama, a cripple and her daughter, an ailing man and woman, and their two malnourished children, out of town without the SS—who sees everything—spotting us. Assuming we can cover the two hundred miles to my base without being stopped by our own patrols or blasted by *Jabos*. Assuming I can get us onto my base unnoticed. Assuming I can commandeer an aircraft large enough to fit us all. Assuming we can evade the Luftwaffe if we get in the air. Assuming that we can fly to the invasion beachhead in a German aircraft without Allied patrols blowing us out of the sky. Oh yes, it's quite possible."

He too recognized how far-fetched it sounded. And he too managed a grin. He put his hand on my shoulder. "Well then, let's get moving, shall we?"

A few minutes later, my father was relaying the bad news of our imminent flight to my astonished mother.

"I don't see why we should have to leave," protested my hopelessly bewildered mother as she and Father hastily tossed some clothing into his old steel-gray bag from the Great War. "Karl, this is our home!"

He continued jamming his shirts into the opening of the bag as if violently stuffing a goose. "There's no time to explain. But we must hurry."

"But our life?" she pleaded.

He stood up and slung the bag over his shoulder in a motion he hadn't performed since his discharge in 1919. "Our old life is over," he said.

SS Sturmbahnführer Keitel sat deep in thought with his gleaming calf-hugging boots propped up on his desk, twirling his Luger pistol on his finger. On his wall hung a photograph of the Führer's triumphant entry into Paris. Other artifacts and memorabilia from Russia were scattered about his office. A captured Soviet banner. A Red Army helmet, which he now used as a candleholder. The emblem of the *Totenkopf* in fine crafted gold served as his paperweight. A real human skull on the shelf. He'd been campaigning a long time, and done his Führer's bidding unquestionably. In Russia he had carried out the Commissar Order and shot every Communist and Jew he encountered with unflinching expediency. And now he felt honored with the assignment to clear this part of Germany and the surrounding countryside of spies, traitors, and all enemies of the state. How could we win the war in the field while enemies still lurked in the shadows at home? He was just the man to find them.

Today his patriotic work would continue. But how best to approach this? Amelia was up to something. He could feel it. After all, he knew her well enough to have once been engaged to her, even if it was her father who said yes and not her. That he never got to share a bed with her filled him with unsatisfied longing. But not after today. She would learn that when it came to finding treachery against the Fatherland, more than a few unfortunate Bolsheviks, partisans, and special prisoners of war found that he had *Fingerspitzengefühl*…intuition at the fingertips. And his intuition was screaming at him today to just break into the blonde tart's house and find out what was going on inside.

Normally that would be simple. As SS commander, he was the absolute authority and could do whatever he wanted. He found this notion intoxicating. And nothing was more thrilling to him than the total power he had in the basement of the offices here, which were once those of a prominent Jewish doctor. The doctor was gone now, of course, sent away with all the others, but he had obligingly left behind his medical devices, forceps, scalpels, clamps, and needles, which Keitel had put to good use. And the damp and candlelit basement, carved from stone like a mine, and which once housed the doctor's exceptional wine collection, kept the shrieks and pleas for mercy hidden from pedestrians above as if in a vacuum. Oh, the rush of excitement he found when inflicting pain upon another! The total and absolute power he possessed. He could make them say or do anything to end his interrogations, which if done right could last for hours before the criminal either passed out or expired. That, he mused, was what a god can do.

He thought about Amelia and felt the familiar stirring of flesh hunger. What fun it would be to get her down into his little laboratory. Naked, vulnerable, strung up by the wrists as he sliced, probed, and prodded. Her heaving breasts, nipples hard from fear and the cold. Offering him anything if he would just make the pain stop. Finally she would be his. It was a delicious thought.

But he'd decided to wait. Something told him that if he played his cards right, bigger game could be snared in his net. Who exactly, he didn't know for sure. Her demeanor yesterday, combined with his own observations and those from the Hitler Youth informant, told him there were other players in whatever game she was playing. How to do this? And then came a knock on the door.

"Come," he barked, straightening up to sit stiffly at the desk. He put the Luger down and began shuffling through papers as if caught in the middle of something very important.

The Luftwaffe first lieutenant stepped into the office and tucked his visor cap under his arm. Unsure how to approach an officer in Hitler's personal bodyguard, he courteously snapped his arm in the air. "*Heil* Hitler."

Keitel looked at the fighter pilot with queer fascination. He stood up and raised his arm to acknowledge the greeting. "*Heil* Hitler." The pilot glanced down at Keitel's sidearm on the desk and then stood in silence. The SS officer held out his palms. "Well? What can I do for the Luftwaffe today, First Lieutenant?"

Josef Mueller forced himself to speak. With each word he felt as if he was carving away at his soul.

49

Things were taking too long. It seemed that my parents couldn't get out of their house. Whether through Father Anton or Gregor, word had gotten around town that young Paul Becker was the latest to give his life for the Fatherland. Soon after we returned to the house, neighbors and friends began to come by in driblets to offer their sympathies and inquire as to what they could do to ease the pain. More than a few were perplexed at the sudden morning burial, but they just chalked it up to the understandably irrational behavior of grieving parents who'd just lost their youngest boy.

Amelia had bolted back to her house to get the Krupinskis ready, but I had to stay out of sight, as I knew by now that Mueller would've carried out his orders and flown back to base. So I stayed hidden upstairs while the interminable visits from the townspeople dragged on. Each brought over something to eat if they had any extra. For the women of Stauffenberg, many of whom had lost their own sons to the fighting, this had become a familiar ritual. Some of my mother's closer acquaintances stayed for tea. They sat around in the parlor and comforted the distraught Greta as her increasingly edgy husband checked his watch with growing frequency.

At one point my father excused himself and came upstairs to find me.

"We have to go *now*," I whispered insistently.

He put his finger to his lips and made a calming gesture. "Easy, Son. We must appear natural."

"But—"

"Harmon. There's always the chance that we may have to come back to this place," he reminded me. "I'll not put your mother in needless danger. This has to play out naturally."

He was right, of course. If we couldn't get out of town, or if, for whatever reason, they had to return here, their conduct now, if it were in any way peculiar, would become suspect. Among their visitors could also be informants. I had to a keep cool head, even as my heart raced. My father's wisdom and maturity over me was showing.

By the time the final visitor departed, I looked out my bedroom window and was surprised to see that the sun had gone down. Still no SS. Josef must have stalled before seeing Keitel, either to give me a head start or to steel himself for so unsavory a mission. But how much longer did we have?

I raced down the stairs, imploring my parents to hurry. "We've little time," I said. "Take only what you can carry."

Along with his packed duffel bag, my father hastily retrieved his old haversack, also from the Great War, and rummaged through the pantry, jamming the sack with anything he could get his hands on. Rolls of bread, jelly, canned fruit, a pocketknife, and so on. He also grabbed his winter coat. I stopped what I was doing to question him about the need for a heavy jacket in the middle of June. "We may yet need to try and go over the mountains. Either way I hear it gets cold up in those airplanes of yours."

I marveled at his ability to think so clearly at a time like this. "I'll get one for Mama," I said with a nod.

He looked over to her, still seated on the couch with a cup of tea and a saucer in her hands. She was staring blankly at the far wall. I tried to imagine what this must be like for her. When she had gone to bed last night, although she fretted over the war like everyone, she still had both of her sons, her home, and her country. By the end of today, all of that, save for me and Father, would be ripped away from her.

"Papa," I asked quietly. "Is she up for this?"

"She has no choice," he said grimly. He looked down at his bags and patted them reassuringly. "Well, that's everything."

I stepped over to my mother and knelt down to look at her. I set her teacup on the table and squeezed her shaking hand. "I'm sorry it came to this, Mama," I said. "Please forgive me."

She looked up and put her hand on my cheek and gave me a motherly smile to warm the iciest of souls. "There's nothing to forgive. You are a good boy."

"Come on," I said, and gently lifted my mother to her feet.

We left through the back of the house. My father was the last to leave. He stood in the doorway and paused before closing it behind him. He was taking in his home for the last time. He knew, deep down, that he would never be back here again.

While I suffered from anxiety upstairs in my home, Amelia made it a point to appear "normal," so she strolled the town. Her aim was twofold: to get provisions for the trip ahead and to scout out if any SS were showing themselves. She wore a floral dress and even washed her hair. Her brief half hour of leisure included a trip to the baker to pick up the first batch of bread he'd baked in a week and then a visit to Koppel's store. Stefan was sweeping as she entered. He watched her enter the little store and exchange pleasantries with the coughing Herr Koppel, who was suffering again from a summer cold. She purchased a wedge of cheese, soap, a head of cabbage, a bottle of cooking wine, and a small bouquet of wildflowers for the house.

Stefan followed her movements about the store. He moved closer. After she paid and Herr Koppel wrapped everything except the flowers into a parcel, Frau Koppel called to her.

"Amelia, dear."

Amelia turned with a start. "Oh!"

Frau Koppel, a heavy woman with a face like a radish and her hair pulled back in a tight bun, laughed. "My, aren't you the nervous little duck."

Amelia smiled. "I'm sorry. I don't know what's come over me lately."

"It's all the damnable air raid warnings." The woman grinned. "You've nothing to fear here. I just wanted to ask your opinion on some fabric we're going to use to make draperies. I have the samples in the back of the store."

Amelia looked around for a clock but saw none. In the interest of normalcy she put down her parcel. “I'd be happy to give you my thoughts.”

They disappeared into the back. While Amelia stood over a table in the middle of the small storeroom looking over swatches of lavender- and plum-colored flowered drapes, Stefan swept his broom past Amelia's goods and bouquet.

When she returned to the front of the store with Frau Koppel's gratitude, Stefan had resumed his sweeping. Herr Koppel, busy stocking shelves, noticed nothing out of the ordinary. And a very distracted Amelia went on her way with her parcel in hand.

My parents and I arrived at Amelia's house ten minutes later. With no SS in sight, I began to wonder if Mueller had disobeyed his orders to report me, but I dismissed that as impossible. Amelia was actually not in her house, but walked through her front door carrying a parcel just after we slipped in the back.

“What the hell is that?” I demanded. I couldn't believe that at such a time she had actually gone shopping.

“Mother will need extra food for the trip,” she said. “And I figured I'd look less suspicious than if I stayed hiding in my house peeking from behind the curtains on such a beautiful evening.”

“How long were you gone?” I asked.

“A half hour maybe,” she responded, annoyed at my doubting her judgment.

“That was stupid,” I said. “Are you sure you weren't followed?”

She dumped out the contents of her package on the table and glared at me. “No, I'm not sure. Are you?”

She had a point. “What about our friends?” I asked. “Are they ready?”

“They've been ready for years,” she said with passion.

I looked around. “Where are they?”

“I don't want to bring them down until we're absolutely ready to go.”

I declared now was a good time. “We'll use the darkness to our advantage.”

"Let me get Mother first," she said. "I told her to get dressed. We'll be out in one minute." She disappeared into the bedroom.

When one minute stretched into ten, I knew something was amiss. I quietly poked my head through the bedroom door and beheld the saddest of scenes.

Amelia was perched on the edge of Hanna's bed shaking her head. The dim light of a single lamp softened the room to a blend of velvety shadows. The shades were drawn. Amelia sat crying, pressing her mother's clammy hand to her bosom. "Mother, I can't leave you here," she was saying with panic in her voice.

Hanna smiled and ran her weak fingers through her daughter's golden hair. "There's no way I can possibly make it, child. You know that."

"Then I'm not going," she resolved.

Hanna sat up with a groan. She coughed furiously, to the point where she almost passed out from lack of air. Then she took hold of herself again and squeezed her daughter's arm firmly. "You have to leave. It's the only way to get the family out of here and still save yourself."

"But Mother, what about you?" she pleaded. "You can't expect me to just leave you."

"Amelia, you must ask yourself this question. If you were in my place, if it was your daughter whose life was on the line, what would you have her do?"

I quietly nodded to Hanna and then studied Amelia in the yellow light. She knew the answer. And with that she began to weep openly. "Oh damn you and your logic, Mother! You are so impossible sometimes."

Hanna laughed. "You should look in a mirror." Then she cocked her head and turned towards the window. "Now go. Go! I can hear them coming."

Amelia was unsure what she meant, but I immediately bolted back into the family room. "Come on, let's go. We need to make a break for it while we can."

I ushered my family to the rear of the house out the back door into the garden. It was now very dark under the new moon, and they disappeared into the shadows by the back fence. I strained to listen for any sounds of danger. I sensed that others were hiding in the blackness, watching us, but only the deceptively soothing *cree-cree* of crickets greeted my ears. I wheeled back into the house and bounded across the living room to Hanna's room. I burst in with more force than I intended and yanked Amelia off the bed.

"Harmon, you're hurting me!" she cried.

I let her go and paused. Amelia, panting with shock, brushed a lock of yellow hair from her forehead. I glanced down at her mother, who was watching me not with concern but approval. "I'm sorry, Amelia. It's time." I looked over to the old woman and nodded. "Your mother understands."

"You would have made a good son-in-law," she declared. "Go with him, child!"

"Goodbye, Hanna," I said while I leaned over to kiss her on her damp forehead. Shaking off the sorrow, I smiled to her and then pulled her weeping daughter out into the living room. "Oh Mother!" she was crying.

Now it was back to business.

"I'll get Leo," I said.

I turned to race up the stairs when suddenly I heard a faint rapping on the door. I froze in mid-step, and an electric terror raced through me.

The knocking persisted, this time with more insistence. I whipped out my Luger and quietly moved with Amelia over to the door. Again, the rapping. Now it was accompanied by a boy's voice. "Hello? Fräulein Amelia?" We both breathed a sigh of relief as we recognized the cracking voice of Stefan.

The last thing we wanted to do was appear suspicious. The lights were on, and with Hanna there, it was obvious that someone was home. I holstered my pistol and stepped over to the heavy wooden door. Cracking it slightly, I peered out into the darkness. It was the faint shape of the young man carrying a bouquet of wildflowers. I opened the door more fully to allow for light to pour out and highlight his young face. Amelia came up behind me to peer at him over my shoulder. Stefan regarded us both and smiled.

"What is it?" I asked with a scowl, as if he'd interrupted a good game of Skat.

He clicked his heels and said: "Herr Captain. I'm sorry to bother you at this hour…but Fräulein Amelia, you left this at Herr Koppel's." He held out the bouquet.

Amelia smiled at her absentmindedness. "Oh my goodness, you're right, I did. Thank you, Stefan. You're very kind to me." She stepped out onto the porch and he presented her the flowers like a gentleman caller. I followed her warily out into the darkness.

Amelia took the bouquet in her hands and patted the boy on the shoulder. She buried her nose in them to inhale the fragrant aroma. The woman was always a sucker for wildflowers.

I was about to question the boy further when I felt the cold metallic circle of a gun barrel press up against my temple. For a brief moment, time stood still. And then I saw the familiar figures of SS men appear from each side of my peripheral vision. There were two of them. Each had a machine pistol lowered at my chest. The flowers fell to Amelia's feet and her nails dug into my arm. Meanwhile, that little spy Stefan quickly retreated down the step. With my heart racing, I turned slightly to my left to see who held the pistol to my head. But it was just a formality, as I knew it could be only one man.

"Good evening, Captain Becker," said Keitel. "I think we should have a little chat."

50

Keitel roughly shoved both me and Amelia back across the threshold and into the house. His soldiers followed us in and quickly took flanking positions. Instinctively Amelia and I, standing side by side, flung our hands into the air. Keitel kept his pistol trained squarely on my temple while he reached for my holster and removed my Luger, tossing it onto the floor to the feet of one of his *Sturmmann*. The stormtrooper picked it up and laid it on the mantel above the fireplace.

Keitel then stepped back and studied us like a man who had unexpectedly come upon a fortune in gold bullion and his mind was racing on how best to hide it. His black eyes were fixed on Amelia, who was shivering with fear, and he gave her a look of mock pity.

"What do you want with us, Johann?" I said weakly. But I knew I was in no position to demand anything with a pistol and two submachine guns aimed at me from three sides.

Keitel ignored me. Instead he slithered over to Amelia and yanked her into his arms with a force that looked like he snapped her back. She tried to scream but found her mouth suddenly covered with his, his tongue forcing its way practically down her throat. She made guttural protests and tried to fight him off, but he held her immobile to him. His sticky lips were coated in a film of vodka and acrid cigarette smoke. Then her nails found his exposed neck, hooked into the skin and raked down, ripping his flesh and creating three parallel streaks of blood like plow lines down to his throat.

He shrieked in pain and pushed her off of him. "You fucking bitch!" he screamed, and whipped her hard to the floor. Her eyes rolled back as she hit her forehead on the mantel and fought to stay conscious. He was panting hard, standing over her as she struggled to grab a chair and pull herself to her wobbly feet. I noticed blood trickling down the side of her forehead, and my anger at Keitel rose to a boil.

"If you touch her again, Johann, I swear I'll kill you!"

His men leaned forward with their weapons in a gesture that said, *No you won't.*

He just glanced at me before returning his attention to Amelia, who'd somehow managed to stand back up. "We'll continue this later, Fräulein. In private," he promised. "But for now, let's just see who's upstairs."

Keitel turned and barked an order to one of his men to go up and search the attic. "*Jawohl!*" he said, and quickly ascended the stairs. His heavy boots pounded on the steps as if someone was hammering above us.

Amelia and I looked at each other. It had finally happened. Just as I'd known it would. We were both dead now. The rest was just a question of how and when. I could see that she was starting to shake violently with fear. I tried to move towards her but Keitel pointed his Luger at my face. "Ah-ah," he said in a patronizing voice.

"Are you okay, Amelia?" I asked.

She nodded unconvincingly as blood trickled down her brow.

The *Sturmmann* descended the steps just as noisily as on the way up. I couldn't bear to see the faces of the Krupinskis, from little Elsa and her doll to a hunched-over old Leopold, being shoved down the stairs by an SS man. But I still had to look. I followed the SS *Sturmmann* and saw that behind him trailed…*no one*. Amelia looked over to me, unable to hide her shock. I tried to remain poker-faced. Keitel, on the other hand, looked as if he'd been bluffed into folding a golden hand, leaving a fortune on the table.

"What the devil?" he snapped at the *Sturmmann*.

The man shook his head. "There's nobody there, sir. But it's obvious people have been living there for quite some time. Also, I found this."

The man handed Keitel a piece of yellow cloth. He took it in his free hand and quickly revealed to all of us that it was a Jewish star. Left behind as a symbol of defiance. I smiled inside. It had to be Jakob's handiwork. But where were the Krupinskis?

Keitel's face went white. So he finally had his answer to the unsolved riddle of the Jewish *Musikmeister*'s disappearance. The other Jews in the town had long been accounted for. But he always thought this family had escaped him. Fled the country. How could he have been so obtuse! Love and unquenched desire had blinded him. That Jew-loving whore had made him the fool. For years! And now he wanted to know one thing. Where had the Jews gone?

He placed a gun to Amelia's bleeding forehead to find out. "Alright, you traitorous fucking whore, what've you done with them?"

Amelia recoiled in terror from the gun, but I could tell that mixed in with her fear was genuine confusion. She honestly didn't know. And she told Keitel just that.

Keitel ran his fingertips down along the scrapes of his neck as if to draw rage from them. He looked over to one of his other men. "*Sturmmann*."

"*Jawohl!*" he shouted, still training his eyes and his weapon on her.

"Go to the bedroom. Bring that old hag to me."

Hanna! We'd forgotten about her in the excitement. But Keitel had not. "No, Johann!" screamed Amelia as the SS man disappeared into the bedroom. "Please. She has nothing to do with any of this."

Johann stood impassive, pistol pointed at Amelia's forehead. "I'm sure you're right."

We heard Hanna protesting loudly in a shrill voice and the SS man screaming obscenities. A few seconds later the soldier reappeared, dragging the sickly old woman violently by her white hair. Her hands were clutching his forearms so her hair wouldn't be torn out at the roots. Something inside me grew viscerally angry and I stepped forward to help, but was shoved back by the other guard.

Amelia's mother was screaming. "Get your bloody paws off me, you devil! You're hurting me!"

The stormtrooper dragged her over to the hearth and let her go, shaking his arm out of her weak grip. She fell to the floor like a sack of potatoes. Amelia was screaming at the soldier to leave her mother alone. The SS man ignored Amelia and reached down to pull Hanna up to a kneeling position in front of the fireplace and then released her.

Hanna, breathing hard as she fell forward onto all fours, looked up at Keitel through a loose strand of white hair. "Whatever you're going to do, Johann Keitel, do it now."

Amelia glanced down at her mother with a look of both pity and guilt. "I'm sorry, Mother."

Hanna smiled up at her. "I'm not." Then she closed her eyes when she felt Keitel's gun barrel against the top of her head.

"Now, Fräulein Amelia, I'm going to ask you one last time. Where are your Jews?"

Amelia stammered. "I swear I don't know, Johann. I'm telling you the truth." His trigger finger tensed, and Hanna went stiff waiting for the bullet.

"He's going to do it," I warned Amelia.

Then Hanna looked up at the man lording over her with a gun to her head and said in a meek voice: "I sent them away."

Amelia's eyes widened. "You? How, Mother?"

"Yes. How, Mother?" repeated Keitel, loosening his finger on the trigger.

Resigned to her fate, the old woman looked over to her stunned daughter. "When you told me to get ready to try and leave town, I knew the game was done. It meant that you must have had these vile beasts breathing down your neck or you'd have never considered something so desperate as to run. With you out of the house, I had to tell Leopold so he wouldn't be trapped up there should these cowards break down the door. He felt it best to get out of the house and into the dark, where he had avenues of escape."

Keitel spat: "I guess you can climb stairs after all, you bag of bones?"

She gave him a look of outright contempt. "You'd be surprised how much strength an old woman can muster when friends' lives are in danger." And then she actually looked back to Amelia and winked. The woman had a gun pointed at her face and she winked! For my own self, I was almost paralyzed with fear. It was one thing to be in the adrenaline rush of air combat. It was quite another to have a cold-blooded murderer aiming a loaded sidearm at your head. Hanna Engel was a remarkable woman.

Her daughter swallowed hard and nodded her goodbye as a tear ran down her cheek.

Way off in the distance, we could hear the low hum of approaching aircraft. But we were all too preoccupied with what was happening before us to pay them any mind.

Keitel, now frustrated to the boiling point, removed his visor cap and wiped his brow with his forearm, like a man who realizes he's been conned when it's too late. He casually replaced his hat and aimed the gun at Hanna's head again. This time, though, it was as I feared. His knuckles went white as he squeezed the trigger and an ear-splitting gunshot popped, made all the more deafening by the echo of the confined space of her living room.

Hanna's body flopped over violently facedown, though still on her knees, like someone peering down through a knothole in the hardwood floor. Amelia screamed, "Mama! Mama!" and I stared in shock as the dark crimson fluid pumped from her head wound in spurts, creating a spreading puddle lapping at our feet. The oily smell of gunsmoke filled the room. Because my ears were ringing I couldn't hear the droning of the aircraft growing louder as if they were on a course to directly overfly the town.

Without pause, Keitel turned his gun back on Amelia. He looked at me with a satisfied grin. "Too bad it's come to this, Becker. You were a good soldier once, but now you and your Knight's Cross will be hanged as a traitor. But…if you come peacefully, nothing will happen to your Jew-loving bitch." The two guards stepped over Hanna's prostrate corpse and made a move to take me by each arm.

I looked at Amelia, who was overcome with the shock of seeing her mother executed before her very eyes. I realized then that I had no choice. "Okay, Johann," I said with quiet capitulation. "You win." It was all over. Wherever the Krupinskis and my parents were, I knew further resistance would just lead to more bloodshed. So this was the end of the road.

51

I never found out whether the RAF Lancasters over Stauffenberg that night were deliberately targeting the town or were off course on their way to Adelstatz and Keitel's munitions factory on the Main.

As the ringing gunshot that murdered Hanna Engel faded from my ears, I could hear the engines, the distinctive bass-note drone of in-line Rolls-Royce Merlin engines practically right over our heads. Amelia wept openly but I wasn't watching her, nor was I even considering the SS men before me. It was the vibrating crystal in her cabinet that set off the first alarm in me that a far graver threat than three SS thugs was now bearing down on us.

Keitel, his ears attuned to aerial threats more so than mine from years of fighting on the ground, pulled his attention from his moment of triumph to consider the low rumblings that were now the unmistakable intonations of an air raid.

"What the hell's going on?" one of the SS men shouted as the din grew louder.

I looked at Keitel, who was looking up at the ceiling.

Suddenly he screamed: "They're bombing us!"

I didn't need to be told of the danger. "Amelia, get down!" I shouted, and I lunged for her and practically tackled her to the floor. Amelia, still in a daze over her mother, didn't resist. As my face hit the dusty hardwood, I had the unpleasant vision of Hanna's lifeless eyes staring back at me, my hand caked in her blood.

Keitel, too, wasted no time in dropping flat to the ground. By now the drone had grown to a deafening roar of hundreds of powerful engines rattling everything in the room as if a malevolent giant had picked up the house and was shaking it angrily down to its foundations. Torrents of soot poured out the chimney, and a fine dust began to rain down upon us as the enormous Lancasters passed directly over our heads like a fast-moving cyclone.

The two SS men with Keitel finally realized the danger, but their moves to hit the floor came a fraction of a second too late, as a blinding sheet of bright orange lit up every window like a direct lightning strike. My ears felt like someone had boxed them from the concussion of violent explosions that ripped through the house, sending a tornado of deadly glass shards and wood splinters flying in all directions. Even before the reverberating boom of the explosives impacting all around registered in their ears, the two SS men were cut down by a hail of debris like the soldiers of old before a battery of grapeshot. The dead men slammed against the walls, with their helmets flying in one direction and their machine pistols and torn limbs in the other.

I could see Keitel lying spread-eagle on the ground with his hands folded behind his head to protect himself from the shower of plaster and wood and glass that soon covered us. *BOOM! BOOM! BOOM! BOOM!* One after another the orange flashes continued unabated, the percussion of high explosives mingling with the bright starbursts of incendiary bombs pounding my eardrums, and it felt as if the entire world were disintegrating. As I lay there helpless, trying to cover a now frantically screaming Amelia as best I could with my own body, I thought: *So this is what happens when the Allies get through our fighter screens.* And I remembered all those bombers I'd watched over the course of the year continue on to their targets even after our squadrons had their run at them and thinned out their ranks. God have mercy on my country! Clearly the Allies were showing none.

As quickly as it had come upon us, the violent thunderstorm of the bomber stream passed. But as the hum of the heavy Lancasters faded to the west, the sounds of chaos and fury and suffering, firebells clanging, sirens screaming, people shouting in panicked voices, calling out the names of loved ones over the roar of the flames—the death throes of a bombed-out town—greeted our ears. The room was filled with smoke, and the dancing light of a village ablaze illuminated the scene as if a million flares had been shot into the air. The raging fires spreading through the town like relentless floodwaters after a levee breaks projected a sinister crimson aurora upon the night sky.

Having been on the receiving end of shellfire and bombs before, Keitel was quickest to recover. He got to his knees and shook the white plaster dust out of his eyes and hair. Coughing, he frantically searched for his dropped Luger. He wasn't done with us yet.

"Get the hell out of here!" I shouted to Amelia, but if her ears were ringing half as badly as mine, then my pleas came to her as muffled sounds at best. I pulled her up to her knees with me and forced her face to look into mine. "Go!" I cried again as loudly as I could. She got the message and nodded. She then shifted her gaze to just behind me and her eyes widened, and I whipped around to see Keitel crawling for the pistol, which was lodged in the fireplace grate behind the mangled body of one of his men.

I pushed Amelia towards the direction of the blasted-out doorway and then made a move towards Keitel. I lunged at him and caught his thighs in my blood-caked hands. Startled, he turned to see me and violently kicked at my face with his heavy jackboot. It hit the top of my head and I saw white spots. But in my rage I quickly shook off the blow and managed to crawl on top of him and pull him away from the fireplace just as he reached for the weapon. He never got it. We rolled on the ground trapped in a grotesque corridor formed by Hanna's body on one end and a parallel SS man's on the other. Keitel was stronger than he looked, and very soon he got the better of me. My ordeal of flying a mission, taking Paul home, and burying him without sleep and little food was taking its toll.

Soon Johann and I were face-to-face, and his knee sat on my chest, pinning me to the floor. I could see in the light of the flames slowly creeping down towards us from the upstairs of the house that he'd gone delirious with rage. His eyes were set on killing me, and with the added strength that hatred provided him, he set upon me. I could only cover my face as I felt the hammer blows of his fists rain down on me, one following another until warm, wet blood flowed between my fingers.

I reached out for him in desperation and managed to catch both of his eyes with my clawing thumbs, which I pushed deep into his sockets. Shrieking in pain, he quickly pulled away from me, as to stay where he was meant blindness. He was still planted firmly atop my midsection, just like I used to pin Paul down to tickle-torture him, but his back was arched towards the now burning ceiling, his fists massaging his eyes furiously. Wiping the blood from my face, I made a powerful movement to heave him off of me while rolling to one side, but his arm quickly fell upon my shoulder to hold me down flush with the floor. I was spent. Trying to force his arm off of me, I could feel any remaining strength draining from my muscles. There was little more I could do but lie back and muster the energy for one last ditch defense, when he suddenly produced a field knife from a scabbard sewn into his boot. The blade, gleaming in the light of the flames, rose high above me, with his hand firmly grasping it in his fist. I felt like a human sacrifice upon a satanic altar as he looked down at me in mad triumph. In a way, I just wanted him to be done with it and this nightmare mercifully ended. I was prone on my back, my one arm pinned by his, the other held tight to my side by his firm knee.

"I'm going to enjoy this, Becker," he said with a demonic grin. I looked up at the fire now spreading over the ceiling, flaming globs of plaster dropping down upon us like candle wax in the intensifying heat, and waited for the stinging pressure of the blade cracking through my sternum and ripping into my heart.

"I'm going to enjoy this more," is what I heard instead. A confused Keitel spun his head around to see Amelia Engel aiming the Luger he'd just used to execute her mother straight at his face.

She stood there with the pistol in both hands, quivering. "Kill him!" I screamed.

But Amelia just wasn't one to take a life. She gave life…and that's what she did for Johann Keitel. It was more than he deserved. I can say that I'd have had no qualms about emptying the entire magazine into him had it been my mother lying on the floor with his bullet in her brain.

Despite the buzzing in my ears, her determined voice, which masked her fear, came through loud and clear. "Drop the knife and get off of him, Johann, or so help me God I'll shoot you."

"I'd do it, Johann," I said, supporting her bluff. Instantly he considered me, then the gun barrel again. He knew Amelia to be a peaceful soul, but he'd also just executed her mother in cold blood. It wasn't worth the risk. He dropped the knife onto the floor, where it made a dull thud, and slowly eased himself off of me. When he got to his feet, he stood in the billowing smoke and intensifying heat with his hands up.

I hoisted myself up slowly, using the mantel for support. Blood poured from a laceration in my scalp but, though messy, I knew it was a superficial wound. Panting heavily I stood face-to-face with the man a moment before was poised to ram a knife into my chest.

"You won't get away with this," he declared in a cocky tone despite his circumstance. "There are SS men all over the area looking for you. I wasn't stupid enough to come here without a backup."

At first he seemed right. But when I gazed past him out the shattered windows to the streets beyond, I could see nothing but flames and smoke, with ghostly figures running frantically back and forth in confusion and panic. "They're out there?" I asked him sarcastically as I pointed to the town. "There is no 'out there' anymore." I heard a groaning from the wooden ceiling beam that bisected the parlor and was now starting to burn from end to end just over six feet above us.

"Harmon!" Amelia coughed. The heat was growing unbearable, and sweat poured down my face in sooty rivulets. "The house is going to collapse."

"What about him?" I demanded. For the first time I saw Keitel show a hint of fear.

"Let's just get Mother and go!"

I stepped over to her. Years of combat had chased away any scruples I might have had about killing this man. "If you won't do it, then I will." I ripped the gun out of her hand and pointed it at my SS tormentor. That was when bona fide terror finally broke through his conceited mask, and his knees buckled. It was a gratifying sight. I aimed the barrel straight at his chest and pulled the trigger without another word. But all I heard above the crackling of the fire engulfing everything around us was the unmistakable click of a misfire. I tried to unjam the weapon, but there were just more clicks. Keitel breathed easier and even managed a smirk as his cockiness quickly returned. He was a tough one to ruffle for long, that's for sure.

In exasperation I strutted up to him before he could regain his wits completely and violently pistol-whipped him across the face. He reeled back onto the stone mantel and banged his head on the hard surface. His eyes rolled back, and I figured I'd actually killed him then and there or put him out long enough for the encroaching flames to consume him.

I tossed the broken gun to the floor and quickly retrieved mine laying in a corner of the smoke-filled room. Now it was my turn to show some sense. I tugged at Amelia and tried to usher her out the door and the burning house, but she resisted. "Not without Mother!"

"There's no time!" I picked her up with both hands and manhandled her, kicking and shouting, out the door.

"No! No! She'll burn!"

When we made our way to the relative cool of the garden, I put her down. "She's already dead, Amelia." Then I borrowed the wisdom of my onetime friend and wingman: "But we still live."

All around us, stretching well into the town center, were licks of roaring flames reaching like malevolent, glowing tentacles and belching up columns of thick smoke blacker even than the night sky. A ruby-red halo hovered over the devastated village; all of Stauffenberg from the river to the hills was burning. I wondered how anyone could have survived such a pounding. Then I realized that there had been others outside waiting for us when the bombs fell.

"Oh my God," I shouted to Amelia. "Where's the rest of us?"

Racing into the garden amidst a virtual whirlwind of flaming embers, I could see a cluster of figures in the far corner of a stone fence that had somehow managed to survive the raid. The trees beyond it burned like torches. The wind whipped as the vortex of a howling firestorm engulfed the center of town. In the radiance that now illuminated everything for miles all around, I recognized them as the Krupinski family, huddled up on their knees in what looked like a prayer meeting. I counted all four of them. "Krup!" I shouted to him. Jakob, his face blackened with soot and dirt, turned and stood up, tapping his father on the shoulder.

The rest of them rose slowly to their feet and gave me queer looks. Their faces, caked in ash, gave me a start as they appeared like apparitions from hell. What was going on? Then I realized two people were missing.

"Leo, where are my parents?" I said with a mouth suddenly gone dry.

The family bowed their heads and stepped to one side to reveal the twisted bodies of Karl and Greta Becker lying still on the grass. I gasped in horror, and my legs almost fell out from under me. Amelia immediately ran to my arms. But I couldn't take my eyes away from them. "Momma? Papa?" I said blankly. "Oh please no."

Krup approached me and above the din of the roaring fires and chaos all around, he said: "The bombs just started falling. They never knew what hit them."

For an agonizing moment I continued to peer down at them. My lifeless legs refused to bring me any closer, as I couldn't bear the sight. "I'm so sorry, my boy," added Krup in a voice that seemed to fade in and out of me. Then I suddenly fell to the ground and wretched, acidic vomit splashing onto the grass at my blood-caked fingertips. I really felt at that moment that I might be struck down dead from the profound sorrow. Both of my parents, the centers of my world for most of my life, gone. Could this be? I had just seen them alive and well not a half hour before. But when I opened my eyes, the dark picture remained very much before me. Karl and Greta Becker had gone on to find their lost son, leaving behind an orphan—one they knew could find his own way in this world gone mad. As I closed my eyes again, I swear I could hear my father's voice calling out to me through the burning ether: "You're on your own now, Son. You're the survivor. The only Becker left. Rise up and live!"

And that's exactly what I did.

"Harmon," Amelia said, putting her hand on my arching back. "Harmon!"

I snapped my head to look at her and Krup, waiting for my next suggestion. With one last spasm of anguish, I reached deep into my reservoir of a father's love and snapped out of it, hoisting myself to a stand. My legs regained their strength and began carrying me away from this cursed garden. As Amelia was forced to leave Hanna, so was I now compelled to leave my parents. I had people still alive depending on me.

"Come on," I said, firmly in control again. "This is far from over."

We gathered the rest of the Krupinski clan and darted to the *Kübelwagen*, which also, thank God, had been spared in the raid. It was a tight squeeze. I drove while Amelia sat up front with Elsa perched on her knees. Leo, Constanze, and Jakob crammed into the back. Sick as it sounds, the smoke surrounding the car had mercifully rid the seats of any trace odor my dead brother's body might have left behind. Without pausing to assess the damage, we peeled out of the blazing bonfire that had been our village just an hour before as fast as we could. We bounced our way through the debris-filled streets, dodging overturned carts, mangled horses, and many dead men, women, and children caught out in the open when the RAF finally introduced Stauffenberg to the war.

52

The eerie crimson glow coruscating from the burning town of Stauffenberg was still visible in the night sky to the southeast even after we'd put several miles between ourselves and the crumbling Main Bridge. It wasn't until several more twists and turns along the mountain road that evidence of the town's fate was completely hidden from our view behind a wall of towering escarpments covered in evergreens.

We drove in absolute silence for the longest time. How could any of us put into words all that we'd experienced this terrible day? Amelia and I had each lost our entire families. Our once beautiful town of Stauffenberg, a hamlet whose medieval charm inspired roving artists to stay awhile, had been erased from the map by the RAF in a matter of minutes. I knew instinctively that not one building could have survived the inferno, save perhaps the stone-and-mortar Saint Gerard's church and the Rathaus tower, which would serve as mute witnesses to the horrors of this night. I no longer even recognized the world I lived in, nor my place in it. But then I looked over to the Krupinskis and my heartache was eased somewhat. Yet I knew even this brief twinge of optimism was a foolish indulgence. I was well aware that even though the Krupinskis were free from their prison of Amelia's attic, they were not safe.

For several hours we drove in the darkness, shielded from view by the undulating folds of the hills and crevasses carved out by fast-running rivers fleeing the Alpine altitudes behind us.

We must have made one hundred fifty miles by my estimate as the ground began to flatten into more familiar territory. Pretty soon a million stars were splashed across the mantle of a dark ceiling made all the more brilliant against the backdrop of the new moon. I glanced over to Amelia, whose head bobbed and weaved as if on a loose spring as we bounded along the road. Elsa was asleep in Amelia's lap and she held the girl close, every now and then lovingly kissing the top of her curly-locked head.

Her eyes stared straight ahead as a torrent of memories poured through them. "Tired?" I asked her. She looked over to me and caressed my cheek with the back of her hand. "Me too," I said.

In the back seat, the Krupinskis tried to stay awake but to no avail. Soon they were all sitting with their eyes closed and chins buried in their chests breathing in a slow rhythm. I thought I could hold out, but as my vision started to blur I had to face the fact that I, too, was at my limit. I needed rest.

We eventually pulled up to a partially destroyed farm cottage nestled in a patch of woods just off the road. It looked like it'd been ravaged by bombs. On the barn situated behind it, a wall had collapsed on one side, and surviving chickens set free from their coops by the blast mingled with the bloated bodies of dead cows and horses.

I ordered everyone to wait outside as I entered the blasted-out house through the intact front door. Its creaking broke the silence of the still night, and I wondered how far away it could be heard. Inside the dark home, I waited for my eyes to adjust so I could make my way around without tripping over anything. When my night vision kicked in, I found myself in a debris-cluttered salon, a fireplace to one side with a kettle suspended over a pile of charred embers. On the stone mantel sat two photographs. One of an older gentlemen in a Wehrmacht colonel's uniform. The other a younger boy in the black uniform of a *Panzertruppe* sergeant. Both frames had a black ribbon draped diagonally over their corners. Two more offerings at the insatiable Nazi altar. In front of me a flight of stairs beckoned to the blackness of the second floor. Under the steps' frame was a tall closet for hanging coats.

Another doorway led to a small kitchen, and in the darkness I pushed my way through. It was far from a gourmet restaurant, but the neatly set table and stocked shelves told me it had been lived in just recently. I raided the cupboard and found a loaf of pumpernickel bread that was rock-hard stale but edible. To my disappointment, the cheese was vile and molded. I did find a few cans of peaches and preserves. I rummaged through the kitchen drawers but was unable to locate a can opener in the pitch dark of night, and I dared not light the lamp. The real meal would have to wait for the dawn, which was not far off.

I retreated to the salon, cautiously navigating upended chairs and some plaster slabs that had been ripped off the walls from the concussion of the bomb blast. Amelia and the Krupinskis stood in the doorway. I tossed the bread to Krup. "Feed your family," I said to him. "Just save me the heel. I don't have any water, but there's probably a pump by the barn. Let me just check the rest of the house first and I'll get it for you."

"I'll get it," offered Jakob.

That was fine with me. "Don't make too much noise." He nodded obediently and felt his way past me and through the kitchen to the back door. Krup ripped the loaf into chunks and handed some to Elsa and Constanze.

"Well," I said to Amelia. "It's not the Stauffenberg Inn, but it's better than we could have expected." She smiled and tugged at my elbow as I turned to go up the stairs. "I'll be careful," I assured her and then cautiously ascended the steps.

I could see even from halfway up the stairs that part of the roof had been ripped away, as stars appeared above me when I leveled off in the second-floor hallway. I was about to step forward to inspect the rooms when I glanced down and was startled to find the body of the *Hausfrau* in her tussled dress and bloodstained blouse lying facedown on the clapboard floor. By her sickeningly sweet odor, I figured she'd been dead for about two days.

Stepping gingerly over her, I noticed that a debris field of broken glass, twisted nails, splintered wood beams, and roof shingles covered the floors, the beds, in fact everything, making the upstairs unusable.

Suddenly I heard the floorboards creak behind me. I whipped around with my pistol drawn and found myself relieved and annoyed to be aiming at the forehead of my future wife. She, in turn, was staring down at the dead woman as if in a trance.

"Jesus! Are you *trying* to get killed this week?"

I holstered my pistol, stepped back over the dead woman, and ushered Amelia away from here. "Who is she?" she asked, as we both descended the rickety stairs.

"I suppose this is her house."

"I wonder what happened?"

"Stray bomb is my guess. Probably dropped by *Jabo* under attack."

"We should rest here, Harmon," said Krup, who was waiting for us at the bottom of the steps.

I nodded. "There's nowhere upstairs. We'll spread out in here for the night. We have a few hours until daybreak. I hate to travel in the light, but we should be pretty close to Andeville by now."

"And then what?" asked Amelia.

I eased down to sit on the floor and leaned my back up against the wall. I removed my boots from my aching feet and let out a sigh of relief. Closing my eyes, I could already feel myself drifting away while the rest of the crew tried to get themselves oriented.

"I'll figure that out in the morning," I said. And then merciful sleep overtook me.

It seemed that within a minute of nodding into a deep sleep, I was awake again. But a quick glance at my wristwatch revealed that I'd been unconscious for the better part of four hours. I slowly opened my eyes and noticed that, although the house was still dark, streamers of bright sunlight fingered through the spaces between the drawn curtains and the window frames. It was morning. Sitting up straight to get my bearings, I noticed the Krupinski family huddled together in one corner of the room like a pod of sleeping sea lions. I craned my stiff neck to find Amelia not curled up somewhere but instead sitting on the floor by the window and peeking around one of the drapes, her attention riveted on something outside.

Instinct told me to crawl rather than walk over to her, and when I did she didn't shift her gaze to me. "You let me sleep," I whispered.

"Shh," she said in a reprimanding tone. Then she motioned for me to pull back the curtain just a hair and take a look.

I gave her a quizzical frown and then did as she said. My mouth, already parched, went drier still. A *Kübelwagen* and an Opel truck behind it were parked in the lane along the stone fence right outside the front of the house. They must have just arrived, as their engines were idling. Three men in combat tunics with which I was now all too familiar, were grouped around the car. Another group, which I counted to be five men, had already fanned out to search the property.

I quickly withdrew from the window. "Waffen-SS," I said. "In full field gear."

"I hope they don't plan on staying."

"Doubtful," I said. "They look like they're on the way to the front lines."

I felt especially happy with my decision to park the *Kübelwagen* behind the remnants of the barn, about fifty yards off the road.

My self-assurance was short-lived however, as right in the window above our heads we could make out the silhouette on the curtains of an SS trooper trying to peer inside. He was so close we could hear his boots crunching on the gravel. Watching him in reverse from a cracked mirror that hung over the fireplace mantel on the opposite wall, we could see that all he had to do was break the window and reach in and he would touch both of our heads.

His form disappeared, but by tracking his footfalls we knew he was making for the front door. I turned to Amelia and hissed: "Hide."

"What about them?" she asked, pointing to the sleeping family in the corner.

"I'll take care of them. Hurry."

She nodded and crawled into the kitchen, folding herself into a broom closet.

I scrambled over to the Krupinskis, trying not to make too much noise. I shook Krup as gently as I could on the shoulder so as not to startle him. "Leo," I whispered.

His eyes opened, and he looked at me through the fog of his interrupted sleep. "Harmon? What is it?"

"SS men are outside. Get your family hidden." I looked over to the door and saw that the knob was starting to rotate. Krup noticed it too, and his eyes went wide with comprehending fear. He quietly roused his family and motioned for them to get moving even as they rubbed the sleep from their eyes.

Time was running out. "Where should we go?" he asked, as much to himself as much as me. I looked around. Upstairs would be too noisy, plodding up the creaky steps. Then I noticed the cracked door of the coat closet under that same stairwell. "In there," I said.

"Papa, what's wrong?" demanded Jakob. "Tell me what's happening."

Krup looked at his son and put his hands on his young shoulders. "The SS are right outside. We must hide under the steps."

Jakob quickly obeyed and ushered his mother and younger sister into the closet and then slipped in himself. "Will this never end?" I heard Constanze ask herself as they crowded together in a space designed for jackets and soggy boots, not four jammed human beings.

The front doorknob jiggled and then stopped as the man on the other end realized it was locked. I looked at Krup and then at the gaunt faces of his family peering out from the closet, ashen with terror. There was no more room. He knew what I was thinking before I said it. "You go in, my boy. I've lived long enough."

"Nonsense," I replied.

"Harmon, there's room for only one more. You've done more than I could have ever asked of you. Please get in."

For a brief instant a part of me thought the probing SS man would just move on, since the door was locked. But no such luck. A glass pane from the little window carved into the wooden door shattered, and broken glass fell to the floor. The soldier's rifle butt, like a battering ram, withdrew and then his hand reached in to unlock the door from the inside.

Without saying another word, I shoved Leo gently but firmly into the crowded closet with his family over his whispered protests. I leaned back against the door until I heard the click of the latch catching. The Krupinskis' muffled chatter stopped when I gave the door a good thump with my heel.

Now what about me? As the knob turned, I desperately scanned the room. My only hope was to bolt upstairs, but just as I was turning towards the first riser, the door creaked open. I stopped cold. My heart hammered and my legs grew weak with fear. As the door swung open and light poured into the room, I opted for the only trick left in my bag. Hiding in plain sight. I stood in the corner, waiting for the SS man to find me. I had one last role to play as an officer in the German Luftwaffe.

A lone figure stood like a shadowy apparition at the threshold. His baggy uniform, crisscrossing haversack belts, and field cap were unmistakable. His gun was no longer drawn but swung casually around to hang at his back again. Why should he be on guard in his own country, away from the front lines? As he stepped into the house he called out: "Hello? Is anyone here?" He paused to wait for a response. As he stood there, both of our eyes adjusted, his to the dimness, mine to the light, and we sighted each other simultaneously. I recognized his *Wolfsangel* insignia and cuff title as that of the Waffen-SS, *Das Reich*. An awful notion ran through my head, but I immediately shook it off as being impossible.

He tilted his head as he processed what he was seeing. Standing in the darkened corner, I didn't make a sound at first. He just gawked at me dumbly. But he didn't go for his weapon, which was a reassuring sign. With more confidence now I stepped out of the shadows towards him, revealing my full figure to his surprised eyes.

"Well," I finally said with an air of authority, "are you going to tell me who you are, *Sturmmann*?"

He collected his thoughts and drew himself to attention, his heels smacking together. "*Heil* Hitler!"

I took another step forward. "*Heil* Hitler," I replied earnestly.

"Captain," he stammered. "I, uh, didn't expect to find anyone here. Least of all a pilot."

I casually strolled past him, trying not to let him see my quivering hand. "Yes, well, I didn't expect to be here."

He began looking around the room, which made me nervous. "How did you get here?" he asked.

"I was shot down about a mile from here." I smiled and added for effect: "I can handle one Thunderbolt. But eight?" Then I made a twirling motion of my plane spinning to the ground with my finger.

He chuckled. "I can't even imagine. Is there anyone else here?"

I shook my head. "The *Hausfrau* upstairs, but she's dead."

The stormtrooper seemed satisfied with that. He made for the door. When he glanced back at me, he noticed that I wasn't following him. "Are you coming, sir?"

"Am I coming?" I replied. "No, no, Sturmmann. I need to rest some more before making my way back to my unit. I'll stay here a while longer."

He chewed on that. "Why don't you come outside with me? We have food and water. And you may need medical attention."

"I'm fine, really," I said rather more insistently than one would expect.

He paused. This was a boy in the SS who'd known only a totalitarian state and was, by his very association with his unit, totally committed to its dogma. I pegged him as one who, like that little rat Stefan, reported on his neighbors. His suspicious mind was not fooled by even the authentic cover of my grimy flight suit.

"I really think you'd better come with me."

"No," I blurted out. "Now go. Leave me, Sturmmann. That's an order."

He smiled wryly. His suspicion was now palpable. "You're giving me an order?"

"I'm a captain," I said rather petulantly.

"And I'm not in the Luftwaffe," he reminded me sternly. "I'm in the SS." Then he called out the open door. "Herr *Sturmbahnführer*!"

This was getting too intense, and I tried to diffuse the situation by appeasing him somewhat. The last thing we needed was for more SS men to enter the house. I had to, if anything, steer them away from this place.

"Very well," I said. "I'll go with you. Do you have water?"

He looked at me coldly. "I said we do. Come with me."

I followed him anxiously into the sunlight and towards the small gathering of men huddled around the hood of the idling *Kübelwagen*. I could hear them chatting amongst themselves, and the gist of the conversation centered around a map spread out before them in a scene eerily familiar to me.

The *Sturmmann* kept turning around to make sure I was still with him. I noticed his hand now resting on the assault rifle slung about his shoulder. The other men heard our approach, looked up from the map, and gawked. A filthy Luftwaffe pilot was not what they expected to see.

"What's this all about, Mats?" asked a lanky *Untersharführer*.

"Where'd you find the pilot?" inquired another fierce-looking *Sturmmann*.

Mats, as was the suspicious SS corporal's name, wiped the sweat off his brow with his field cap as we made it over to them. "I found him inside."

The only person who seemed not to care about our presence was the commanding *Sturmbahnführer* he'd to called to from the house. The SS major stood with his back to us, still intent on studying the map. I noticed that under his visor cap a bit of white cloth showed. A thick head bandage.

My wary escort stood before his commander's back and clicked his boots. "Herr Sturmbahnführer! I beg to report I was unable to complete the search of the house, as I found a comrade in need of aid inside."

The officer folded the map and then slowly turned to face me.

I felt as if I'd fallen through a trap door.

I couldn't believe it! The black eyes pierced through me and I fought off a sudden wave of nausea. A terrible smile spread across his pale face as he tucked the map into his uniform pocket. Johann Keitel simply said with utter euphoria: "Oh my, oh *my!*"

My expression must have shown abject desolation. I really wanted to sit down and cry. I just didn't care anymore. How many times could a man escape death just to fall back into its clutches again? And with the same demon prodding the trident in his back. I had been right to try to kill him, and I found myself silently damning the piss-poor gunsmith who'd made that Luger.

"Sir, I found him inside. He was shot down." The familiarity of Keitel's greeting was lost on young Mats.

Keitel played along. "Shot down? Is that what this man told you?"

Young Mats nodded. Keitel put his hands to his side and stepped up very close to my face, his breath reeking of onions. "And where were you shot down, Captain?"

I said nothing but looked straight ahead. The small group of soldiers watched in curiosity. It was quite possible that one or two even recognized me, as this was the same unit that had butchered the inhabitants of Sainte Laurie-Olmer that winter. But if they did know me, they remained quiet. It was obvious that something bad was going on between

me and their commanding officer.

Keitel's expression went from giddy amusement to dark, intense hatred. "You'll talk soon enough," he hissed. With that he backhanded me hard across the face. The men stepped forward, shocked to see one of their own slapping the face of a Luftwaffe officer…especially one with a Ritterkreuz pinned to his uniform.

"Stand fast!" Keitel shouted, and they obeyed. My face started to swell on one side. "*Untersharführer!*" he barked to a sergeant while still glaring at me. I recognized the burly man as that same NCO who had treated me after my crash. Again, if he did recognize me, he gave no hint as such.

"*Jawohl!*" He snapped to attention.

"Take some men and search the house. Rip it apart if board by board you have to." The man immediately obeyed, and soon a group of four men raced past us and burst into the house. He then commanded Mats to bind my hands.

There was no point in resisting, so I willingly submitted to the boy's motions as he took my pistol. Then he wrenched my arms behind me and proceeded to wrap my wrists in what felt like a leather strap. He cranked my shoulders until tiny flares erupted in my joints.

From inside the house I heard the now familiar screams of "*Raus! Raus!*" which told me that my band of refugees had been discovered.

Keitel looked at me with a haughty expression. "I guess we've found your Jewish rats in another hole."

A few seconds later the Krupinski family and Amelia emerged from the darkened interior with their hands up, squinting in the sun.

Not even in the aftermath of the destruction of Stauffenberg had I seen Leo look so defeated. His family followed him in single file as they were muscled by the SS men, who'd enacted this scene many times in the past few years, over to Keitel and me. Anger burst through me as I saw the pathetic figure of little Elsa being roughly ushered through the door at gunpoint, her face awash in confusion and fear and innocence, her frail arms up in the air in a pathetic gesture of bewildered submission.

Amelia trailed behind them separately. As she stumbled along with a stormtrooper's grip firmly clamped over her bicep, she looked to me as if by summoning divine inspiration I could devise an escape plan for us all. I gave her a dejected look, and she knew. I was powerless. It was all up to Johann Keitel now.

Keitel, in fact, ordered the men to herd us past him and around to the back of the house near the blasted-out barn. He aimed a finger at me. "Him too," he said to Mats, and I was roughly shoved along behind them.

We weaved through the cluster of liberated chickens clucking mindlessly. When we got to the barn, Keitel ordered the men to line the Krupinskis up against the only intact wall. He ordered one man to stand about twenty yards off to the side to keep an eye out on the road. The rest formed into a single rank and stepped several paces back, and I immediately knew what was happening. They'd formed a firing squad.

Amelia stood on the other side of Keitel, still in the firm grasp of the SS man. Panic showed on her young face. After the years of hiding, the constant, chronic fear and tension, the helpless pleas of friends who so completely trusted her to stand between them and the Nazis, that it should end like this. That her charges were to be machine-gunned down behind a barn of a bombed-out farm in a corner of far-western Germany amidst a brood of clucking hens.

"Johann," she pleaded in desperation. "I know that you have admirable qualities. My father saw them in you as well."

Keitel snorted. "Your father saw a handsome fortune, Amelia. Nothing more."

"I saw something."

"You saw him," he sneered, pointing his gun at me, not taking aim but merely extending his hand gesture.

"It never meant I disliked you," she offered. *Keep it up, Amelia*, I thought. *He may just go for it.* "And I know even now, with all you've seen in this war, that you do know right from wrong. That's why I couldn't get myself to pull the trigger yesterday." She let that thought float in the air between them. "Please, Johann," she said. "Don't do this."

Keitel turned to face her. He stepped forward until their noses practically touched. But she didn't turn away. She poured affection into his eyes. And he managed to even break into a soft smile. He still loved her, no doubt. For some reason, even as I looked on while an innocent family was about to be murdered by him, I felt a tiny flutter of guilt over the pain I'd caused him in stealing Amelia away.

Keitel exhaled and nodded his head. He took Amelia by the waist and kissed her, this time with gentle sweetness. A symbolic show of affection between a man and the woman he loved. I thought, *She's reached him!* Even Johann Keitel had a shred of humanity left. My eyes darted to the Krupinskis, who were watching the theater with their heads bowed but eyes raised. Perhaps we may live yet.

Johann released Amelia from his clutches and turned to one of the SS men taking this all in with a quizzical gaze. "Her too," he snapped.

An electric shock ran through me. "No!" I blurted out in reflex as one of the soldiers shoved Amelia roughly up against the wall to stand alongside with the rest. She turned and looked at me. "Harmon?" Terror showed in her wide eyes.

Keitel laughed. "You think I'm an imbecile? I was going to maybe let you live, you slut. For a while longer at least. But that was before you tried to play me like one of Harmon's saloon pianos. To hell with you all. You left me to die by fire. And yet here I am. You should always make sure your enemies are actually dead before moving on." He laughed mockingly. "Hell, I suffered far worse blows in Russia."

"Let them go, Johann," I finally said, clearing my dry throat. "It's me you want, isn't it? Well here I am."

"You, Harmon," he began dispassionately, while surveying the scene, "will accompany me to Berlin, where you will face public trial for both desertion of your post and treason to the Fatherland for harboring Jews. No matter, either one is a hanging offense."

I shuddered to think of myself suspended lifeless at the end of a rope. And I felt abject panic start to rise in me. But then I realized that my friends were in more immediate peril. So I persevered.

"Then take me to Berlin," I said. "Hang me for all I care. Kick out the stool yourself if it pleases you. Just let them go. What does Germany want with a wretched family of Jews and their stupid girl shepherd? They'll leave the country and never come back. You'll be rid of them just as if you'd killed them yourself. And if God is watching, he'll remember your mercy." In one last spasm of false hope, I thought I might have gotten to him.

Then he turned to me. "Please don't try piety on me, Becker. You think I give a rat's ass about these *Untermenschen* living or dying? This one, that one, I couldn't care less. Does a rat catcher care about the individual rats he kills?" Johann stepped over to Amelia, who was standing with her eyes to her feet. He cupped her quavering chin in his hand and tilted her head up to look him in the eyes. "And as for this whore, I'll be doing myself a service. Killing her will rid me of an open sore. You're already a dead man, Becker. If I didn't think I could profit by delivering you up to the Führer, I'd shoot you right here and now. Suffice it to say, I will enjoy watching you suffer their deaths until your meeting with the hangman."

That was that. We'd just been condemned to die. For everyone but me it would all be over in a few minutes. Keitel marched back over to me and then pivoted to face his men.

"*Achtung!*" he shouted, and the seven men in line drew themselves to attention like machines. Constanze clutched Elsa, who was now weeping at what she didn't even fully understand. Krup and Jakob put their arms around each other in a last gesture of love from across a generation. Amelia simply closed her eyes and softly recited the Lord's Prayer.

"Ready!" I heard the metallic sliding of rounds being loaded into their chambers.

"Aim!" Keitel raised his hand and glanced at me to savor my expression. I gritted my teeth and shut my eyes. If my hands weren't bound behind me, I'd have placed them over my ears in a vain attempt to block it out completely.

Then I heard the command. "F—"

RAT-TA-TA-TA-TA-TA-TA-TA-TA-TA-TA-TAT!

The unmistakable sound of a submachine gun being sprayed back and forth split through the humid air, and I cried out in anguish without even hearing my own voice above the rattling din of the gunfire.

Then the firing stopped, and the echo was carried away with the summer breeze. I couldn't bear to open my eyes and look upon so heartbreaking an image as my friends and my lover lying strewn across the ground in a pool of their own blood. Silence still. Now it was almost too long of a pause.

Then I felt Keitel's hand on my shoulder. But it was not forceful; rather it was as if he were using me to support him from falling over, as a drunkard might. Then I opened my eyes and was utterly astounded by what I saw.

53

Before even giving Keitel my full attention, my eyes opened to reveal a row of bodies lying in grotesque poses on the blood-soaked grass. But they were the bodies of SS men…not Amelia and the Krupinskis. My eyes then darted to the barn wall, where my group of refugees was crouched down clinging to each other and crying. But they were completely unharmed! How could this be?

Keitel's grip on my shoulder weakened, and when I turned to face him, a look of astonishment and pain was plastered on the pasty gray pallor of his face. Blood spurted from the corner of his mouth, and his legs buckled. He tried to speak but he just gurgled, making an awful slurping sound. In a last vain gesture he made a dreamy motion to reach for his pistol, but he had no strength left. His arm went limp to his side, and the Luger dropped harmlessly to the grass. I noticed a deep purple stain spreading across his uniform's mid-section and realized he'd been nearly sawed in half by a hail of bullets. His eyes glazed over, and I knew he was about to die.

I shoved him off me, like casting a boat away from a pier, and he fell back onto the grass. He was dead before he hit the ground with a dull thud. All of the SS men were dead, in fact. At first I thought it might have been the Maquis, but the aim was too precise to have come from any of the distant woods, and the grass was too low to hide anyone closer in. And besides, we were still on German soil. And then I saw the lone SS soldier whom Keitel had ordered to watch the road standing with his smoking submachine gun lowered to his hip and aimed squarely in the dead men's direction.

At first I didn't know who this guardian angel was. As my condemned fugitives were first coming to realize that they were still alive and their executioners dead, I stared at the rogue stormtrooper. I didn't even bother to watch them all hug or come running over to me whooping and crying for joy. They must have thought I somehow did this, as they embraced me and even Jakob ruffled my hair. But I focused on the odd soldier. Then he removed his steel helmet and I recognized our savior immediately.

"Loos?"

Oberschütze Emil Loos stepped over to the bloody heap of dead men lying facedown in the grass shoulder to shoulder as if still in their rank. The boy was hyperventilating as he gazed down at his former comrades. He raised his head and I could see that he was overwhelmed by what he'd done. As if he didn't understand himself what had just happened. My friends went silent as the enormity of their luck sank in. But I wasn't ready to declare us out of danger yet.

"Captain Becker," Loos said to me wanly. "I…"

"Put the gun down, Oberschütze," was the first thing I could say. He still could have killed us with the pull of a trigger. The teenage private obediently dropped the smoking weapon to the ground and walked over to me.

"Are you okay, sir?" he asked while he produced a knife. He came around behind me and cut the leather bands, freeing my arms and bringing a merciful relief to my burning shoulders. I rubbed my wrists and gawked at him. What could I say? He'd just wiped out his entire squad to save us all. These were those very same men, including his paternal sergeant, who'd so clearly shown playful affection for him when we rode together in the truck just six months before. But why?

"You should get out of here," he warned. He sounded more in control now. "The rest are only two miles behind."

Still in mild shock, I managed to ask him: "What about you?"

He just shook his head forlornly. "I don't know."

I turned to Amelia. "Get everyone into that truck," I ordered, gesturing to the larger Opel. She didn't say a word. No one did. They just filed around the house to the idling vehicles on the road. Only Jakob stayed back for a second. He went from dead soldier to dead soldier, collecting their canteens. He was thinking ahead. He didn't take a weapon, though. Jakob, for all his piss and vinegar, was a peaceful boy. I found myself admiring him even more. I hadn't been so grounded at his age. But, of course, I didn't have an entire nation out to kill me. I also had no delusions over what lay ahead, so I grabbed Keitel's Luger that lay in the grass at my feet and slid it into my holster.

"Loos," I then said. "You're coming with us."

"Why? And to where?" he asked.

"We're going to make a run for the Allied lines."

"No, sir," he said deadpan. "I'm done for."

I took him by the shoulders. "Look, boy," I said. "I haven't the vaguest clue what just happened here, but we're getting out of the country, and right now that looks like your only option short of suicide." He looked at the ground and kicked some grass mindlessly. I knew what he was thinking. "No, Loos. I won't let you do it. You're coming with us."

"You'll never get through," he said. He made a gesture in the general direction of France. "It's hell up there."

"We have to try, dammit!" I snapped. I knew he was probably right, but I didn't need to hear it said aloud. "Get in the truck, Loos. That's an order."

He looked up with resigned despair. "*Jawohl*," he answered quietly. I patted him on the shoulder, and we made our way to the truck. I figured that he'd tell us why he did what he did when the time was right. But for now we had to get the hell out of here before the rest of the SS column arrived.

As we walked briskly around to the front of the home, I glanced back at the body of Johann Keitel lying on his back in the grass. Although the man seemed to reincarnate at will, I knew that this time our paths had intersected for the last time. His lifeless black eyes, shark's eyes, stared unseeing into the sky and the face of an angry God. I could only think that as I believe there is a heaven, so must there be a hell, as balance is one of the great truths of the universe. I think I have a good idea of where Keitel ended up. But what of a pilot who fought, as Krup observed bitterly, to prolong the horrors perpetrated by the thousands of other Keitels throughout the Third Reich? I can only hope and pray that my actions of these most desperate days of my life somehow will be my redemption.

54

We were back on the road. This time in the larger Opel, as the SS men had no more use for it. I was driving again, since I was the only one who even had the remotest idea of where we were. A sheet of high, colorless clouds had drawn across the sky, giving my eyes a welcome relief from the glaring sun. Again, the going was slow, as now more than ever I made sure we stuck to the backroads through whatever forest cover could be provided. My serpentine route probably added at least fifteen miles to our journey, but I had images of bands of SS men hot on our trail, hell-bent on revenge for the deaths of their comrades. I had one consolation: that Loos's massacre had taken place on German and not occupied soil. The retributions in France or Belgium would have been horrific.

So far no one had bothered us. The few civilians we saw along the roadside didn't even give our truck a second look. To them, we were just another supply truck passing through on our way to the fighting in Normandy. In a way this felt more like a Sunday drive in the country than a desperate flight from the war. Much of this pastoral area, lacking any targets of opportunity, was unscathed.

It wasn't long before Loos climbed from the back of the truck over the seat to plant himself in the cabin to my right. He continued to display that long stare into oblivion.

"Is everyone okay back there?" I asked.

"They're all asleep."

"But you couldn't sleep," I observed.

"No." After a prolonged silence he asked: "Do you know where we are, sir?"

"I reckon about thirty miles from my base," I said, while maintaining a fix on the narrow dirt road in my windshield. "I know we're in Belgium."

"How can you tell?" he asked. "It all looks the same to me."

I called his attention to one of the wooden road signs at a dusty crossroads. "They're in French."

"Oh." He seemed satisfied with that. Then he retreated back into his shell.

"It's Emil, isn't it?"

"Yes."

"Emil," I finally said to him. "I want to thank you for what you did."

He shrugged, barely acknowledging my gratitude. I could tell his actions had deeper meaning than merely helping out a family of Jews and traitors.

"Why did you do it?" I asked.

He leaned his head back in the seat. He didn't look at me but rather stared blankly out the window, not even registering the beauty of the passing greenery. At first he said nothing, and I took that to mean he wished to remain silent about what he'd done. I was just about to change the subject when he began to speak in a hushed, remorseful tone of one offering a confession.

"About a month before he took his leave for home, Keitel ordered us to move into a little French village near Nancy. I don't remember the name. Doesn't matter now. We were there to pacify the town. You know what we mean by 'pacify,' don't you, sir? Much the same as when you and I first met. But the crime of this place was not that they supported partisans but rather that it was a haven for Jews. None of us could figure out how Keitel knew this. We just assumed that an informer had squealed or a partisan had broken under interrogation. So, we rounded up all the villagers and drove them into a field. All the men were handed shovels and forced to dig a long pit. You could tell they realized what this meant by that look I've come to know. It's seared in my memory. Some of the condemned stare at the ground, as if by not making eye contact with reality it will pass them over. Some look around, soaking in their final images of this world. Others weep openly."

He swallowed hard, and his already high-pitched voice piped up a semi-tone.

"Then the men were all lined up along the edge of the pit, and before their families we shot them all. We went methodically down the line, one by one. Very efficient. They fell nice and neatly into the hole, lying like cordwood. Then we did the same with the women."

"And what of the children?" I asked in a whisper.

He turned to me, and his face was a mask of unbearable torment. "I was tasked with this myself as the youngest of the lot. I must have shot twenty children, no older than little Elsa back there. One round to the back of the head. The very small ones, kindergarten age and younger, were lined up one in front of the other…to save a bullet. Like an assembly line." He mimicked the motion of pulling the trigger with his forefinger, reliving the horror in his mind. "One…two…three…four. Do you know it's always the children who never flinch, even as they know what's going to happen? Halfway down the line, I had to pause to change my magazine. The next little boy in front of me. He was maybe nine. Eyes like buttons. He turned to me and asked in the most polite voice: 'Am I standing straight enough, Uncle?'"

That was all he could say before breaking down into a fit of heartfelt sobs as he reclaimed his humanity that for years had been suppressed by the ice-cold doctrine of Nazi ardor. I put my right hand on his shoulder while holding the wheel in my left.

"My God!" he cried to the roof. "Oh my God, please forgive me! What have I become? I'm just a boy!" Then he cupped his face in his palms, and I let him be.

When he'd cried himself out, he composed himself, wiping the tears from his face with his gray sleeve, the words "*Das Reich*" on its cuff title. Then he looked at me with the clearest conviction in his eyes. "I do not want to survive this war."

55

Evening. A mere six miles from Andeville. Still no one harassed us. I was once more approaching exhaustion. Loos offered to drive, but I didn't want anyone else behind the wheel. I was a shepherd jealously guarding my flock from what still could be an SS wolf in sheep's clothing. Plus, the boy seemed to be unraveling inside. He might have missed a turn in the road or steered us into a ravine or worse.

I tried to know the boy who had saved me. Emil Loos was from Westphalia near the Black Forest, and had enjoyed hunting and rowing since he was a boy. Like all the young men in his town, Loos was absolutely enthralled by Hitler; when he saw the fine lines of SS men parading through his town during a visit from the Führer himself, he vowed to be one of them. And so he was. Until today.

When I considered this lad, it was hard for me to remember that he'd massacred children in the past. He was, perhaps, a little too much like the rest of us for comfort. Emil Loos was not a monster. He was far worse. He was just a simple boy…a dark reflection of us all.

"You should come with us," I repeated to him. "There's nothing for you here."

He just sank back in his seat. "There's nothing for me anywhere."

"What about America?" I asked, vaguely recalling his ironic desire to see his enemy's country.

"I'm a war criminal, Captain. There is nothing." I let the matter rest after that.

As the sun began to sink behind its thin veil of gray into the western sky, I cast my eyes about for familiar landmarks that would lead me to my base. I told Loos to be on the lookout for any sign that pointed to Andeville.

The land now composed of gently rolling knolls topped with neat ranks of poplar trees. Thicker forests lay on the road ahead, giving me another hint that Andeville was near. I was growing anxious to get to the base, as the needle on the truck's fuel gauge showed the tank was near empty.

Amelia poked her head through the canvas flap behind our shoulders.

"Did you sleep?" I asked.

"Some. How about you, Harmon?"

"There'll be time to rest. The sun's almost set. We can't do anything tonight anyway. Even if I get us to my base and find a suitable aircraft, I'd have no idea where I'm flying in the dark."

Actually, I needed the night to think this through. I didn't really know what to do once we got to my aerodrome. It was mostly single-seat fighters. And the cockpit of a Focke-Wulf was not exactly suited for six, now seven, people. My hope was that one of the transports might be there. Otherwise we risked crossing over Belgium by land into the Normandy front. As I had told my father, the odds of safely slipping through the lines into that boiling cauldron of death were slim.

Amelia glanced over to Loos, who seemed transfixed by something in the distance. He leaned forward to peer through the windscreen. "What is it?" she asked him.

He abruptly raised his hand to cut her off. Then he grabbed my arm insistently. "Stop the truck!"

"What?" I said.

"Do it!"

I was surprised at his urgency and immediately slammed on the breaks. We both lurched forward, and Amelia nearly fell over the seat into our laps. I heard astonished utterances from the back, and immediately Krup peeked his head through next to Amelia.

"What is it?" he asked. "Why did you stop so quickly? Have we hit a mine?"

"Quiet!" Loos demanded. For an agonizing moment I thought that maybe this SS boy had led us into a trap. That it was all an elaborate ruse. Perhaps up the road he would be a re-animated Keitel. Still alive, still hunting us. Never stopping until we were dead. Then I heard what Loos heard. Our SS pursuers may have been dead, but mortal danger came in many forms out here.

"Can you see them?" I asked. Loos and I both stepped out of the truck and peered upwards, scanning the sky.

"No, sir. But I hear them. Maybe they're in the overcast. Unless my ears are toying with me."

"What are you looking for?" said Amelia, who followed us onto the side of the rural lane while Krup stayed in the vehicle.

"There," I said. "Hear that?" We stood motionless, our ears straining at the sky like radar discs. Then it became more audible. The low growling of heavy radial engines echoing off the trees.

Loos spotted them first. "*Jabos!*" he cried, pointing to the southwest. He jabbed his finger at the clouds just above the tree line of a distant forest. My eyes followed his arm until they locked on two silver shapes, like shiny coins, moving low and fast just above the horizon. They pulled up in unison to about five hundred feet and banked over towards us. They were heading in our direction.

"Shit!" I cried. "Thunderbolts."

I could make out the distinctive oval cowlings of two P-47s coming straight at us. I stared up at them, paralyzed with fear. The huge propeller arcs made wide yellow haloes around their massive radial engines. The elliptical wings jutting out from the fuselage carried eight fifty-caliber guns and plenty of ammunition. The enormous planes swooped in so fast that they were practically upon us before we could even move.

"Get down!" shouted Loos, and he dove for the ground. But with a rush and a roar the planes over-flew us before Amelia and I even twitched a muscle. I marveled at the pilots who maintained that airspeed while buzzing so close to the ground that their propeller blades might clip the trees behind us as they screamed past. Only then did I stop to consider that had they opened up with those machine gun batteries, they would have blown us all to Valhalla.

Loos leapt to his feet. He followed the two fighter planes as they gained altitude before turning in unison in a gentle chandelle. "Get everyone away from the truck!" he called to me. "Quickly!"

As I followed the path of the two *Jabos*, I could see that they were winging around to make another pass. Then I considered the black military cross painted on our truck and I realized that at first they didn't want to risk disintegrating some poor Belgian farmer on his way to the market. But now having positively identified us as German and thus fair game, they would bear down with guns blazing.

Amelia bounded to the back of the truck, whipped open the canvas flap and let drop the tailgate. The Krupinskis were already on their feet preparing to jump out of the truck bed and onto the road. "What the hell was that?" asked Jakob as he leapt to the earth with a grunt. He turned to spy the American fighters in the distance banking over to line up on us again. "Oh crap," he muttered. "Elsa! Mother! Here, take my hand!" He helped them down and then assisted Leo as well.

I raced over to them and then pointed to the forest only fifteen yards off the road. "Come on. Into the forest. Let's go! Run!"

The whining of the gargantuan two-thousand-horsepower, eighteen-cylinder engines grew more pronounced as they throttled up to maintain their speed through the chandelle. The distant silver specks were now in their groove, and suddenly they were coming for us again. This time more menacing, roaring in for the kill. I could almost feel their gunsights lining us up.

We hurried towards the woods and before we knew it we'd entered a dark outcropping of trees with thick underbrush. "Keep going!" I urged the others as thorns reached out to rip little bits of skin off our faces and forearms. The howling of the engines grew in my ears. "Everyone down!" I yelled, and Amelia and the Krupinskis ducked into the thick green undergrowth, hidden, I hoped, from view. I was about to do the same when I heard another mechanical sound. It was the sputter and cough of the fifty-five-horsepower Opel truck engine turning over. Then I realized we were one person short.

"Loos?" I turned and tripped back to the very edge of the woods. I spied the truck sitting exposed on the open road. Loos had climbed into the driver's seat and was shifting the revving vehicle into gear.

"Emil!" I shouted as loud as I could over the din of airplane and truck engines. The Thunderbolts were almost upon him now, and they were flying no higher than fifty feet, following the contours of the road so tightly that at a certain angle it might have looked like they were *on* the road. I doubt if their propellers, thirteen feet in diameter, would have cleared a haystack should one have appeared from nowhere, or even a slight rise in the ground. "Get the hell out of there!" I screamed.

Amelia called to me from behind: "Harmon, for God's sake, get down!"

I ignored her and instead focused on Loos, who must have heard me because he turned his face to me. With a shake of his head and a faint, resigned smile he stomped on the accelerator and lurched forward along the road. I realized what he was doing for us. He was drawing the *Jabos'* attention away from the trees and towards him and the more enticing target of the truck. Even though they could've sprayed the woods with bullets and surely ripped us to shreds, they forgot about us entirely and focused instead on this SS boy in his puttering vehicle.

As the truck gathered speed and bounced down the rough road surface away from the rest of us, I shifted my gaze to follow the two fighters racing after it. Still standing, but hidden among the heavy underbrush, I covered my ears as the Thunderbolts howled past me so close that I felt their prop wash as they kicked up a dust storm behind them.

Emil Loos never had a chance. And I knew he didn't want one. For him this was his redemption. His final nod to his humanity before answering to God for all he'd done.

It was over in seconds. Just as the huge war birds screamed by so close I could make out the pilots' determined faces, I saw puffs of smoke from their wings and heard the *POW! POW! POW! POW! POW!* of heavy machine guns blasting away. They sounded different from the outside. I'd only heard them before from the enclosed womb of my canopy. I never realized how much power was in the weapons that had been trained on me, and shuddered to think that I'd been in the line of fire of such guns in the past with nothing but the skeletal frame of a fighter plane and a half-inch steel plate behind my seat as my only defense. They seemed like overkill against a single truck.

A fountain of dirt chased after the lumbering Opel until it overtook the hapless vehicle, which disappeared in a shrieking tornado of smoke and sparks. An orange fireball reached into the sky; at the same time I felt the concussion of the thunderclap as the P-47s blew Emil Loos and his vehicle apart. The fighters whooshed through the black pall of smoke from their burning target and pulled up again. Satisfied with their work, they continued to climb for the gray clouds until they disappeared above them. Only the fading acoustic shadows of their engines echoing this way and that off the trees gave any hint at who had just been here. On the road the motionless truck was a flaming hulk, and I could just make out through the ripples of heat Loos' charred body, like one of those figures from the Pompeii ruins, frozen in time in his death thrall, draped out of the open driver's side window.

I bowed my head and thought, if I did not say out loud: *Well, boy, you got your wish*. Oberschütze Emil Loos was dead and, yet again, it was we who still lived.

Behind me the five remaining members of my flock raised their heads above the greenery. Twigs snapped behind me as they formed beside me along the edge of the woods. "Oh, Harmon," cried Amelia as she looped my arm in hers. "Has the world gone mad?"

Constanze tried to shield Elsa's eyes from the gruesome sight of the boy's charbroiled remains, but after all she'd seen, who knew how sensitive this child's psyche could have been at this point? Jakob and Krup stood in silence as they watched the vehicle burn. It was as if we were observing a moment of solemnity to honor the brave lad who had saved us twice, but knew he could never save himself. I know that his sins were many—I witnessed them myself—but perhaps in his last act of self-sacrifice he escaped the damnation he so feared. Either way, Emil Loos made it possible for me and my friends to live another day.

56

But now we had a practical matter to contend with. It was getting dark, and although I could sense my base nearby, we had no means of transport to get to it. I considered my ungainly procession of refugees. A sickly man, a physically weakened woman, and her little girl. Jakob was still relatively robust, as was Amelia, but we were all suffering the debilitating effects of little sleep and less food. I decided we should rest here for the night within the cover of the woods. Fortunately, Jakob thought to bring the SS canteens. We should have been laid low with thirst otherwise.

With the blackened shell of Loos's truck still smoldering on the roadway out in the open, we hid in the woods and lay with the biting insects in the dirt. Nighttime brought with it a cool breeze from the northeast and a much-needed rest for all of us. We were relatively safe here, but soon we would be out in the open once more and dangerously exposed. Andeville was just over the next rise several miles away. The next day would show whether my extraordinary luck would hold.

The heavy clouds of the previous day slid off to the east as we slept. A mantel of bright stars greeted my eyes as I awoke about a half hour before the dawn. My mouth was parched, and I took a last swig of water from my canteen. *Well*, I thought, *now comes the hard part.*

Everyone was curled up in the dewy underbrush as they lay with their eyes closed, breathing deeply. We were all so tired that we could have found sleep on a bed of pinecones. I went from person to person gently shaking them awake. "Amelia, get up.… Come on, Leo, Constanze, we have to get moving.… Jake, get your little sister up, it's time."

After draining the canteens we left them behind, well-hidden in the brush, as we moved on. We were headed towards a nest of German soldiers on my base, and had we been found with SS canteens we would've been implicated in the massacre of Keitel's detachment, surely long since discovered, and shot on the spot by Seebeck.

"How will we get to your base?" asked Krup, fearing the answer he already knew.

I looked around at this pathetic band. "We walk," I said. And so we did.

We trekked for what felt like several miles through the edge of the woods following the road to Andeville that cut through them, but careful not to show ourselves in the open. A thick mist shrouded our movements. I knew we had to make it to the base by early morning. It was right around here. Everything looked familiar to me now. The tree lines, the roadways, the scattered farmhouses along the narrow lanes. Even though the sun was just showing its full self through the trees, already an intense heat was building. I took stock of my hapless band of refugees and knew that they would not be able to go much farther. Krup's breathing had grown steadily more labored, and Constanze, her ragged frame weakened from years of inadequate diet, was on the verge of fainting. For a while I carried Elsa on my shoulders and she made a game of it by plucking leaves from the branches that she could now reach and snag with her little fingers. I saw Jakob smiling up at me as we stumbled through the undergrowth, grateful for the kindness I was showing his baby sister.

"Captain," he said at one point.

"It's Harmon," I said. "I was only a kid when you were born."

"Harmon then." He smiled. "I'm sorry for all I said about you."

I patted Jakob on the back. "There's nothing to apologize for. You were right." I looked over to see Amelia almost in tears as she watched me with Krup's children. Even though I stooped at times to prevent Elsa from being clotheslined, I felt taller than I had in many years.

"Do we have much farther?" asked her big brother. He looked back to his parents, who were lagging behind us. "I don't know how much longer they can last."

"We'll be there soon," I said. "Trust me."

Jakob nodded. "I do trust you, Harmon."

No sooner had I made that prediction than we came to where the woods abruptly ended. At the apex of the corner embracing the trees like an inverted *Y* was a road junction. About a hundred yards down the *Y*'s stem was a checkpoint. The red, black, and white gate, manned by two helmeted guards, was the southern approach to the new airbase, which literally was just an open grass field. Farther off, well in the distance and barely visible, stood the ruins of Château LeClaire, in whose warm embrace I'd been comforted through much of the struggle. Now it was just a bullet-riddled exoskeleton of stone. But actually it was better for us that the base was no longer on the grounds of the estate. The old one was much more expansive and open, with no covered approach to the airfield. Our new base was more like a hideout, in which the shroud of the woods was used to conceal our parked fighters from marauding *Jabos* until they were ready to burst into the clear and make a quick scramble to take off on the lawn.

"We're here," I announced, lowering Elsa to her feet. She'd amassed a bouquet of leaves and seemed to have put the horrors of the past twenty-four hours out of her mind in a way only children can. "But," I cautioned them, "we have a little more walking through the woods to do still. We need to avoid the guard stations on the road."

The Krupinskis groaned at that. "Harmon," said an exhausted Leo. "I think I am spent."

I trudged over to him and took his hand in mine. "You can do this," I said with conviction. "Leopold Krupinski did not spend years in an attic and come all this way to give up in sight of his freedom."

"I see only more woods." He sighed.

Constanze stood up straight. "Come on, you old goat," she mused to Leo. "You're not rid of me yet."

With that he nodded and found the strength to trudge on.

It was just a little farther until we got to the improvised hangars, which were just tents among the clearings hacked into the woods. The distance was actually less than I'd thought. It seemed that within a half hour we were crouched in defilade in the shrubs at the border of the woods gazing at the new sylvan home of JG 32. It was difficult in the morning mist to make out the shapes of the fighters scattered and camouflaged among the poplar trees. Birds twittered but not another living creature made its presence known.

At the far end of a clearing stood a neat row of camouflaged tents, which now served as the crude quarters and mess for the skeleton crew. There were maybe a dozen serviceable aircraft that I could make out through the haze. The Mustangs had gotten the rest the day I left. That day seemed more like an eon than a mere fortnight ago. My life I once had known was already receding into the distant past. I tried to put the faces of my parents and Paul out of my mind for now. I would have time to mourn later. Right now I had other matters to contend with.

It didn't look good for us. Here we were, ready to make a dash for a plane that could take us away, yet I saw nothing but single-seat fighters. My roll of the dice had come up craps, and I honestly wasn't sure what to do next. I felt my spirits sinking into despair at the thought of traveling on foot to France with my weakened band. That was when I heard the faint echo of idle chatter from across the field. I crouched down low as I observed Sergeant Ohler and one of his corporal assistants lazily walking across my field of vision until they stopped at what looked like a very large haystack. They began to pull down shocks of straw, and to my astonishment a glass nose cone and then twin propellers with bright red cowlings revealed themselves. More branches and shrubs were removed, and what had once looked like a garage-sized pile of straw was, in fact, a forest-green Heinkel He 111 medium bomber.

The battered old gas truck then emerged from the mist, and two more men stepped out and hooked the hose to the plane's fueling gasket. I turned behind me and signaled with my finger to my lips for everyone to be silent. If they fueled the plane up quickly, we could make a dash for it. It was our only chance. It had come down to this one window of opportunity. And as the base was now stirring, it was a long shot, but I was in desperate straits.

In less than ten minutes the little gray truck pulled away and disappeared in the haze towards the faint outlines of tents down at the far end of the field where the woods began again. I was glad to see that the corporal drove off with them, leaving no one but the bullet-headed Ohler, who was too busy tinkering with one of the landing gear struts to notice anything else around him.

"Amelia," I whispered to her. She crawled up to me. I cringed as twigs snapped beneath her knees, but at least her wool dress muffled the sound. "You all follow after me when I get to the plane."

"Be careful," she begged.

"I've lived this long, haven't I?" I winked. She took my hand and squeezed it tightly, and I kissed her quickly for luck. Then I rose to my feet and emerged from the woods and out of the fog like a lost soul.

57

I could hear Kurt Ohler humming contently to himself as he did what he enjoyed most: working on machines. His tools made metallic pings as he adjusted a strut here, tightened a screw there. He was standing underneath the right wing of the large Heinkel, which was the versatile mainstay of the Luftwaffe level bombing fleet. His thick, grease-stained forearms were buried in the bowels of one of the engines doing some last-minute pre-flight maintenance when I approached him cautiously.

"Is this machine ready to fly?" I asked in a hushed voice.

At first he didn't deviate from his task and only responded: "I should hope so or else I'm sending the supply officers up to their doom." He closed the panel that gave access to the in-line engine and locked it. He turned around. "She's flying to Frankfurt in about two—" At first his face was stone. But then the bushy mustache rose on his cheeks and his yellow teeth showed through. "Captain Becker!" he exclaimed. "By God it's good to see you, sir! We all thought you'd left us."

I raised my hand and pointed the Luger at his stomach, and he squinted in confusion.

"I have left you, Kurt." I made a flipping motion to the plane's open hatch with the gun barrel. "Get in."

His expression changed to alarm. "Sir, please, I don't know what this is about."

"There's no time to explain. Just get in the plane. Now!"

He didn't say another word and obediently scaled the extended ladder into the side ventral gunner 'bath tub' position that led into fuselage. I followed him up, keeping the gun trained on him. Once inside the narrow interior, I ushered him through the empty bomb bay and into the cockpit, which was enclosed by the distinctive birdcage glass and strut nose of the aircraft. We could see through the windscreen Amelia hurriedly escorting the rest of my charges along the grassy runway until they disappeared below us. Then they popped up one by one into the plane's belly and found places to sit in the cramped fuselage. Amelia crouched behind us in the cockpit, holding on to the pilot's seat for support. Jakob shoved past Kurt, got on his hands and knees, and crawled onto the bombardier platform, which was in front and to the right of the pilot seat. A twenty-millimeter cannon jutted out of the tip of the nose, which was offset to the right so when manning the gun for defense or strafing, the bombardier wouldn't obstruct the pilot's field of vision. On the other side of the bomb bay, in the center of the aircraft, Krup sat in the right waist gunner's seat and Constanze the left, with Elsa on her knees. Ohler looked back over his shoulder at them with a mixture of curiosity and confusion.

"Who the hell are they?" he asked.

"Shut up, Kurt," I snapped. I tapped Jakob on the shoulder and handed the gun to him. "If this man makes a move, shoot him."

Jakob took the gun hesitantly but, realizing that he needed to make a good show of it, sat up on the platform with his knees tucked in and firmly grasped the weapon. He placed his finger on the trigger, aiming it straight at Ohler's face. (I didn't bother to tell anyone I'd left the safety on. I had no intention of hurting my good crew chief, either on purpose or by an accidental discharge.)

I situated myself in the pilot's seat and ran my fingers over the many dials above my head with one hand while taking the wheel in the other. "I've never flown anything so large," I muttered mostly to myself. "Okay, let's just go through this by the numbers, Harmon."

I did an accelerated pre-flight check as best I could remember and then strapped myself in. Ohler was warily looking around for something to hang on to, as there was no co-pilot seat. "Not you, Kurt," I said. "Once we hit the runway you can go." He gave me a suspicious look and then pointed at Jake and the gun aimed at his forehead.

"Will you please tell this...boy to point the gun away?"

I ignored him. It was time to go.

"Hang on, everybody. This won't be smooth," I warned. I primed both engines and then depressed the starters, first the right and then the left engine. There was a protesting whine as the propellers reluctantly began to rotate and then the submissive coughing as the engines turned over and the real power with their cylinders took hold. The grass and hay and leaves behind the wings began to whip around violently in the prop wash, as I lowered the flaps and very gently eased the throttle to move us out of the wooded cove and onto the open field of the runway.

"Is everyone either strapped in or holding on to something?" I shouted back to my frightened passengers, who'd never flown before in their lives. The Krupinskis nodded unconvincingly from the gunners' stations. Only Jakob seemed to be relishing the moment. That he was actually aiming a gun at a Nazi soldier as opposed to the other way around was especially gratifying to him.

I taxied out to the far end of the field opposite the rows of tents in the distance. The glass nose offered me excellent visibility, which I needed as I sloppily lined up for takeoff, trying to figure out the best angle to run down what was really just a pasture. I did one last check, revving the engines to 80 percent throttle while applying the brakes to check the manifold pressure. Everything checked out. And we were topped off with fuel. *This might just work*, I thought.

One last act remained. "Okay, Sergeant," I shouted over the din. "This is the end."

Ohler's eyes widened in disbelief and fear. "You're going to *kill* me, sir?"

I frowned at him. "Of course not! You've been a fine crew chief. I've always liked you, Kurt. But unless you wish to accompany me to England as a POW, I suggest you get out of this bird now."

"Sir," he protested. "What's gotten into you?"

Jakob was less patient with this man who was just the uniform of an oppressor to him. He stood up and grabbed Ohler by the collar (even though Kurt outweighed him by at least eighty pounds).

"Get out, you Nazi scum!" he shouted.

Kurt was shocked to hear such a taunt, and whipped his head to find the boy aiming the pistol straight at his face. At this point I was wondering whether leaving the safety on was a good idea. But I saw Ohler's eyes travel down Jake's sleeve to spot a tattoo I'd never noticed before on his pale forearm. It was a Star of David. Ohler resigned himself at that point to getting out before he got shot. With one last glance to me and then a disapproving scowl, he sidled his way in between the two bomb compartments and leapt out of the ventral hatchway that was still dangling open. He fell with a roll onto the grass as the plane passed above him. He stood up and brushed himself off to watch the Heinkel pick up speed and race down the field. As Jakob pulled up the hatch and then made his way back to the platform to my right, I gently increased power until I could feel the plane rise off the uneven airfield. Then I eased back on the yoke, and after bouncing a few times on the rough surface, the landing gear cleared the ground and we were airborne.

Through the nose cone I could see men emerging from tents in front of us as we passed overhead, buzzing the field. Very soon we were clear of the base and over the trees. I maintained our course and airspeed in order to gain altitude. Having flown only single-engine aircraft since 1940, it took some time to get used to the slower and more labored responses of the bomber's flight characteristics. It felt like climbing to cruising altitude would take all day.

Jakob marveled at his first views of the world from the air. To our right, barely visible in a sea of ground fog illuminated by the morning glare, was the little hamlet of Andeville. Beyond it the crumpled remnants of Château LeClaire and my old aerodrome. "It's beautiful," exclaimed my teenaged passenger.

Amelia was in the seat directly behind us and was leaning forward to also take in the splendid scenery. The placid green of the fields laid out before us and the serene sensation of smooth flight gave a false sense of security to my passengers that was underscored by Amelia's hopeful inquiry: "Are we safe now?"

I answered her while my eyes darted back and forth from the instrument panel to the sky before me. "Not by a long shot. Even if no one comes after us from my base, we're flying a bomber with Luftwaffe markings into Allied airspace over a combat zone. They're bound to have strong patrols out."

I reached for the radio headset and snapped it over my ears. Then I began fidgeting with the dials.

"What are you doing?" asked Jakob more from curiosity than anything.

"I need to get on to an enemy frequency. I need to announce to the Allies who we are and what our intentions are so they don't shoot us down. There's only one problem," I cautioned.

"What's that?" he asked.

"The Luftwaffe will pick us up too."

"Do you think they'll bother to come after us?"

"I don't know, Jake." I lied. I knew the answer. Because I knew Major Hans Seebeck.

Seebeck at that moment was standing half-dressed outside his tent furiously waving his arms as he berated poor Sergeant Ohler for letting us escape. The major paced back and forth on the wet grass while Ohler stood stiffly at attention. "But, Herr Major," my former crew chief protested. "He had a gun on me."

"Who?" the irate major demanded. "Becker?"

"Well no, sir," replied Ohler sheepishly. "A boy."

Seebeck shook his head. "A boy? And who were these people again?"

"I don't know, Herr Major. A woman, an older couple, and what must have been their two children. I believe the family at least were Jews."

"And why is that?" asked Seebeck.

"The boy had a tattoo of their star on his arm."

Seebeck stared at the clear sky, his frustration growing. How could he be having this conversation? Whatever had happened to that Keitel fellow in Stauffenberg?

Exasperated, Seebeck asked one last question. "Do you have the slightest idea where they may be heading?"

Ohler thought about it a second. “The captain spoke of England.”

Seebeck shook his head. “England?”

“I can’t be sure, Herr Major. Like I said, I had a gun to my head. But he said something about England and being a POW.”

Seebeck pondered the meaning of that. “Traitorous coward.”

The major scanned the base and searched through a band of pilots emerging from their tents to find out who was the inconsiderate sot who’d rudely awakened them so early in the morning. Among the men was a quieter-than-usual First Lieutenant Mueller. Seebeck called to him.

Mueller immediately obeyed. “Herr Major,” he said with a crisp salute.

“Did you carry out my orders in Stauffenberg?”

“I did, Herr Major,” said Mueller, staring straight ahead.

Seebeck tried to detect any deceit in the flier’s eyes, but there was none. The major had no idea what series of events had led to this morning. He would have to take it up with Keitel at another time, but right now needed to get to the bottom of all this.

“First Lieutenant, are you aware that it was Captain Becker who flew off with my plane just now?”

Mueller looked at him, visibly surprised while trying to maintain his soldierly manner. “No, Herr Major, I most certainly am not.”

Seebeck again wanted to doubt the man’s veracity, but it was clear that Becker’s wingman was as surprised as anyone, if not more so.

“He was with a woman. And a family of Jews.” He stepped up closer to Mueller. “You know this man better than anyone here. Do you have any idea who they might be?”

Mueller thought for a second and then nodded. “I do, Herr Major,” my wingman answered. “Or at least I can offer an educated guess.”

“Well?”

“The girl I met yesterday. Her name is Amelia Engel. His sweetheart.”

Seebeck curled his brow. “His lover? Huh. But what of the family?”

“I don’t know, sir. Perhaps his piano instructor and his family. He’s the only older man about whom the captain speaks with any affection.” Then Mueller’s expression changed, like someone solving a riddle. “*Well I know four Germans who are* not *going to die.*" My words bounced around in his head. "I wasn't aware they were Jews. But now I understand."

"What do you understand?" sneered Keitel.

Mueller cracked a knowing smile. "He's saving their lives, sir."

Seebeck was taken aback. His best pilot was risking his life to save a pack of Jews? Inconceivable. Yet it was the only logical explanation for the strange events unfolding.

"So, the man who wishes to be above it all has suddenly become Moses," he said. He turned to Ohler. "Very well, Sergeant. Prepare Becker's and Mueller's planes for takeoff, immediately."

"*Jawohl*, Herr Major." Ohler saluted and trotted off to fuel up the two Focke-Wulf 190s. "And arm them as well," he added. Ohler paused and then proceeded to go about his task, calling to several ground crewmen to assist him.

"You're coming with me, Mueller."

"Sir?" Mueller blinked in surprise. "Coming with you where?"

Seebeck gazed up at the clear blue sky towards the west. "Up there," he said.

Mueller was more than a little hesitant about flying with Seebeck on his wing. He was, in fact, downright terrified. With a sky filled with Allied fighters, it seemed to him that going on a mission with the cycloptic Seebeck, even if it was to shoot down a lone bomber, was suicide.

"Herr Major, with all due respect," said Mueller diplomatically, "are you up for flying? It's been a while. And the Allies will have their fighter umbrella up."

Seebeck threw him a look of contempt. "I'm still a fighter pilot. Be ready to take off in ten minutes. He'll not get away from me."

Mueller was unconvinced. And the thought of having to go after his old friend, even if he was deserting and harboring Jews, was something he was having a hard time reconciling with his sense of duty. After all, had he not swallowed hard on his standards already and done as the major ordered by reporting his trusted wingman to the SS? Wasn't that enough to ask of him? But a soldier's lot was to do more than expected at all times. It was the nature of excellence. Still, he made one last attempt to stay neutral.

"Herr Major. I respectfully request that I be excused from this mission."

Seebeck gave him a searing look from his good eye.

"Request denied. Now go." Then more to himself he added a footnote of finality. "This ends today."

Fifteen minutes later, while the rest of JG 32 chattered amongst themselves about the mysterious takeoff of the Heinkel He 111, a pair of fully armed Focke-Wulf 190As roared down the grass and lifted off, heading west with the morning sun behind them.

58

We'd been flying for a half hour now, steadily chugging westward, and so far all was well. I leveled us off at ten thousand feet, as any higher might have made breathing difficult for the sickly Leopold. The mood in the aircraft began to improve as a sense of security that accompanied seeing the Third Reich disappear farther and farther behind us cheered my passengers. Amelia moved directly behind me as I scanned the skies while keeping my hands on the wheel. I felt her arms around me and her chin on my shoulder.

To my right, Jakob continued to gaze in wonder through the strutted canopy at the marvelous sights of Europe two miles below us. I recognized his face. It was the same one I had worn when I first climbed into a trainer biplane and saw my country for the first time from above.

Krup and Constanze sat in silence with heads turned to each other as the choppy air bounced us along, both watching little Elsa as she slept in her mother's lap. I could only imagine what they were feeling at this moment. Freed from their prison, but now wondering what lay ahead. Was Germany the exception, or were Jews unwelcome everywhere? What was the world like after years of near isolation? It must have been a bittersweet moment for them.

"Well," whispered Amelia. "You did it."

It was time for a dose of reality. "I've done nothing yet. Look around you. We're flying a German bomber towards a battlefield. The Allies will have clouds of fighters overhead. If I don't raise them before they spot us, we're dead meat." Her smile faded after that, and she sat back and let me work. I adjusted the headset so it covered my ears securely. Then I adjusted the dial to find what I knew to be a commonly used open frequency, over which we'd often eavesdrop on the Amis' chatter when they weren't observing radio silence. "I only hope my English is not so terrible."

I clicked the talk button and began to call out to all who were in range—German and Allied alike. In broken English I said:

"This is Nebel-One calling on an open frequency to any Allied controller or aircrew. We are a Heinkel He 111 with German markings on a route west to Caen. Exact coordinates unknown. We are a single aircraft. We are not hostile. Repeat, we are not hostile. We have refugees onboard. I request an escort to English airspace. Please come in, any Allied air personnel…"

"…come in, any Allied air personnel."

What on earth are you doing, Harmon? thought Mueller as he tweaked his whistling radio set to more clearly hear the crackling voice of his friend over the airwaves.

"Mueller, is he a madman?" came the cry from the plane with which he was flying in pack wing formation. Mueller tried to stay in a wingtip configuration with the FW-190 to his right, but the man flying Becker's plane was no Becker. His aircraft bounced and weaved to and fro as if on a roller coaster. Twice already they'd nearly collided, and so Mueller gave the aircraft he'd once felt comfortable almost touching with his a wide birth. He never realized how smoothly he and Becker had worked together until he attempted to fly with someone he considered a rank amateur. He was quickly coming to despise the mission and even more so the man who had ordered him on it.

"I cannot say, Herr Major," responded Mueller, deadpan.

"Well he's a damned fool for sure. Ground control has a fix on him now."

"They are off to your eleven o'clock, Hanny zero zero, about forty miles. You will see them soon," chimed in the ground controller. "Estimate contact in five minutes."

"Victor," responded Mueller robotically.

As I continued to make my desperate plea over the radio, Krup quietly appeared in the crowded nose and put his hand on my shoulder. I stopped talking long enough to pat his hand in reassurance.

"Harmon," he said solemnly. "I heard about Paul. Now your parents too. I have no words to tell you how sorry I am."

I closed my eyes as the memories of those I'd lost came flooding back to me. "There's nothing to say. What matters right now is getting out of here. Or we'll be with them sooner than we wish."

Krup was going to say something else, but I held my hand up to silence him as the first response to my radio shouts came through my headset. My heart sank. It wasn't what I wanted to hear. "Leo," I sighed. "You'd better sit back down with your wife. This is going to get rough."

"Becker," said the familiar, shrill voice over the wire. "You have two FW-190s on your six o'clock high."

"Shit!" I cried.

Jakob whipped his head to see my face. "What is it?"

I looked up but couldn't see them in the overhead rear-view mirror.

"Jake," I said. "Run back to the gunner's station and tell me what you see."

The young man nodded and scurried behind us through the fuselage until he found a dorsal glass hood with a mounted machine gun a quarter of the way between us and the tail, just in front of where his nervous parents and sister were seated. Carefully he poked his head up and scanned the blue skies behind us. At first, he thought that all was clear, but then he spied two black shapes rapidly approaching out of the eastern sun. They were fighter planes moving fast and closing the range on us. Jake didn't need to be told whose side they were on, and an electric current ran up his spine.

He quickly ducked his head back down and found his parents, who were pale with airsickness, looking at him with fear. "What's wrong?" asked his father. Jake ignored him and reported directly to the cockpit.

"Well?" I asked.

He looked at Amelia. Then to me. "I saw two fighter planes. Coming out of the east. I think they're German."

At that moment, as if to add confirmation to Jakob's report, Seebeck's voice again pierced through my headset.

"Becker, if you do not turn back now we will open fire."

Then I heard Josef's voice pleading with me: "Please, Harmon. Do as he says."

"Mueller," I barked over the radio, "if you know what's good for you, you'll shoot down the bastard next to you and follow me to England. Get out of this war while you still can."

"Harmon, do you even know what you're saying?" he responded.

"Enough, First Lieutenant," I heard Seebeck interject. "I'll take the shot."

"Oh Christ, Major!" I shouted to him. "Let it go! Let us go!"

Silence but for the hissing of the radio. Then: "Cover me, First Lieutenant."

I felt ill. Looking around I saw no clouds to hide in. I thought about taking evasive action, but I knew that the agile Focke-Wulf 190A could literally fly loops around this lumbering machine. I was desperate. And so, I did something desperate. I turned to Jake, who was sitting behind me in a crouch, biting his nails.

"Was there a weapon in the gunner's station?"

"I saw a machine gun, yes," he said.

"Was it armed?" I asked.

"I'm sorry?"

"Was there a belt of ammunition running into it?"

He nodded. "Yes. I think so. I mean, yes. There are bullets, yes!"

I stood up. "Shift places with me," I said to Jakob.

"What?" he asked.

"Do it!"

He quickly slid into the pilot's seat. "Put your hands right here," I said while placing them on the yoke. He just gawked at me. "Dammit, boy, just do what I say!"

His hands gripped hard on the wheel. My instincts so far were correct, as I knew this boy had an affinity for machines. He looked quite comfortable at the controls. Only a single bead of sweat running down his temple betrayed his anxieties.

"Okay," I said, removing the headset. "Keep your hands steady. Pull back to go up, push forward to go down. But don't do any of it. Just keep her straight and level and pointed west. It's not hard to fly a plane if you don't need to take off or land." I pointed to the altitude indicator. "Watch that line. Keep it straight and level. I'll be right back."

I shoved my way past Amelia. "Harmon," called out Jake from the pilot's seat. "Are you sure I can do this?"

"You already are, aren't you?" A grin spread across his face and he turned to face the sky through the nose cone.

Amelia stayed hunkered down behind him but said not a word for fear of distracting our teenage pilot. As I made my way past her in the tube of the aircraft guts, Constanze asked me: "Harmon, who's flying the plane?"

"A very bright young man," I said as I manned the gunner's station. The plane violently yawed clockwise and I almost fell over. "Dammit, Jake, keep your feet off the rudder pedals!"

"Sorry!" he called back. And then to my relief we leveled off again. The lad was a natural in the air.

I grabbed a pair of headphones to listen in on the chatter and pulled back the bolt of the MG52 machine gun and loaded the first of the long belt of rounds into the chamber. And then I waited.

Suddenly the two fighters appeared in my field of vision. My first thought was actually one of annoyance. *That swine's flying my plane!* Then I threw down the proverbial gauntlet. "Come on, Hans, let's do this."

At the moment, that swine was too slowly pulling back on the throttle and would soon over-shoot our slow-moving Heinkel.

"Sir," cautioned Mueller. "If you don't slow down, you'll fly right past him."

But Seebeck remained silent. He needed all his concentration to compensate for the lost depth perception of only one eye. "Just a little closer," he said to himself.

As my former fighter plane crept so close that I could now see the man in the cockpit and even make out the flower petal-like pistons cooking inside the radial engine cowling, I lined up the gunsight.

Mueller's voice was railing at him over the radio. "Sir, if you don't fire now you'll either over-fly him or collide!"

"One more second!" said Seebeck to his wingman.

"Good boy, Jake," I muttered under my breath. "Keep her steady." Then to Seebeck, whose plane now filled my sights. "That's it, Major."

"Almost there." Seebeck was coaxing himself. I could hear his labored breathing.

Mueller suddenly noticed my form in the gunner's position over his nose and called out to Seebeck: "Watch the gunner!"

"What gunner?" I heard a confused voice reply.

Mueller banked hard left and pushed the stick forward to slip under the bomber and clear of my aim.

But it was too late for Hans Seebeck. He was at point-blank range at no more than forty paces. As I squeezed the trigger and let the rounds fly, there was no way I could miss. My gun shuddered, and white flashes burst from the muzzle that was aimed right at Seebeck's face.

The Krupinskis screamed in terror as the gun just behind them blasted away, dropping sizzling spent cartridges on my feet and even their shoulders. I didn't have to concern myself with conserving ammunition with short bursts, so I doused Seebeck's plane with a steady stream of projectiles as if from a garden hose.

The hail of bullets sprayed into my commander's exposed radial engine and windscreen above it. Sparks pinged off the propeller blades from the rounds that were deflected away. The rest of my volley scythed into the machine. I saw several flashes in the cockpit and could tell that I'd hit the pilot right between the eyes.

Seebeck's fighter violently flipped over in a snap roll and went inverted and fell away. Leaping down through the fuselage to the gunner's ventral gondola below me, I strained to get a better view of the crashing fighter. I could see through the glass panes a smoking Focke-Wulf 190A spiraling towards the ground. I saw no parachute. Immediately I knew that Major

Seebeck was dead. I should have felt more, but after everything I'd been through, I'd turned quite callous about killing those trying to prevent us from getting away. "One down, one to go," was the only eulogy I could muster.

I scrambled back into the cockpit, where Jake was maintaining a respectable control over the machine.

"What's happening?" he asked. I looked to Amelia. "My major's dead."

"You got one of them?" replied Jakob, excited at my exploit. Amelia, on the other hand, bowed her head. There is only so much killing one can take in a period of time.

I had no time for reflection. I quickly shooed Jake out of the pilot's seat and took the controls. "Good job," I said, sliding on my headset with one hand while gripping the wheel with the other.

"Thanks." He beamed. "Are we in the clear?"

"Not yet. We still have one more out there."

His eyes lit up. "You want me to take the gun? I can shoot as straight as I fly."

I patted his head. "No, Jake. I assure you this one's no Seebeck."

Amelia squeezed my arm tightly. "Mueller would still come after you after your commander's dead?"

"I'm afraid so," I reported sadly. "Dammit, I need a cloud. Any other day I'd pray for this weather for flying. Now it may kill us."

"But I thought he's your friend?"

I shook my head. "He is. But he's a soldier first."

As if on cue, Mueller's distressed voice hissed in through my headset. "Harmon, come around to a new course on me."

"Sorry, Josef," I said. "I'm only going one way."

"Please," he continued. "I don't want to do this."

Krup, hearing one side of my conversation, momentarily left his bawling wife and daughter to peer up through the gunner's station to look for Mueller's plane. "I can't see anything," he said with a wisp of wishful thinking.

"Did you hear that?" echoed Amelia hopefully.

"He's in the sun," I said, squashing their momentary relief.

"How can you be sure?" she asked.

"That's where I'd be," I offered grimly. "It's right behind us, and so is he."

"Harmon, I repeat, I do not want to do this," he said. I could almost hear his voice quaking. I briefly considered weaving the Heinkel left and right to both present a more challenging deflection shot to him as well as pull him out of the sun's rays. But that would just prolong the inevitable. I had to try to reason with him. After all we'd been through, for one of us to die at the hands of the other was absurd, and I told him so.

"Josef, you don't have to do this at all. The man who gave you the order is dead."

"You know that doesn't change the order," he replied.

"Dammit, man, it changes everything!" I protested. "Are you more than just a robot? Either come with me to safety or turn around. But I'm not heading back with you if you choose the latter."

There was a pause. Then he responded, more deadpan: "I have my orders."

I was growing more frustrated than scared at this point. "Orders! Josef, it's time to forget protocol and think about tomorrow. You have a chance to get out of this unholy mess with your honor intact. No one will fault you for not murdering a family of refugees just wishing to leave."

That didn't work on him. He was a child of totalitarianism too. And he'd had no Leopold Krupinski or Amelia Engel to show him the way as I had.

"I told you, Harmon, there is no tomorrow. Only the here and now."

As I banked slightly just to stay on course, Mueller followed to reveal himself out of the sun. A menacing, stalking machine that seemed to be coming right for Leo and his family. Krup cried out from the gunner's spot with panic. "There he is! He's right on us!"

There was nothing I could do to get away. Our only hope was to try to get my old friend to come to his senses and remove his blinders through which we'd both once viewed the world, but I'd since discarded.

"That's where you're wrong," I protested. "Listen to me, Josef. We are friends. You've always trusted me as I you. Trust me now when I tell you that this war is over. Germany has lost. I think it's even for the better. All that will matter in a year or two is how you conduct yourself right now. How you behaved as a man. What will you tell your children about this day?"

Again, I had no effect. "I'll tell them that I was a good soldier who honored my sacred oaths and did my duty and obeyed my commands."

I spat, thoroughly disgusted. "Commands from who? A madman like Hitler?"

"Stop it, Becker!" he pleaded.

"A fat oaf like Göring? The Hans Seebecks of the world? Why should you surrender your life to such lesser men?"

I could tell he was having an internal dialogue. We would have otherwise been dead by now. Of that much I was certain. I gunned the Heinkel to full throttle, but the little fighter effortlessly kept up with power to spare. This was the final moment of truth.

"Harmon, I'm giving you one last chance to turn back." And with that he fired a warning burst over our heads. But one round must have spun wild, because it smashed behind me through the windscreen and pierced me below the left shoulder. I'd been shot yet again. Amelia screamed when she saw the bullet thump into my flesh and me grunt in pain.

"My God!" exclaimed Jake.

"What? What's happened?" cried out Constanze. "Harmon, are you alright?"

Gritting my teeth, I tried to shake away the burning pain, but I felt my left arm losing strength. And yet I was more angered than anything. Angry that my friend would actually take a shot at me. As the French countryside passed below us in all its emerald glory, I screamed into the radio: "Dammit, Josef! There are children aboard!"

"Can't you get away from him?" begged Jake.

"Quiet, boy!" yelled his father.

"In my pocket," I said to Amelia weakly as I motioned to the zippered compartment of my flight suit pants. She unzipped it and reached inside the pocket to find the handkerchief she'd made for me those many years before, after Kristallnacht. Amelia looked at it with a faint smile. The "*HBN*" embroidery lovingly hand-stitched on it brought back the sweet memory of our first night together. It was now my field dressing. She pressed it up against my wound to stem the flow of blood seeping through the shoulder of my flight suit. "I keep ruining your handkerchiefs," she said, trying to deflect my concern.

"This time it's my blood," I grunted.

"I'll get you another when we get to England," she said with that crooked smile. I nodded back to her.

"I said turn around and I meant it, Herr Captain," commanded Mueller again.

"Listen to you. '*Herr Captain*'! You think you'll still be a soldier if you shoot us down? You'll be a murderer, Josef. A butcher of defenseless women and children."

"I'll be an executer of enemies of the Reich. A warrior."

I couldn't believe my ears. "A warrior for what? A morally bankrupt cause. What good will that do you but offer you a collection of dusty medals and tattered ribbons! When your children ask of your wingman and friend, Harmon Becker, what will you tell them? 'I shot him down because he saw the truth'? In the name of humanity get out of here, Josef!"

Then I heard him click off his radio, no longer willing to endure the emotional torment. But I knew he wouldn't leave. It was just not in him to abandon his mission. So, I gave one last look at my helpless crew. I with my bleeding shoulder. Amelia with her kerchief trying desperately to stem the flow. The Krupinskis, all four of them now, huddling together again. This time in a narrow tube that was now to be their coffin, two miles above France, almost within sight of the English Channel and freedom.

Mueller adjusted his gunsight to rest on the intersection of the lumbering bomber's broad oval wings and narrow fuselage. This time he switched to cannon. There would be no more warnings.

As he choked back a tear, he gathered all of his training to prepare himself to carry out this most difficult of orders. But carry it out he would. He was a soldier. And his oath to Hitler bound him to the will of the chain of command. This was what made him different from Harmon. He knew where his duty lay. Harmon had lost his way. And now he was an enemy.

"I'm sorry, my friend," he muttered to himself as he flipped up the safety on his control stick with his thumb. He took a deep breath and prepared to fire. Then he squeezed the trigger.

59

In my mind's eye, the last thing my friend Josef Mueller saw before his death was a bright sheet of orange filling his field of vision. There was a sudden loud rush of sound and searing heat, and then all went dark. I hope he never even felt his body plunge to the earth below with the other pieces of his disintegrating fighter plane.

"What was that?" I said as I listened to the swishing of cannon rounds streaking over our aircraft from out of the west, followed by the thud of an airplane exploding in mid-air behind us. Before anyone could answer, the humming of Allison in-line engines screamed all around us and a blur of twin-engine fighters blew past, coming from the opposite direction as if in a game of chicken. Through the conical windscreen I watched in marvel as a second wave of speeding aircraft appeared from seemingly out of nowhere before they too zoomed past us, two over us and two under.

I knew in an instant what had happened. And with that realization came the knowledge that the Krupinskis' long nightmare was finally over. I almost wept with relief. But the throbbing in my bleeding arm reminded me that I still needed to focus on flying this plane and landing it before I passed out.

"I think we're okay," I assured everyone.

"What are they?" cried Jakob, who didn't know whether to be scared or relieved. Amelia too gripped my good arm with fear.

The last time I'd seen American P-38 Lightnings, they were on my tail peeling apart my mount. Today, they were not my pursuers but my saviors. We used to call them "fork-tailed devils." Not this day. For me, "angels" came to mind.

Soon the fighters banked around—I counted eight—to form up on either side of our plane. To my relief they held their fire. Apparently, they'd heard my distress calls. They were sleek, futuristic machines. Their curious lines were made all the more intriguing by their shiny silver color scheme and black and white "invasion stripes" painted on the twin booms for their engines and their knife-like wings. In the center, between the booms, sat the pilots in their cockpit nacelles. The one nearest to us looked us over with curiosity and, I assumed, suspicion.

I waved at him, and he waved back. Then a young, robust voice crackled in my ears. In English he spoke with what I would later come to recognize as a Texas drawl: "Attention, Heinkel He 111. State your intentions. Over."

"My English is not so good," I said. Struggling to remember the proper words, I continued: "I am Captain Harmon Becker of Jagdgeschwader Thirty-Two. I have onboard five, eh, stowaways? Refugees! Yes, refugees. Including two children."

Jakob, the relief washing over him, even managed some bravado. "Children," he said, rolling his eyes. "I just flew a plane, didn't I?"

"Shush!" said his beaming mother.

"I request an escort to England as your prisoner," I continued. "We have a wounded man onboard."

"Roger that."

"Do you see any more Luftwaffe fighters?" I asked.

"That's a negative," responded the American pilot with the confidence that only air supremacy can muster. "Follow us in. If you deviate from our course, you will be shot down. Is that clear? Over."

"Victor," I said. "I mean, yes, I understand."

I fought off a wave of dizziness and then shook my head and focused hard on keeping the Heinkel level.

Amelia studied my color with growing concern. "Are you okay?"

I nodded. "I'll get us in. Don't worry." And then I saw a brilliant gleam of orange and gold, like a sheet of lustrous metal, spreading out before us. It was a body of water, glistening in the morning sunlight. I pointed for everyone to see. "The English Channel."

But water was not all I saw. I considered the entire scene around me. Escorting *V*s of P-38 Lightnings flanked us, bringing us in like sheep-dogs would a lost lamb. Below me, an endless collection of black shapes in the water. We marveled in awe at the Allied invasion fleet stretching out as far as the eye could see, almost all the way back to England. From smaller transports to LSTs to great warships cruising back and forth, lobbing their massive projectiles as far as twenty miles inland for support. The sky was filled with aircraft coming to and fro. All sporting either the American star or RAF roundels, on their way to or returning from their missions. All of this power was concentrated for one purpose: to pound my country to dust. To hurl us out of the lands we'd taken by force, and if it meant killing every German there was, then so be it.

Ever since I'd seen that map in the Berghof, I'd had a general, nebulous notion that the war was lost. It was a vague concept that drifted listlessly in the back of my mind. But now the full reality of our doom was laid out before me. To this day I cannot describe the sinking feeling I felt when I saw the power arrayed against my people. All I could do was sum it up to Amelia in three words:

"It's all over."

And so it was for all of us. Krup would live; I would live; Amelia would live.

And the Third Reich would die, taking the megalomaniacal dream of Hitler and his nation of acolytes with it.

60

I feared I might pass out before we reached my escorts' base in England, but soon the jagged edges of the British coastline appeared below us. The Lightnings formed a virtual net around us as we began a gradual descent towards a sprawling airfield that was barely inland from the rocky cliffs overlooking the channel.

The closer I got to it, the more this expansive complex of runways, hangars, barracks, towers, canteens, mess halls, anti-aircraft batteries, and a swarm of aircraft lined wingtip to wingtip out in the wide-open space with no fear of *Jabos* pouncing on them impressed me; especially in contrast to my base, which was reduced to a dozen planes crouching to stay out of sight in the woods. How could we have ever thought to overcome such might? Now I felt not just ashamed of my country, but stupid to have been duped for so long by the fantasy proclamations of the high command.

"Heinkel 111, this is the nearest aerodrome. Since you have wounded onboard, you're cleared to land here," said the Southerner again over my headset. "Make your approach from the northeast. I remind you that you'll be shot down if you deviate. Other than that, welcome to England, Captain. Your war's over."

The pilot in the plane to my right who'd stayed at my side throughout the trip across France and over the channel waved. I waved back weakly. Then he rolled ninety degrees and gently arced towards his squadron to oversee our touchdown before heading off to his own base farther west.

My head was swimming, as the loss of blood saturating Amelia's kerchief was affecting me. "Come on, Harmon," I said to myself. "Just one last push."

I shook my head spastically to clear away the fog as one might do when nodding off at the wheel of a car. Then I gently banked the Heinkel around until the landing strip appeared as a flat trapezoid in my windscreen. I extended the landing gear, making sure I had green lights all around, and then eased on the throttle, tapped the flaps until fully extended, and pulled back slightly on the yoke to slow us to a safe landing speed. "Hold on, everybody," I called out to my weary passengers. I let the bomber gradually descend until the runway rushed up to fill my windshield. A pair of Lightnings stayed with us like chase planes, then peeled away before stalling.

The greatest feeling I have ever known, besides the first time I kissed Amelia and the birth of my baby, Dora, was that initial bump of the landing gear skidding along the concrete surface of the American airstrip. A few more bounces and jolts and then solid terra firma beneath us as the floating sensation died and our full body weights returned. The aircraft slowed to taxi speed as it rolled down the long runway.

My field of vision was closing in around me as the continued blood loss was reeling me into a dream state. Even though it was June, I suddenly felt so cold. Amelia noticed the alarming change in my complexion from flesh tone to gray and realized I was slipping into shock. "Hang on, Harmon," she said coolly. "You did it. Don't you go soft on me now." There was no longer fear of the unknown in her voice. Although we were in the heart of enemy country, we were the safest we'd been in years. And the four good people we had spirited here need no longer dread the knock at the door. It was an incredible sense of accomplishment. One that Amelia and I shared together.

In my reduced vision I watched through the windscreen as a little jeep, painted olive drab with a white star on the hood, drove out to meet us. In the back sat two helmeted MPs carrying carbines, one of whom waved for us to follow them and pointed to an empty space at the end of the field where I could park the wounded bomber. I lowered the throttle so that we were now slowly taxiing over the web of runways and approach lanes behind this little vehicle. As we moved, an ambulance truck pulled up to follow alongside, its canvas covering painted with a soothing red cross. Other jeeps, also loaded with MPs, followed in a crude procession.

I had to muster all of my remaining strength to stay conscious and get this plane the last fifty yards. Waves of lightheadedness washed over me and then receded. Vision blurred, cleared, blurred, went dark, and came back again. The Krupinskis were speaking in excited tones, with Jakob pointing out to Elsa the different types of cars and aircraft that were parked in this enormous aerodrome. All around us were row upon row of those massive Thunderbolt fighters, painted in olive and sky-blue camouflage, their cowlings coated in bright scarlet.

Just under the cockpits of so many of these heavy fighters were those little crosses or swastikas painted in neat rows along the fuselage, each representing a German kill. I couldn't bear the sight of so many of these decorations. Each marking was a record of the final moments of men like Borner, Gaetjens, Mueller, and Paul, who had died for a cause whose ugly face was now fully visible to me. And there were bases like these spread along the length and breadth of Great Britain.

Finally I brought the bomber to a halt in the designated area at the end of the runway and cut the throttle. My head slumped forward as I felt a gentle sleep overwhelm me. As if I were underwater, the last thing I heard was Krup asking: "Harmon. Are you okay?" I just needed to rest a bit was all. I felt myself fall sideways into the arms of my old master as I drifted away.

When I opened my eyes again, I wasn't in the plane but staring up at a huddle of faces looking down on me with the clear sky behind them. I was lying on a stretcher with a blanket up to my chest and staring up from the tarmac, contemplating everyone around me. Some of the faces I knew. Amelia, Jakob, Krup. Others were strange men in olive uniforms. They were US soldiers and Army Air Corps personnel. Wary MPs with their hands resting conspicuously on their sidearms stood guard over me. But I was in no threat to anyone. Kneeling to my left was a medic holding up a glass IV bottle with a drip that went into my exposed forearm. Another was applying a heavy bandage to my wounded shoulder. Someone had cut away my grimy flight suit. "You'll be alright there, Cap'n," another medic was saying in a reassuring tone. "Just try to lie still."

Krup managed to wedge himself into the scrum enough to kneel by my right side, clasping my hand in both of his. Amelia hovered above and behind him, smiling down at me. When I saw her expression of relief, I knew I'd survive. Then Leo spoke to me. "Harmon," he said with a husky voice ready to go to pieces. "You've saddled me with a debt I can never repay." I tried to say something, but I was too weak. "Save your strength," he said.

I don't know what possessed me to do what I did next. Maybe it was an act of contrition on my part. Maybe it was a repudiation of all I'd fought and killed for during this damned war. Or maybe it was a final token of affection for my old *Musikmeister* who'd saved me as much as I him. Whatever the reason, I raised my free hand to my neck, unclipped my Ritterkreuz, and offered it up to Krup.

He stared at it and then at me. "No, my boy," he protested. "I cannot take this from you."

I took his hand that was holding mine and opened his palm, wherein I placed my Knight's Cross and closed his fingers around it. I pushed his hand away and dropped my arm to my side. Then I closed my eyes again. Sleep once more was invading my world.

I heard strange voices in foreign tongues. Enemy soldiers all around penetrated my darkness. "And up!" said one of the medics, and I felt myself lifted into the air and carried as if in a dream.

"*Bitte*," said Amelia in a confused tone. "*Lassen Sie mich mit ihm bleiben.*"

An MP held her at bay. "Sorry, lady, I don't follow. You and your friends go with the chaplain. This man needs medical attention."

Still moving along with my eyes shut, I could hear other voices drifting in waves in the darkness. Some men were none too happy to see the enemy in their midst. "Hey, Joey, get a load of this. That a friggin' Heinkel?"

"Yeah, just landed. The Kraut officer's some hotshot ace."

Another insisted: "Someone oughtta shoot the Nazi sombitch."

Still another said: "Easy, Sergeant York. The guy called 'uncle' fair and square."

Then I could feel myself being slid into the back of a truck and the engine rev as we sped away. The medics never left my side. "It's okay, Cap'n," the one kept saying. "You're gonna make it."

The other simply added: "Now this ain't somethin' you see every day."

And then the most relaxing sleep I've ever known washed over me.

I awoke with a start to find myself in a military hospital among a row of beds. I don't know what time it was other than it was the middle of the night. I seemed to be alone but for an armed MP who sat motionless on a stool by the door. Careful not to dislodge the intravenous line running into my forearm, I rolled over to face my guard and an electric pain pierced my bandaged shoulder. I moaned and the MP sat up in his chair. He may have been dozing.

I was at least comforted by the fact that, though the pain was throbbing through my shoulder, my arm wasn't in a sling, indicating nothing was broken. But it hurt like the devil.

Still, my curiosity overcame my discomfort, and I sat up on the edge of the bed to take in my foreign accommodations. I noticed at once how much more advanced and well-stocked this hospital was than our own. Supply and logistics were not an issue here. Rows of empty IV bottles lined the wall waiting for patients. Each bed had fresh linen. Medicine cabinets on either end of the room practically burst with supplies of morphine, aspirin, iodine, penicillin, bandages, and anything else a sick or wounded man needed.

I wondered if my father had felt this sense of helpless resignation when he was captured by the Allies in the Great War. That thought brought the memories of my dear parents and brother in front of me for a moment, and I had to remind myself they no longer existed. That I was alone. Oh how I ached for them! There would be plenty of sobbing in the weeks to come over the deep cavern in my heart. A cavity that would be filled in time with the love of Amelia—who at that same moment was somewhere else on this enormous airbase, confused, alone, and suffering her own anguish over the loss of that incredible woman, Hanna.

But that night, my first night as a POW, I was still in shock from the staggering level of violence and bloodshed I'd left in the wake of my exodus from the war. But I also took comfort in the knowledge that four innocent people were indeed alive, just as I'd vowed to my hopelessly misguided friend Mueller, one melancholy morning before.

I stood up and contemplated my comfortable cotton hospital nightclothes. The IV drip followed me on its wheeled stand as I hoisted myself to my bare feet and shuffled over to the doorway. The MP went to intercept me. I had to remind myself that I was now a prisoner of war on an American airbase.

"Problem, Captain?" the gruff soldier said warily. He gripped his sidearm.

I poked my head through the door to look up and down the barren hallway coated with sterile white light reflecting on an ugly linoleum floor. At the end of the hall I noticed an old Wurlitzer spinet piano on a wheeled base, which they used for entertaining patients. I made an instinctive move to exit into the hallway until I felt my guard's hand on my uninjured shoulder restraining me.

"Sorry, but you can't leave this room," he said. Then he paused. "You speak English? Uhh, *sprechen Sie English*?"

"Yes, I speak some," I said. "I was wondering if I could play your piano."

The MP shook his head. "I don't think so. You ain't supposed to leave your bed. Besides, you took a thirty-cal. to the shoulder this morning. Don't you think you oughtta cool it?"

I looked down at my burning shoulder and then to the American. "*Bitte*…please. I play. It has been a, how do you say, 'a bad dog day.'"

The guard softened at that. I was clearly harmless. "Close enough," he said. "Come on." With that he led me to the piano and even pulled out the bench for me. I groaned as I eased myself to sit under my guard's curious eye. My shoulder let my arm move only with some shoots of pain, but I ignored my bullet wound's protest and placed my hands on the keys.

I could feel my confidence growing as I entered into the first measures of Beethoven's Sonata Pathétique, second movement. I was confident that I'd done a good thing. Confident that my friends were safe, that my future wife need no longer fear the deranged obsessions of a jealous and sadistic SS officer. And I was relieved that I was going to live through the war. As a prisoner of the Americans or British, yes. But alive nonetheless. As the music filled my world and blocked out all around, I felt the deep abyss of mourning for my family that existed now only in my memories. They were the victims of a nation led astray. Paul, so naive and young, never even got the chance to live. My parents, good and simple folk, didn't deserve to die violently as they had. But the war took from us all. It was up to me to go on from this moment and make their sacrifices count. Deeper I fell into the notes and phrases that now surrounded me like golden leaves whipping around on a windy autumn day. And through these notes I reflected upon my lost nation. Upon the faces of men I'd known, mostly dead, who were on the wrong side of the wrong fight but were too wrapped up in it as I had been to see the truth. That I had an old *Musikmeister* and the woman who had harbored him in my life to show me the way was an extraordinary stroke of luck for me. That I could return the favor was my gift.

Playing the piano before a soldier of my enemy was my last action as a German officer in the Second World War. The killing across the channel would continue unabated until May 1945. Millions more would die until the Western Allies and the Russians met on the Elbe, sealing Germany's fate. Berlin would be razed to flaming ruins as the Russians exacted their final orgy of vengeance upon their brutal invaders. And Adolf Hitler, once master of all Europe and the center of my world, would be reduced to a cowering existence deep in his subterranean *Führerbünker* below the Reich Chancellery building. He would end his mad reign with a self-inflicted gunshot through the mouth, surrounded by his deluded henchmen, who remained under his spell to the very end as *Götterdämmerung* raged in the streets above them.

No, Germany's chapter was not yet closed. But my war, finally, was over.

61

Rachael beams at me while sifting through a torrent of emotions. I am indeed the man. All her concerns about wasting her time had steadily washed away as I unpacked for her my real story.

"Well," I say with my palms out. "There you have it. Shall I go on?"

"I think I know the rest," she says with a warm smile. She flips through her notepad to the writing on the last page: "You spent two years in Old Coulsden prison."

"That's right. After my initial interrogation at Cockfosters, I was given a white patch, which they issued to those of us with no loyalty to National Socialism, and sent to the camp in Surrey. We were put to work building pre-fabs. They treated us well under the circumstances." Oddly enough, a fond memory flashes before me. One I haven't thought about in years. "We used to carve little wooden aircraft models and give them to the local children."

Rachael continues: "You stayed in England until offered repatriation to Germany in 1946. But you never went back to live there. Why not?"

I sigh. How to explain this? "Amelia and I decided to stay here. Almost twenty-five thousand of us did, you know. We considered moving on to America, but I was able to get placed at the Royal Academy of Music here in London through the help of one of the English families for whom I did work as part of my captivity. Anyway, it made sense to stay. I didn't wish to go back to Germany. And I'll tell you why. Germany after the war was as Krup had predicted. There were no Nazis to be found. Oh, there were the Nuremberg trials of course, but that was just for the big fish like Göring and the like. But if I may extend the metaphor, do you know what feeds the really large sea creatures of the world?"

Rachael nods. "Plankton?"

"That's right. The smallest organisms. They have little appendages for flailing about in the water, but really their moves are dictated by the larger currents that move them. And they seem so insignificant until taken as a sum of the whole. More importantly, without them the giants cannot thrive. The Allies brought the whales to justice—most of them. The millions of enablers just disappeared into the fabric of post-war German society. They are still there, some of them, to this day. Although the younger generations have taken responsibility for something their parents and grandparents refused to acknowledge. You see, as far as I could tell from some of my correspondence with old friends, or when I would tour there, most of the older Germans felt that the war was a mistake…but not because it was an immoral act of aggression at the behest of an evil man. But rather they saw it as a bad thing for Germany, well, because we lost. A disastrous error in strategic judgment. The cries of the children of Sainte Laurie-Olmer and countless others like them from France to the Balkans to the Ukraine were lost on them. Their response when I tried to tell some of Johann Keitel's crimes? Often a shrug followed by: 'Well, it was war.' After a while I just stopped telling anyone at all. I'm sorry. I could not go home and live as a party to the lie. My country was overflowing with Nazis until 1945. Where did they all go? Hmmm?"

The reporter jots that down. Perhaps another story from this? Who knows. But it explains why she's interviewing me in London, and not in Münich or Berlin.

"Although you did visit Germany while touring, you never returned to Stauffenberg? You never looked for your parents' graves? Someone must have tended to them."

It pains me to think of that lovely village on the Main. "All of Stauffenberg was effectively leveled. There weren't enough people left alive to rebuild it. I believe it is a game reserve now or something. I don't know. Even the cathedral was leveled. Only the Rathaus tower remains."

"And what of the Krupinskis?" she says with what I read as an almost mischievous look in her eyes. "Did you keep in touch with them?"

"No. I spent two years in captivity with no real connection to the world outside of England. And Amelia was in a more awkward position than I if you think about it. My role as POW was defined. And I was treated well by the RAF and US Air Force, who were naturally eager to interrogate an officer with such extensive knowledge of the other side. But Amelia, well, here was this German woman in the heart of England during a war against her country. A civilian on the wrong side of a line. Not a prisoner, but an enemy nonetheless. In fact, the authorities were not sure what to do with her. But then through an extension of the POW program, she was taken in by a generous old couple in Coulsden who'd emigrated from Austria years before and were citizens of the Commonwealth. They treated her like the daughter they never had. She learned English better than I ever did and was eventually accepted into the community. Meanwhile in Germany, my heroic death in combat over Normandy was reported and National Socialist accolades were posthumously bestowed upon me. Even Göring was said to be moved by my death. Anyway, not until I began limited touring of Europe did many figure out that Harmon Becker the pianist and Harmon Becker the dead flying ace were one and the same."

"Why did you not write about the Krupinskis? You have a publisher. Wouldn't they want such a story?"

I shake my head. "They're a German military press. They needed no morality lectures from their authors. I suggested it to my editor once…as a purely hypothetical proposal. You know what he said? 'Ach, Harmon. Enough of the Jews already. We need to get past that bit of unpleasantness.' I guess I didn't want to be the one to start pointing fingers at my own people. They would have just viewed me as a traitor anyway. 'My country right or wrong,' remember? I didn't need the scorn. Maybe that makes me a coward."

"You're not a coward, Mr. Becker," Rachael assures me.

"I wonder whatever happened to the Krupinskis?" I say with a distant look to the far windows. "Amelia heard Leo moved the family to America, but that's all I know."

Rachael throws me a vulpine grin.

I look at her, perplexed. "What? What are you smiling at, young lady?"

She leans in. "Leopold Krupinski left England as soon as he could make arrangements and eventually settled the family in Lake Placid, New York, where he became a high school music teacher. He died in 1951 from complications due to pneumonia and his long stay in your wife's attic. The climate of the mountains was not good for his damaged lungs, but it reminded him of his lost home. Constanze died ten years later. She would always say that the last six years of Leo's life were the happiest for him despite his ill health, because he knew his family would live on. They did contact the US government to find your whereabouts, but many records were lost in a fire…and they didn't exactly have software back then as backup. It was a frustrating experience for them, and they gave up and just moved on. The rest of the family drifted to New York City after Constanze died."

I raise my white brows in astonishment. So enthralled am I with Rachael's unexpected denouement to my story, that I don't even hear the knock on the door or the shuffling of Dora's feet as she descends the stairs to answer.

"How do you know so much about Leo's family?" I ask. "I mean, why would you know? You're the only person I've ever spoken to about this in such detail in decades. You must already know my connection to them, don't you? What's going on here?" I cough and then clear my throat. "I think it's time you fulfill your quid pro quo and tell me why you are really here today."

She reached out to take my hand and calm this nervous pilot. What a change in attitude from her first condemnation of me as an old Nazi. I gaze down at her hand holding mine. It's more calloused than I expected. She clearly lives life on the front lines.

"Mr. Becker," she says with a glint in her light eyes, "I know about your relationship with the Krupinski family because I am Leopold's and Constanze's granddaughter!"

My eyes widen.

She startles me even more as she gets up and steps around the coffee table and leans into me, throwing all pretext of the professional journalist to the wind.

"Oh, Mr. Becker!" she cries. And then to complete my shock, she hugs me tight and buries one side of her weeping face into my sweater. I am unsure what to do. Should I hold her? I opt to give her a soothing pat on the back the way Karl Becker often showed affection to his boys. She continues as her tears dampen my sweater. "My mother's name was Elsa Azerad. But Azerad was only her married name. Her maiden name was Elsa *Krupinski*. And I'm alive and here today because of you and what you did for her!"

I feel her sobbing intensify. It reminds me of when Amelia first cried as she contemplated my going off to war. But I can tell these are tears of joy and gratitude. I stammer as I try to contemplate the significance of this revelation. "But Elsa's a little girl," I insist.

"Not anymore," Rachael says, pulling her face off my chest. She wipes the wet part with her sleeve. "She grew up, married, had children of her own, and lived a happy life. I have no doubt she'd have died a little girl like Anne Frank in the gas chambers but for your courage. Pancreatic cancer took her last winter. She went fast. And it wasn't until I stumbled upon your book by chance at a book fair just a month ago that I got to wondering. Same name. But no mention of Mother's family? That made no sense. It can't be him. Becker is a common enough surname. But also a fighter pilot *and* pianist named Harmon Becker? I kept coming back to your face on the cover. A good man's face. And as I flipped through the pages, the timeline fit and I realized who you were. They'd all given up finding you. There was no internet in their day, remember." She opens her palms up, alternately laughing and weeping. "But they raised a snoopy reporter. And now here you are."

Then another voice comes from the doorway. "Yes, Harmon. Here we all are."

I look up as Rachael wipes her eyes and then sits down beside me. She sees my expression go from confusion to ebullient recognition. Standing at the French doors with Dora at his side is a distinguished man in a finely tailored suit and tie; he is in his early seventies, though he looks a decade younger. His bronzed face is thicker than I remember and deeply creased, and his coiled black hair has gone white and thin, but I recognize the sharp eyes and intense demeanor immediately. Still so alert and bright. And still very much alive.

"Jake," I say, shaking. Jakob Krupinski nods and steps into the room with his hands extended out to me in affectionate greeting.

I make a move to stand up, but he implores me to stay seated. He turns to his niece. "I'm sorry Rachael, but I couldn't wait at the pub any more. I had to see for myself."

Though he had gone on to found a company that manufactured rocket engine parts—sold to General Dynamics in 1998 for an unholy sum—I still see that young boy looking at me with such suspicion from below the hood of that 1922 Ford so many years ago. Against his protests I stand to face him. He comes to me. We shake hands. A handshake is inadequate and it becomes a manly embrace. Then we step back and each view the other up close, through the lens of time.

I notice he bears something in his hand. A rectangular case. I glance down at the curious item. It appears to be a leather jewelry box. Perhaps it's a watch. It has that regal yet earthy smell of freshly tanned hide. "What's this?" I ask. "A gift for me?"

Jakob smiles at Rachael and turns to Dora, who stands in the French doorway observing the curious scene. She has her mother's smile. "This is something that belongs to you, Harmon. My mother wanted you to have it. Constanze never got to give it to you herself."

I open the case and am astounded by what I hold in my hand. I cannot contain myself, and I fall back seated on the couch. "Oh my goodness," I say. Displayed in this fresh case is my polished Knight's Cross.

"Jake," I say.

"You gave this to my father a long time ago. I think he understood why. And I know before he died he felt that you'd earned it back in a way. It belongs to you, Harmon."

"But I gave this to your father," I protest weakly. "To remember me."

"And now his son is giving it back to you. When I think of that entire hellish trek, I remember most the kindness you showed Elsa."

I clear my throat as I run my trembling fingers over the sharp points of the edges of the eight-point Maltese Cross. The smooth fabric of the ribbon. Like a man reading Braille, I feel the decoration's every contour, from the embossed "1939" to the terrible swastika that serves as a reminder of the vicious depths into which we are all capable of sinking if the stars align and evil is offered the reins of power.

But it also tells me that it takes just one person with courage and moral clarity to break the spell and lead generations into a better world. This cross then is Amelia's more than mine. She was, and will always be, my champion. The bravest person I have ever known. Someone whose grit was matched only by her decency, made all the brighter in its contrast to a dark world in which she alone faced the crucible of defying Hitler. She was not my wingman…I was hers. These people are in my house today because of my wife, who is no more.

"I only wish my dear sister were here to share this moment with me," Jake laments.

I extend my free hand to Rachael and she takes it in hers. "I think Miss Rachael here is a fine substitute, don't you?"

"She is indeed."

Jakob looks to his niece with adoration, seeing his own sister Elsa alive in her, and himself alive because of an unlikely pair of saviors a long time ago.

62

Just outside of London proper is a cemetery dotted with crumbling headstones marking the final destinations of generations of British farmers, craftsmen, artisans, and others who've lived and died in these fields since the Norman Conquest. An old gated archway constructed of five-foot-diameter stones beckons visitors to the top of a dale, where the wind never seems to stop gusting into the faces of those who come to pay their respects to those who rest here. Even on this sunny day, there's an autumn bite in the frigid November air. My face grows numb and my cheeks and nose show a bright pink, but I'm glad to be here.

I stand over the most recently set grave within these walls. The ground is still churned, though no longer that black moist earth of a freshly dug hole but dried to khaki. It speaks of a newness that implies a grief still being borne by those who love the person lying beneath our feet.

I'm not alone. Rachael, Jakob, and Dora stand beside me like fighter escorts. Two taxis wait patiently in the nearby gravel lane. Their engines are turned off, but their meters still run. No matter. The Krupinskis insisted on making this pilgrimage before heading to Heathrow Airport and then across the Atlantic back to their adopted home, America.

All stand in reverent silence as I recite a soft prayer for the soul moved on from the decaying body beneath us. For Rachael, the headstone brings the true reality of what Amelia and I did for her family into clear focus. And once again, this woman who has seen children die of horrible wounds in their mothers' arms in far-off lands cannot seem to squelch her tears. Her Uncle Jakob holds her tight, offering that he has never seen his usually stoic niece display so much raw emotion.

But Jakob, too, cannot fully shut the floodgates of oft-muted feelings triggered by the memories of a childhood trying to survive in a country immersed in the acid bath of manic hatred. For him, seeing this old fighter pilot one last time, ravaged as I am now by the lashings of time, and then standing here at this place today, brings back long-forgotten imagery to be recaptured for good or ill on the canvas of his fertile mind. There is much pain in his past. But today also offers him the sweetness of triumph as well. And so Jakob Krupinski comforts himself with the notion that one has to have survived the whirlwind to remember at all. He remembers fondly that I gave him life. I and the woman beneath the headstone, which reads:

Amelia Becker
B. 1920–D. 2004
Devoted Wife, Loving Mother
Giver of Life When Others Turned Away

We each take our turn laying a rose on such an unassuming stone for so incredible a woman. They seem so utterly incapable of articulating the depth of our sorrow. I stand immobile and read her name again and again. "Amelia," I say, as if my spirit fled this world when she was taken from me.

Dora takes me by the arm. "Come on, Papa. You'll catch a death in this wind."

I turn to my daughter and ask: "Would that be so bad?"

"Oh, Papa," she says while taking me in her arms.

"I miss her so," I sigh while my body shakes. "I feel hollow. Scooped out inside."

Rachael puts her hand on her uncle's shoulder. She doesn't know what to do now. They can no longer tarry if they hope to catch their flight. Yet how can they leave me in such a way?

I must give them leave to go. I compose myself and say to the pesky Yank reporter, "Well, Miss Azerad. I guess you have your interview."

She offers me a loving smile. "I have much more than that, Mr. Becker."

I put a hand up to dismiss her. "Your uncle will tell you. It's Harmon."

"Mr. Harmon," she says, trying to lighten the heavy mood. I make a motion for her to come close. She leans in. "You," I say, "have a better sense of humor than your grandfather."

She laughs. "Thanks to you I've had a better life. Goodbye…Harmon."

I take her in my arms like another granddaughter. In some ways I suppose she is. She backs away and tries in vain against the wind to right her hair fluttering across her sharp nose and high cheekbones.

I then turn to Jake. "Look at you," I say with not a little pride and some sense of accomplishment at my having lit the fire. "Did you ever learn to fly?" I ask.

"I've had my pilot's license for years now," he says with a deserved sense of accomplishment. "I'm even certified to fly a 737, my company's jet."

"More Boeings," I say, rolling my eyes. "I see enough in my dreams already."

He laughs. "At least commercial jets don't have machine guns."

"Thank goodness for that! It must be difficult to fly."

"Believe it or not that Heinkel was trickier," he says.

"Bah!" I say. "I have no doubt you can handle anything with wings. I was there for your first flight." I shake Jacob's hand at first. Then I give him a final hug and a manly slap on the back.

"Well, Harmon. Let's just say if it was me flying one of those 190s, you wouldn't be here today," he jibes.

"Oh really," I say. "I don't know about that. But, I will say that if it had been anyone but you with me in that Heinkel, you're probably right." We laugh together. Cocky pilot to cocky pilot. As it should be. The world turns and life moves forward.

"It's too bad we flew together only that once," he says. "But we made one helluva team, didn't we?"

I tap him on the bicep. "We're here, aren't we? Oh Jake, it was good to see you after so many years. I can't thank you enough for coming."

His jocular demeanor dies. "And you, Harmon. I only wish I'd made it before…" His voice fades as he looks towards the headstone.

"I know. Still, I cannot help but think she's watching us right now. Probably figuring out how best to get you two safely to Heathrow in this traffic."

"Of course. Getting us out of tight spots is a Becker specialty." He pauses. "I'll never forget you, Captain."

"Nor I you, Jakob." A pause and then I break the long goodbye. "Now go before you end up spending another day and risk losing the good weather we've been having." I look up at the clear sky above us. Wisps of fine clouds against the blue. "It's a good day to fly."

Rachael looks up with me. "I suppose it is."

I nod my head. "And a good day to finish it."

At first Dora is unsure what to make of this. "Finish what, Papa?" she asks cautiously.

"Yes," echoes Rachael. "Finish what?"

I wink at them. "Finish my book. I have some chapters to add."

Relieved, Rachael laughs. "You may need this." She retrieves the little recorder from her purse. She pops it open and hands me the micro-cassette.

"Keep it," I say. "It's all stored away in my memory as if it happened yesterday. And between you and me, I wouldn't mind reading about myself in the papers. It's said that concert pianists and fighter pilots have tremendous egos. You can only imagine what goes on in my head!"

After one more round of farewells, hugs, and handshakes, Rachael and her uncle Jakob climb into their taxicab.

"Heathrow then?" asks the taxi driver. An old man with a scarf peers at them through the mirror. It's as if the London tourist bureau purposefully picked them to drive home an image of all that is charming about this ancient city.

Dora and I stand arm in arm next to Amelia's flower-topped stone and wave goodbye as the first black cab peels off down the lane.

"I would have liked to spend more time with them," I say with regret.

"Maybe you'll see them again, Papa," my daughter reassures me.

Maybe, I think. Who knows? My life with the Krupinskis has already taken so many unimaginable twists, why should one more be out of the question? I look back at my dear wife's memorial one more time before my daughter escorts me down the hill to our waiting taxi, as the red sun sets to the west behind us.

EPILOGUE

"Whenever I play, I try to penetrate the mental state of the composer as I interpret his work. What was happening in his life when he wrote this? What fired the creative furnace to forge such a beauty? When I launch into Chopin's Revolutionary Etude, I try to become that young distraught Pole, far from home, flailing away with pen to sheet in an angry stream of defiance to the Czar's violation of his nation. Music has a supremacy among the human expression. It is unique among the arts in that it pulls you into the mood of the creator. You are powerless to resist it. The ear is touched, the head bobs, the fingers drum, and the feet tap. Your emotion is now in a different place. All you can do to prevent the metamorphosis is plug your ears and flee from the sound. Otherwise you are a prisoner of the air. There is no neutral ground.

"Nations are like that. If I think too hard I find myself astounded that an entire people can more easily turn a deaf ear to the pounding resonance of a monstrous injustice—indeed the suffering of millions—than it can hold back a single tear at the first measure of a Mozart aria. How is this possible? This question plagues me. It has haunted my dreams for sixty years. I still have no answer for it."

—Excerpt from *My Cross to Bear: Bitter Skies—The Rest of My Story*, by Harmon Becker. Select chapters featured in the *New York Times Magazine,* with a foreword by Rachael Azerad.

It's late and yet I cannot sleep. In my pajamas I heave myself out of my lonesome bed and slide into my robe and slippers. I need not be quiet or mindful of turning on the lights anymore, as Dora's now back home with her family in Dover, where she belongs. It's not anxiety or sadness that robs me of my sleep. It's not even the fact that I've finished re-writing my memoirs to include my true story and that of Amelia and the Krupinskis. I've sent off the manuscript to Rachael Azerad in New York, who thinks she can do much with it, as my old German publisher has chosen not to release the updated version. We shall see.

What arouses me from my bed is the simple desire to play one more time before my forever sleep. My health is now deteriorating rapidly, although I haven't led on to anyone close to me. Why should they worry? Death isn't so bad for an old man like me. And I know it's caught up to me now. These fleeting moments feel like they will be my last on this earth. It's okay. I've lived longer than most, and the prospect of being with Amelia does little to stoke the flames of self-preservation. Besides, I've cheated the reaper so many times in the course of my life that I owe him the final victory. I no longer run from him. My heart flutters, and my legs wobble below me. And as my breathing grows shallower, and my head swims, I now ponder what shall I do as I ride out these last precious minutes?

I'll do what has always given me the most pleasure. I'll ease myself, with some pain and fading strength, down the stairs and stumble my way through the French doors to the piano. It waits in dignified silence to welcome me as an old friend. I'll lower myself before the keys, and sweet music will careen off the walls of the empty flat one last time. Two items will sit in my field of vision as I play. They will be the last images I see. So weak will the trek down to the conservatory make me that I know I'll not be able to get up once I'm settled at the instrument that has kept me alive when I should have been dead many times, along with the rest of the world.

I'll click on the lamp that overhangs my Steinway, and my eyes will linger on the photo of Amelia and me on the boat just off the Channel Islands. We both look away from the camera, as if remembering a different time when we shared such danger and excitement together that tempestuous June of 1944. Opposite the photo rests a shiny Ritterkreuz, always there for me to remember when I reached the decisive moment in my life, and can drift away from this world knowing that I made the right choice. That God will forgive me my many sins when weighed in the balance.

My hands will continue to move across the keys, but their strength will dwindle until only a slight hint of *pianissimo* breaks the silence. All will grow dark around me as the Mendelssohn Fantasy comes through to me only in gentle waves by the last measures. And then I'll be off to a place where the skies are always clear, where all people can stand upright in the sunlight, unafraid of what is to come, and my love will be with me until the end of time.